D0298454

BLOOD FROM STONE

Also by Frances Fyfield

Blood From Stone

FRANCES FYFIELD

sphere

SPHERE

First published in Great Britain in 2008 by Sphere

Copyright © Frances Fyfield 2008

The moral right of the author has been asserted.

A CIP catalogue record for this book
is available from the British Library.

Hardback ISBN 978-1-84744-074-7
C Format ISBN 978-1-84744-075-4

Typeset in Plantin by M Rules
Printed and bound in Great Britain by
Clays Ltd, St Ives plc

Sphere
An imprint of
Little, Brown Book Group
100 Victoria Embankment
London EC4Y 0DY

An Hachette Livre UK Company

www.littlebrown.co.uk

In memory of Magdalen Nabb.

With heartfelt thanks to Ian Goldup, and Rebecca Cobb, Coroners, for facts and information.

Thanks also to Judith Dorey, for giving me the atmosphere of a place where clothes are lovingly restored.

All errors are my own.

PART ONE

CHAPTER ONE

Scene 1

Following his acquittal, which happened without too much of a fanfare but with dramatic abruptness on the fourth day of the sixth week of his postponed and protracted trial, the Defendant waited outside Court 3 in the Central Criminal Court long after everyone else had departed. He was admiring the older part of the building. He had been granted the accolade of the original, seventeenth-century courtroom that had once led, via a trapdoor in the floor, to the cells of Newgate Gaol beneath. Two centuries ago, prisoners would enter the court via this hole in the ground; it was said that the judge would hold a perfumed nosegay to his face to mask the smell of incarcerated humanity. *Ring a ring o' roses, a pocket full of posies, Atishoo, atishoo! We all fall down.* Or maybe, as Ms Shearer, QC, his learned Counsel for the Defence had said, this ditty referred to the plague years.

He was waiting specifically to say goodbye to her. He knew very well she detested him as thoroughly as anyone of her bloodless and ruthless temperament could entertain such an emotion. He had his own, foul smell. She would be better at carefully concealed contempt than she would be at affection and as for sentiment, Jehovah forbid. She was fifty-one, walked like an aggressive ballerina, acted like a wheedling prima donna specialising in outrage on behalf of her clients, and had the ability to make herself believe in them absolutely for as long as it took. Her desire to win was lethal. He had charmed her at first, but that was a long time before. Ms Shearer had got what her ugly face deserved.

The trial had gone wrong on her, with the right result, certainly, one achieved through exploitation of weakness, legal argument, bullying, manipulation and luck. The suicide of the prime witness could only be called a misfortune. A thoroughly professional hatchet job on her part, in other words. It was for the prosecution to prove their case and for her to destroy it; she had done the latter but the result would not cover her with glory simply because it would be seen as an outrageous piece of cruel luck, rather than advocacy.

She would not want to say goodbye. She would never want to see him again, but he was fresh out of jail and for the first time he was leaving the court via the front door and not via the prison van. The prison van, he had told her, was an exquisitely uncomfortable mode of transport, like travelling on the inside of a human time bomb complete with moulded plastic seats and manacles.

Freedom could wait. He knew she had to come through that door over there in order to find her own way out and he knew she would be hoping he was long gone, never to be seen or heard of again, but he wanted a chance to stress to her how much they had in common, to *thank* her, of course and above all, to let her know exactly *what* they had achieved between them. As if, after all those hours spent together, she did not know already.

She wore her high heels as if born in them, clicking over the tiled floor, hesitating when she saw him, alone apart from the security guard who waited to see them out. The space was suddenly vast. His small legal team had melted away as soon as the Judge left his seat. No one else wanted to say goodbye. The Prosecution's pathetic posse of lawyers and disgruntled police had exited stage left, shepherding away that bitch of a girl with a bag who would have spat at him in passing if not held back. They might all be elsewhere, rending their garments like biblical penitents. So, it might just be the two of them, then; after all those hours spent together saying goodbye.

Her hesitation, a slow little click-clack of the black shoes, as if pausing in a dance, turned into certainty. Ms Shearer would never give herself the option of running away.

'Still here, Richard?' she said. 'Doesn't the fresh air beckon or something? It's over.'

'I wanted to thank you.'

She was standing back, but he reached forward and touched her arm above the elbow. She was heavily laden with leather panniers of paper over each shoulder; her face was old and cold, paler than his prison pallor, a face devoid and exhausted and still ugly.

'No need to thank me. I was only doing my job.'

'So you were. Can I carry your bags, miss?'

'No. My luggage is my own.'

She began to steer her way round him, her distaste palpable. He was furious. *After all those hours.*

'I only wanted to walk out of here with you. My saviour. And you can't even bear to do that?'

5

She put down the document bags and rubbed her right shoulder, weariness overcoming her. Spoke loudly in her harsh voice.

'No, I don't want to walk out of here with you, even if it's the wrong time of day for the newspapers. You wanted to say goodbye, so goodbye, Rick Boyd. I've done the job and I've got another. Another innocence to prove.'

'Shake hands, then.'

In an automatic gesture of politeness – she was good with gestures – she extended her right hand towards him. He glimpsed the long, ringless fingers with the talon nails he had seen so often turning the pages of paper in his presence, looking for the weaknesses in the words and always finding them. In the last second, her hand trembled and he imagined what she would want to do after she had shaken his. She would want to wipe away all traces, stroke her damp palm on the cloth of her skirt to get rid of the slime of him and maybe she would not even wait until he was out of sight. He seized the proffered hand in both of his own and bent back the first finger until he could hear the crick of bone.

'Beautiful hands,' he murmured. 'I got the dear Angel to display hers on the kitchen table. I do so love a woman's hand. She'd varnished her fingernails for me. She was admiring herself, hands splayed on the wood, when I took off the first digit. The blood went in the soup and salt went in the wound. She slept very well, I assure you. I'm sure she doesn't miss it. Anyway, I really did want to thank you for springing me. Magnificently done. Every single trick in the book.'

He struggled with pride, straightened his shoulders.

'I suppose we killed her, really,' he murmured. 'But I didn't mean it. I'll find that other bitch. Anyway, thanks.'

The hand he relinquished fell to her side. She flexed nerveless fingers, took a deep breath, hoisted her bags of robes and papers and clicked her way across the floor. From a safe distance, she half turned, checked the mobile phone in her breast pocket, spoke over her shoulder, 'I'll put it all in my memoirs, Mr Boyd,' and then she went out. The guard followed her, leaving the Defendant alone.

He did a little dance on the central design of the tiled floor. Free.

Conscience was something which belonged to other people. The hot summer sunshine outside on the street was as sweet as she had promised, not that he noticed the seasons. Truth never hurt anyone except his victims, and victims lied, did they not? Lied, while only one of them had died. Who cared? They were cut from the same cloth, Ms Shearer and he. They didn't *do* suffering.

Rejoice.

Only, out in the daylight, he knew she had not done it right. She had not proved he was INNOCENT. What memoirs? What book of revelation of all those long hours? She never loved him and she still had his life.

Scene Two.

It was early in the morning of a cold January day when Paul Bain was crossing through from one busy road towards another, admiring the contrast between this street and the one he had left and wishing he was at home in bed. The tree-lined street was quiet, containing ambassadorial-style residences and a discreetly expensive hotel with six floors and a façade of Edwardian splendour. He was wondering what it would be like to be a rich London tourist and stay in a place like that, reflecting that an overnight stay would cost him a month's wages and this was not the career he had in mind for himself. Artist reduced to dosgbody. It was a day for feeling bitter. He had his camera ready for the morning's unglamorous task, which was photographing road works in an evidence-gathering exercise for Westminster City Council. He hoped he did not look the part and he did not want to reach his destination, so he stopped and looked up for a spot of dreaming, and that was when he saw her.

The woman was sitting on the balustrade of the sixth floor balcony of the hotel, framed by a couple of box trees behind her with her booted feet dangling in front, supporting herself on her hands. She was fully dressed with a flash of colour and looked small and odd, perched up there. A window opened in the room next to hers; someone stepped out on to their balcony and spoke to her. It all seemed very relaxed, if eccentric, as if it was a normal, early morning chat between chambermaids, all under control. The camera was in his hands. He trained it on her the better to see. She had shiny hair, which caught the light as she shook her head. He thought he saw the suggestion of a reassuring smile through the lens, as if she had seen him or someone she knew and liked, and then she jumped.

She leapt. In one split second she was safe, if precarious, on the broad stone balustrade, a person teasing danger rather than in it, and then she pushed herself off with her hands, spread her arms wide and floated down like a bird shot from the skies. He recorded her agonisingly slow progress through the lens: he knew the meaning of time standing still as her disfigured shape fell and became a blur as it hit the road with a deafening sound. The noise was like a distant car crash causing vibrations through his feet and skull, a muted explosion sending the birds in the trees flying away in screaming protest. He simply stood there with his camera frozen to his hand until his knees began to tremble and the buildings around him seem to shake, shrug and become still. He had forgotten his own name.

Then he let the camera drop and looked back up to the balcony with his naked eye. The person who had been speaking to the woman had moved back from the edge and covered her face. The silence was unspeakable. He did not move; nothing moved. He stood there for some time, like a child waiting for someone to collect him. He had the perverse feeling that someone ought to ask him how he was, because he was cold on the shady side of the street and he felt weak and sick and lonely. In the midst of all of this, after an ambulance arrived and people fussed over the dead thing in the road and no one came near him, he found himself obscurely angry with her for subjecting him to this, and at the same time it occurred to him that all disasters created opportunities and if he wanted to be a member of the paparazzi, he should learn to think like one. With those colours, she looked as if she might have been a celebrity. It might have been a film stunt gone wrong. As soon as he had seen her, he had remembered a startlingly similar happening only a week before, when another woman had leapt from a building in the cold light of day. It made all this seem like an unreal sham, simply a harmless death rehearsal and a perfect photo opportunity.

So he sold her. Her, pictures of her. Ms Marianne Shearer hit the news with more force than she had ever done even in the most infamous of her trials as a champion of justice.

'Celebrity' and 'well known in certain circles' amounted to the same thing. It was a dull week too soon after New Year.

Throwing oneself from a window was enough to secure temporary celebrity status, especially when the suicide was rich, well qualified, successful and without any apparent problems, thus providing more of a sensation than the last self-inflicted demise. Bain's excellent quality mementos were published the next day following an auction for the rights. There was intense interest and considerable outrage since the selected newspapers were the first to bear the bad tidings to most of her friends, family, colleagues, etc. They all learned of her ending by watching her in free fall, captured in newsprint on a morning when there was no other news. The insensitivity of sensationalised death on camera and the cold voyeurism of the opportunistic photographer gave the deceased an added dimension of tragedy. She floated to earth in a brown blur of glory, famous at last, as she might have wanted, or not. *A woman at the top of her professional tree/a fearless practitioner of the law/protector of human rights/the innocent/owner of three-bedroomed Kensington apmt worth one mill, loved by friends and surviving brother. British citizen, born in NZ.*

Strangers who never knew her at all shed tears. Poor, wretched woman, for whom money bought nothing but the price of a lofty hotel room hired for the express purpose of throwing herself out of it. A failed love affair? Seasonal blues? Whatever. Poor, lonely rich woman, a lesson to us all. Tributes from friends.

One person looked at the first edition of the *Daily Mail*, having been drawn to buy it like thousands of others purely by the front page photograph of a blurred silhouette plunging down the side of a building, with promises of more on page three. She looked closely and was also moved to tears until she found the details and name. Then she threw it across the room. Why didn't she kill herself sooner, before she did so much damage? And then she cried herself angrily into sleep, because this wasn't justice, it never was.

The photographer came to consider it was the worst thing he had ever done, to be in that street, at that time and to sell what he had seen. It paid his debts and more, but she owned him after that. He could no longer hold his camera to his eye without his hand shaking; he could not believe what he saw on the screen and the images blurred along with the observations which haunted him, such as how careful she had been about the choice of a place to jump, so that she avoided the hotel portico where she might have fallen against the flagpole, or the room to the right, where she might have become entangled with the tree which reached the fourth floor, from whose bare branches the birds had flown with their anxious screams. He was trying to find something which indicated she had not meant it; that it was accident or homicide rather than self-destruct. He was also looking all the time for the third figure beyond the box tree ornaments on the balcony and into the room beyond, searching for the shadow he wished he had seen, someone who would explain. There were no pictures of anything before the moment when she had jumped, nothing until she pushed herself away and that full skirt had slightly checked her fall, but there were the pictures he wished into his mind of the same figure, flying back.

A third person saw the photographs and simply laughed. Serve you right. You wouldn't walk out of there with me. I knew I scared you rigid, I saw it in your face. I passed on the baton of conscience, all right? You fell with your hands outstretched and it looked as if you had no thumbs at all. You thought you were immune. Who'll write the memoirs now?

He remembered how the last time he had seen her, she had fingered the mobile phone in her pocket as if checking. She recorded everything. He also remembered how it was with her, how nothing she did in public, not even the smallest gesture, was without a purpose.

She might have lost her grasp, but she still had *his life, his soul*. On record, on paper, she still possessed all that knowledge of *him*.

An old man sat with the evening paper, which he examined closely. He smoothed the fine mohair fabric of his jacket and picked off a small lump of fluff. It was the only time she had ever intruded into his home. From the far end of the house, he could hear his grandchildren.

Then his plump wife came in with his tea.

CHAPTER TWO

Shearer—Marianne Jane, on 4th January, aged 51, at Kensington, London. Private cremation to be arranged. No flowers, please. Inquiries to T.Noble@NobleandCo.com.

It was a beautiful flat, if you liked that kind of thing, which Thomas did. It was an estate agent's dream for the client worth a million, requiring nothing more than space without a single piece of evidence indicating a previous occupant of any kind. Cream walls, cream carpet, a kitchen full of stainless steel, a single, neutral sofa, marooned in the centre of a large living room, alongside a small perspex table so transparent it melded with the rest. A blank canvas, to be written upon, with no writing as yet.

The newspaper, left open on the floor, provided the only contrast. Black, against the white, looked almost shocking. One longed for the odd wine stain, even for blood. Any sign of life would do.

The taller of the two men, Thomas Noble, picked up the

newspaper, which was offensive to him for several reasons. His shorter companion stood a good way off, leaning against the window with his arms crossed and admiring the view outside with a proprietorial air. The irritation which percolated between them was in control. Thomas had rarely disliked anyone with such intensity, and marvelled at the fact he could so loathe on sight a person who was the brother of someone he had counted as a close friend, but then, that same great friend had obviously been a bit of a mystery in her own right. Her failure to confide despair rankled like an itch. After all, she seemed to have confided so much. Marianne could be shockingly frank. Not so her brother. Thomas shuddered, imperceptibly, and in order to say something, picked up and read from the newspaper article she had ringed with the red felt pen. It provided the only colour in the room.

'I have the feeling that this is the only evidence of why she chose to do it the way she did. It makes me sad.'

Frank Shearer continued to look at the view outside the window, enjoying it, listening without caring.

'Pardon?'

'She was reading an article in the *Daily Mail*,' Thomas explained. 'Page three.'

'I thought she never got further than the law pages in *The Times*.'

'She did this time,' Thomas insisted. 'She was reading an article about an unemployed woman who died in a bedsit in North London and was only found two years later. Almost a record. Two years! Doesn't say much for her neighbours, who reported a foul smell, and then nothing after a couple of months, which according to this,' he handled the newspaper carefully, it was evidence of a kind, after all, 'is hardly surprising. She died with the heating full on, and it never went off. TV still murmuring away in the corner, central heating going full blast after two winters and a summer. Place infested, of course, but even the bugs had perished.'

'Are you making a point?'

'Yes. The point I'm making is that Marianne read this article which is dated two days before she died. It gives a clue to what she was thinking. She was thinking that if she stayed in her own flat, no one would notice she was dead. She didn't want that.'

'Your point was?'

'The woman in the newspaper. Marianne definitely didn't want to be undiscovered for two years. Or two weeks.'

'So she jumped instead? And if she *had* died here, how long would it have been before the body was found? How long before a friend like you would have worried enough to break the door down?'

Thomas shrugged. He and Marianne Shearer met for civilised evenings as often as twice a month. That was his version of close friendship.

'Knowing my sister,' Frank Shearer said, 'she might just as well have been reading the article to try and discover what type of boiler and TV that dead woman had. The sort that works for two years without servicing. She'd be looking for the same make and model. Or maybe it was just envy of someone who didn't have to pay any bills. She was cute with money, my sis.'

He shook his head. 'No, I don't think it was that, even if she did leave this newspaper. There was that other woman who jumped out of a hotel window the other week, wasn't there? Wasn't she some kind of lawyer, too? Photos of her in the paper, but not nearly as good as Marianne's. Marianne would have seen that and thought she could show people how such things ought to be done for maximum impact. Make herself the definitive hotel suicide. She did like having the last word in everything.'

Thomas knew that Frank Shearer and his late sister had not been close because she had told him. *Bloody ne'er-do-well, sponger, with a touch of the vicious about him, you know? Workshy, that one, spoiled rotten. No time for him.* Frank Shearer had absolutely no interest in her life, only her death. The physical resemblance was there. Frank had her eyes and her hair, without any of her backbone; he was soft where she was slim and muscular. He was handsome: she was not, although she could be striking. *That's why I had to succeed, Thomas, I didn't have the option of hanging around and being pretty.* Thomas Noble, solicitor; friend of the deceased whom he had accompanied to many a football match in pursuit of a shared passion which surprised them both. If she wasn't winning herself, she was certainly wanting someone else to win. She might have evolved into a hired assassin in another life, and if he had been a heterosexual man himself, he would have run a mile from her. As he was, he was free to appreciate a frightful friend and consider himself a mentor, although how much he had succeeded in that was sadly in doubt. Marianne had said nothing about what ailed her – that was insulting – and it seemed that she had never followed his advice to make a will. All the same, he had to admit there was something in what Frank had just said. There had been a similar suicide soon after Christmas, and Marianne could never resist upstaging another woman. This was surely an unfair thought, although it lingered because of the similarities. Marianne's was definitely different. All she had done, on the same day she had read the newspaper article about the woman dead for two years was transfer money into his bank account, with the cryptic email saying *Look after stuff, and have fun with this will you? Use Peter Friel for the business, he's dull but dogged. Mx*

He coughed. It followed from this that he was appointed in the role of her legal representative in the absence of anyone else. There was no one better qualified to sort the mess. It also followed that this foul, definitely homophobic man needed him, since Frank did not know where else to start and Thomas held all the cards. Frank was a car salesman with a history of debt and he needed a lawyer, since, as things stood, under the rules of intestacy, he the undeserving was going to reap the fruits of what she had sown. Ms Shearer's brother was practically salivating. Worth nothing last week and now worth enough to strut like a cockerel.

'Great apartment. The newspaper said it was worth a cool mill. And recent life insurance, you said?'

Thomas shook his head.

'I doubt if the flat's worth that much. And there's a mortgage. She was a barrister for twenty-five years, but a Life of Crime doesn't make you a millionaire. If we,' he stressed the 'we' in the interests of companionship because it was important they did not fall out . . . yet, 'don't find a last will and testament, or other known relatives apart from yourself, then this,' he nodded at the white walls, 'falls to you. Subject to tax et cetera. The verdict at the inquest will have an impact on the amount, of course.'

'How's that? What do you mean?'

Oh Lord, signs of animation at last. If not grief, at least anxiety. Thomas was a conscientious lawyer, but he still liked alarming the client and enjoyed it when people gave themselves away. It always amazed him how mere information had the knack of creating anger, which was something he preferred to witness rather than experience first hand. Hence the love of football. Ritualised disharmony. Also Wagner. Anything with a tempest included watched from a safe seat.

'She insured her life, of course. She would have had to have done that, to get the mortgage. I did the legal work, I have those papers. A verdict of suicide, as such, can invalidate life policies. Most coroners are careful these days. A verdict of accidental death would be better. You aren't really supposed to take out insurance and then kill yourself, any more than you're allowed to insure your wife and then kill her. Simply not sporting. But yours, all yours, old son, pending evidence of other instructions, of course.'

'So we want the Coroner to say something like accidental death while balance of mind disturbed?'

'Yes. Especially if the insurance policy she took out on the mortgage has a suicide clause. It would diminish the estate quite a bit. Coroners rarely give a verdict of suicide. Even murder would be more convenient.'

Frank barked with horribly satisfied laughter.

'How do you pay the bloke to get the words right? Get him to say she didn't really mean it when she's thrown herself out of a window in front of witnesses? For fuck's sake, there can't be much doubt about that, even if she was copying someone else.'

'We all need doubts, Frank, no doubt about that.'

Thomas turned the old newspaper over in his hands and slipped it under the sofa. It was offensive. Let someone else take it away. He supposed that the money Marianne had left in his care was for practical things, like paying for cleaning and a funeral. Three days after her last occupation, and the place was already dusty. She had been the owner for less than a week. There was a bed, sofa, the rudiments of furniture. The rest she was going to buy new. There must be things stored with other friends.

'You don't pay coroners,' he said. 'You pray for their discretion.'

'Surely Marianne would have known that suicide could invalidate insurance policies? She was a lawyer after all.'

'One of the few female Queen's Counsel, and the even fewer who made crime pay,' Thomas answered. 'But speaking as one who acts as a humble, domestic lawyer to many other lawyers, I'm beyond being surprised about how little they know about law outside their chosen field. And how little they take the legal advice they either dispense or receive. Such as making a will, minimising tax, that kind of thing. I doubt if she read her policies. Don't worry, there'll be plenty left. She was clever with property. She invested wisely.'

Frank Shearer moved from his view over the gardens at the back and sprawled on the sofa, testing the springs with his weight, as if already deciding whether he would keep it or not. Or maybe regretting that she had depleted what was going to be his inheritance by purchasing such a thing. He pulled a cream cushion on to his lap and picked at the braid around the edge, actions designed to irritate. The last buttocks to occupy that sofa were those of his dead sister. The indentation of her behind was still present, next to him. Thomas would have scalded himself rather than sat on it. Oh why, oh why, had she not made herself clear? There were too many whys buzzing around here, like angry wasps, trapped in a room, such as why she had done it at all. There were all those possessions of hers, no doubt hidden with some *other* friend, maybe the will was there, too. Hope sprang in his mind and he kept his face bland. You're like an old cat,

Marianne had said. No one knows what you're thinking, even when you purr.

'I'm sure she didn't make a will,' Frank said. 'Because, if she had, she would have told me what to expect. There was no love lost, if you see what I mean, but I'm still her only brother. Perhaps she jumped because she'd invested her all in the dream flat, and then found she was still fifty-one, past her sell-by date, still ugly and as lonely as ever.'

'She wasn't lonely,' Thomas protested, guilty for leaving out the fact that beautiful she was not.

'Don't tell me she was popular.'

'No . . . I mean yes. She never needed to spend an evening alone unless she wanted. She was a workaholic, not lonely. Have we finished here?'

He could not bear the sight of Frank Shearer unpicking a cushion as if he might find money inside it. Frank grinned at him.

'Shame you don't like me, old boy,' he said. 'Cos we're stuck with each other for a bit, aren't we? That's what she would have wanted. Everything sorted out fair and square in strict accordance with the law, and you in charge, looking after me.'

'I don't know what she wanted,' Thomas said. 'But I'll act for you in the matter of her estate if you pay me. I'll need to advertise and hire a probate researcher, just to ensure there's no other beneficiaries. I've got Peter Friel on hand to do that.'

'Look out those insurance policies, old boy. Smile at the taxman, cosy up to the coroner, throw a few hissy fits, kiss arse and sleep with the enemy. That's what she would have done, that's what she did all the time. Anything for a result.'

The phone rang, eerily loud in the empty space. Thomas

looked around for the source of the sound, coming from the small room stage left of where they were. He hovered, for once uncertain about a bizarre piece of etiquette such as who should be the one to answer a dead person's phone. There was no precedent for that one. He moved towards it and Frank moved faster.

'Hello, what d'ya want?'

'Marianne? Is she there?'

'Don't you read the newspapers? She's dead.'

Thomas stepped forward, seething with anger and grabbed the receiver from Frank's hand.

'Hello, who is this please?'

There was the sound of tumultuous breathing, like someone struggling for air.

'I'm so sorry for that response,' Thomas said. 'You got Ms Shearer's brother. He's upset. Can I help you?'

More breathing. He waited.

'I don't read any newspapers, I make things for her, I have this dress, ready for her, and . . . I so sorry. Why she die?'

Why, oh why? Not enough to say I don't know.

'It seems she was very depressed,' Thomas said, gently. 'So depressed, she took her own life.'

The breathing became sharper.

'Tha's a lie. She not *depressed*. How can she be depressed? She had this *dress*, beautiful dress, she wanted it so bad. I don' believe you. Someone gotta pay. She love it. Oh, nooooo . . .'

He paused. Another challenge to the good manners that dictated his life.

'Can you give me your name?' he asked quietly. 'And send details of any outstanding bills to me? I assure you, they'll be paid.'

He recited his address as he listened to the sound of noisy weeping.

'I send what I want. I keep the dress, maybe. Now I'm the one depressed. Someone kill her, you hear?'

The phone was slammed down and the sound rang in his ears. He went back to the living room, shaken. Frank was on his feet, chucking the keys to the place from one hand to another, itching to move all of a sudden. The cold of the place got to them. With her usual efficiency, Marianne had turned off the heat before she left from her new home here, to go to a room in a hotel a hundred yards away in order to kill herself. She had been sure she would not need warmth when she came back.

He took the keys from Frank and Frank took one last look around. Thomas remembered as he closed the door on the empty space what it was that had impressed him about Marianne Shearer when they had first met, a decade before. Not beauty, for sure. Style. He wondered for the first time what exactly she had been wearing when she jumped.

It was warmer outside.

Chapter Three

Always colder by the sea.

The wind was howling round the door, tugging at it. Henrietta could not imagine how her mother had found the strength to pull it closed so quietly in order to plod alone head down, up to the beachfront as she herself did now in cold pursuit. She remembered that Ellen Joyce was strong; wind and rain were her favourite hazards. It was her father who stayed indoors and refused to follow. When she found her mother this time, Henrietta was likely to kill her.

She could hear someone screaming.

Saturday afternoon, cold and gusty, children drawn to the playground of the beach, standing at the edge of the thundering sea with a dog which barked in tune with their shrieking. They were screaming for the sake of it, adding to an orchestra of sound. Then they ran away. Maybe her mother had heard them and gone out to watch; maybe she was simply being perverse in wanting to sit in the cold until it froze her. It would be the third time in a long week that

Hen had embarked to find her. Dragged her back with gentleness no longer quite genuine while all she felt was impatience with the nagging edge of fury and compassion, and anger at the dead. Perhaps better to let her mother die in whatever way she wished, but then her father would be helpless, and she herself would be trapped in a worse vortex of conscience. Her own life had been on hold for a year and she wanted it back. It was too soon for this. Her parents were hardly ancient and yet they had grown older than the hills.

Striding against the wind, Hen thought that there was a great temperamental difference between her father and mother and herself. She, Hen Joyce, believed in the creative power of anger, which was not something either of them understood. That was half the problem. Mother was wallowing in grief the way she had always wallowed in worry, instead of being like the eldest of her daughters, devoted to action rather than reaction, interference rather than reticence; *damn* her, where was she? Mrs Ellen Joyce always said everything would turn out all right, and it didn't. She had always told Angel that it was all right to be plump and insecure as long as you were loved, because that alone was enough to make you beautiful. Rubbish; you were what you made yourself. Even when you were crippled by your name. Hen and Angel, I ask you. How could they do that to us?

What a day. Squalls of wind, little interludes of deceptive calm, bolts of sunlight and flurries of rain, as if to say, got you, just when you thought you were safe. The sea was broiling along the promenade, prowling against concrete, laughing and threatening, growling and roaring like an old bear, then scuttling back with a snarl. No children to watch now. Four o'clock, darkness coming down with a bitter, gusting chill. Hen pulled her coat around her and wondered if

Mother had bothered to cover herself at all. The instinct to shout at her increased with the cold, and then died in her mouth. Her mother had grown so thin.

Ellen was in the furthest bus shelter along the seafront, the smelliest, most miserable sheltering place on the whole promenade, sitting upright in the corner with her handbag clutched to her waist, leaning over it as if it was warm. She looked fully in command of all she surveyed, serene in the face of hypothermia with her small feet in her damp slippers. Henrietta knelt at her feet among crushed glass, beer cans and litter brought in by the wind, took hold of her mother's cold ankles and began to knead them warmer. Mother stared out to sea. It was her refusal to look anyone in the eye that had always infuriated.

'Come home, Mother, there's a dear. It's getting dark.'

Ellen Joyce inclined her head in an approximation of agreement, nodded, then shook her head and held her handbag tighter.

'But it's so nice out here,' she said.

This could only have been spoken by someone with a neurotic love of the sea and Hen ignored it. It was foul out here. Dismal, bleak and ugly. Everyone else was quite right to avoid it. Ellen was surely crazy, but the gaze she turned upon her daughter's hands was merely confused, as if she had woken from sleep. She shook herself and stood up, awkwardly, stumbling into Hen's arms, and then pushing her away almost in the same movement. Hen let her lead the way slowly out of the bus shelter and begin the walk home. They did not link arms, Hen measuring her steps to keep pace with her mother's slow progress, all the time wanting to break into a run. Darkness descended like a blanket as they turned the windswept corner into Alpha Street and saw the lights of the house on the corner shining a mocking welcome with the Christmas tree still in the window. No one had the energy to take it down. Ellen held on to the wall, wanting to say something before they went in.

'I'm not *mad*, you know, Hen. Really I'm not, but coming out here and sitting in the midst of it, well, it's the only way of feeling alive. I have to get very cold so that I can feel the warmth, if you see what I mean.'

Hen did not see. She saw an awkward woman with an infectious grief she refused to relinquish. She said nothing, pushed open the door and watched with some satisfaction as her mother was propelled over the step by a gust of wind. The stairs to the second floor faced the entrance to the house. Ellen clutched the banister as if shaking hands with a long-lost friend and went straight up. Soon there would be the sound of running water, the prelude to a deep, hot bath in which she would stay so long that Hen would begin to worry about her all over again. She went into the living room on the left, where her father still sat by the fire, apparently absorbed by the television and entirely unperturbed. Hen could have throttled him, too. She decided to ignore the fact that he was entitled to relax after a morning in the storage warehouse which was his business and his pride and joy. The worker of the house was entitled to the fire.

'All right?' He asked, smiling.

'*She* is, yes. I suppose so. Would you have gone after her if I hadn't?'

'Eventually. Maybe, maybe not. Why don't you sit down? You never sit down, you're always standing or leaning. You're so restless, Hen.'

'You would have left her, wouldn't you?'

Hen realised she was shouting and moderated her voice. It

made less of a strident sound in this room, what with the shifting crackle of the fire in the grate and the sound of the old plumbing filling a bath.

'Sit down!' he said quietly as if he was training a dog. It made her feel like a disobedient thirty-one-year-old bitch. Called Hen. She sat.

'I need to talk to you.'

'I've been trying to talk to *you* for days.'

'It's not always the best thing, Hen. Not always appropriate. I don't go after your mother when she goes for a walk because I think she knows what she's doing. She's only trying to get some sensation into her bones.'

'By freezing herself to death and then boiling herself alive?'

He sighed.

'It's probably as good a cure as any. Like having a sauna and running out into the snow, only in reverse. Look, Hen darling, I think you ought to go.'

She sat, stunned. Her father was telling her to *go*. Fetch. Come. Sit. Go. Her utterly dependable father: the man who could bore for Britain on the subject of removals and self-storage. The man who never dismissed anyone.

'Go?' she echoed stupidly. 'Go?'

He nodded. 'Go. As in leave this house. Go. To your own home and your own life.'

'Why?'

'Because you simply aren't helping here. You're making it worse. Oh, I know it's with the best intentions, but that's what you're doing. Making it worse. We can neither of us rest with you around.'

A wave of heat rose from her neck and into her face. There was an instinct to weep, scream and also to remain completely still, numb with hurt. This was *her* home. She looked at the framed tapestries on the wall. All sewn by the restless, painstaking hands of her mother. Hen wished Ellen could sew now.

'You don't want me here.'

'We'll always want you here, Hen. But not at the moment.'

'If you're telling me to go, I might never come back.'

He was silent for a moment and then smiled again.

'When you were a child, you were always threatening never to return,' he said. 'And you always did.'

'But all the same, it's a risk you're prepared to take.'

He was, she could see it in his averted eyes. Her dear, ineffectual father. There was nothing she could do. You could never make people love you and you couldn't mend anything by simply loving them. She knew that, but what she had not realised until now was that her presence was an irritant. Her mother shrugging away her supporting arm should have told her that, likewise her father turning a goodnight hug into a pat on the shoulder. They may as well have loathed her. All they wanted was Angel, and Angel was dead. Angel had used her secret cache of pills to overdose herself into endless sleep; if only they had not left her in peace. There, there, they had always said to Angel, you don't have to do anything you don't want to do. And in the end they blamed Angel for nothing and Henrietta for everything. If only Hen had not interfered. You never know when to leave a thing alone, Hen. She saw the newspaper he had stuffed behind the cushion of his armchair, where it had remained because he could not throw it away. She had thought that dramatic photograph of that hateful woman in free fall would have helped, but it had not. He was not that kind of man. Watching her watching him, he took the newspaper and threw it on the open fire.

'Poor woman,' he said. 'Do you know what I dreamt last night? I dreamt you'd killed her. I don't know how you would have done it but I wouldn't put it past you, Hen. You didn't kill her, did you?'

'No, Dad. I wrote to her, that's all.'

Henrietta Joyce went upstairs, past the locked bathroom door where her mother hummed in the bath, into the tiny bedroom which had been designated hers since childhood and had always been too small. She packed a few things into her single holdall and was back downstairs again within minutes, picking up her coat from where she had dropped it in the hall. There didn't seem much point in saying goodbye. It was not so much the fact that her mother and father did not like her much, but the fact that they did not know her at all. They would not have dreamed that it was she, Henrietta Joyce, who needed them. Being in danger had always been Angel's sole prerogative. Her privilege, her inalienable right. Angel always had to be rescued: Hen, never.

She walked along the promenade in the opposite direction to the one her mother had taken, moving easily with the wind behind her towards the centre of town. There was a train at five thirty: she knew the train timetable by heart. Anger gave way to mourning, and the sea seemed to mourn with her. It took twenty minutes to reach the station. She had made this journey to London hundreds of times.

Sitting on the slow train, she tried to feel relieved. An hour and a half would take her to a different world of light, bustle and optimism. Work, friends. She might never have to make this journey again. The heaviest thing she carried in the carpet bag was the file. She had covered it with a binding of red rust velvet, the colour of dried blood, because she liked to handle soft material and the luxury of the cover belied the nature of the contents. The colour was accidental, but it went with the muted, autumnal colours in the material of the bag itself which sported a motif of abstract flowers growing from the handle and over her shoulder as she strode along. People remembered the bag. The file was beginning to wear a hole on one corner.

The file contained a history of everything that had happened to Angel, from the moment when she herself had found out and intervened. Found Angel and dragged her back, which was not exactly what Angel had wanted. There was stuff in there she had never shown anyone and never let out of her possession, not quite knowing whom she was protecting. She had found Angel in a dump and everything of *his* that could go into the carpet bag had gone with them. Shame there had been no money. The photographs were obscene, enough to convict him of something if ever they had been used, but Angel had wept and said, no never.

I am thirty-one years old, called Hen. I'm not going to look at this file, now, although I shall when I get home. I have the older sister syndrome of knowing best. I am still so angry about everything that happened I give it off like an infection. And it's all over, or it would be if I had not written to *her*. I wonder if she was inspired by that other woman who jumped? One hour to go on this train and all those stops ahead of me and I can't even bear to read. Paddock Wood, Tonbridge, into London commuter land. She rummaged in the bag and brought out her sewing, leant against the window and made stitches with quiet precision.

Peter Friel got on the train at the penultimate stop before London, on his way back from his brother's house and aiming for home, relieved to be returning to normality after a day with other people's children, marvelling at the carnage created by a birthday party for his four-year-old niece and considering that life in the suburbs really was red in tooth and claw. A quiet drink or three, accompanied by adult food and possibly, a phone conversation with Thomas Noble, was what he had in mind for the rest of the evening, and then he saw that bag, alongside a woman sewing. It was the bag he recognised first because he had seen and admired it often enough before. Then he registered the novelty of a young woman sitting and sewing in a half empty train carriage, knew who it was, Angel Joyce's sister, the nondescript girl who had come to court with her, sat with her patiently through the long delays, always accompanied by that colourful bag. The girl who gave evidence first, was cross-examined first, and then kept apart, waiting outside Court One while her sister was grilled, bullied and humiliated inside, until she could bear it no longer. Angel's blotchy face and badly tinted black hair made a mockery of her name and Marianne Shearer had cut her to ribbons. Peter had always resented the fact that a good-looking victim was always more convincing. It gave them confidence, and Angel had none of that. It seemed unfair. The last time he had seen Angel's sister, she had been running away from the building and he had wanted to stop her.

Peter hesitated, then went and sat opposite the girl whose name he could not immediately remember, although he could remember the words of her statement. Last time he had seen her he had been in disguise, a faceless lawyer/junior prosecutor wearing a wig, part of the legal team who had thrown Angel Joyce to the wolves in the interests of justice and had been powerless to protect her. It was the case that had shattered his belief in the system, the vision of her collapse haunting him for months now, coming back in strength because of what had happened this week. He had to talk to her. It occurred to him that he would be the last person in the world she would want to speak to, but by that time it was too late. Hen carried on sewing a hem on a piece of emerald green silk the size of a handkerchief. The train trundled through London Bridge station. He had five minutes to do what he had wanted to do six months ago. Apologise.

'Ms Joyce?'

Henrietta, that was the name. A jolly-hockey-sticks kind of name that did not suit her any more than Angel had suited her sister. She folded up the piece of cloth and began to stuff it into the bag, ignoring him. She closed the bag with a clumsy leather clasp he also remembered and began to move out of her seat.

'What are you making?' he asked. 'It's a beautiful colour.'

She looked at him warily, poised for flight. Of course she recognised him. The features and the roles of every person involved in that case were etched in her memory, wigs or no wigs. She had watched them come and go and despised them.

'I was junior counsel for the Crown, last May, and . . .'

'I know,' she said. 'And what?'

'I wanted to apologise. I wanted to say how sorry I was.'

The train was pulling into the station. They were standing by the door, with her clutching the bag and refusing to listen. He found himself talking to her urgently. The doors opened: in a moment she would be able to run.

'Look Ms Joyce, please listen to me. Can I buy you a drink?'

She took off down the platform, hoisting the bag, and he caught her at the ticket barrier when she stopped, cursing, and started fishing in the pockets of her long coat for the damn ticket. No bloody ticket. A second chance, then, as she crouched by the bag and began to search through it. The ticket was wrapped up with the material she had been sewing. Fate intervening again. It had to be right.

'Can I buy you a drink? Please?'

She suddenly looked weary, her hand holding the ticket shaking as she went through the barrier and turned to face him, some instinct either of manners or tiredness making her stop. She had no energy to run any more.

'Why the hell should I talk to you?'

What was there to say?

'Because it isn't all over,' he said. 'And because I need you.'

He did not know the magic in those final words, more particularly the word *need*. Plus the fact that he had eyes like a dog pleading for food and he was as thin as a rail, and she did not want to go towards her own, empty, complicated home just yet. She shrugged.

'OK.'

Why not? Someone had said they needed her. After all, Hen thought to herself, I'm a makeshift daughter whose parents have at long last told me to fuck off, and I've been waiting all my life for that to happen. I've got nothing to lose.

And he's right. It can't be all over, because that bitch jumped.

Chapter Four

She had been in almost silence, trying to talk for the last ten days and then she had been told to go. Later, Henrietta Joyce used that as her excuse for why she agreed to go for a drink with a virtual stranger she had met by unhappy accident on a train. It was the sight of crowds which did it, the prospect of remaining in a place full of chattering people, instead of the view of the sea from an upstairs window and a house full of silent recrimination. Also, the knowledge that if she had not found the ticket, the man with the Labrador eyes would have paid the fine, all for the privilege of sitting with her. She must have something he wanted, and if she was not wanted for herself, this was a good substitute.

She did not trust him as far as she could have thrown him, but that did not matter. This wasn't personal. Whatever else was on his agenda, it did not include flirtation.

'It may seem strange to you,' he said, far more composed after he had done his manly thing and steered her towards empty seats in a pub within fifty yards of the station and bought a bottle of red wine, 'but I've dreamt of meeting you. To say sorry.'

She let him do the talking and did not acknowledge the apology. It was, as a lawyer would say, irrelevant. Hen had never blamed the secondary people for the debacle of the trial that featured her sister as victim, even though their powerlessness amazed her. They were not the enemy. The Defendant was the foe, along with his Defence Counsel, Marianne Shearer, QC. She shook her head, dismissing his words. She was here, she told herself, because it was cold out there and warmer in here, and a part of her was back with her mother on the seafront, instead of being vaguely, indeterminately, needed, which was one step away from rejection. It clarified the mind. Let him talk first. She was starved of chat, with a head full of things she wanted to articulate: she would have talked to a dog.

'But the other reason for seizing the opportunity to talk to you . . . well there are many. I keeping thinking of it all, you see, especially now. And then Marianne Shearer . . . well, she died. Did you know that?'

'Jumped. Yes. She was in the paper. Front pages, too, I expect she would have liked that.'

He nodded vigorously, ignoring the bitchy note in her voice.

'It set me thinking all over again – as if I'd ever stopped – because it means it isn't all over, is it? I can't help wondering why she died. I know that the officer in the case thinks Rick Boyd may have something to do with it. Maybe he got to her somehow. May even have seduced her, too. Heaven knows, he wasn't fussy about looks. Oh God, what an awful thing to say, I shouldn't have said it.'

He seemed like a man who frequently said things he

should not have said and that reassured her. Not such a careful lawyer as he had seemed six months before, nodding and bowing in Marianne Shearer's wake like a dinghy behind a yacht. They had all done that, even the Judge.

'Yes, you should. There's no point pretending that my sister was beautiful, but she did have youth on her side, and naiveté, and lack of confidence. Sorry, Mr Friel, but I can't see that bastard having a crack at a dried-up old walnut like Shearer, she'd have seen him coming a mile off. You mean he might have seduced her after he was acquitted, but why bother? He specialised in the insecure, didn't he? She wasn't one of those. And what would be the point? She'd served her purpose brilliantly. Although you might be right, and he manipulated her, too.'

That was the greatest number of words she had said so far and at least it proved that he had her attention. He sat back and sighed; most of him consisted of legs and arms, with a concave torso, a bad haircut and amazing colouring. Pale skin, red hair, freckles, and casual clothes that appeared, on a second glance, to be spattered with egg. Not a man who noticed his own appearance.

'Boyd might have put pressure on Shearer because she knew so much about him. Maybe she was going to have a word with the police about all the other things she knew. Join up all the dots so they had a proper profile of him for next time. No, she wouldn't do that. It would be like being human and socially responsible. Maybe she was simply influenced by that other woman, Mrs Ward, who also jumped and got a headline.'

He was thinking aloud, talking to himself as if he had known her for ever, as if they had something instantly in common simply because they were discussing a subject about which they knew more than anyone else. Hen had noticed the same syndrome when she was working; the rapport of otherwise isolated experts, fascinated by an obscure book or a design, ready to gnaw at ideas forever with complete strangers made instant friends by rare, shared knowledge, but still she bristled. She did not want to talk about Ms Shearer, QC, except venomously.

Mrs Ward was sad and depressed, pour soul,' Hen said. 'She'd tried to kill herself before, hadn't she? It was spontaneous desperation in her case and it's insulting to her to equate her with Marianne Shearer in any way. She was a good woman, for a start. Not like Shearer at all. It looks to me as if Shearer staged it all for effect, probably hired the bloke who filmed it. It would be nice to think she killed herself for shame,' Hen continued. 'After all, what had she done with her life but defend scumbags and get them off?'

'I think the earlier suicide might have influenced her in some way,' Peter said. 'She copied it in certain respects, but I very much doubt if shame had anything to do with it. She regarded defending people as a mission, a good use of talents, a fight for justice for the underdog. Shame doesn't come into it. Probably not part of her psyche at all, and why she couldn't understand its existence in your sister, except for something to be exploited. It would have to be a far worse sort of shame than getting someone wicked released – she revelled in that. It's what's known as *winning*; it's the opposite of losing. Look, I'm sorry. It's hardly kind of me to talk to you like this, but the reason it was such a lucky chance for me to meet you is because the whole thing haunts me and I can't let go of it, very unprofessional, I know. It's as if he won out over everybody. Infected every life he touched, you know. Even Shearer's.'

Hen felt she was being used in a way she didn't understand and was irritated rather than angry. She had just about lost the habit of being angry. How upset could he really be? It wasn't his sister who had died last year. He had never been mauled by Ms Shearer in court.

'You're upset, and everyone else you know is bored with you talking about it, is that it?' she said, jeeringly. 'So you mug someone on a train, just because you think you've seen a fellow obsessive who'll listen to you for the price of a bottle of wine? Not particularly sensitive, Mr Friel, especially if that someone is me, sister of the first deceased, on her way home from a visit to still grieving parents who can't bear the sight of me, because I remind them of her and they blame the whole thing on me, and oh, shit . . . I'm going to cry. And I've got no money, and my business is on the rocks, and what the fucking hell, you want to discuss it like it was something for a thesis? Just because that harridan jumped to her death and you feel guilty about something? Oh, get a life, what do you really want?'

She thought for a dreadful moment that he was going to clasp her in his arms, or seize the hand which was delving into the carpet bag for a cigarette, forgetting no-smoking laws. Instead, she could see through the mist that he was looking crestfallen and holding out a capacious handkerchief which she seized from him. She could tell by the feel that the cloth was fine linen and could see that it was an interesting shade of blue. It was nice to the touch; she would have accepted it as a gift, anytime, and she sniffed it, instinctively, the way she always did with cloth. There was a smell of lavender.

'What the hell's this?'

'Sorry. One of my sister's table napkins. I've just been to her kid's party, didn't know I'd got it. Must have put it my pocket.'

Kid's birthday party? A young uncle.

The mist cleared and she wiped her eyes on sweet-smelling linen, drained the glass of wine and watched him pour the next. No more apologies from him; if he had not had any plan for this conversation in the first place, he had one now, without room for sentiment or sympathy.

'I want to get rid of a ghost,' he said. 'And I did want to apologise for the magnificent cock-up we made of that case. And I do have a professional interest, but basically, I want to know what happened, and that's all really. I hate getting part of the truth and not all of it, as if one ever could. There was so much evidence we couldn't use, for instance. There was so much *missing* evidence. They couldn't call all sorts of stuff after so much evidence was disallowed, and I can't bear only knowing half of it, and yes, I do want to write a thesis. And I'm probably in the wrong job. Not my business to know about the background, but I do want to know what really happened. And all the stuff that Angel suppressed. Stuff that he'd hinted at and thought that she might have had, only she didn't. You must know more than I do. I only know what I saw on paper. It isn't over, you know, because he's out there, doing it again, just like he did before.'

'Doing what?'

'Raping, debasing, stealing. Kidnapping, disfiguring if necessary. Life-poisoning. Another victim. There were three before Angel, two running alongside. He's a con man, that's what he does and he isn't anything like old yet.'

He sat back, embarrassed by his own gabbling, but not enough to stop.

'And you thought you might discuss it with Marianne Shearer,' she said. 'Only now, you can't. So that leaves me.'

'His modus operandi is this,' Peter went on. 'He finds a

vulnerable, self conscious woman, flatters her, seduces her, makes up a story of poor, poor me, gets her to part with her money and then keeps her prisoner, working for him, because she's too weak to run for cover. Once she's down, she's down. In the hands of competent Defence Counsel, the story's reversed, so that it's *she* who's the predator, *she* who gives him no alternative but to leave her obsessive self; she who is the unreasonable tyrant. He was so credible, I could have believed him, if it weren't for the others. We got a bit bogged down in similar facts, didn't we? Sorry, how would you know, you weren't in the room during the legal arguments. Shearer and that spineless judge won them all. I want to learn. It does tend to make one ruthless. I want to know what Angel was like and what evidence you suppressed. I really, really want to know. And, since you're never going to be a witness ever again in a case involving your own sister, you might feel free to tell me.'

'Can I keep this?' she said, folding the sweet-smelling napkin into her fist.

'Please do,' he said.

She sipped the wine, clutching the napkin as if it was a lucky charm. She quite liked this insensitive objectivity and she was sick of people not wanting to know. Sick of hiding things from Mum and Dad. It made her talk as if a dam had burst.

'So many lies get told when people are feeling guilty,' she said. 'Is there ever such a thing as an entirely innocent victim? Angel was sweet, but she wasn't perfect, nobody is. She was amazingly affectionate and everyone loved her, but she found it difficult to stick at things. She was my little sister and I was the bruiser. I left home as soon as I could; Angel tried one thing and another and kept going back. She always needed reassurance about everything, all the time, it was as if there was a big hole in the middle of her. Angel was always picked up and hugged and she got to rely on it. It was a kind of spoiling, really, because she was always treated as if she was special until she knew, not so deep down, that she wasn't. It's pointless trying to analyse her, but she was a whole mass of insecurities by the time she met Rick Boyd. She'd been on half a dozen training courses, failed the lot and this one was for learning how to be a carer. Boyd worked for the taxi firm the college used. He brought her home a few times . . . well, you know the rest.'

'Not what made her into a victim.'

She crumpled the napkin in her hand, then straightened it out and folded it neatly, trying not to cry, brushing away tears before they fell, hating him and wanting to tell him *he knew she could sew*, and then saying something else.

'Angel was always hung up about her appearance. She hated almost every aspect of it, with the surprising exceptions of her hands and feet and she was very vain about those. Anyway, she was always trying to change the way she looked. She thought she was ugly and fat, but she wasn't really, she was just ordinary with an ordinary weight problem. Rick cured that, didn't he? She wasn't so fat by the time he'd finished with her. She never had an ounce of dress sense, and she wouldn't be told. She should have stuck to sewing, like me. She was waiting all the time for someone to wave a magic wand and make her feel beautiful. I guess he did that. She was . . . needy.'

He waited but she said no more.

'I see. Just his type, then. Like the others who wouldn't talk. Insecure, immature.'

She nodded, miserably, cross that he might imagine she

41

had not thought of that, when she thought of it all the time. She closed her hand into a fist.

'I wish I understood *him*,' she said. 'I can understand being a con man, making a woman adore you, getting sex and adoration for nothing, extracting money from credulous parents for his so-called business, doing all that. Mum and Dad have a storage business, they'd done all right. They were so pleased she'd found someone personable, they would have given him anything, and did. I can see the money angle, but why did he have to be so cruel? Why this power kick, why debase her, why put her in prison and disfigure her, when she would have done anything he wanted for another promise? Why didn't he just leave her?'

'Because she'd got wise?' he suggested. 'Because *she* was going to leave *him*, is that why? Nobody leaves Rick Boyd.'

'Dead right, they don't. Not even his QC. And Angel wouldn't have done either, if I hadn't pitched up. She'd got way beyond being able to leave, even if she wanted to. They'd been gone a year, supposedly working together at this mythical bar in Birmingham and she'd long since stopped calling home because he'd taken her mobile. There was no bar: she had a two-bit cleaning job in a pub and he took the money, rationed it out in pence. Then one night, I think it was soon after he chopped off her finger, she phoned me, from the job. She phoned because he'd left and she thought he wasn't coming back. She wanted me to find him. I went the next day. You know what I found.'

'No, I don't. Not exactly. I know what you said you'd found.'

'Bloody lawyers. You never believe what you hear.'

'We can't afford to.'

Hen poured the last of the wine into her own glass and put

42

the napkin in the carpet bag. Now she had run out of words and held on to the watch she wore on a piece of ribbon round her neck. He noticed that the ribbon was red and gold and she herself was a mass of colours. He was slow to notice, but when he did, absorbed every detail. She did not seem to mind his scrutiny. She was calm after storm, spring after winter, a woman composed for the witness box.

'There's one thing about Angel you have to know, Mr Friel. She wasn't very bright and she wasn't pretty, but she was loyal and sweet-natured. She was born to look after people, should have got a job looking after animals, something simple. She may not have believed in herself, but she was utterly incapable of telling a lie.'

'You must have loved her very much,' he said.

She was shaking her head, wincing at the cliché. Love, yuk.

'No, not all the time. She was exasperating and there were times when I actually disliked her, but I wanted the best for her. Look, I wanted her to give evidence because that was the only thing which would give her back her dignity and stop her being a victim, and also because she had the power to stop him doing it again. I thought she had an absolute duty to use her experience to put him in prison for a long time and I was going to make sure that she did. Only the worst happened. Your bloody Ms Shearer used every trick in the book to spin it out, knowing every delay would make Angel more of a nervous wreck than ever. He knew that and she knew it too. The final trick was to take my evidence first; it gave her more fuel to undermine Angel before she even appeared and it kept us apart. And then she made her look a fool. Angel's worst nightmare comes true. She wasn't going to be believed. She was being accused of being a liar, which was the one thing she wasn't, and she was being exposed for everything she feared she was. A clinging wretch of a woman who'd never grown up and was willing to drag a man down into her own dirt. A madwoman who would mutilate herself to make him stay.'

'He reversed it, didn't he?' Peter said. '*She* was demented and he was sane. Very clever. He made himself a mirror image of her. I don't think it would have worked, you know, if only she'd had the strength to go on. It would all have become clear when he gave his evidence, we could catch him in so many lies. He was her diametric opposite, one of those who'll lie about everything even when there's no need. If only she'd completed her evidence. There was no real case without her. Not even with you.'

He sounded genuinely sad. Hen did not know if this was pity, or regret for an opportunity missed. She was feeling cold, but oddly grateful for finding her tongue. She touched the handle of the carpet bag, reminding herself of its presence, wanting to go, wanting to stay, needing to explain and not knowing what.

'If Angel had completed her evidence, then she would have to see herself as others saw her. The ultimate, stupid victim. I think anything was better than that. She may have wanted to end it all, she may have wanted just to sleep herself into oblivion, I don't know. She just could not bear to go back into that courtroom. There should have been screens . . . there should have been every protection fucking Shearer argued away. There shouldn't have been Boyd's fake illnesses, there shouldn't have been a weak judge allowing all those delays. Don't tell me you don't know that. And I should never have let her out of my sight, not let her go home with Mummy and Daddy, to be put to bed and told she didn't have to do anything she didn't want to do. Look, I must go home myself. Thanks for the drink.'

'Can I see you again? This is where I am.'

She put the card he gave her into the bag and smiled. With both of them standing, the top of her head was level with his shoulder and he was unnerved to notice how small she was. Her sister had been a strapping girl, once. The sort a kind aunt would have referred to as bonny. They bore no resemblance to one another at all. He walked down the road with her, wondering if he dared offer to see her home, or if that added to his impertinence. No, Peter, don't push your luck. You know where she lives and she might, just might phone you. Saturday evening crowds were gathering, looking for warmth on another cold, January night.

'Can I get you a taxi? I've kept you late,' he said, hurrying along beside her.

'No. I don't do taxis, except for work for carrying things.'

She wanted rid of him now and he felt awful, leaving her, as if he was letting one of his nieces cross the road on her own.

'What exactly do you do, Henrietta?'

Not a good question. He remembered what she did. Something menial and dull. Shearer had sneered at it.

They had stopped at a bus stop and he could see one waiting at the next traffic light, ready to pull up and take her away.

'Me?' She sounded surprised at the question, sticking her hand out for the bus, not looking at him. 'Me? Oh, I look after things. Clothes are so much more reliable than people. It's all in the trial transcript. She gave me a job description, didn't she? You can look up my website. Frockserve.com. You could do with a bit of scrubbing up yourself.'

She was looking him up and down with a glimmer of amusement; she in her mass of muted colours, and he, bland and rumpled and egg-stained. 'And,' she added as the bus slowed and a cyclist cut across, slowing it further, giving her the chance of the last word, 'don't think I don't know your game, Mr Friel. You don't care about my sister or me. It's Marianne Shearer you care about. Your club, your kind. Your brotherhood.'

He stood rooted to the spot, because she was right.

The bus rolled her towards home. Henrietta Joyce pulled out the emerald square and sewed a few more stitches. Then she pulled out the lavender-smelling napkin and blew her nose on it, thinking how people imagined she was always in control of herself just because she seemed as if she was. They would make unconscious judgements about her because of the clothes and the way she sat, long before they had even really looked, but everybody did that with everybody. If manners maketh man, colours maketh woman. She decided that despite the doggy eyes and the egg on the shirt, she did not like Peter Friel for accosting her on a train in the evening of a dark day and pretending he cared.

Damn Peter Friel and her own need to talk. Damn the woman for jumping. It made her question everything she had done, as if she had ever stopped. Angel would have come home and licked her wounds, Dad said.

Which wounds do you mean, Dad? A missing finger? A terrible affliction if you needed to sew. Perhaps I felt that more than she did. That would have been the worst thing, for me.

She walked twenty yards from the bus stop and took the key out of the pocket of the coat he had noticed last of all, which didn't help him any, since she was proud of this home-made coat, slept in it many a time and the thing came out brand new. She had wrapped Angel in it to take her away. She opened the door, and thought, yes, her parents were right, it was high time to come home. There was a long march upstairs, past the empty shop premises on the ground floor and up, up, up. She had the top two floors and the thing she called the laboratory in the basement. You had to watch against moth, detect the smells, behave with decorum. There was a small nest of rooms in the attic which was hers alone. Bedroom, living room, kitchenette. That was all Angel needed, then, or so it seemed.

Forget Angel. Hen had been away for two weeks: there was work to do.

She sniffed the air in the kitchen, which was stuffy but clean. Jake, the old man who once lived here, still had a presence not quite displaced by the other more recent ghost. There was still a missing space where a treasured coffee percolator had been and the sound of his kind, scolding voice, saying, *NO, not that way, this way.* It was her business now, he said; he was sick and tired of it. She missed him.

Hen moved into the bedroom, took the card Peter Friel had given her out of the carpet bag and put it on the table by the bed. She still needed to talk about it, and he was right, they didn't know the half of it. If he was that fascinated by the subject, maybe he could be her unpaid therapist. After all, she had exhausted everyone else. None of it was real life, not any more.

Out of nowhere, a strange feeling of peace and homecoming stole over her. This really was home now, and she need not share it with anyone else, not even phantoms, spectres and memories. She hurried from the kitchen, down the stairs with the key and unlocked the door of the floor below, fumbled for the switch with her eyes closed only so that she could open them again.

Lights, action, spectacle, sensation. A workroom full of colour; a red cloak edged with purple hanging against the far window, a shimmering shawl over her chair and the halogen bulbs illuminating a rack of gorgeous skirts and dressed in the hues of a dozen subtle rainbows. The brash and the sophisticated, garments for tarts, queens and bishops and actors keeping company with one another, waiting for her in neat orderliness, a vision of loveliness. Cloth of silver and emerald silk, and a wedding dress that shone with an ivory sheen. Aladdin's cave. It was a room of dreams and she sighed with relief.

My sister's death, my parents' mortality, is not my fault or my blame, it's all over, now. I must say my prayers and go to sleep. It's me and myself for all time, now. I've nothing to protect any more, except this.

In his own neat flat, Peter Friel reprimanded himself for being a liar. Not exactly that, but certainly a little economical with the truth. His need to apologise to her for the inadequacies of the law was certainly genuine, but the bottom line of the truth was that he was now hired by the hour to find out why Marianne Shearer had jumped in the way she did on the day she did, and what her legacies were, and the pay was good and he had to do it. One way or another, someone in that case had pushed her into despair. *R* v Boyd, featuring dead Angel Joyce, Marianne Shearer's last big case, with a copy of the transcript on his desk. They all had them. She had ordered dozens of copies.

She had jumped to her death because of this case. There was no other reason and she followed no one's example.

How pretty Hen Joyce was; he would always think of colours when he thought of her.

He looked up the website, Frockserve.com.

He took out the transcript of the trial, read to dispel his dreams and make himself remember the fine details he had forgotten.

No one was ever as straightforward as they looked, however colourful.

EXTRACT FROM TRANSCRIPT: *R* v BOYD

Cross-examination of Henrietta Joyce by Marianne Shearer, QC

MS. Miss Joyce, you have just told the Court that your sister phoned you from her place of work almost a year after you had last spoken to her. You have said that the last thing you knew was that she was with her boyfriend and was happy and you were happy with it?

Witness interrupts.

HJ. I didn't say that. You're paraphrasing. The last thing I knew about Angel was that she was apparently all right. She'd been on a training course, chucked it, met a man and gone off to live with him in Birmingham. I said our parents were happy with this, I didn't say I was. I didn't say I knew anything beforehand about what her real situation was, because I didn't know. I said I hoped she was happy. Please don't twist what I say.

MS. No need to be aggressive, Ms Joyce, just answer the questions. So, you hadn't seen your sister in a while before she phoned you?

HJ. No.

MS. How long?

HJ. *Sighs* I saw her intermittently before that, mostly when I went home to visit my parents once a month or so. Angel was usually there. She never really left.

MS. So, how close were you to Angel? You'd fled the nest, and she'd stayed dependent? How much older were you?

HJ. I do wish you'd only ask one question at a time. That was three, wasn't it? Can I answer in reverse? Angel was eighteen months younger than me. We were very different in

50

temperament and development, but we learned the same things and we were close.

MS. Ms Joyce, would it surprise you to know that the other Ms Joyce, Angel, your baby sister, told my client, the Defendant, that she was *not* close to you, in fact, that she did not like you at all? You had always bullied her and she disliked you intensely. Hated you, in fact?

Pause

HJ. No, it doesn't surprise me. She might well have said that. Although I must say it hurts. I didn't always approve of her, or she of me, for that matter.

MS. Your sister said to the Defendant, 'She's a control freak.' She said you would always try and stop her. You tried to control your parents and her. You always went to the rescue when there was no need. You were bossy, domineering, jealous, even, and you always knew best.

Witness shrugs.

HJ. Takes one to know one, Ms Shearer.

Fuss in court.

MS. Just answer the questions.

HJ. I thought I was.

MS. Your sister phoned to say she was in distress. You stated she told you she wanted to leave the Defendant.

HJ. No, I didn't say that.

MS. You said so, Ms Joyce, in your evidence. You said, quite clearly, that you went to Birmingham to rescue her *because she was distressed.*

HJ. If you had listened, Ms Shearer, you would have heard that I said in my evidence in chief that I went because *I* was distressed. She sounded lost and alone and she told me she wanted me to find him, because he had left her.

MS. Ahh. Is it not the fact that you found your silly, angelic sibling alive and well and whingeing about the fact that her boyfriend was in the process of leaving her? A common enough occurrence in a young woman's life, surely? As well he might, after she had drained him dry and driven him mad with her infantile dependence and her spendthrift tendencies?

Witness clutches rail of witness box.

HJ. I found a rat in a trap, Ms Shearer. I found a starving, brainwashed woman in rags. With polished nails and a missing finger. No one would keep a dog like that. Not even a silly bitch.

MS. She didn't want releasing, did she Ms Joyce? She wanted to wait where she was until he came back?

HJ. She didn't seem to know what she wanted. She was terrified of him at the same time. She was paralysed.

MS. Terrified? And wanting him to come back?

HJ. Yes.

MS. The two don't go together, do they? Isn't it true, Ms Joyce, that you found your spoiled baby sister weeping and wailing because she had driven her boyfriend away, and it was you, not him, who finally kidnapped her? You did not do as she asked, which was look for him. You took her away and you took everything else you could find with you. You wanted to be back in control of the sister you bullied. What have you done, Ms Joyce?

Witness is silent.

MS. You knew she had to be the centre of attention, to the extent that she would injure herself to get it. She would even starve herself, she'd done that before, hadn't she? You knew that.

HJ. No, I didn't know that. It isn't true.

MS. You knew she was unstable and demanding. And yet

you, Miss Joyce, from the depth of your experience, con-
demned my client for the symptoms of your sister's mental
instability. What qualified you to judge?

*Ms Shearer turns pages of witnesses deposition, reads from
it.*

You do dry cleaning, Miss Joyce, that's your job. What does
doing laundry tell you about life? Does it make you obsessive? Since when does being a dry cleaner make you God?

Witness remains silent.

His Honour Judge McDonaugh. That isn't helpful, Ms Shearer.
I think we'll adjourn now, until tomorrow.

CHAPTER FIVE

'Pray stand for Her Majesty's Coroner.'

They stood obediently as the Coroner entered from his own side door, at the back of the raised stage which held his vast desk, ushered forward by the Coroner's own Sergeant. HM Coroner was a thin man with a large head; he took his own seat, easily, while the Sergeant sat below, busily arranging his papers. The Coroner smiled on those assembled, adjusted his jacket, checked the position of the gavel on his desk and folded his hands in front of him, as if waiting for something to happen. The room was wood-lined and oblong, with a raised, square witness box to the left of the Coroner's dais, so that only a witness would be at his eye level. The rest of the oblong was occupied by three rows of benches with elongated narrow desks, all surrounded by plenty of open space and a few plastic chairs at the back for spectators. Thomas Noble always found the place reminded him of a church without decoration, its very plainness speaking volumes about the anonymity of death. It was a little like the inside of a large communal coffin.

Frank Shearer sat next to him, and on his left, the photographer, Paul Bain and on the far side of him, a plain-clothes police officer. There was really no need for any of them to be there. Thomas recognised the Coroner as the new model, the type who made it his business to make light of formality and talk in plain English. Speaking for himself, he preferred pomp and distance, because at least one knew where one was. Obfuscation was usually better than straight talking. There was never any comfort in a Coroner's Court, however much the coroner's purpose was dressed up or dressed down and Thomas did not like it if he himself was left with nothing to explain.

'Mr Noble?' the Coroner said.

Thomas nodded.

'Good. I can rely on you to explain that this is all a bit of formality. I shall open the inquest into the death of Miss Marianne Shearer, and then adjourn it, once I've explained what I do and why you have to listen to me, OK? Can I just check who's here?'

He produced half glasses to look at his papers.

'Mr Frank Shearer, brother of the deceased, Mr Bain, witness to the death of the deceased, DC Jones of the Metropolitan Police, Mr Thomas Noble, legal representative of the deceased?'

They all dipped their heads in dutiful acknowledgement, like a row of puppets.

'And those sitting at the back?' the Coroner asked. 'Are these family members?'

Thomas turned to see the three sitting in the spectators' plastic chairs. Two journalists, which was one more than normal, and a man in a heavy coat who sat with his arms crossed. Thomas could have sworn that he winked. As he looked, a small woman came in and sat at the end of the row, nearest the exit door. She was carrying a bag of many colours which she placed on her lap. Everyone looked straight ahead.

'No, sir, not family members,' the Coroner's Sergeant said, gazing disapprovingly at the newest incomer.

The Coroner looked down at the front row. No signs of terrible grief, no wailing women. He could be brisk.

'Good. No need for anyone to take the witness stand at this stage. I've got statements from you all. Ms Shearer jumped from a sixth floor window at eight a.m. on Jan fourth, and it's now Jan ninth, OK? Are we agreed?'

Nods all round. He wrote it down.

'I'm assured that this incident is not related to the death of Mrs Ward, ten days ago. Similar circumstances, very different people. I should stress that the latter case is not within my jurisdiction and is not being considered by this court, so we should dismiss it from our minds.'

There were further nods.

'And you, Mr Bain, saw her fall, and you, DC Jones, were present when death was certified and you accompanied the body to a place where it was identified by Mr Noble in the presence of my sergeant, and you, Mr Shearer, are the next of kin? And Mr Noble's her executor?'

Again, they all nodded.

'Right. There is therefore no doubt that Ms Shearer is the deceased, and equally no doubt that further post-mortem enquiries have to be made. For those present, I must explain my own, very humble role in all this. To put it plainly, whenever a person dies in out-of-the-ordinary circumstances – without having received medical attention within two weeks of their death, for instance; not old, not unwell, basically, death not expected – there has to be an inquest. That means an inquiry. The Coroner's role is to establish *cause* of death, nothing more nor less. Not to say why this person died, but what caused it. Not who was to blame, if anyone was, but *cause*. In the case of what looks like a self-inflicted death, which this certainly does, I have four possible verdicts. Accidental death, Death incurred whilst the balance of mind was disturbed, an Open Verdict, or Suicide. The last means definite evidence that the deceased was determined to make away with him- or herself and actively planned to do so and only that last verdict requires proof beyond reasonable doubt.'

There was the sound of the exit door shutting. Thomas turned. The girl with the carpet bag and the two journalists had already left, as if realising nothing more was going to happen. The Coroner frowned.

'I'm adjourning this for two months, by which time I expect to see evidence which will make my verdict inevitable. Not blame, not analysis, evidence.'

'Pray stand for Her Majesty's Coroner!'

He was gone.

'Charming,' Frank Shearer said. 'Why the hell were we dragged halfway across London for that? He could have written us an email or phoned.'

'Not allowed,' Thomas said. 'We have to be here, present and correct, and show ourselves. The Coroner is an ancient institution begun in the days when you had to turn up to prove you existed. I think we have to go. You might like a word with Mr Bain.'

'Why?'

'To see if he has anything to add.'

'The one who took the pictures?'

'Be nice to him, Frank. He isn't the one who jumped. He could be useful.'

They crossed the dismal waiting room, where another posse of people waited their turn with the Coroner, shuffling to one side to let them through. It reminded Thomas of the ruthless efficiency of a crematorium. Thomas had read the Coroner's daily list. Short cases and adjournments first, full hearings next. The man had a long day.

Paul Bain, equally bemused by his role in the day's procedure, stood outside, smoking, along with other waifs and strays who were wondering what to do next. The suppressed anxiety of the courtroom spread into the street, despite the brusque kindliness of officials who marshalled them in and marshalled them out. There was an air about Bain which said, 'Is this it?' He looked like someone who expected to be punched.

'Good of you to come, Mr Bain,' Thomas said to him with his frightening bonhomie.

'I didn't have any choice, did I? Are you the lawyer? Will I have to come next time?'

''Fraid so, Mr Bain. Next time, you'll have to give evidence, verbally. I wondered if we could talk to you about that.'

'I've given a statement to the police. That's all I'm doing.'

You gave your statement to the newspapers, you little swine, Thomas wanted to say. You've had your lucky moment and you don't look as if it's made you happy, yet. Tough luck.

'I'm looking after Ms Shearer's affairs.' He almost added 'in her absence', and thought at the same time that the choice of the word 'affairs' was unfortunate. Marianne must have had Affairs, in the improper use of the word, and he might have to find out about those, too. Distasteful, but she was leaving him with no choice. There was some elegant man to whom she had alluded but never described.

'And I simply wanted to ask you, as the only observer of her untimely death, if there's anything else you noticed. It must have been a terrible shock.'

He managed to make the sympathy sound genuine. Bain had a face like a weasel and the stature of a small, disappointed man to whom life had not been fair. He was defensive, belligerent and apologetic at the same time, trying not to admit he was out of his depth and still suffering something he did not deserve. Being paid well for the evidence of his own trauma was not a palliative. He was still owed some sort of compensation for feeling bad. Frank Shearer stood to one side, saying nothing, but hemming him in. Paul stubbed out his cigarette. Frank took out a packet and offered him another. It came across rather like a command to stay still. He took the cigarette. Frank lit it for him, solicitously, holding the lighter far too close.

'What else could I have noticed? I noticed her, that was all. You couldn't really notice anything else.'

'Yes, I understand that, but now you've had a few days to consider, do any other details come to mind?'

'I don't know what you mean. I saw a woman jumping off a fucking balcony, that's what I saw.'

'Could you see inside the room?'

'Not beyond the curtains, no. I remember them blowing outwards, there was a bit of a breeze, I had my coat on, oh shit.'

The cigarette trembled in his fingers and he took a deep drag on it. It seemed to calm him.

'You didn't by any chance see anyone else on the balcony?'

'Would have been in the pictures, wouldn't it? There was someone on the next balcony.'

'Yes, I know that. I mean, could you have seen someone else behind Ms Shearer? You know, in the room itself.'

'I couldn't see . . .'

'Not even a shadow? A teeny, weeny shadow? A movement? Perhaps you'd like to think about it,' Thomas said, smoothly proffering his business card. 'And then, when you have, come and see me and discuss it? I'll pay your hourly rate, of course, whatever that might be. Thanks so much for your time.'

He shook Paul Bain's hand, warmly, watched his face turn from puzzlement to shrewdness, and ushered Frank away.

'What the hell was all that about?' Frank said as they sank into a taxi. 'What exactly are you up to? Christ, Tom old boy, you were practically offering the guy money up front for something. Whose money and why?'

'Don't ever think I don't work hard for you, Frank. I'm always devoted to the interests of my clients. I was just acting strategically, that's all, taking an opportunity, just in case. I told you we don't want a verdict of suicide. I've looked at the policies. The damn policies are about all I've got. If it's suicide, the estate could be short of rather a lot of money. Mr Bain has already shown that he's absolutely corruptible, so it occurred to me that he might be willing to muddy the waters a little. The mere suggestion that there might have been someone else in the room *behind* Marianne does exactly that.'

'But you don't think there was? The police would have found that out, wouldn't they?'

'*I* don't think there was anyone else there. I think she deliberately chose to be alone. The room was booked for a single occupant. But there *could* have been someone else there, and as for the police going through the place with a fine-tooth comb to see if there was any *evidence* of a visitor, well I know the police and I doubt if they did. Suicide isn't a crime, and it wasn't a crime scene. All pretty cut and dried as far as they were concerned. No one got into her room until about twenty minutes after she jumped. They would have taken away her stuff and responded to pressure from the hotel to get the room back in service as soon as possible. Apparently she left it very tidy. They wouldn't have dusted it for fingerprints. So there's room for suggestion.'

Frank laughed in admiration.

'My God, Tom, you're a cold fish.'

'No, merely devoted.'

Thomas looked out of the window of the cab and watched the rain begin. Bloody January. Cold and dark and a good time to die. He wanted to be back in his homely office in Lincoln's Inn, where he could watch the rain from the window. It occurred to him as he watched a girl running for shelter, teetering on high heels and hopelessly dressed for the weather, that Marianne Shearer had also been inappropriately dressed for her death. That ridiculous skirt. He felt utterly depressed, covered it with words.

'I'm only doing what you told me to do, Frank. What I suppose she would have wished me to do. Which is to look inconvenient facts in the eye and twist them if possible, especially if there's anything to be gained, no matter how small. That's what she would have done.'

'Good, Tom, good. Keep at it. You can drop me off here.'

Disgusting man. Disgusting servitude. A bloody mess, but at least the rain had stopped. Thomas Noble took a turn round Lincoln's Inn Fields to calm down. He could not yet admit to Frank Shearer what a legacy his sister had left, not just a mess, but also a deliberate mystery. Somewhere there was a record of what she really wanted; there was a sense of threat if he did not find it. He must explore the looming possibilities of the *affair*, the existence of some secret, trusted person holding her papers and unwilling to come forward. It would have to be a man, a lover of sorts since she neither trusted nor liked women. Maybe someone who did not even know she was dead. He could see Marianne jeering. He had the policies, the deeds to the flat, and the minimal mementos sent on from her chambers, the bulk of it being the transcript of that damn trial and that was all. As if the transcript was everything. Nothing personal, she was saying, talking through a mist in which her ugly face became blurred.

It was grey and misty in Lincoln's Inn Fields. He hesitated at the door of the John Soane museum, wanting to go inside for the solace of beauty and its celebration of the collector's constructive greed, but he saw the queue and walked on. Marianne loved it in there: the use of space was as crafty as she was. Thomas walked round the rim, watching the people walking their dogs, or rather, the dogs walking the people, and noticing, not for the first time, how animals and owners resembled each other.

It was indeed depressing to realise that one became quite like one's own client, rather like people came to look like their dogs. Why was he doing this, when he would have loved it if Frank Shearer never got to inherit a single undeserved penny? Frank did not improve with acquaintance. He had a habit of touching the person who was nearest on the arm or shoulder which made Thomas want to recoil because it was the opposite of affection; more a desire to control with his own bulk or to tease a homosexual man with his heterosexual superiority. A little bit of suppressed violence, always poking at things in order to feel for weakness. He did not like to think what Frank was like around women. A womaniser, Marianne had told him. Been sacked for it, couldn't keep his hands off them, which is why he ended up selling cars. Without doubt, a rather male environment.

So why was he working so hard for him? Because it was second nature to give the maximum effort to any client, just as it was instinctive to try every trick in the book to get the better of insurance companies, the Inland Revenue and the all manifestations of the State. It was a game, and it did not matter for whom he played it. It was all about his bounden duty to save the client's money and there was something perverse and personal in his attitude to the current project. First, he did not want the verdict to be suicide, he really would rather she had been murdered or simply mad enough to think she could fly; and secondly, he had the feeling she was manipulating him, amusing herself at his expense, giving him a challenge to prove the friendship from beyond the grave and watching what he did with some other purpose in mind entirely.

Not that the body of Ms Shearer could be given the courtesy of a grave as yet. The remnants of it remained in a mortuary and he did not like to think in what condition. The scant possessions in her hotel room were being delivered to him, along with, God help him, the clothes she had worn.

He was fond of his tiny office in Lincoln's Inn Fields, because of its associations and because of the view. The room was small, its old-fashioned ambience the result of deliberation and neglect, with the result that clients of a certain age found it reassuring, and the younger clients, of whom Thomas had very few, disliked it for lacking anything obviously associated with efficiency. He had all the technology of computer, fax and phone, of course, and a receptionist shared with the other occupants of the building. Sole practitioners in the law were anachronistic and rare these days – few lawyers would take the risk – but Thomas only needed

63

the clients he had chosen, most of whom only defected way beyond death. He specialised in probate, personal problems, personal services and debts. He was a sounding board, a keeper of secrets, and the clients stuck with him not only because he was cheap, but because he knew where the bodies were buried. So his morals were malleable, his consistency admirable, and his discretion was guaranteed. The pickings were adequate and this way he could devote himself entirely to one client at a time.

There were features of this office space that made it invaluable to Thomas's unusual practice. There was the lease that meant he was secure for life and then there was the position. Proximity to the Inns of Court where most of the barristers lurked ensured him a steady stream of clients who mostly came via word of mouth. He liked the cachet of Thos Noble, the lawyers' lawyer, although it was scarcely true. The highest flyers and top earners would always go elsewhere, which was entirely up to them; more fool them since when it came to the matter of sorting out estates, the amount of money involved really did not matter or make it more or less complex. Testators could be equally mischievous and divisive in the way they wrote their wills whether the sum to be inherited was large or small, while the inheritors themselves would fight for their so-called rights to a hundred pounds as viciously as they would for a share in millions. It was the same process, requiring a dogged brain rather than Einstein.

The third irreplaceable feature of Thomas's office was the room itself. There were tall sash windows going down to the floor, giving a view on to the large square that was Lincoln's Inn Fields. In high summer, it was Thomas's joy to gaze out, not at the trees and greenery which afforded their own different pleasures in spring, but at the people, shedding clothes on hot days, eating lunch on the grass and lolling like puppies. In all seasons, mid morning, he watched the older man who practised tai chi on the lawn by the tennis courts. Persons of other persuasions leaned out of windows on the far side of the Fields to watch girls play netball. He was drawn to the dog walkers with their frolicking, ambling dogs and found he envied them most of all although he was never tempted to pat. Dogs were allowed without a lead; people were encouraged to sit semi-naked on the grass; really, Lincoln's Inn Fields was a hotbed of quiet depravity. In the depths of winter, like now, when he arrived and departed in the dark and the view of people was limited by the light to see them by, he could draw down the blinds and turn his contemplative gaze towards the fireplace. It was a gas fire with convincing flames and it seemed a proper addition to an essentially Victorian lawyer's office, even more vital than books. With the fire lit, he could imagine himself as a young Bob Cratchit, wielding a quill pen and warming his chilled hands against the flames, flexing his fingers the better to avoid mistakes. The fire, although rarely lit, was a positive aid to ambience and concentration.

Quietly seething with rage, Thomas was now contemplating the question of rights. Not Human Rights in the larger sense, but people's personal and largely misconceived rights to inherit money. No one had the right to either property or money unless they had earned it. He had no quarrel with the inequalities of earning power, as in a pop star or footballer earning millions while the receptionist downstairs earned peanuts, as long as it was *earned*. You could only *earn* inheritance rights by loving someone faithfully. It was the right to grab what you had not earned in any way at all which infuriated him; it was clients and the children of clients talking about their rights to Daddy's cash and Mummy's house, while really, they had no rights at all. What was the legal phrase? *Spes succession*, hope of succession, was no hope at all. Frank Shearer's *right* to his sister's property was not really a right, it was an unjust windfall which the law turned into a right, and dammit, he had the duty to make sure the frightful man got every penny. Still, he supposed that was marginally better than letting the whole thing go to the State.

Coroners' Courts made him sad. He had attended one too many, never with quite such an enraging sadness. It would pass: everything did. He turned from the fire to the window, trying to see whatever he could in the fading light and wishing Marianne would talk to him.

There was a man on the bench on the other side of the railings sitting and looking up at Thomas's first floor window. He saw Thomas looking at him and turned away. The man was wearing one of those awful, vaguely mustard-coloured camel hair coats which he rarely saw round the Inns of Court now, except on older men or misguided younger ones who thought such a coat made them look establishment. It was what he called a member of the ruling classes coat. The last time he had seen such a coat, it had been earlier in the day. A coat looking incongruous on a plastic chair.

There were plenty such coats: they were built to last. Like the moss-coloured German variety and the bomb-proof Burberrys which he did not like either. Camel hair belonged on camels.

Thomas was thinking to himself how much Marianne would have enjoyed that observation when the receptionist phoned from downstairs and said a man wanted to see him. About making a will, or something. Thomas never denied the walk-in trade who had included his better clients, directed by someone else who knew this convenient address. The plate outside advertising his presence was very small. One had to know. When the man in the camel hair coat walked in, Thomas was pleased and unsurprised because after all, he wasn't the first to wait outside on a bench before coming in and he himself desperately needed distraction. Even hardened lawyers regarded consulting another lawyer on a private and confidential matter as something akin to going to the dentist, but all the same, it was unusual to wait in winter. Never mind the coat; the tone of voice adopted by the downstairs receptionist suggested that this one not only passed muster but was OK to look at. Shirley knew his criteria for acceptability in the male of the species, which were roughly similar to her own. Any man allowed into the premises without an appointment had to be reasonably dressed and body-odour free. Being perfectly formed was a bonus.

The man who came into Thomas's office had shed the camel coat which he carried and emerged from it as an athletic figure, in fitting jeans and short leather jacket which offset a neatly turned bum, a narrow waist and slim hips. His eyes really were the most startling blue against a tanned skin. He had an innocent way of turning and shutting the door behind him that showed every aspect of his physique with the modesty of a shy schoolgirl. He seemed to be twirling and asking, Should I do this? Where would you like me to sit? Is this the right thing to do? What he said was, 'How kind of you to see me, may I sit here?' speaking in a pleasant, low-pitched voice, while extending his hand. Thomas took it, charmed.

'Rick Boyd,' the man said.

Then the handshake made him whimper, disgracefully. The man had a hand as big as a spade. It enclosed Thomas's hand up to the wrist and felt cool and almost metallic. His thumb seemed to gouge Thomas's palm painfully, so that he breathed in sharply, and gritted his teeth for the brief moment the sensation lasted and once released, disguised his reaction in the quick business of sitting behind his own desk. Rick Boyd sat gracefully, maintaining eye contact with Thomas, smiling and pleading for his attention with a slightly apologetic air. Once he was seated, he looked smaller and vulnerable and Thomas decided that the brutality of the handshake was either sheer clumsiness or his own imagination. He was trying to remember why the name was familiar and registering the fact that Boyd was really quite alarmingly attractive.

'What can I do for you, Mr Boyd?'

A familiar name, only just swimming into focus. Someone he had heard about rather than met. Rick Boyd ran his huge hand through his black hair, making it stand on end, adding to his air of uncertainty and making him look youthful. He had the kind of face that would always look young, what with high cheekbones, those eyes and white teeth, although he must have been thirty-five at least. Thomas was no good at guessing ages, everyone seemed young to him. Boyd: Marianne. Something clicked.

'Wills and probate are my main trade, Mr Boyd,' Thomas said, putting on his well-rehearsed avuncular act. 'But you do look a bit young for that kind of thing.'

'I haven't come about making a will. I came to ask about Marianne Shearer. The *late* Marianne Shearer.'

He emphasised the word *late*, with exaggerated respect and kept his voice low.

'Oh.'

'Perhaps I should have written, but I was passing by, and I

was away, and I only just heard, and I went to the inquest, and, oh dear . . .'

He looked as if he might be overcome with emotion, then recovered and leant forward, clasping the enormous hands over his knees as if he was afraid to let them out of his sight.

'Your name was on the record at the Inquest, so I thought you might be able to help. I wondered if, as her executor you could tell me *Why*? Such a lovely woman. So successful, so professional. We were close, Mr Noble. Extremely close. The fact is, I wanted to find out if she had left me anything. I don't mean money, I mean a memento.'

Thomas gazed at him. A beautiful, disproportionate man whose name he remembered, now. Not a toy boy, although it would not have surprised him if Marianne had at least one of those about her person. She might have been over fifty but there was nothing wrong with her appetites for any number of things. Mr Boyd and Ms Shearer had certainly been close and she had talked about him at length, without ever alluding to his charisma. Other people had, though, and Thomas could feel the first stirrings of acute unease. In the face of it, ignorance was the best policy and he let his own blandness speak for itself.

'Why?' Rick Boyd murmured, brokenly. 'Why did she do such a thing? I can't understand. She knew I was coming back. She knew I would have helped. Why didn't she say anything? She promised she would send everything to me.'

Thomas resorted to pomposity to hide his surprise.

'Really, Mr Boyd, I'm afraid I can't tell you anything about what might have led to my client taking her life, let alone the manner of it. It's a mystery to us all and I'm afraid I don't know anything about her extensive acquaintance, or to whom she was close. I'm relying on everyone else to enlighten me,

I'm merely an administrator. Please accept my sympathy. Time may unravel the mystery, it very often does.'

Boyd placed his hands in a position of prayer and spoke with greater determination. He did not seem to like platitudes. Thomas gazed at him, finding the flaws in a handsome body, the hands too big, the curved torso too long for the rest of him.

'Having done *time* myself, Mr Noble, I can understand that, but I don't want you to misunderstand me. I'm not after money, and I'll wait for explanations, but she had something she promised to send me. She had something of mine, to say nothing of what she had of my heart. I poured my heart out to her, you see and she recorded it. She made notes about me on paper, on her laptop, her phone and she would have kept them all. She said she would send them all back so no one else would ever see them. She's the only one who knows me, and since we adored one another, I'm sure she'd want me to have what she promised.'

Thomas had been disposed to like the man because of the way he looked, but the demanding tone irritated him. He had him placed now and his appeal faded abruptly. Boyd, as in *R* v Boyd, Shearer's last big case. The subject of that messy box of paper, over there. A triumph for a maligned man, she said, but that surely did not entitle him to anything, not even ten minutes of his, Thomas Noble's time, not even if he had the novelty value of being the first, the only person to express grief over her death.

'A dead person's personal effects, their notes, love letters, records, their whatever else, remain theirs until disposal, Mr Boyd. Her brother, Mr Frank Shearer, has the final say in that. He's the sole heir of her estate. I've no idea what precisely it is that you want, but Ms Shearer's notes and records are hers and hers alone.'

'I don't want them all, sir, I just want the confidential information which relates to me. I'd like it now, before it falls into the wrong hands.'

He was out of his seat now, advancing towards the desk with his fists clenched and then, as if realising what he was doing, he retreated back to his seat with his head held in his hands, sobbing.

'I loved her, Mr Noble, I loved her. She saved me, you see.'

Thomas maintained his best inscrutable look while clenching his own hands under the desk to keep himself under control. He loathed displays of emotion, especially when they failed to convince him and he had begun to find the person opposite more than a little frightening. Boyd. Charged with kidnap, abduction, rape, grievous bodily harm, and in Marianne's words, *Quite deliciously ruthless, dear, but only a danger to very silly women.* Nonsense. Involuntarily, his gaze shifted from Boyd to the boxed transcript in the corner of the room. Boyd wiped his eyes. Genuine tears, but so were those of crocodiles. Thomas wanted him to leave. He wanted it with an intensity of revulsion that unnerved him and it occurred to him that Boyd would not go unless given some sort of promise. He would stay where he was with his big hands and his intimidating weeping. Thomas managed a smile.

'Mr Boyd, let me explain. As Miss Shearer's executor, I shall have to go through her effects and find anything that is relevant to her estate, as well as anything that could be relevant to the mystery of her death. At least that's what I'm going to have to do when I can lay hands on her records, which I'm afraid I haven't been able to do so far.'

'Have you anything here? Anything I could look at now?'

Thomas found the question deeply impertinent, as well as touching a nerve. There was so little to look at.

'No,' he said. 'Not yet.'

'But her things will come to you?'

'I live in hope, Mr Boyd. We lawyers do. She'd just moved house, you see, so certain items seem to have gone astray. All I can tell you is that when I get them and go through them as I must, should I come across anything unduly personal which refers to you, I'll be sure to let you know if you leave me your number. Other people's lives really aren't my business, you know, only hers. I've no wish to withhold anything. And,' he added in a moment of mischief, 'perhaps I could put you in touch with her brother? I'm sure you'd like to share your grief and he knows more than I.'

'Oh yes. Her heir, you said? The only one? How sad she had no children.'

Thomas wrote Frank's address busily, then beamed, gravely, getting up and going towards the door while Boyd wrote down his own number and left it on the desk, muttering thanks, suddenly humble and charming all over again. Thomas remembered to keep his hands on the door to avoid another crushing grasp and listened while the Defendant went downstairs, taking his awful coat and moving very quietly. Thomas shut the door and found himself leaning against it. That had not gone well, no, it hadn't gone well at all. He was short of breath.

The files in the corner of the room were all he had of Ms Shearer's personal effects, sent from her chambers. They consisted of pens, pencils and otherwise entirely of that box labelled *R* v Boyd. It contained nothing but a transcript in six volumes. There was nothing of the usual, untidy detritus of a trial, no old notebooks, photos, bits of paper. Just the transcript, as if she was begging him to read it. Marianne had talked about it. She always talked about her triumphs, but he had never seen her in action. Idly, he began to read, picking passages at random.

After an hour he was thinking what a bitch, and wondering why he had ever liked her at all. Then another parcel arrived. It was more than he could handle. Thomas phoned Peter Friel, expecting, and receiving, an immediate reply.

'Get over here, Peter. Don't argue. I know you're unemployed with nothing better to do. Need to discuss. What the hell was she playing at? I can't open *this*. I need you. Get here NOW.'

EXTRACT FROM TRANSCRIPT: *R* v BOYD

Cross-examination of Angel Joyce by Marianne Shearer, QC

MS. So, *Mz* Joyce. Are you Ms or Miss? Speak up. No? OK, I'll call you Missy, if you like.

You've told the court that the Defendant, my client, kidnapped you. That's a charge which has been argued away, but I take it you know what it means. You made it. Basically it means you were taken away against your will, but you went willingly, didn't you?

AJ. *Whispers.* Yes.

MS. In fact, it was your suggestion, was it not?

AJ. NO.

MS. Oh, come on, Angel. I know you aren't very bright, but can't you at least concede that it was a joint idea, perhaps? Unless you're saying you never have any ideas of your own? Clearly not. Speak up, Miss Angel Joyce, otherwise the Court can't hear you.

AJ. It wasn't my suggestion, but yes, I went along willingly with it at first. Rick said he had a business opportunity in Birmingham, provided we got some money, it was there for the taking. That was part of the reason why I went. I got some money.

MS. You tried to seduce him with the prospect of money, didn't you, Miss Angel? Sorry, I mean Ms Joyce. I do apologise, but I simply can't call you Angel, it's such a silly name for a woman of your age, but I don't want to get you confused with the other Miss Joyce when I come to repeat suggestions she's already made in her evidence. Anyway, Miss Angel, you wanted to get him away from the temptation of students far prettier than you.

AJ. No.

MS. There must have been plenty of those. He wanted nothing to do with the money your parents were willing to give you both just to get rid of you, did he? It was *you* who offered it, wasn't it?'

AJ. *Long pause.* He ... asked me about money the first time we were together.

MS. Slept together, you mean? The first time you fucked? *Interruption: Ms Shearer explains to HHJ McD that it is important to use plain language.*

MS. All right. The first time you were together, in a manner of speaking, *he* expressed concern for *you* because you didn't look like a person who took care of herself, a bit of a fat slob. If he mentioned money to you then, it was to offer it to you, wasn't it? Don't just shake your head, please. The shorthand writer can't record a movement.

AJ. I don't remember.

MS. What do you mean, you don't remember? You've just said you did. Oh come on, Miss Angelic, it wasn't your first time with drink, drugs or sex, was it?

AJ. No.

MS. But it was the first time you'd been with any man who was good-looking and cared for you and wanted a future with you?

AJ. Yes.

MS. And you would have done anything for him?

AJ. Yes. No. Yes. Anything. Not anything, yes, no yes.

MS. Which is it, no or yes? Please stop this pathetic whispering. You were loud enough when you complained. Speak up, the jury can't hear you.

CHAPTER SIX

It was dark by the time Peter arrived. People scurried across the Fields like lemmings, towards the underground station at Holborn. He had to push his way between them out into the cold air. On his way to Thomas's office, he noticed that the museum he had never yet managed to visit was closed. One day he would get there.

'Rick Boyd said *what*? He came *here*?' Peter Friel said. 'What on earth for?'

'I thought you might be able to tell me. I was rather caught short, if you see what I mean. He revealed all my inadequacies in one fell swoop. First I fancied him, then I loathed him, then I put him in touch with Frank Shearer, ha ha! Interesting to see if those two touch base, they're as awful as one another. I forgot, you haven't met Frank yet, have you? Ah well, a pleasure best postponed. I've had a horrible day, then that parcel arrived.' He pointed in the direction of a large paper sack in the corner. The office looked positively littered. There was the sense of an inner sanctum being invaded, quite different from when Peter had visited first the day after the death.

'Then I started reading bits of paper from that awful trial you've got to tell me more about, and got to thinking nastiness might run in the Shearer family. Marianne was quite a clever brute in court, wasn't she? I've got to read the whole thing, I suppose. There's nowhere else to look for clues. It's absolutely all I have got of hers. That's why I feel so bloody inadequate. She left me to deal with her estate, but nothing else. No will, no explanations, all her personal possessions disappeared or stolen. Do you know the most despicable fact about sudden death is the opportunities it creates for theft? Especially a well-publicised death. Someone's got her stuff and can't see why they should give it back. Someone's nicked it.'

'You don't know that,' Peter objected, always wanting proof of an allegation before it was made. 'It's probably shipped off to a friend, held up in a queue somewhere, a mix-up . . .'

'Yes, but where? She's not given us a hint, no records, no receipts, damn her eyes. I was relying on the stuff they sent me over from chambers, but all they had in her office was that.' Again he pointed, this times to volumes of paper spilling out of a box, 'Nothing else, she hadn't been in there over Christmas. Bugger, bugger, bugger. I hate being given a job without the tools.'

The best description for Thomas at the moment was of a man not quite himself. His sangfroid was sinking in alcohol; he was smoking cigarettes as if his life depended on it in a littered room overlooking dark Lincoln's Inn Fields with the window open and a bottle of whisky on the table, his nerves shot. His language was all over the place, words scattered like spat-out crumbs, a frightened man. They were talking in non sequiturs.

'So what is it exactly that Rick Boyd did?' Thomas said crossly. 'Only he's got these bloody great big hands and I can feel them round my neck.'

'Rick Boyd is a fantasist and a serial abductor of young women,' Peter said crisply. 'He got them to fall for him, spun them a yarn about being a poor orphan or poor man on the run, extracted as much money as he could, took them out of their own environment, and then, once the money ran out and he was tired of them, kept them, or persuaded them to keep themselves, like spiders keep dead flies in a web. He had a woman in Peterborough, one in Milton Keynes and the last one, Angel Joyce, in Birmingham. Three in a year, provided a generous income.'

Thomas snorted.

'I don't believe it. In this day and age? What rubbish. What the hell kind of female would allow that? Women rule the world and they know it.'

'Not his kind of woman.'

'Where the hell has Marianne deposited her bloody goods?' Thomas yelled.

'I don't know. I don't know her, haven't got a clue,' Peter said. 'I keep telling you I didn't really know her. I worked with her, and latterly against her. I don't rightly know why I'm here, except for the fact that in some funny way, she may have quite liked me.'

Thomas pushed the window open wider. Even with the fire, it was freezing in the room.

'You're here because you're a clueless failure and she knew you might be available for whatever fucking game she wants to play, and you're going to find out where the stuff is. I

78

don't know. If I were to think of a single reason why you're here, it's because there's obviously a connection between that last big case and her suicide. That brute coming in here today, gotta connect, hasn't it? Anyway, that aside, I wanted you here at this precise moment because they sent along her clothes from the mortuary and I don't like being alone with them. What's she wearing now, sunny boy, what the hell is she wearing now, poor soul? High heels in hell?'

Thomas took a slug of whisky and shuddered. He flexed his fingers as if trying to restore his own circulation.

'You're here, dear boy, because while you're otherwise useless, I want someone present. They bagged up her clothes and sent them on. I know it's not usual. They probably wouldn't have done it if she hadn't been a lawyer and I hadn't demanded it. I must have been out of my mind, and they may have to go back, but I had the crazy notion she might have hidden something about her person and I wanted someone there when I opened them.'

It was hardly the time to feel offended by Thomas's version of why Marianne Shearer had elected him to assist her friend and executor in the sorting out of the aftermath of her death, although he did pause to find the reasons unflattering. She had named him not because he was honest and doggedly curious, or because she had flirted with him a long time ago, like a glamorous aunt to an innocent nephew when she had been his pupil master. *Pupil mistress, darling*, she had said, please. I'm not here to teach you anything; you're here to carry my bags. He had been elected only because she knew he would be available, but that could have applied to any number of younger men with whom she had had contact over the years and he still did not quite understand Why me? It was humiliating to think she had chosen him simply because he was idle and penniless enough to say yes, and to know that when she was alive, that was the way Ms Shearer had described him. He could hear her strident voice, discussing him over a drink with Thomas Noble. *He's so* wet, *my dear; he actually believes in Justice and Truth; he wastes so much time and energy being* sorry *for people.* Ah yes, she had seen him coming, but still, she was way too canny for there not to be something else on her mind, such as him knowing all about *R* v Boyd and what she had done with it. Alternatively, she might have thought she thought she owed him something for getting him drunk a dozen years ago.

'Is that what she said about me?' he asked Thomas humbly. 'That I was so useless I'd be up for any humdrum task? That I might otherwise be sweeping the streets and glad of any old job?'

'Not in so many words, no,' Thomas said, irritated and ready to move on. 'That's simply what I surmise. Yes, all right you've worked with her before that last big case and she talked about you, like she did about everyone. We loved mutual gossip about people we didn't know. She said you were way too soft and you were never going to make it.'

'There are other ways of making it than her ways,' Peter said.

'Not as far as she was concerned. The only way to win she said, was wanting to win at all costs, and people like you don't want it enough, have never been hungry enough, so you lose every time. Oh, for God's sake, I can't even remember what she said. Except she also said that if she'd ever had a son, she'd have liked him to be something like you. Now, can we get on?'

Peter had an uncomfortable memory of being twenty-one and assigned to Ms Shearer as pupil *mistress*, to follow her round from court to conference, doing her research, until at the end of six months, that drunken evening to celebrate his fitness to take a case all by himself. He could remember waking up at three in the morning in a back alley behind the pub, covered in filth, with the sound of her laughter in his ears, and the note pinned to his chest in her cool hand. CLAPHAM COURT, 9pm TOMORROW. That was Shearer's kind of training, otherwise known as learning how to function with a hangover, no money, and with the contempt of the court and the client oozing out of every pore. He shook his head. She had been kinder then: perhaps she meant to be kind now. She had taught him his own incompetence by reverse example and in *R* v Boyd she had been at her utterly competent, dreadful best.

'Pooh,' Thomas said, settling into the wheeled office chair he used to propel himself around his small office space. 'Pooh, pooh, pooh, everything smells of that awful man. Perhaps Mr Handsome Boyd and dear Frank Shearer will go off into some glorious sunset together now I've introduced them, but meantime the business in hand is looking at these blasted clothes. Will they smell, too? Here goes . . . No, I can't, I absolutely can't. You do it.'

He had trailed his chair towards the pile in the corner, where the *R* v Boyd transcript spilled out in disarray from where Thomas had selected the afternoon's reading material. Next to this mess which Peter had an automatic desire to tidy, there stood the lopsided brown paper sack with labels on that Thomas had pointed towards earlier, securely fastened with staples.

'I think,' Peter said, 'it can wait for a minute. First, I'm going to tell you about Marianne's last trial. Save you the reading. You really shouldn't judge her by it, you know.'

Thomas winced.

'Be brief, dear. Please be brief. I've read enough and it sounds unpleasant. I only want to know why she might have been ashamed of it.'

'As I said, Boyd's a fantasist, and I suspect a revengeful one. Basically, a no-hoper without much education but plenty of high life dreams. Not much going for him but the looks and charisma you noticed, plus an enormous amount of perverted cunning. He's plausible because he believes himself. Always on a power kick and full of injured innocence. He'd probably been robbing women for years, believed his own fantasy of life owing him a living. Basically, he got jobs in clubs or colleges where he could meet the right kind of girl. He'd pick the dumbest or the most vulnerable, overwhelm them, persuade them to run away from home with him, and he knew how to pick. I should tell you about the trial, rather than him. Originally there were three sets of counts on the indictment. Three victims. The identities of the first two only came to light through correspondence taken from a flat in Birmingham by Angel Joyce and her sister. Three women, kidnapped by deception. Boyd persuaded the first that he was on the run from the Mafia and not only did he love her, but he needed her protective cover and her money to stay in hiding. Then he put her on the game to finance him. The second believed there was a price on his head because he had informed on the Mafia; she too was besotted and agreed to move cities and live with him. The deceit with Angel Joyce was less dramatic. Angel had money from parents that she gave to Boyd on the understanding that they were going to resurrect a business he had inherited and already owned. In fact it was a disused factory where he had a squat. God alone knows why any of them believed him, but his plausibility and sexual prowess, perhaps, made them credulous slaves. They were overwhelmed. They went to work for him. If they questioned him, he beat them, or worse. All three had scars. All three of them were going to give evidence. It was going to be a sensational trial, tales of sex slavery and cruelty, plus fascinating psychological insights. Scenes of torture and two lost fingers.'

'What?'

Thomas had been looking sceptical. Now he looked faint. The whisky had gone to his head.

'What happened next?' he said.

'Marianne happened, but the texture of this extraordinary evidence was already wearing thin before she did. The first trial began. Then Boyd sacked his Counsel and the whole thing was postponed for months. That happened twice. No one else wanted to defend him. There was this overwhelming similarity of evidence and despite the whole scenario being unbelievable, it had to be believed. He frightened people. The next defence team withdrew. Then Marianne took up the baton. She would always take on the untouchable. Remember? That brutal paedophile, the robber, the rapist? That's what she wanted. Anyway, the witnesses were dreading their turn in the witness box long before Marianne appeared. What woman is going to look forward to admitting being brainwashed and duped? Especially when terrified of the Defendant. They got weaker with every delay. Then Shearer got started.'

Thomas groaned.

'She'd managed to draw the weakest and most nervous of judges on some political basis. He couldn't cope and he wouldn't withstand her. Then she claimed Boyd had a heart murmur. More delay. He looked like butter wouldn't melt. He was groomed to look like a waif. Then she sprang legal arguments at the last moment and got away with it. The jury would be sent away again and the witnesses left waiting. She got the Judge to agree that the screens used in court to protect vulnerable witnesses should be dispensed with. They were all grown-ups, she said. The first two victims received mysterious, intimidating letters, hinting at knowledge of their sexual preferences. Shearer denied these could possibly have come from Boyd, saying they must have made them up. She argued away some of the charges. She argued away kidnap; she argued away the law on similar fact.'

'The two missing fingers?'

Peter sipped the whisky Thomas handed to him. He was going on too long because he needed to rehearse it to himself. Connect. Revenge. Why would Boyd want revenge?

'I can't be brief, because that wretched trial went on and on. Charges were knocked out before evidence really began to be heard. Rumours abounded about how Shearer was going to lay into these girls once they were in the box. The diminishing of the charges meant Shearer had a case for Boyd to be let out on bail. She applied for it, failed for once, but the first girl, the other with the missing finger, got wind of it and just quietly disappeared. She'd been summoned to court five times and never called. She sent a message saying she wasn't coming back. So, the similar fact evidence went out of the window. Sorry, I'm losing the thread, and that's another long story. We all lost the thread, except Boyd and Shearer. The second victim withdrew her evidence rather than give it. She had a nervous breakdown and couldn't be forced. So the trial of the century was left with only two important witnesses. The third victim, Angel Joyce, and her sister. A trial that should have lasted three weeks had gone on for eight months. We were left with their word against his.'

'A question of interpretation. Which of them was the fantasist?'

Thomas lit another cigarette and coughed, pointedly, to spur him on.

'Marianne insisted that the Prosecution called Henrietta Joyce first. I don't know why my learned leader agreed, but he'd lost the will to live by that time. Shearer did a hatchet job on the first Miss Joyce. It was as if she had been instructed to exact personal revenge on her, which makes sense, because after all, it was her intervention that led to the charges in the first place. Also, Hen had something to hide. Marianne could find the smallest untruth like someone else finding a needle in a haystack. It was vital to undermine her and she did. Then she had a whole two days with Angel Joyce in the witness box, toying with her like a cat with a mouse. Angel Joyce went home with her parents on the second night and, either by accident or design, killed herself. Some variation of shame, or just too tired. Case collapses, end of story. It was a brilliant job. Sorry not to be brief, but it has occurred to me in the telling why Rick Boyd might have come here today. What it is he might really want, apart from revenge.'

'Revenge on *whom*, dear boy? Surely he'd got it? He was acquitted, wasn't he? And it sounds as if he'd driven his accusers demented. Isn't that revenge enough?'

Peter shook his head.

'No. Not for a man like that. He might have been acquitted, but he wasn't proved innocent. He wasn't exonerated, he was merely let out of prison, and that wasn't enough for his pride. Plenty hubris, this man. Acquitted, but exposed,' he slapped his hand on the desk so hard that Thomas jumped and Peter winced. That hurt. He was so clumsy, always bruising himself, not good in a courtroom. His nephews loved it, but no one else laughed. His sister said he was a man who could cut himself on paper.

'Sorry. Two things. Connect. What is the connection? Boyd, here. Boyd everywhere. Boyd hates Marianne, because although she's done a great job, she hasn't restored him, and never cared about him anyway, because she never cared for anyone.'

'I take exception to that.'

'*But*, also, she's got all the notes, all the instructions, personal material, everything he wanted to say when he took the stand, all the stuff, and she knows, down to the last detail exactly what he's done and she's the keeper of that knowledge. She had to know the truth about him in order to defend him. She's got enough for a book. He wants that back. He may have hounded her to get it back; he might have threatened her to get it back. She's got him, his words written and recorded, his *soul*, if you like.'

'Where has she put her THINGS?' Thomas yelled. 'WHERE are they? That's all I want to know.' He stopped. 'Wait a minute, that's what he said. He said, "she knew me better than anyone." How very uncomfortable. The second thing?'

'Revenge. The trial was supposed to get him revenge. But he didn't get it. He used Marianne to expose the Joyce sisters. He sat in court, hating Henrietta Joyce like poison. She made her sister report him and she led to the finding of the others. She was the catalyst who put him into prison. There was something she kept back, something he said she stole . . . Oh, hell, I've lost the plot.'

Thomas was sober again, and tired, but he knew a good storyteller when he saw one.

'Well, yes, I'm hearing what you're saying, but I can't quite see how I should make it my business, unless he actually came up behind Marianne and pushed her out the window. In which case, it is my business. Shall we look at these wretched, smelly clothes while you're here? Please say yes.'

Peter swam back into the present, with a terrible gut ache interfering with his breathing. He was remembering the awful feeling of impotence and inertia and fury. Charismatic, persuasive Rick Boyd. Marianne had won, but there were no winners, only losers and unfinished business.

'Sorry. Let's do it.'

Without waiting for further invitation, knowing what Thomas wanted, Peter went towards the labelled paper bag unstrategically placed in the corner of the room, exactly as it had been delivered and treated as contagious ever since. He could quite see why. Thomas handed him a pair of industrial-sized scissors with huge black handles and blades like heavy-weight saws. He thought, irrelevantly, how useless they would be as a combat weapon, no good for stabbing, only for cutting. A vital piece of equipment for a lawyer's office; as useful as the paper clip. In the face of such scissors, it was disappointing to find the tough paper so fragile. No exhibit labels, no seals, therefore, no crime; although everything about him screamed out to say there must be. He simply laid the bag on its side and cut across the top.

The skirt spilled out like something live, a fantastic vision of crimson, red, blue, a creature escaped from a cage. It expanded as they watched, and settled on the floor, breathing out and breathing in, crumpling, finally, amongst its own folds and settling down. Both of them took a step back, watching it deflate like a parachute. The garment seemed to be made of tightly pleated delicate material, which increased from its own folds into volumes of cloth that needed to breathe. The colours took Thomas's breath away, they were so unexpected. In the photographs of her free-fall death, this garment had been a blurred mass of dark fluff. Thomas regretted it on her behalf. So unlike Marianne Shearer, in her killer black suits, so horribly alive in its own right. She never wore skirts; she wore immaculate trousers. There were so many yards of material in this it should have changed the direction of the fall.

It was Thomas who tipped out the rest of the bag. A boned corset, stockings, suspenders, a heavy silk slip embroidered with lace, camiknickers in lockknit silk. Small, heeled boots not for walking. The delicate but substantial undergarments were split, bearing the soak of what little blood there was. Death instantaneous, external bleeding to the torso minimal, contained in the undergarments, leaving the skirt almost fit to be worn. The delicate, pleated silk moved with the breeze from the window. Peter thought it was beautiful.

There was a very long pause. Thomas filled the glasses and sat back on his office chair, old, slumped and bewildered.

'Why did she die dressed like that?' Thomas howled, crying into his whisky. 'What the hell kind of funeral garment is that? Could she have hidden something inside it?'

'I don't know,' Peter said. 'But I may know someone who does. I'll take it all away, shall I?'

Thomas threw his glass through the open window. They both heard it smash on the pavement.

Frockserve.com.

Henrietta Joyce rescues clothes and knows all about them. And might need rescuing herself, if Boyd was around. She had something of his.

Peter put the clothes and the shoes back into the bag.

CHAPTER SEVEN

'I can't pay much,' Hen was saying to the new girl, 'because I never seem to end getting paid very much myself, and at the moment I use most of what I make to buy something else. Increase my own stock and buy the chemicals.'

The girl, whose name was Ann, was looking round herself, turning this way and that and saying Oooh, ooh, look at that, bustling around with wary enthusiasm.

'And,' Hen said, 'I'll have to be very careful about what I let you do. Don't want injuries or you drawing blood on scissors. We'll stick to alterations for the time being, shall we?'

'I don't care what I do,' Ann said. 'I just want to be here.'

That was nice, and made Hen smile, because it was exactly the way she felt herself. The feeling might not last beyond a day or two in a newcomer, but it had lasted in herself for years, or anyway so long she had stopped counting. A room like this, full of clothes, a myriad of colours and textures catching the light from the big window and looking like an invitation to dance. To the left, a selection of five evening dresses, carefully hung from the waist, as if they were making a bow and shaking out their own creases. Green and scarlet and midnight blue. Next to them, a row of sombre black jackets, hung from the shoulders, all showing on closer inspection that black was never really black and no black quite the same. A selection of multicoloured shawls draped themselves over the shoulders of the black clothes, as if they were embracing each other. On the hanging rail to the right were some shabby wool suits and voluminous skirts, next to a small selection of cloaks, which gave way to the whites and creams of a wedding dress and a selection of large pieces of lace. On the shelves high above the garments were the hats, tilting towards them on wire stands, showing off every colour of the rainbow. Beneath the hats were the shelves of knitted clothes laid flat.

'You always lay the knitted stuff flat,' Hen said. 'Preferably not on top of one another. They take up a lot of space. If you fold them, you have to fold them another way every so often. Creases weaken the fabric. If you hang them, they stretch. I'm not sure what I'll ever do with these.'

The centre of the room was empty space occupied by a very old and worn rug in various faded shades of rose madder and olive green. At the far end of the room was the workstation, a large, old pine table that could have seated six and was spotlit from above. The surface was covered with two sewing machines, boxes of threads, scraps of material. From the open door of the shelved wardrobe that stood behind it, Ann could see small samples of cloth and pieces of other clothes, stuffed in and spilling out against a large roll of muslin propped against a wall. The mirrored wardrobe doors reflected the room and doubled the light.

'Never can quite get enough light in here,' Hen said. 'Light might be good for the eyes, but not always for clothes, not in the long run. I'm not skilled enough to know how things fade, but I know they do, and you can do a lot to restore stuff but you can never put back the colour. Doesn't matter so much for these things. They're work in progress, might not be here long. Storage is another matter. Here, look at this. I shan't make you wear it, promise.'

From amongst the black garments which were not really black, she pulled a Victorian maid's dress with a boned bodice of bombazine and a full wool skirt which fell in stiff, pockmarked folds, the severity of it softened by the addition of cream lace at the neck and wrist. The hooks and eyes fastening the front were orange with rust.

'Don't know what the hell I can do with it. It's a learning garment, like a sampler. I've ruined it, really. I tried freezing it to get rid of an infestation, which did the trick, but moth eggs are organic, they rot, so when you freeze them and they dry out, you get mould spots.'

She could see the girl hesitate.

'It's sort of . . . quaint.'

'Not very comfortable unless you happen to be a Victorian midget and don't mind the same dress every day. Its been mended almost to death and it's the oldest dress I've got. I'm not into costume, although you never know. The kettle's over there. May as well start as we mean to go on. Tea, every hour at least.'

Ann wrinkled her nose, crossed her arms and shivered in pleasure, forgetting that unpleasant word *infestation*.

'A dressing room,' she said. 'With its own stage.'

Hen laughed.

'Well, I'm glad you like it, because I love it, but I'm afraid when the sun comes out you might see it for what it really is, which is one big room full of tat. Second-hand rubbish of no value to anyone but the owners, a scrapyard really, but the scraps made of cloth rather than metal. It looks better in the dark, in winter. This is the fun side, where I try and make something out of nothing for people who want it. The business end's in the basement. Everything that comes in here is already damaged, but it has to go through the basement, first, to be cleaned. Only comes here when either it's fit to mend or fit to turn into something else. This room's for sewing or trying things out. Downstairs is more serious: other people's clothes. Do you have milk and sugar in your tea?'

Ann nodded, still looking round. A nice, insecure girl, with a mother who despaired of her and wanted to find her something to do. She likes sewing, the mother said in disgust; she wants to learn to sew. Nice girl or not, Hen reckoned she would get through the day and no longer. Not every teenager could stand a job in a room with no company other than a grown-up and the radio. What had been Hen's idea of heaven might become Ann's idea of hell, especially when Hen gave her the first task. Which would be to unpick the bodice of the Victorian maid's dress, let out every seam and put it back together again a whole size larger. That way, they would see if she could sew.

Making the tea, sitting down at the table in the wardrobe room, Hen felt a moment of uncomplicated contentment, because although in this room she might make mistakes, she could do no wrong to anyone, except perhaps mislead a newcomer to her own black arts about the financial prospects of sewing and cleaning for a living. They were as doubtful as they always had been. She frowned to herself. It wasn't quite right that she could do no harm to anyone in here, and she looked at the girl with a touch of worry, because she did not want to care for her. She did not want responsibility for another human being, however temporarily, and she did not want to have to be cheerful. Too late, the girl was here; she had promised, and that was that.

'I don't exactly know what you do with all this,' Ann said. 'Only Mummy says what you do with stuff is priceless.'

'Priceless? As in ridiculous?'

'No . . . no, I think she meant beyond price.'

'What a kind woman your mother is, but I doubt it's true, and it's probably a bit of an exaggeration to call it a business, more like a surgery, but such as it is, it's based on sentiment as well as frustration. Because your modern man and woman seem to have all the choices in the world when it comes to clothes, but they don't really. Enough people want what they simply can't find in a shop or a catalogue, some people don't know what they want, and a lot of people just like old stuff, or want back what they've seen, or owned before. And some yearn for haute couture, I know I do, or they want old things made new, or they want a clean slate. I'm not doing very well here, am I? That's what I want the business to be, but the bare bones of the thing is all about dealing with rot, stains and bugs and that's in the basement. I just love old clothes. I can't bear them dying.'

Mustn't lecture her, Hen told herself. I've nothing to lecture about, because I really don't know enough. I've learned on the hoof, and from Jake and it's all my mother's fault. Ann was looking at the maid's dress.

'I think it's been let in and let out lots and lots of times.'

'Exactly. Probably had a dozen wearers and none of them owned it.'

If ever Hen was asked for her job description, she either said she messed about with clothes or that she was a cleaner of clothes, both accurate. There was, she would say if asked, a difference between conservation and preservation; you conserved a thing for further use, while you preserved it for posterity. She was never sure if she had the definitions right, but what she meant was that she was making things wearable again, even in another form. She was giving garments another lease of life, and if they were really at the end of their natural span, turning them into something else. There was a customer who mourned the loss of a red moth-ridden skirt and a blue cashmere coat, both beyond redemption, so she used the surviving material from both to make a patchwork waistcoat now worn with jeans. The remnants of a favourite silk dress, faded with age and hopelessly torn and stained, had the makings of a scarf or a sash. Old could be restored or incorporated with new; an old quilted jacket could be lined and bordered with emerald silk, radically revamped with buttons. Hen had an ongoing love affair with buttons. Buttons had weight; she had thousands of buttons. She would rescue, redeem, conserve anything for anybody, let out, let in, remodel, persuade against remodelling, recreate, tear apart, treasure and above all, clean. She would also buy what she could. This room was not a museum, it was a tailor's shop where someone might also come and find something which suited what they were, or what they had been, or what they might become, rather than what current fashion said they should be. I rescue things, she said. I have a Bachelor of Science degree in chemistry that did not lead to this, and I blame it all on part-time jobs and my mother's dressing-up box.

Hen sat, in her favourite room of all time, sewing. She had coveted Peter Friel's linen napkin as the perfect lining for a small pouch of a handbag made out of a badly perished embroidered linen jacket. What are you, Hen? What do you do for a living, Hen, with all your qualifications? I'm a scavenger, trying to make a business out of doing what I like, and today, for the first time in ages, I feel content. I think I'll stop doing wedding dresses, though. They simply don't adapt; too many dreams attached.

'How did you start?'

'My mum teaching us to sew, and then her dressing-up box, I suppose. Then I was a dogsbody in a theatre for a while and I liked the costumes more than the plays. I met a man in the wardrobe room who cleaned the clothes they wore on stage. He was the real expert with a little business at home. A specialist cleaner. He owns this house; he set it up for cleaning. He's retired, now, but he persuaded me into this because he needed help and I hated the job I had. Like I said, the bare bones of this is cleaning rather than making. Restoring rather than creating; I'm not a designer. But cleaning's the basis. Only it has to be expanded, even Jake agreed on that. Cleaning doesn't pay the bills, however much fun it is.'

Ann's face was puzzled. Cleaning as fun did not figure. She would not last, but it did not matter. She wanted to sew.

'Here,' Hen said. 'Unpick this bodice. Doesn't matter how long it takes.'

A nice silence, with a cup of tea, while Hen thought about what she had said and went into a dream with the material in her lap. She was trying to tease off the surviving lace from the wrecked, moth-eaten border of a skirt of a bridesmaid's dress, circa 1950, so that she could use it. It's gros point de Venise, Jake had said, developed in seventeenth-century Italy, but I reckon this is another, nineteenth-century version. Guipure lace to you, doll. There was a bloke called Doucet who made evening gowns out of ribbons, flowers, braid, beadwork and embroidery, and wedding dresses out of this lace. Fantastic stuff, as delicate-looking as cobwebs from a distance, tough as old boots close to, and heavy. Take off the rotten backing and keep it.

Oh hell, memory lane. It was the dressing-up box, that trunk in the corridor outside her childhood bedroom that did it. Donations of unwanted stuff for the amateur dramatics society in a small seaside town, way before car boot sales and everything having a price. The dressing-up box, repository of grandmother's knee-length knickers in pink silk, shawls in lockknit silk, taffeta frocks and petticoats made out of tired net, underskirts, nineteen-fifties gathered skirts in jazzy cotton, faded velvet curtains fit for something else, pre-war home-made dance frocks sewed with sequins, cotton nighties. All fit for make-believe on endless rainy days playing with the relics of difficult-to-keep-clean clothes abandoned as soon as polyester and nylon took the stage. Those heavier, shiny, sparkling materials never otherwise seen acting as a contrast to dull school uniform; a way to become a princess in a minute and act the role for the rest of the day. How to discover what it felt like to dress like a boy and walk like a duchess and wonder, why can't I be like this all the time? What's this made of, Mummy? That feels soft, while this stuff prickles. Then the market stall on Saturdays where thrifty Mrs Joyce bought material to make curtains and Hen purloined leftovers for a shift frock with big red poppies all over. The glamour of the dressing-up box fading in the desire for jeans and big shoes just like everyone else, but never disappearing. She always collected buttons; couldn't throw a thing away without removing the buttons.

Then the ideal student job in the back rooms of that

theatre where they staged opera, ballet, musicals, pan-
tomimes, extravaganzas and where she was nothing as grand
as a dresser or seamstress, simply an errand girl for the
frightening people in the wardrobe room. Collecting damp
costumes worn by ballet dancers and opera singers and pantomime queens; chasing down cramped corridors to dressing
rooms to deliver the newly mended and collect the burst and
torn, noting how perspiration could rot cloth more than anything else; it was as if they were sweating acid. She had
watched the speed with which the ball gown was altered for
the understudy, standing in the wings and seeing it was still
not right; learned how no performer ever owned what they
wore on stage. Costumes belonged to everyone. The pre-
vailing scents in the mad sanctuary of the wardrobe room
were body musk, perfume and anxiety, and the wardrobe
people were the only ones who cared more about the clothes
than the song, the dance or the play. Where cleanliness was
akin to godliness, not for hygiene but preservation.

Wish they wouldn't wear deodorant, Jake would mutter. *At
least sweat shows. Sweat plus chemicals is sweat hidden. There's
nothing stops sweat or moths. They love sweat, see?* Was it there
it began? Or Jake getting old? Hen ignored the lure of the theatre but loved those durable, hard worn, handmade clothes
and watched how they transformed those who wore them.
She had dressed herself on wardrobe remnants; she was a
walking patchwork.

Was that where it all really began? No, it was all earlier
than that. It came into focus on that fateful day when she had
gone into her parents' storage business, to help a customer
collect the clothes stored in a container for two years and
found them eaten to death. A whole wardrobe infested with
live moths, chewing into ugly lace and still moving. She never

forgot it. Cloth was only food for mice and moth; unwashed clothes, all natural material, carried nourishment for its own verminous predators.

She unpicked the end bit of lace and laid it aside. It was pleasant to be doing something for which technology had few short cuts. There was no machine substitute for this.

'I've got to warn you,' she told Ann. 'In this line of work you only ever to get to meet older women and gay men. Shall we go and look at the basement? Cup of tea first.'

She was dreaming again.

How absolutely stupid, to go to that inquest, only to see *him*, sitting there in an old-fashioned coat she had noticed first, then clocked in to who it was, felt his presence from twelve feet, registered it and ran. Not because she was afraid of Rick Boyd, but because she might have scratched his eyes out. Hen let the moment of remembered panic fade. She favoured redbush tea, iced in summer, to be followed by a pint of wine in the evening. She might live without the wine, but never the tea.

Peter Friel had phoned in the morning. It was afternoon now and he was due in two hours time. She would take him to the basement.

'My mother says you're too kind for your own good,' Ann said. 'She says you really try to make people feel good about themselves. She says you're the kindest person in the world.'

'Well, well,' Hen murmured, touched to the point of blushing. 'She must know the other part of the saying. You have to be cruel to be kind. Let's skip the basement, for now. Next time, I'd like you to help me sort out buttons and braid. I've forgotten what I've got.'

All of a sudden she wanted her out of here. Ann reminded her of Angel, not pretty, not secure, vulnerable. Angel could sew; they had both been taught to sew. Angel was quicker and defter; she had better eyesight; sewing could have redeemed her. She could sew, but she had no eye for colours or shapes, no feeling for texture, no patience. All the same, she could stitch, embroider, embellish and make perfect buttonholes. Hen turned her head away, so she could not see the shadow of Angel sitting there in the dark, dressed in that black corset and stockings, her lips and her nipples painted red, waiting for him, a mad, corrupted Angel.

Ann said goodbye, and yes, she would come back, but not until the weekend, was that all right? Hen hoped she would and hoped she wouldn't and said yes, any time. As soon as the door shut, she was going over that conversation with Peter Friel on the phone this morning. How ironic that he should think of her as an expert. Ah well, in the country of the blind, the one-eyed woman is queen. Half an expert was better than none.

It's Peter Friel. I need your help. I got your website. What do you mean, dry cleaner, you're an expert.

No, I'm not, I'm a cleaner. Whenever you like. Five would be fine. I'll be waiting. Ring the bell. She was intrigued and reluctant at the same time.

Peter Friel was waiting at the door of the house with a suitcase, looking as if he was coming to stay and for a brief moment she wished he was. Hers was a narrow Pimlico street of tall houses and her door was the small red one between two shops. He had remembered instructions. He was looking into the next shop window as if he was waiting for it to open and he felt a little shifty, as well he might, Hen thought, with a suitcase containing a dead woman's clothes. Hen had been oddly unsurprised by his call and his request. Nothing surprised her much these days and of course she had been wanting to know what Marianne Shearer had been wearing at the moment of her death ever since she had seen that photograph. She was also relieved that this might be the real and only reason why it wasn't all over.

'This is very kind of you,' Peter said. 'Kinder than I deserve.'

'It isn't kind,' she said. 'You said you had a garment to inspect. You had me interested, that's all.'

She led him down the stairs, past the shop and through the door to the basement. The workroom was too personal a space, with too much of herself in it, while down here nothing much happened except overnight. He was allowed to see how she worked, not how work overlapped with how she lived. He did not seem to notice.

There had been a great misty cold outside, which made the interior of the basement seem warm as well as stark in the neon light and the blue of the insect repellent lamp that stayed on all the year round. It was entirely without the comfort of the sewing room. Upstairs was for creating; downstairs was for cleaning and destruction. There were two large tanks of stainless steel, one long enough to hold a body, the other smaller and deeper. The shallower tank held a piece of lace, soaking in solvent. The tanks had drainage pipes leading below the floor. Hen knew how to filter the used solvent, to examine the dirt it displaced. The whole place smelled cleanly of benign chemicals, acceptable, useful poisons. There were gallons of solvents in plastic barrels, and a stone sink with smaller barrels of liquid detergent. A workbench, also stainless steel, half covered with a dress. A ventilator, a low-wattage heater which kept the room no more than warm, but not warm enough to tempt Peter to take off his coat. The smaller tank reminded him of a deep fat fryer in a fish and chip shop. On top of it, sitting in a basket-like sieve, sat two antique teddy bears, drying out like freshly draining deep-fried chips. They were bedraggled and defiant and they delighted him. He liked the smell and feel of the place: it seemed to clear his head. He put down the suitcase and went towards them, stooping down to speak.

'What are you doing here?' he asked. There was no reply.

'They've been dunked,' Hen said, touching them affectionately. 'Moth got them. Remarkable survivors, moths. If you soak them in solvent long enough, you deprive the eggs of the oxygen they need, kill them and dislodge them, so their dear little carcases should be dropping into the filter, right now. But moth eggs are pernicious little buggers, they seem to be able to live for years, and some of them might come back. So Gilbert and Bob have to stick around while I see what I collect and what happens next. At least they have one another.'

Peter Friel fondled the ears of the teddies and looked. He seemed to have forgotten his mission in his curiosity, or maybe he just liked the smell.

'*Dry* cleaning's a bit of a misdescription, isn't it?' was all he said. 'Everything seems to have to get wet.'

He was peering into the tank which held the lace, then looking above him to the wooden three-tiered hanging frame suspended from the ceiling over the sink and the freezer. He grinned at her, inviting explanations, and she warmed to him for actually wanting to know. He remembered Marianne Shearer in court. *You're a dry cleaner, Ms Joyce? No wonder you wanted something else to do, or do you just love meddling in other people's dirt?*

'No, It isn't *dry*, not in any sense of the word, but solvents act differently to water. Water swells the fabric, and then shrinks it in the drying. Solvents are less invasive, stay where they touch, dry quicker. Colours remain stable in the right solvent, but you still have to soak the thing in liquid for long enough for it to work. More than once, sometimes, until you get it right. If you can cut out a piece and test, you do that first. Again and again. Sometimes water's best. Like this . . .'

She loved to explain and he wanted to listen. She could lose herself in her own excitement, as long as someone would listen. Angel never listened. That was her problem. Hen was by the workbench, pointing at the dress. 'Water damage,' she said. 'I tried everything. Solvents didn't work. But if I put a towel underneath and drip boiling water on to the stain, it begins to go. Like with like.'

The enthusiasm began to feel out of place. He stopped looking around and remembered that the errand was more than an excuse to see her again.

'If this is too difficult,' he began, awkwardly, 'perhaps you could recommend someone else.'

'It isn't difficult, although I'm not an expert, yet. I often deal with dead people's clothes, although I don't usually know how they died. Museums do the same, don't they? It doesn't affect me. Put it here, let's see.'

He put the suitcase on the table, opened it and let her do the rest. He had twisted the skirt to contain the buoyant folds of it, watched as she lifted it out, and saw how it expanded as soon as it was freed.

'Oh,' Hen said. 'Oh.'

'Could you describe it in words?' Peter asked. 'Only I couldn't begin to do that.'

The skirt seemed to fill the room, as it had in Thomas's office. She handled it confidently, the way he had seen a dealer in antiquities handle a precious object. In the bright light, the skirt looked durable and strong and Hen's pleasure in it was obvious and slightly repellent.

'It's really rather fantastic.' She turned the cloth, held it this way and that and her voice was high. 'Look, it's made of hundreds of ribbons, stitched together vertically with the tiniest of seams to make the basic material, and then pleated. Four, no five, different colours of ribbon to give this effect, all in these stiff, accordion pleats, so that it flares out, structured and full, if you see what I mean. There must be a thousand seams in this cloth, and there's metres and metres of fabric compressed into these pleats. It's made for twirling round, because it moves, and then comes back and falls straight back in shape. No wonder it seems to bounce, no wonder it seems to float. It's like a pleated rainbow. Description in words? Exhibit A consists of silk grosgrain ribbons, artfully combined for stunning effect. How marvellous that it survived such a fall. It's delicate, but tough, like the best silk is. Would you like a drink? I would.'

She put the skirt down, carelessly, over a chair. *Delicate but tough*, like she was. It shocked him a little that she should be so objective and yet so welcoming, but if clothes were Frockserve's business, as they were according to her website, he supposed it followed that they were more important than their own, personal associations and whoever the hell had worn them, dead or alive. Didn't matter whether worn by a dictator, sadist, pope, social butterfly or executioner. They were all pieces of cloth.

He said, yes, please, and sat, feeling strangely at home in her laboratory, hardly conscious of the suitcase between them. Hen was easy to watch and did not seem to mind being watched as she fetched wine from a shelf and presented him with a glass of deep red. The colour of it reminded him of the predominant colour in the skirt and he looked at it again, sitting there, over the chair, like a second guest. No, red was not the colour that predominated: they all did. Dark crimson, burgundy, purple, maroon, and it made him dizzy. Hen sat too, raised her glass to the skirt, nodding towards it deferentially, entirely without sentiment.

'I've seen a cape made out of material like that, once,' she said. 'I'll take you to see it, if you like. I doubt if anyone's ever patented that use of material. The design of the thing I saw was American, 1940s, real haute couture. You couldn't put a price on this skirt, you know. It's precious and unique, might have taken a year to make. It's *built*, rather than simply made. It would have cost a bomb. So, was she rich, or did she inherit it?'

Thomas sipped the wine that tasted good. Must not spill: must listen to her closely and must explain.

'The thing is, I told you on the phone, I have to find out what Marianne Shearer was up to, and that's my job at the moment. All her records are missing: there's no record of what she might have been thinking, except, perhaps, *this*. Her executor got hold of the clothes she was wearing in the vain hope there was some message hidden somewhere in them; well, there isn't, is there?'

She smiled at him, slowly, propping up her chin with her hands, laughing at him perhaps, he neither knew nor cared.

'Hmmm. Messages hidden in clothes, you mean, like sewn into clothes? What a nice idea, but not, I fear in these tiny, delicate seams. Nice, creative thinking borne out by history. I like it. I mean, it could be true, couldn't it? Think of the Tsar's family, fleeing Russia with their jewels sewn into their clothes. Think of royal messengers, with precious documents and written orders sewn into the inside of the cloak so they could walk around empty-handed. The stones from a ring set into a button. Think of a Turkish wedding, where the bride stands in her voluminous finery and the guests pin banknotes to the hem of her dress. Clothes as big, fat, hidden pockets for secrets. Its been done, but it wouldn't work with Lycra.'

'No.'

'Not that it's far-fetched, not really, but why? I think you might have this the wrong way round. It's not that the elusive Ms Shearer left clues in her clothes. The clue's the clothes themselves.'

He was listening; he could have listened and watched for a long time. She drank that first glass as though it was water; so had he. She fetched the bottle.

'What this woman is telling you by wearing this precious garment to her death is that she had another life. A life with entirely different priorities. If she was woman who possessed an outrageously extravagant, beautiful garment like this, you can bet your bottom dollar that it wasn't the only garment like that. You get used to them; you can't wear lesser things. She's telling you what she was. It's a collector's item, and I'll bet she was a collector. I bet she had a collection of clothes, beautiful, spectacular clothes. Damn her eyes, damn her, damn her.'

She felt the hem of the skirt with the fingertips of one hand, and held on to her glass of wine with the other.

'She damned herself.'

'No, damn her, because I now find it impossible to hate her. I've sustained myself by hating her, to be honest. But to think of her jumping out, wearing this, I have to think of the *other* woman who wore this, and it's tricky. I always wanted to be able to laugh at her, scorn her, and now I can't. Because of this skirt. I wonder if she hated herself or loved herself, to wear it. Hell, you've got me hooked.'

She was smiling. A rueful smile, he noticed, but still illuminating. She was an appealing woman when she smiled. He had not noticed the smile in court, when there had been no place for it, but seeing it now confused him. She did not look like a woman who was capable of hatred, or not for long. She looked like someone who should smile more often. This time, he noticed what she was wearing. Businesslike black jeans, black polo-neck sweater and a rust-coloured waistcoat with large triangular buttons, no jewellery, but small silver studs in her ears. Simple but striking on her small, neat figure. It made him think of Holly Golightly in *Breakfast at Tiffany's*. He wondered who her friends were.

'Did you hate her so much?' he asked.

'Oh yes. When I was standing up in court answering her questions, I hated that woman with every fibre of my being, because then I knew what she was going to do to Angel and I knew that she'd already destroyed so much of the case against *him*. I hated her because she believed him, and that made her capable of anything. And she hated me, because he did. She was like a wolf protecting a cub, all teeth and claws.'

'It's just one way of doing it,' he said, lamely to his own ears. 'Not my way. There's no need to maul a witness to make a point. You don't have to wrestle them to the ground and stab them to death to create a reasonable doubt.'

'Don't you? Surely you have to, sometimes, if it's the only way of undermining the evidence? If the only way of casting doubt on what a witness says is to make them look a fool, sneer at them until they start doubting everything themselves, then surely you have to do it. I didn't hate her for that in the end; I hated her for *enjoying* it.'

Yes, he understood that. Marianne Shearer had relished going for the jugular. She got high on the kind of interrogation that made a witness writhe with confusion. She was flushed with triumph afterwards, like a hunter with a wounded animal, not even wanting to watch the kill. Points scored by the wound, relationships ruined by unnecessary revelations; too bad. The witness stand was a lonely place and if you volunteered for it, you were fair game. Win, win, win. Sitting in this sterile room, he was suddenly glad he did not have the killer instinct and at the same time, he wanted to defend her, because the dead deserved defending, or at least understanding, and the mere existence of this garment, sitting there, filling the room, was a very significant sign that no one had understood Ms Marianne Shearer at all.

'You've gone on to another planet,' Hen said. 'Can I look at the rest?'

'If you're sure . . . There's bloodstains. It was really only the skirt I wanted you to see.'

'Not so difficult to remove, blood,' she said, briskly. 'We all have some of it on our clothes. Usually in our pockets where we put our cut fingers. I'm always finding blood.'

She was rummaging, looking in the suitcase, talking to herself, picking at undergarments, removing a pair of boots last, reciting an inventory.

'Rigby and Peller corsetry, basque, thick vest thing with sleeves, sixty-denier stockings, black panty girdle, laced, knee-length boots with three-inch heels. My, she was very well upholstered, wasn't she? I suppose it was a very cold day. Glamorous stuff, but practical. Several layers. Oh dear.'

Hen put everything back but the skirt and closed the lid of the suitcase. She looked pale and reached for her glass of wine with an unsteady hand. Wine did not look as if it belonged on a steel bench. The glass made a noise when she put it down.

'I wonder if you're thinking what I'm thinking,' Peter said. 'I've been thinking about it all day and night. That she wore the layers to contain herself. Keep herself in when she imploded on the pavement. Soak up the spillage. Staunch the blood.'

'Oh, really?' Hen said. 'I didn't think she had much of that. No heart, no bloody veins.'

She drained the wineglass. Peter wondered if he was outstaying his welcome, and got up from the table.

'Sorry,' she said. 'Rather a tasteless remark, in the circumstances.'

'Rather tasteless circumstances. Very tasteless of me to involve you at all.'

She smiled at him again, and he found himself smiling back.

'But you have, and I am. Not that I was ever uninvolved, you see, not ever since I saw that photograph. Which is why I went to the inquest, yesterday. Just to sort of make sure she was dead, and it wasn't some elaborate hoax. Maybe I'm just addicted to inquests. The last one I went to was Angel's. It only took ten minutes. She wasn't important any more. An overdose, death while balance of mind disturbed. The post-mortem report was interesting, though. I sent a copy of it to Ms Shearer at her chambers address. She didn't acknowledge it. I don't suppose that's turned up amongst her things?'

He was taken aback by this conversational turn.

'The point is, that her things haven't turned up at all. She's hidden them, or they've been stolen. Or lost. All we have is what she was wearing. Not even a mobile phone. Why on earth did you send Angel's post-mortem report to Marianne Shearer?'

She looked away, stood to fold the precious skirt carefully, then unfolded it, and put it back where it was, reluctant to put it away out of sight in the suitcase.

'I'll tell you the rest sometime, I hope. You were, after all, brave enough to accost me on a train. And you were on the right side of justice, once, even if you aren't any more and you were too junior to interfere. And I do have a lot of guilt to resolve. Not guilt, mistakes. And whatever kind of blood-less bitch she was, it must be awful for her family not to know. They must deserve better.'

Peter thought about Marianne's only known family, Frank Shearer as described by Thomas. Not interested in anything but the money, couldn't give a fig *why*.

'Anyway, about this skirt, can I keep it for a day or two?'

Peter could hear Thomas saying *you did* what? *You gave our only evidence to someone who might burn it or spirit it away? You incompetent idiot. It belongs to Frank Shearer.* Hen could see the doubt in his face. This time, she liked his face, also the broad shoulders that seemed too willing to bear other people's burdens. It would be easier to confess to Peter Friel than to anyone else. Someone had to know. She watched him hesitate, on the brink of trusting her when, really, he should not. She was waiting for him.

'Yes, if you tell me why.'

'I'd like to get it clean,' she said. 'Since she was so careful to preserve it, I'd like to get the blood out. That's what she would have wanted. That's what it deserves.'

He was stunned. She went on.

'Because, as I said, the woman who owned this thing was probably passionate about clothes. This might have been one of her best things, for her to choose to die in it, but there would be other things of similar quality. I'm sort of sure about that. It said in the newspaper that she had just moved house . . .'

'Yes. Sold most of the contents of the last, hidden everything, but we don't know where.'

'Hmm, yes. I doubt she would have moved far from her precious clothes. Got them stored, carefully. Or given them to someone. There are specialist storage places for theatrical costumes and clothes. I could ask around. See if anyone in my line of business, the richer end of it, I mean, could have an idea of where they might be. Maybe she's hidden away other personal things along with them, but whatever, she would always have looked after her clothes.'

Peter went home without the suitcase, lighter for the lack of it, and feeling better. He felt he was sharing a burden, but above all, he wanted to share hers and he wanted to know what was in her carpet bag.

His flat seemed horribly colourless when he went indoors. A place with beige walls and no distractions except for the piles of paper which were still the heft of a legal practice – despite the computer, the disks, the online research, they were all, still, fixated by words on paper. It was second nature to come indoors on any evening and start reading.

He did so, now.

The transcript of the trial, in neat folders.

Everyone had a copy as a souvenir. Marianne insisted.

Why did Henrietta Joyce send the post-mortem report on her sister Angel to Marianne Shearer? Was this an act of malice?

His phone went at midnight. Thomas Noble despised mobile phones, always used the landline, waiting for people to come home so he could get them there and had no idea of what were sociable hours. He phoned when it suited himself, and when he was excited.

'Peter, dear boy, I've found the lover. Did you hear me? I've found the lover. No, he found me. Yet another person who wants to know if Marianne left anything around referring to himself. Very nervous, very distinguished, very cagey. Very. I've had to promise him extreme confidentiality. He won't come in tomorrow, only the day after. You can use tomorrow for searching. I'm resting. Perhaps you'd better be there on Thursday afternoon? On second thoughts, better I deal with him myself. I'll keep you posted. We'll all take it easy tomorrow.'

Peter went to sleep, dreaming of floating garments made of silk, and Hen Joyce.

He woke early in the morning, and dragged out the manuscript of the transcript again. There was so much detail he had forgotten and it was somehow important to remember it all. He would keep going back to cross-examinations rather than evidence in chief. Cross-examination revealed more, although it was arguable whether it revealed as much about the person who asked the questions as it did about the person who answered.

Continuation of cross-examination of Henrietta Joyce by Marianne Shearer, QC.

MS. To continue, Ms Joyce. I hope you're feeling better today?

HJ. How do you expect me to feel?

MS. Like someone foolish might feel, I suppose. Unless you're telling me you're unfit to give evidence, it's not really my business how you feel.

HJ. You asked.

MS. So I did, but it was only to see if you were fit, and a matter of courtesy, and you're here, so we'll just get on. I want to ask you about what happened after you brought your sister back to London from Birmingham. Can we agree she was in a sorry state, even if we might not agree as to the reasons for that state? She wasn't well, can we say?

HJ. She was ill.

MS. I'll go with that. She was a bit poorly and she was claiming she'd been raped, successively, hence some of the charges against my client. She also claimed he'd chopped off her finger. She told you this, you said so in your evidence in chief. You believed at the time that she had been seriously abused. So why didn't you take her to a doctor?

HJ. I did.

MS. And? Why don't we have a medical report of that consultation? Why didn't you take her to the nearest police station and claim rape, like you did later? I've got your statement here, Ms Joyce and even you can't quarrel with that. You kept dear little Angel in your flat, away from her parents and everyone else for three whole days. However ill she was, you kept her there.

HJ. I didn't. I drove her home, my home, and put her to bed. She was ill. She was raving—

MS. At least you admit she was raving mad. Not amenable to reason, was she? Perhaps you thought you might dry-clean her up, is that right?

Laughter from jury/reprimand from HHJ McD, who also smiled.

MS. OK, I take that back, Ms Joyce, but why didn't you take her to a doctor immediately if she was so ill? And ranting and raving etc.

HJ. I did. I took her to Accident and Emergency on the way home. Then I let her sleep, and eat, and talk, and then I took her to a doctor.

MS. So where's the report from A and E?

HJ. I presume it's part of the evidence. I don't know.

MS. I'll tell you why you don't know. That medical report doesn't exist. You never took her there. You simply said you did. Nor did you take her to a doctor.

HJ. Isn't going to a hospital the same thing?

MS. It's for me to ask the questions, not you. You kept her at your flat for three days, until you had both concocted the right kind of story. *Then* you went to the police.

HJ. I took her to Accident and Emergency as soon as we got back. There was a queue. If the records of that are lost, I'm sorry. The next day I took her to the police after she was rested. It wasn't three days after I brought her back, it was twenty-four hours.

MS. Why not take her to hospital in Birmingham if she was that bad?

HJ. I thought it better to get her out of that place, bring her away. Get her clean, make her feel safe. Besides, I didn't know then how bad it had been. I didn't know the extent of what he'd done.

MS. Isn't it true, Ms Joyce, that the only evidence of

what my client had allegedly *done*, was what Angel *told* you he had done? There was no real evidence of abuse inflicted by *him*. There was only your belief in what she told you?

HJ. She was seriously malnourished with visible bruises. Her right index finger had been severed.

MS. But why did you assume that implicated my client? Why my poor client, when your sister's real complaint was that he had already left her?

HJ. It was obvious.

MS. Obvious to whom? Wasn't there another explanation? Didn't it occur to you that you sister might be lying, creating a story of systematic, violent abuse in order to cover up what *she* had done to herself?

HJ. No, that didn't occur to me. Angel's a truthful person.

MS. My client always thought so too, Ms Joyce. He's never suggested otherwise. Which leads me to this. Could it be that *you* helped her with the invention you both took to the police? Two minds working on it, with yours predominant, concocting a story for them which would hide Angel's shame and reinvention?

HJ. That's nonsense.

MS. I suggest it isn't nonsense. It's the only sense, isn't it? If Angel was such a truthful person? You pushed her into making fantastical allegations.

HJ. I didn't.

MS. It was your way of cleaning her up, wasn't it, Ms Joyce?

Silence from witness.

Sigh from Ms Shearer.

MS. Please answer.

HJ. The suggestion's beneath contempt.

MS. So be it. You went to the police. They were shocked by the finger and the bruises and they accepted the allegations, hook, line, and sinker. You were sent to a place for vulnerable persons and handled with kid gloves.

HJ. Not kid gloves, surely. They mark so easily.

Objection from Prosecution Counsel. Pejorative statment, Counsel must stick to questions and refrain from comment.

MS. All right. We'll move on. Ms Joyce, if the allegations of sexual abuse were true, why was it that your sister refused a full medical examination?

HJ. Did she?

Objection by Prosecution. Witness cannot speak for what was going on in another witness's mind outside her presence. Unfair.

MS. All right, point taken. Shame's a powerful factor, isn't it Ms Joyce? You wanted her to push her shame on to someone else. You say you don't know why intimate medical examination was refused, but I suggest you do. You didn't want anyone to know how little she had suffered. How much did you really know about what was in her mind when you persuaded her to refuse?

HJ. She didn't want to be touched. She didn't want anyone to know . . .

Witness falters. I know she did not want to be touched.

MS. Didn't want anyone to know, Ms Joyce? Wasn't it you who didn't want anyone to know how much your sister was capable of inventing? How corrupted she was?

HJ. I waited for her to come out. That's all I did. I was waiting to take her home. I don't know, didn't know if she was examined. I thought she was.

MS. You didn't know? Surely you told her to refuse.

Otherwise I could see your surprise. Angel Joyce refusing a finger up her vagina? That would be a first, wouldn't it? *Interruption from Prosecution; rebuke from HHJ McD.*
HJ. Stop. Please stop.

PART TWO

Chapter Eight

All women were bitches. That was the only sentiment upon which he and his sister had agreed.

The moment would be soon. Frank Shearer could feel it in his bones. It was not quite near enough. In the quiet of early morning the frustration was less, because at this time of day he could feel he was lord of all he surveyed, not quite an emperor, but at least a governor. He could ignore the imminent presence of the manager, due in at eleven or whenever it suited him, ready to bark orders, talk about targets and tell Frank he was a lazy bastard. Between eight and ten a.m., he could lose himself in admiration of the space, the bright lights, the location, the metallic sheen on the bonnet of the nearest, newest Mercedes. He could even turn a key in the ignition, listen to the purring of an immaculate engine, imagine he owned the power of it and could drive it away into another dawn in another place, safe in the pale upholstery.

He could drive away, or be driven. At this time, Frank could forget that his first task of the morning was to dust and remove fingerprints from all fifteen of the models on display without transferring the dirt to his clean suit; or fail to remember how he was the lowest of the low in the pecking order of this business with a job not greatly admired in the larger world, either. His name badge described him as 'consultant', which meant he was a car salesman who could not afford to buy the cheapest of the branded, all-leather interior, air-conditioned Mercedes Benz and BMWs he was employed to persuade other people to buy. He was the slightly ridiculous man who came to work from the suburbs on the tube, to cut a swathe amongst all this mechanised glamour while possessing none of it. Not even a real salesman; the cars sold themselves, or not: the fools who inspected them could not be conquered or persuaded although some of them could be nudged. There was nothing creative about parroting by heart the specifications of every machine: he could blind them with science and even simulate love for the things and the people, while knowing that, at a pinch, he could just about afford to hire one of the Mercs for a whole weekend. Frank was as a man who was employed for his suit and his manner, who longed to punch the manager in the jaw and dreamed of the day when he could tell him what to do with his job. The day was coming, but not yet. Frank took a flying kick at a large cardboard advertising sign which announced the best discounts on BMWs alongside a depiction of a tanned male hand flourishing a set of car keys towards an awestruck woman who smiled with huge, parted lips and ultra white teeth. The message was *Buy this car . . . blow jobs for life*. He sent the sign skittering across the floor to thump into the flank of a Mercedes, the feeling of satisfaction quickly displaced by horror as he raced over to the car and examined it for a scratch. So powerful, these machines, and yet so vulnerable in their perfection. There was no mark, but he caught sight of someone staring through the window to see him leaning over to look for it with his bum in the air. A woman on her way to work laughed at him. That's how powerful he was.

Frank Shearer did not even like motors and yet he was forced to tend them like babies. Should they require to be bathed in milk, he would have to oblige. It was still half dark outside, and cold. At least he was out of the rain, and the location alone saved him from car salesman ignominy.

He told himself, often, that there were plenty of men out there would love this job or at least that was the sort of shit the manager came out with every day, and in one way it was true. Kids of all colours were always hanging round, sidling in, saying any chance of work in here, lingering to admire and inhale the smell of engine power, just wanting to be within touching distance of all that high octane image-enhancing, penis-extending stuff. Stars in their eyes, treasuring vicarious ownership. The distant cousins of the swaggering drug dealers and thieves who also ventured in, ready to buy for cash, but still overawed by the ambience. Not their kind of place, really; too upmarket and respectable looking, a small cathedral for sainted vehicles and at least it had that going for it. The harsh neon lights emphasised the shiny, high colours and gave him a headache.

Frank replaced the kicked-over sign and looked for something else to hit, imagined burying his fist into something softer and fleshier than metal. Such as a mouth, or a sweet, yielding stomach. He drew in his paunch and stood upright.

By his own reckoning, his sister's estate was worth over a million quid; less if the insurance policies were fucked up by suicide clauses, but Thomas would fix all that. It was still a fortune; it was freedom; it was his *right*. He wanted that money so badly, he would happily have liberated the biggest car in the room and run over anyone who got in the way, reversing over the corpse to make absolutely sure. More than halfway there. He stood in a reverie of anticipated happiness.

A man was knocking on the plate glass door of the showroom. It was too early for serious customers, so Frank ignored him. Waste of time to be here at eight thirty, but the manager said someone had to, just in case, as though anyone who could afford this merchandise ever got out of bed before noon, unless it was some city slicker ready to spend the obscene annual bonus on the way to work. Those buggers never slept. The knocking continued, scarcely loud enough to be heard in the silence of the showroom. The glass doors were armour plated; all the glossy stock and its salesman were well imprisoned.

Outside, there was Berkeley Square, famous for plane trees and a song that insisted that nightingales sang there. Frank never noticed either the trees or the birds, not even the pigeons, but it was the West End, adjacent to Bond Street, an excellent address and to say that you worked there did no harm when it came to chatting up women. Frank's never unfashionable Mayfair taunted him with money. Half the people he passed in the street round here would think that a million quid was loose change, while the other fifty per cent were like himself and knew it was a fortune in freedom. He could taste it in his mouth, like blood after a punch, and he curled the fingers of his fist.

You're a fucking loser, aren't you, Frank, and there's nothing more savage than that, is there?

He unlocked the glass door, taking his time about it and looking officious for the benefit of the man outside, not making eye contact as he did the unbolting, first at the top, then at the bottom and only enough to release one of the doors. A sideways glance en route, taking in the frame of the person on the other side of the glass was enough to convince him this was not sales material. It was the coat that did it. Even Frank knew that no one wore an overcoat like that any more unless it was second-hand.

This was a young man, younger than Frank, anyway, sporting the sort of out-of-date coat which might lend another man authority, shivering all the same. Frank's instinct was to say, 'We're closed', but he somehow warmed to the pretensions of that coat, swung back the door and ushered him in. Killing a little time with a bloke who would never buy one of these cars beat the shit out of polishing them. Buffing up bodywork was surely woman's work. Talking was what Frank did best and he wanted company. Wanted to behave like he was already rich and invite whom he liked.

'Come in, come in, what can we do for you?' he said, breezily. 'Just looking? Anything in mind? Or do you just want to browse?'

He turned his back on the stranger and moved away to the office area at the far end of the showroom, indicating that he would leave the man alone if that was what he wanted. Always better not to pressure people in the early stages; it made them more forthcoming.

'I was looking for Frank Shearer,' the man said.

Frank froze in his tracks. These were dreaded words. He did not like the idea of anyone looking for him, because those who had done so in the past had been debt collectors, tracking him down through his chain of employments in pursuit of unpaid rent, the credit card bills not quite resolved, the one time alimony, until she responded to threats, recovered her wits and never asked him any more; the expenses claimed when he had worked for a firm who had been vicious in pursuit of them, and on one occasion, a large man sent to locate a company car he had failed to return. He shook his head, racking his brain to think of anything still outstanding, but he had been clean of all that for a year in a job where the scope for the minor form of cheating he favoured was absolutely nil. All that was in the past, but still he froze, until he remembered that it was only a sense of déjà vu, because he was a man of substance now. Or almost. He turned, smiling.

'That's me. What can I do you for? Nothing personal, I hope.'

The man smiled back, keeping his hands in the pocket of his coat. It was a pleasant, boyish smile which bore no resemblance to any debt collector Frank had ever encountered, but still it put him at a disadvantage, somehow, although his own smile was a legend in the business, famous for catching the halfway-there buyer and freezing him in the headlamps like a cat on a dark road, also famous with women who rued the day Frank Shearer made them laugh before really showing his teeth.

'It was, actually. Personal, I mean, but it can wait. Lovely motors. Don't suppose you've got anything cheap.'

He threw back his head and roared with laughter. Frank couldn't see what was so funny, but in the silence of the place it was strangely infectious and he found himself giggling.

'Don't do cheap. Don't even do halfway cheap. Have a look anyway, make yourself at home. You won't be the first to turn up on a bike looking for something a bit better, so dream on. They're all yours for five minutes.'

The nervousness was gone. Here was a fellow with the story of his life written all over him. Another chancer, surely, still in the league he was about to leave. He, Frank, could afford to be generous and was on his way to make the beggar a cup of tea, advise him, maybe, that the coat was a giveaway, until he stopped in his tracks and remembered that word, 'personal'. Oh dear. On his way to the back room cupboard which was otherwise known as his office, he let his leather-soled shoes sound noisy on the faux wood floor, spun on his heel and came back.

'So what's personal?'

The man shrugged, nicely. 'Your sister,' he said. 'Your divine and lovely sister. I came to offer my commiserations on her untimely death. So sad. She was my greatest friend. My name's Rick, Rick Boyd.'

Frank had a feather duster in his hand, and he let it drop on the floor with a small clatter, stopped, picked it up with a flourish and waved it playfully. He'd have liked to have stuck it down the bloke's throat, for a moment. Shocks like this he did not need. Made him say what he meant. He shook his head.

'Sorry? I didn't know my sis had greatest friends. Or any friends. Unless faggots, and I don't see you as one of those. No disrespect intended, not that you can tell.'

The man advanced towards him and it was all he could do not to run away, but he did not, until his hand was grasped in the biggest paw he had ever felt, and he was gazing into Rick Boyd's eyes and watching those eyes fill with tears. Then the handshake turned itself into a hug that left him paralysed, as if someone had thrown a blanket over him in such a way it was impossible to shrug free. They detached, quickly and simultaneously, with the imprint of Rick's hand, removed from the small of his back, now burning a hole in the elbow of Frank's suit. At least he had not been required to kiss.

'Yeah, well,' Frank muttered. 'Thanks a lot. She was a great lady.'

'Come off it, Frank, she was the biggest bitch unhung. Mind you, there's always competition for a title like that.'

They stood, staring at one another, until a grin passed first over Rick's handsome face and then over Frank's.

'I can't shut up shop, Rick, honest I can't.'

'I know that, Frank, really I do. Just wanted to talk to you, you know? We got such a lot in common. Mind if I look at these cars? You make the tea. Look, mate, I've got something to tell you which might be of interest when it comes to your inheritance and all that, but I promise you, mate, there's nothing I want in return. Just a bit of info, like where the hell did she keep her stuff?'

He was perched on the bonnet of a Mercedes, not splayed on it like some model at a car show, but like another kind of sweet, wild animal, resting for an elegant minute before flight. This one would not leave a scratch. He was a heavy-weight delicacy, nothing clumsy about him. His claws were clipped and his hands were clean.

'She got me off a murder charge, you see, quite rightly, too, since I didn't do it, but we had lots of time together, if you see what I mean. She told me things I'd like to share with you. And, she promised to leave me papers that might get me out of a future hole, only she didn't. I wondered if you had them? Nobody else has her mobile phone, her notes, her anything. Quite frankly, Frank, I could be a bit compromised without these notes and things, and I don't like being in this position. It's like waiting for someone to call in the debts, if you know what I mean. So if you can tell me where this stuff is, I mean the useless crap like Thomas Noble's looking for all over town, I'd be ever so grateful. And, course, there's the other side of the coin. Like another piece of news for you which could really bugger up this inheritance malarkey, but if you don't want to know, I well understand. We can work on it together, OK? Women, eh? Aren't they the limit? The way they worm themselves in and get you in the end. Can't have them winning, can we?'

'A murder charge?' Frank said, ready to faint.

Marianne got people off murder charges, rape charges, theft charges, that was what she did and he'd read about it, but to meet one. . .well. Nothing scared Marianne, but he was a different matter. Frank could scare women, but men scared him.

'Complete fiction, mate, don't worry. I was a police informant at the time and just got implicated, no worries, I can't even swat flies, just got implicated. Did she ever talk about me?'

He had a soft but demanding voice and a face ready to laugh, and he had already said far more than he needed to say. It was making Frank think of what he regretted, such as never really talking to his sister since they were kids. He did have a pang of sentiment about a person who had bailed him out a few times and then left him all the yummy money, even if it was by mistake. A teeny-weeny niggle of regret for not having known her better.

'We didn't talk, Rick. We never did. You know.'

He went into the straight-talking mode he enforced with a customer, only this time he meant it and hoped it was obvious.

'She wanted nothing to do with me, Rick. She'd have crossed the road if she'd seen me first, she really would. She might just stop by to give me a kick if I was down, and I have been down, I tell you. She thought I was a loser, which I'm not, and she didn't want to know.'

Rick got off the bonnet of the car and stuck his hand in the pockets of the coat, shaking 'yes' with his head, and looking at his feet. Good shoes.

'You too, Frank? You too? I knew her really well, and then she went and pissed on my head. Best friends, followed by total reject. Are you sure she didn't mention me? Didn't leave anything with you?'

'Did she buggery. We did Christmas cards, like I was one of her customers. She didn't even know where I lived. I never went to hers. I knew she'd died because I saw a photo.'

'All of them bitches, aren't they, Frank? The only thing that ever turns a man into a loser is a woman. They get you, every time.'

Frank's head was reeling. This was a sudden intimacy, an onslaught on his sensitivities, making him truthful even as he backed away. His first instinct was right and this man was the bearer of bad news, another kind of debt collector. This was the only person he had ever met, apart from long-deceased parents and Thomas Noble, who had known his sister; it confused him and reminded him how she had never included him in her life, always wanted to avoid her baby brother, always shone the bright light of her success on his failures, had always been the irritating example of naked ambition made good. Only bitch he knew who had even made crime pay, made a fortune on the back of it. He recalled snippets of insults, like when he got engaged and she consented to meet the fiancée for a quick drink, leaving only enough time to tell the woman she was a fool to marry her brother and perhaps she should think twice about it if she wanted to keep her looks. The nerve, when it was he who needed that advice. Big sister, always looking down on him, even though she was so small she should have been looking up. Resentment swelled in him and whether he liked it or not, Rick Boyd was bringing it back, making him realise that whatever else she had intended, his sister had never meant to make him rich and might still, yet, take it away.

The darkness outside had lifted, revealing a watery winter sun in Berkeley Square and a day that had been slow to start now meaning business. Another person stood with his face pressed to the glass. The bright light inside seemed bleak and artificial, revealing too much. Frank Shearer wanted to pour out all his wounded feelings about his sister, and bearer of bad news or not, Rick Boyd seemed ready to share.

Boyd had moved from lounging on the Mercedes, stood with his back to Frank, looking out of the window. A woman in a red coat twirled by in shiny boots, looking as if she owned the world, not pausing to look sideways to see who might be looking at her.

'Get a load of that,' Rick murmured. 'I wonder who's paying for her?'

'What do you want?' Frank asked, humbly this time, wanting the man to go, and then wanting him to stay.

'I wanted to buy you a drink, that's all. Commiserate, chew the fat. Share memories. Maybe you can tell why she was the way she was with both of us. Frank, my man, I'm sorry, I've upset you. When do you get off work? I'm so sorry.'

Frank was crying. Couldn't bloody help it.

'I never saw her, you know? Never saw her in action. Never saw her winning. You know?'

'Lets talk about it, Frank. I've got all the time in the world.'

Continuation of cross-examination of Angel Joyce by Marianne Shearer, QC.

MS. Before you met my client, Mr Boyd, you didn't have much experience of life, did you, Angel?

AJ. Not a lot. No.

MS. You were naive, then.

AJ. No, I don't think so.

MS. You'd been a bit spoiled, hadn't you Angel? Never forced to do anything you didn't want?

AJ. I think I might have been, to be honest.

MS. And you were bored?

AJ. Yes – No. I just didn't know what to do.

MS. Come on, Angel, you were bored out of your skull. Small seaside town, boring parents who spoiled you. A dad who would always give you a job in his office. What is it he does? Ah, runs a self-storage unit. Very exciting. Didn't you used to daydream a bit?

AJ. I suppose I did.

MS. You were a failure, weren't you Angel? A stay-at-home loser.

AJ. No. I kept trying . . .

MS. And failing, and running home? High spots visiting your sister in her squat in London? Or so you told my client, didn't you? Not much glamour and sex in your family, was there, Angel?

AJ. No.

MS. Rick Boyd was a way out of failure, wasn't he, Angel? Everyone wanted Rick. He turned you into a winner, didn't he?

AJ. *Quietly* I didn't want to be a loser.

MS. You didn't want to lose *him*. You never won a single

prize for anything, did you, Angel? Then you got Rick. A man your parents liked, which was more than your sister ever had. A real win, wasn't it?
You couldn't bear to let him go.

A day of rest. It was dark by the time he finished reading.

CHAPTER NINE

The best of friends, the very best. The day went quick when you had a good-looking mate who understood you. Mates, muckers, something Frank had missed ever since he had been not quite the dimmest boy in school in the Antipodes, but almost. 'Not academic', was the way they put it. Dim, but OK enough at sport, although everyone pretended he only cheated for fun, instead of from a perverse instinct just to do it, because he could have won under his own steam without taking short cuts. Always wanted to be a team player; never quite made it and being a short-fused bullyboy with a tendency to hit anyone smaller did not help. Not his fault, always someone else's. And now, as he told his new best friend, Rick Boyd, he was really, really going to win because of the sister who had always done better and always despised him. What kind of win do you call that, Rick?

Rick shook his head and patted Frank on the arm.

'A win's a win, Frank, however it happens. She owes it to you, you know? Just be happy.'

'She wasn't so bad, was she?'

Rick shook his head, seriously puzzled. The third bottle was going down nicely. No, not a pub, Rick insisted. Be there, I'll have champagne on ice, because I'm so sorry I upset you. That posh place round the corner where all the tarts go. Something to look at. They had the same vocabulary when it came to the other sex; they were not girls or women if they were shaggable, they were called tarts. If they were preoccupied, they were called tarts; if they were dressed up or down they were called tarts and if they were over forty they weren't called anything.

'I don't know,' Rick said. 'Was she that bad? I mean, I spent hours with her, you do when you're on trial. Hours, days, even. And she did everything right by me, believe me, she was very, very good, and I'm not kidding you when I tell you we were close. Wrote everything down, ever so careful. She did well by me, she showed them all up as liars and framers and they had to cave in, finally, because I was inno-cent and she believed me and I've got to be grateful for that, because she really did believe me. She told me she believed every single client she'd ever got off and that's what worked, her belief. But it was after, when I thought we were friends and it turns out we weren't. I ask her to come out and have a drink with me, she doesn't return the call. I write to her where she works, she doesn't reply. I write to her again saying look, Marianne, I understand, but can you please send me on all those notes you took, all that stuff you recorded with me about everything? And she never did, even though I wrote to her again and said, it is mine, you know, and isn't part of defending me giving it back so I know it can't be framed again?'

He prodded Frank's arm, affectionately.

'Once you've been an informant, see, and you know how
they operate, they'll always be out for you, the cops, which is
why I want my stuff back, but never mind about that. It was
the way she turned her back on me, not quite finishing the
job, like I had some disease or something. Made me feel
smaller than *this*.'

He held his first finger and thumb a fraction of space
apart, close to Frank's face. Frank's eyes were slightly
blurred, but he nodded and a bit of the old anger resurfaced.
Marianne always made him feel so weak. He had the feeling,
nudging at something in the back of his skull, that he might
have talked too much, but what the hell, this guy was talking
back with nothing to hide. You had to trust a bloke who told
you he'd been charged with murder.

'Shall I tell you what really pissed me off, Frank? Well, I
shouldn't really, but I shall. She got the cops on me, well, to
be honest, I don't know if it was her or them. Only one call,
but the day after she died they came round and asked did I
know anything about it? Me? I say, me? I'm getting my life
together, selling space like you sell cars, doing very nicely
thank you, starting over, when this lot are at the door. Even
though there's no question and no reason why there ever
should be, about me; I was at work all night and first thing I
ever knew about her being dead was opening up the paper in
the morning. And I thought was that you, Marianne, my
darling, who doesn't want to know me? Was the last thing
you did was to set the bastard cops on me, coming round and
saying could you shed any light on this tragedy? All mealy-
mouthed, they hated her more than anyone. They were there
first thing in the morning. I thought it must be her, fingering
me, somehow, but she had no malice in her really, did she?
She wouldn't do that.'

Frank Shearer was not following entirely. The world was a blur, but Rick had sure as hell brought luck in his wake. He had sold two cars, just like that. It could take weeks or hours, and it had taken what felt like minutes, because he simply didn't care.

'No. No, she wouldn't. And I don't know where she kept stuff, didn't know where she lived. She never came to see *me*. Never deigned to stoop. Never asked me to anything. Never even sent me a customer.'

His hand wavered towards his glass. A line of coke would do it, Rick thought, but he's not the type. One more round. Frank Shearer was expensive enough so far, with alcohol his only oblivion-making, confession-inducing substance of choice. Next time, Rick would find a more regular, darker, more atmospheric and cheaper place to work the magic. Get him nearer Thomas Noble. Frank's memories swam to the surface.

'She did it to me, once. Set the police on me, once, back in NZ. The cow.'

They drank to that. The last of the day, with Frank knowing he had to turn home to his own little hole in Willesden and Rick knowing something similar, although having drunk half as much.

'I'm sure she had a bloke,' Frank said. 'She must've done, even looking like she did. We used to call her Frog. Small and jumpy, know what I mean? And, oh boy, did she love to dress up when she was a girl. She had enough clothes to sink a ship, tons of stuff, she dressed up out of the movies and she never looked right. She clocked the boys all the time, I remember, even though they didn't have much time for her. Always the wrong clothes.'

Giggles, sniggers.

'Did you ever see her with the white wig they wear in court? Imagine that face with a wig on top, it was a picture, Frank, I tell you. Miss Muppet, frog face in the wig scared the hell out of them all. Good body on her though, at her age.'

They sat back and watched the women lined up at the bar. Businesswomen, saleswomen, all laughing. All tarts. Next time, somewhere dark, without the distraction. Somewhere in Rick's own territory, anywhere near the Old Bailey.

'I think you might be right about that, Frank, about her having a bloke. You can always tell. She'd sometimes look at her watch at four thirty in the afternoon; that's the time to meet your married man, isn't it? On his way home from work. Good luck to her. Why not?'

Glasses were raised. A happy chink, a pause and a grin at one another before they looked towards the bar, thinking of happier times and better times to come. Rick Boyd picked up his glass and sipped, delicately, choosing the right moment.

'Did she ever tell you about her having a baby, Frank?'

'What?'

'About her having a baby, once.'

'No.'

'Like when she was nineteen or twenty.'

Frank put down his own glass clumsily, spilling a bit, leaving it still half full, clutching the base of the glass with his hands around it.

'She didn't. She couldn't have.'

'No, you're right, she didn't have it in her. Not her thing, she'd have been more careful. Only . . .' He leaned forward, so he was whispering in Frank's ear, patted his arm again and leant back, looking towards the oh-so-unavailable women, making sure he had Frank's full attention as he began to absorb this absurd idea, and Rick turned the full focus of his honest blue eyes upon him. Frank's blood was running hot; he could feel sweat bursting into his hair. Rick leaned forward again. 'Only it was something she said, in all those hours together. She had to ask me once, did I have kids, and I said, no, not that I know of, and I was a bit sorry about that, but I'd still got time, and did she? And she said, perhaps just to make me feel at home, yes, she'd had one, once. Then it was gone, just like she wanted, because she hadn't wanted it at all, so it went to someone else. It was only her talking, trying to get close. Probably not true. Oh, you do look ill. Had I better get you home?'

Best friends. United. Nothing freeloading about Rick, he'd paid for it all. He had a job selling advertising space, he said, somewhere along the line, boring as anything, but paid OK if you knew how to sell. Frank liked a man who bought the drinks, and then when he was a bit wobbly, bought another, and waited for him to feel better and then, would you believe, stuffed cash in his pocket towards a taxi. They would meet again, tomorrow and the day after tomorrow, cos we do have to work, don't we, Frank? We could check out Thomas Noble's place, see what he's up to, don't trust him, Frank, he'll shaft you and then we'll go down to one of those proper pubs round Fleet Street where you see the lady lawyers and bankers, and the booze is better, OK?

I think she said she had a son, Frank, but it may have been a girl. It wasn't a gender-specific conversation, it was about kids.

Take no notice, Frank, I've upset you again, but I'm here to help, really. Why should it matter one way or another, might be nice to be an uncle, now that she's dead, no, perhaps not.

Why did she tell you, Rick? Because we had hours together, waiting for things to happen and you get talking, you know? She was good at getting people to talk, open up, you know?

On the way home, feeling sick again, but not too sick to notice the time and find it still early enough for recovery by morning to be a distinct possibility, Frank thought, *And you're not so bad at that, either,* in the briefest moment of suspicion which passed, quickly. They had that in common, he and Rick Boyd: they could both talk the talk and there was nothing wrong with that. He was thanking his lucky stars that Rick had come along because he knew he had found a friend, just at the time when the lack of them weighed on him. He was lonelier than a lost soul in hell, buoyed up by hope of redemption, which just at this moment looked awful shaky. Fancy him coming straight from fucking Thomas Noble as soon as he knew, the very next day. His head had cleared, only now it felt like a hollow drum, supported by his shoulders, with someone banging on it.

The rules of intestacy, Thomas had said, doing his pompous, finger-wagging lecture that had accompanied his first introduction to the client, *mean, as follows. If parents are dead, all goes to children. If no children, to brothers and sisters in equal shares, if none of them, cousins etc. Children first, they take all, so you're a lucky chap, she didn't have any, not her thing. Otherwise, you'd be out of the loop. Nada. And my client would not be you. It would be him or her. Or them.*

Frank's head jarred against the window of the cab, the driver treating him with contempt, cornering fast, lurching around with a prepaid customer, hating the route north away from the fleshpots of Mayfair. Fat chance of picking up another fare in Willesden for the route home. Frank clutched the door handle, steadied himself upright and automatically checked his heart, his wallet and his balls, finding all intact. Not a bad day all round before that last bit, still winning, been dreaming of living in Marianne's all-white flat in Kensington, debt-free, new suits, new opportunities. Before this spectre introduced itself in the form of a grown-up bastard bent on taking it all away with a prior claim of blood that would nullify his. The last revenge of his hateful sister would be this and he could hear her laughing. *I really got you going there, didn't I, Frank? Only nothing was ever yours.*

Rick's words, over the last round, like, I didn't mean to upset you, and then Frank had found himself explaining the point. If Marianne had a child still alive and known, I'm fucked, Rick, I really am.

'No, you're not. Not if it's not interested. Not if it's dead. Not if it lives in another country. Not if what she said in passing wasn't true. Just a woman boasting.'

'Thomas Noble will find *It*. If he knows there's an *It*, a legal inheritor, he'll find *It*. He'll regard it as his bounden duty, the prick.'

'Well, we'd better find *It* first, hadn't we, Frank? And what business is this of Mr Noble's? Who's going to tell him? Everything's confidential with me, Frank.

Here we go; see you, when did we say? There's better pubs down the City end. More intimate. Better tarts, we'll go there Wednesday, drink here tomorrow? Don't worry, we'll sort it out. I've got your number. Go easy, friend, phone me in the morning.'

We. Frank's first instinct had been right. Rick Boyd was the bearer of bad news, but also the bringer of good tidings. He was like a tidal wave of reassurance, bringing the not-so-good news and also the solution. Don't shoot the messenger, or ignore him.

When Marianne was twenty, she was here, in London. He was still in NZ with Mummy and Daddy; none of them would have known.

Rick Boyd watched the taxi trundle away into the distance and hugged his coat around his body. It was a good coat and he was fond of it. He had found it in the open cloakroom of a club into which he had invited himself and selected it on the way out as being far warmer and better-fitting than the one he had worn on the way in. He was trying to remember which club it was: the Groucho, the Travellers or the Reform. It was an old man's coat, indistinguishable from many others; no one would recognise it again. The visiting of such clubs was the cautious part of a wider plan on which he had been working ever since his acquittal. The strategy had formed itself in prison, where his incarceration with exclusively male company had made him realise that maybe he had got it wrong, because men were easier to con than women, equally gullible while demanding less. They required a different approach, sure; none of the physical seduction, although he didn't rule it out; only the befriending, the playing of the role, and so many men were lonely, willing to compromise with the virtual, rather than the actual embrace.

Rick Boyd did well in custody. Model prisoner, barrack-room lawyer since law was his hobby, benign influence on the younger inmates, got even fitter in the gym – done wonders for his upper body strength – and even the warders liked him. Rumour had it he was in for fraud, he looked so smart. That was what gave him the idea, because if you could fool a screw, you could fool anyone. Conning men would be easier than conning women; he should have seen it before. Either way, you got the trust and when you couldn't keep it any longer or the game was up, or they turned sour, you turned on the pain. Picking the target, working out the scam was the hardest bit. You needed someone already halfway to corruption. Rick was congratulating himself. Sweet Marianne Shearer had handed him an heir.

He walked through Jermyn Street, passing the shirtmakers' and shoemakers' shops, into Regent Street to Oxford Circus, passing Aquascutum, Austin Reed with the January sales notices in the windows. Displays of clothes never tempted him any more than the clothes themselves, except for the sweet cleanliness of anything new. He liked the smell of new, unused things; he was rigorous to the point of neurosis about hygiene. That was where prison had hurt and where the humiliation of it was excruciating, the constant smell of men, but at least it did not enrage him like the smell of an unwashed woman. It was the stench of their misery that made him want to hurt them; no such complications with men. Rick was not going to get that close and he was sick of any kind of flesh.

He took the Central Line at Oxford Circus for the long, stop-start ride to home. Leytonstone. Still not late, the ten o'clock lull, with most of the passengers not yet stinking of drink, and plenty of space. He eyed the women. London was one hard city for a small-town man, but tonight, he felt positively fond of it; tried to stop himself smiling. Smile on the Underground and people thought you were mad.

Priorities. Frank. Frank as victim, Frank as weapon; Frank as the means to an end, rich Frank. Frank made to think Henrietta Joyce was the enemy. . . Even the daughter? Implant the idea of a daughter? One more session with Frank would do it. One more day.

He looked down to find he had clenched his fists,

unclenched them and let his hands lie in his lap, peacefully. Henrietta Joyce, the thief of liberty, pride and possessions, who also had something of his.

Then there was the Lover of whom he had been jealous. When *his* Marianne rushed away, she should have had eyes only for him, should have been concentrating on him, not looking at her watch. He had copied the name of the Lover from the open page of an address book in all those hours together. Hate him. The Lover might have the stuff, might be the keeper of Marianne's things, like all the letters she surely meant to send to him.

Rick looked down at his hands, admiring them and himself. Fancy the law giving him the lever. Inspired to suggest that Marianne might have spawned a sprog, the merest suggestion of it enough to turn Frank into putty and make him, R. Boyd, indispensable.

The Lover was definitely true; you could see it in her face some days, the existence of some other priority, someone she loved better. And the bitch; she'd never once mentioned a child, why should she? She never confided *anything*. *She* thought she was immune to him, the bitch, but she wasn't, not really. Just pretended she was.

It was a brilliant piece of invention.

A child, specifically a female child, a daughter.

An invention Frank would pay to eradicate.

He wondered idly, why the hell did she jump?

Must have been him. Couldn't bear life without him.

Continuation of cross-examination of Angel Joyce by Marianne Shearer, QC.

MS. When you first moved with Mr Boyd to Birmingham, you were happy, weren't you?

AJ. Yes.

MS. Insofar as you're capable of such a thing. So happy that you freely gave him your money. Where did that money come from, incidentally?

AJ. My parents.

MS. Who liked my client enough to trust you with ten thousand pounds? They must have been very keen to get rid of you, weren't they?

AJ. *Whispers* Yes, they must have been.

MS. Sick of you sponging off them? Final payment? Good riddance?

Interruption.

MS. All right, let's get on. Boyd was freedom and a taste of the high life.

AJ. For a week or two, that's all.

MS. Then you had to work and you don't like work, do you? Cleaning work – all you'd ever learned to do, wasn't it? Like your sister. With all your opportunities, shame on you both, isn't it? You didn't like work, did you?

AJ. He lied to me.

MS. No, he didn't. More a question of real life intervening and him doing his best, wasn't it? Nothing wrong with being a cleaner, but you resented it.

AJ. No, I didn't.

MS. You thought you were going to be kept in style, didn't you?

AJ. I didn't.

MS. I suggest you did, you resented having to work at all and it was all a bit of a shock since you'd never had to do it. You thought you were going to be kept, isn't that it?

AJ. I didn't like him lying to me.

MS. But he didn't lie to you, Angel. He never said he co owned the bar he talked about. *You* made that up for your parents, to get them to give you the money. You made it up and you embellished it. It was always understood that you'd both get jobs.

AJ No . . . yes. I was going to work with him.

MS. You were obliged to work for the first time in your spoiled little life and you didn't like it. You didn't like the flat he rented for you, you didn't like anything.

AJ. That's not what I said. I liked the place.

MS. Oh, you mean you liked it before you trashed it?

AJ. I what?

MJ. You trashed it didn't you? You said it wasn't good enough and you trashed it?

Interruption; Witness not obliged to answer leading questions.

AJ. Someone came in when we were out and trashed it. We had to go somewhere else, this little cellar. Rick said someone was after him and he had enemies. He said they wanted to hurt him, and me, too, and he got us this place. I was scared, you know? He said it would be better if he went away for a while, he did say that, only I had to stay and hide, we'd be burnt in our bed, otherwise. And that became the pattern. I went to work: he came back for two days a week, maybe. He took the money I'd got and then he'd go again . . .

MS. Who were those enemies, Angel?

AJ. He said he'd been a police informant, got some people put in jail and they wanted to kill him.

MS. You do let yourself down, don't you, Angel? I don't

know what's worse. You, having the gall to suggest my client would come out with such rubbish to appease you, or you admitting you might be stupid enough to believe it. Which is it?

AJ. He said it. I believed him.

MS. Doesn't take long to get through cash with a dope addiction like yours, does it Angel? He had to give you rations, didn't he, so's you wouldn't waste it? He worked and you bled him dry, didn't you?

AJ. . . . And he said he couldn't go to the police because they were in it, too. That's what he said.

MS. He said, he said. We don't know what he said, do we? Truth is, Angel, he had to get you out of the first flat after you'd trashed it and he had to work all hours to pay for the damage?

AJ. No.

MS. Was it then, was it then when you really resented him, was it then that you thought up the idea that he also raped you?

AJ. That's when it began. Not the idea, the raping.

MS. You mean that's when you stopped begging for it every five minutes? You know what rape means? Sex without consent. Four counts on the indictment?

AJ. Yes, I know what rape means. I know what it is.

MJ. You joked with my client, didn't you, Angel? You said the only things you were good at in life were sex and sewing. Didn't you say that?

AJ. I did say that, once. In the early days. That's why he took off my finger.

Peter Friel put away his rereading of the transcript.

He needed to be reminded of the terrible, convincing details.

CHAPTER TEN

After what turned out to be two days of ease in which nothing happened and no one phoned except to cancel, Thomas Noble's office was restored to order. So was his mind. Indulgence in either emotion or alcohol did not suit him so he washed it away with his morning shower and finished the cleansing of his spirit with a Floris aftershave. He was glad of the delay. It gave him extra time to look forward to meeting the Lover.

The opinion that all moral dilemmas were soluble in eau de toilette was one obviously shared by the man facing him over the opposite side of his desk, entirely comfortable in the leather armchair drawn up for the purpose and quite oblivious to the effects of the comforting fire; a cold man who needed no warming, delightfully sweet-scented from his shoes to his collar. The contrast between this man, Frank Shearer, the scary Rick Boyd and the scruffy Peter Friel, who was the last to linger in his space, reminded Thomas that he must flex the muscles of his personal authority, because this old man presented the greatest challenge of them all. This old fellow was the real alpha male. Thomas had no conscience to speak of, save client loyalty, which had made him entertain the most dreadful persons and suffer the most appalling manners. No need to dwell upon these; there were problems and solutions, that was all. Such as where were Marianne's documents and dispositions, apart from that wretched transcript, which he was never going to read any more, if he could help it, and what was he going to find out this morning.? Did this man have the answers? Thomas relished the task and had to admit to a degree of excited curiosity which was, naturally, carefully controlled.

The other man looked as if he was purpose-built for the keeping of secrets. The Lover sat like an elegant statue at ease with his elderly limbs, the sort of exhibit Thomas would have admired in a museum with no hesitation about following the instructions not to touch it. Better from a distance, he thought; not made of a tactile substance and not carrying about his person any invitation to stroke. If he were made of metal, it would be cold iron rather than warm copper, although Thomas considered his face could have been carved out of marble and left with a permanent expression of distaste. Was there ever such a thing as a smiling sculpture? The Lover reminded Thomas of certain statues in parks and squares, looking slightly outraged because they did not want to be there in the first place. Whenever he was at a loss with a person, Thomas would make himself wonder what they were like when having an orgasm. It was a way of cutting them down to size, but in this case, it defied imagination. He could not imagine this divine creature ever losing control or even having the ability to do so. Maybe his manner was dictated by the obvious awkwardness of the situation or by grief; Thomas hoped it was the latter and wondered how he could use the former to the advantage of his own investigation.

The Lover must have been seventy-five if he was a day, albeit with the straight back and long legs of an officer schooled on a parade ground. He looked as if he could still climb hills without breaking stride or drawing breath, a man who made no concession to the years written in his heavily lined face and mottled hands. Surreptitious examination, becoming more obvious in the silence that hung between them, made Thomas conclude that the Lover was more of a dancer than a soldier. He would have suited a ballroom floor and looked ready to glide across the room and away. He was waiting for Thomas to start and he was giving nothing of himself, so that when he smiled, it was perfectly shocking. It took up every line in his cadaverous face and made his eyes disappear into their own folds.

'Have you finished?' he said.

'Finished?' Thomas echoed.

'Your examination of me. I can imagine what you're thinking. What on earth was Marianne Shearer doing with an old hound like myself and were we any good at it? Did we really make the beast with two backs? Yes and yes, although there was rather more to it than that. We did like to dance, you see, long after it was out of fashion. We were devoted to our own style in a cruel, style-free world. We didn't like it out there, so we made our own, occasionally. Marianne was a demanding savage without her clothes, you know. Properly dressed, she moved beautifully.'

Thomas grabbed hold of a pen to hide his surprise and discomfort. He pulled a sheet of paper towards him and wrote down the Lover's name. He was never going to think of him by name, only as the Lover. Or the Dancer. Everything about him was streamlined. His suit was double-breasted cashmere and Thomas was suddenly reminded of the sartorially obsessive Duke of Windsor and his temptress, Wallis Simpson, who had not really been a beauty either, but knew how to wear her clothes. The comparison made him want to giggle, the way he did when he knew he was outclassed. He stroked his own chin, thoughtfully, to massage away the smile and check whether his own neck was half as loose as the ancient Lover's. Not yet, thank God, not yet. The dirty old dog. The Lover was staring into the fire and had not yet once met his eye, until now. The full force of his gaze was akin to being caught in headlamps. Amazingly pale blue eyes, possibly cruel.

'I take it that I can rely on your discretion, Mr Noble. No one, and I repeat, no one ever knew about my affair with Marianne Shearer, and if there is the slightest risk of it ever becoming public, I shall deny it utterly. My name stays out of it. I have a loving and possessive wife who will certainly outlive me, children, grandchildren and I am quite determined to bask in my own reputation for as long as I need it. Marianne understood that, entirely, and I trust that you do, too. She mentioned you in passing, but I did think I was relying on someone else to act as liaison. Peter Friel, she said.'

Thomas was insulted, but did not say so.

'I looked you up in *Who's Who*,' he murmured. 'W. Stanton, Bencher. Arrived at Gray's Inn as a barrister in 1954. Otherwise, dress designer with Charles Creed. What a career of contrasts, if I may say so.'

'Not really. I specialised in patents and the protection and registering of ideas and inventions when I was in practice, not that that has anything to do with anything, but it did provide a sort of continuum. You could say my flourishing in the latter career happened in the late nineteen forties, when all you were allowed to design was economical clothing. An apprentice at seventeen. A challenge, of course, but unrewarding in those limited times, and one needed a living if one wanted the family one had lost. I'm a Jew, Mr Noble. Escaped from Germany when I was five. I was a designer at seventeen, realistic at nineteen, took to the law and started my dynasty. I have lost everything, once, and I'm not going to do it again. Am I absolutely assured of your silence, Mr Noble? Otherwise, there's no point continuing.'

Thomas fiddled with paper and pen, longing for something else to touch. Everyone wanted promises from lawyers and never seemed to realise they could not have them, but then, he was talking to another lawyer, Mr Stanton, QC, who, however long retired, should have known that. He shook his head with suitable sorrow, still feeling for the saggy bit beneath his own chin and relieved to find it not fully formed.

'*You* contacted me, Mr . . .' he almost said Mr Lover. 'And it was conscientious of you do to do so, but if you have anything to say which is relevant to the inquest, I shall have to confess your existence. That's my duty as a solicitor of the Supreme Court . . . I shall have to tell the Coroner about anyone who might have any knowledge about Ms Shearer's death, or indeed, any influence on it.'

'Then I shall leave, now. If you don't mind.'

He rose with a stiff grace, revealing the crease in the trousers of his suit which he had hitched up as he sat and looked round for his coat, determined, but a shade uncertain of where he was. Thomas's temper was on a far shorter lead than he had realised and he found himself shouting, 'Sit down!'

To his amazement, the paragon actually sat, composed himself and hissed, 'I cannot give evidence, Mr Noble, I really can't. You must know that. Where's this Peter Friel she told me about, where is he? She promised me, she *promised* . . .' He paused. 'And I promise *you*, that I have no information which fully explains her death, or her motives. I knew about it from the newspapers, I opened a newspaper and saw her fall. And . . .' He turned the pale blue eyes towards the fire again and for a moment, Thomas thought he had lost him, until the Lover continued in a stronger voice, '. . . she left me instructions. Which I have, and I am fulfilling to the letter.'

'Where's her stuff?' Thomas said. 'Her documents, her will, her things?'

The Lover spoke very carefully, clasping his hands as if testing their strength. His initial, polite handshake had been like grasping tissue paper and even his neck seemed fragile. Not weak by any means, but vulnerable.

'I have some of them,' he said. 'But nothing relevant, I assure you. Letters to me, letters from me. Her instructions; the least I owed her. She was the most undemanding mistress – no, mistress is the wrong word, a mistress is paid, is she not? I never paid her. She serviced me and I her. We loved the same clothes and music and how important is that?'

He sat back in the chair, an almost perfect piece of symmetry, a graceful version of age.

'It matters,' Thomas said. 'Very much.'

The blue eyes were sardonic, making Thomas realise that he did not matter at all.

'How long did you know her?'

The eyes checked the room for recording equipment, obviously absent. It was if ol' blue eyes understood that Thomas could not have managed the equipment suitable for a spy, again, faintly insulting.

'Thirty years, in total, I suppose, although . . .'

The long fingers gripped the sides of the chair and flexed, briefly, before he drew breath and continued, slowly.

'The first year I knew her, she was twenty and desperate, and I was very much older and successful. Perhaps that's why I was so cruel. She could have upset the whole cart. I had a wife with a beautiful face and a body like a truck. Marianne was the other way round, at least you could dress her. All I can tell you is that in the months before her death, she was conducting research into her own family and it upset her greatly. She was also reviewing the so-called achievements of her professional life and that upset her even more. She said, and I quote, that all she had ever done was liberate scum to float back and poison the water. She said she had betrayed the innocent.'

He hauled himself out of the confessional chair, nimbly, strode towards his coat on Thomas's artful coat stand and had the thing halfway on before Thomas could intervene with any vestige of politeness. He was into the coat, perfectly, adjusting its warm lightness in the way it deserved since it was made of vicuña, before he spoke. Thomas was powerless to stop him and felt the Lover's revulsion from three feet away.

'I hate *queers*, Mr Noble. Nothing gay about any of you, nothing at all. I share some prejudices with Hitler. If you want anything more, send that Peter Friel. I'm obeying instructions, that's all. How can you possibly understand Love as I know it? She said you wouldn't.'

'Oh.'

'She said you didn't understand it all. She said you kept it in storage, just in case.' He adjusted a white silk scarf with care. 'Send this Peter Friel, soon. I've given you the address, it isn't exactly far for him to come. It's my bolt-hole away from family, at least once a week. Where I used to meet Marianne. As far as I'm concerned, I've never been to this office at all. My wife would certainly not understand and nor do you. Good day, sir.'

He was gone down the stairs without a murmur from the light coat worn against the cold to preserve the suit beneath. A veritable vision of geriatric loveliness.

Thomas pulled down the sleeves of his white shirt, the better to show his cufflinks. He was suddenly hot, and took off his jacket which the Lover would never have worn and threw it to the furthest corner of the room. It bounced back and lay still and lifeless. That bastard Friel with his shabby clothes. Phone him now; tell him where to go and advise him to dress properly. And as for the phoney old crust, he would shove his reputation up his shrivelled old arse. He was no further forward than yesterday. The Lover knew everything and he wouldn't tell Thomas a thing. Christ, all she'd preserved was that ghastly skirt. Did she go down head first, so she hit the ground the right way up to keep her face clean? The back of her head imploded, he was told. She bled from the ears. Someone had had to sweep up her brain. Someone still was.

Thomas phoned Peter Friel, furious enough to call his mobile. More furious to be told to leave a message.

Peter felt the phone go in his pocket and ignored it. After a day of quiet contemplation, he was bewildered to find himself on the ground floor of the Victoria and Albert Museum with Henrietta Joyce and he was still wondering how he came to be there. Probably because he responded automatically to orders, however sudden and unexpected. He was enjoying himself very much.

'So if I were obsessed with women's clothes of the haute couture variety . . .'

'There are plenty of men who are,' Hen interrupted.

'Only me not being one of them, this is the place where I might start, right?'

'I couldn't possibly advise you,' Hen said, 'unless I knew exactly what you were looking for, what your particular fantasy was. Me, I clean and mend. I know a bit about design, not how they do it.'

'All right. Suppose I were a woman and judging from the quality and design of that skirt, what else might I like?'

Hen considered.

'You'd be into vintage, for sure. Nothing like that available today. Not in a shop, anyway.'

'What era of vintage clothes might I like?'

'Something from the same decade, possibly? Nineteen forties, fifties? Earlier, I'd say. It would depend on your taste and your body shape. I'm trying to remember what Shearer looked like. I only saw her in that black robe, with a wig on. I thought she was ugly.'

'She was slim, muscular, rather androgynous.'

'She could wear anything then. I think she liked glamour,' Hen said. 'A complete contrast to the everyday black. Something that would make her feel operatic and in control, the clothes of a diva. She'd quite fancy one of Catherine Walker's dresses for Princess Diana, a sheath of silk sewn with oyster pearls, worn in 1989, I think, but perhaps a bit modern. She might like that leather evening dress made by Versace, another kind of sheath, but not really for dancing. I think she'd like something less restricting. She might like the sort of evening wear made by Thierry Mugler. Ballet dancer turned designer, made wonderful, flamboyant evening clothes fit for the stage. I can't see her relaxing with Coco Chanel. Lots of classic day clothes from 1916 on, beautifully styled and timeless, you could wear them now. Ideas often borrowed from the male wardrobe, suits and supple dresses; he liked navy, grey, beige. No, she would have had enough of that. She had a bit of an Audrey Hepburn figure, and Hepburn wore Givenchy. She liked colour for sure. 1930s, like Schiaparelli. Schiaparelli invented shocking pink, used dyed fabric and had hidden zips in the same colour. That was about the time when tanned skin became really fashionable. It looks wonderful with shocking pink. What colour was her skin?'

'She always looked tanned. She liked the sun. Maybe she was just swarthy.'

'Hmm. Maybe she was just sallow, like me. I think she'd have liked Christian Dior's 'new look'. Came in the nineteen fifties, deliberately extravagant, a reaction to austerity. Huge skirts and bows. Maybe not. More streamlined. She liked the colours in the skirt. I just don't know.'

They were in the fashion section of the Victoria and Albert Museum, a place where Peter had never ventured before, although he had been elsewhere in the place, like every London school child. Voluntarily to the British Galleries; he had been to see the throne of the Maharaja Ranjit Singh, the Sacred Silver and Stained Glass on Level 3 and the Asian Galleries on Level 1, lingering over carpets, wood and stone rather than the ephemera of clothes. The world divided on entry through the main doors, he supposed, between those who wandered and sat, rapt, and those herded through and those who took notes on the history of every kind of domestic sophistication from the humble to the palatial, to the fruits of industry to those of piracy. He could see why he had been forced on the school trip, in an attempt to see how history connects, all inventions lead to variations upon themselves and how everything, it seemed to him then, stemmed from a mysterious East. He regretted how bored he had been. He was not bored now.

He could see a garment as a work of art, rather than a means to an end. Hen Joyce and everyone else in here looked equally drab when staring through glass at spotlit clothes designed by Givenchy and Calvin Klein. Personally, he liked the idea of crinolines. He was trying to think like a woman, and as a woman he would have liked big clothes because it would stop anyone coming too close. That would suit Marianne Shearer, too. Wig and gown had a similar effect.

'Have you got a favourite in here?' he asked Hen.

She led him to it. From the other side of the glass, he saw a simple dress of sky-blue linen with short sleeves and artful seams delineating a high waist and a skirt falling to ankle length, with large pockets inset at the side. The only other detail was a lace collar and a floppy polka dot bow at the neck.

'That's my dress,' Hen said. 'It smells of summer and happy days on the beach. It's a proper, useful frock for romping around in and playing hide and seek. The sort my mother made for me weren't so different. My mum was influenced by the clothes she had, in the days when fashion was rationed after the war. Mass-produced, using minimal labour and cloth. You could feminise it with padded shoulders and nipped-in waists, but buttons were limited to three, and turn-back cuffs eliminated as wasteful. Hardy Amies specialised. My mother made a little material go a long way. You can see why the "new look" followed. I don't think Shearer would have wanted to wear this linen dress. Too plain.'

'You know so much,' Peter said.

'No, I don't,' Hen protested. 'I'm reading the labels. I'm making it up as I go along. Look, here's that cape I told you about. Similar colours to that skirt. The skirt's a copy of the fabric. It's better as a cape.'

Peter stared through the glass and turned away, blinded by colour.

'1949. . . American. . . They obviously didn't have rationing.'

The lifelike models unnerved him slightly. He wanted them to move.

She led the way out of there, not to the grey daylight out-side which he craved, but to another floor. She walked very fast and he had time to notice what she was wearing: cropped trousers, a cardigan with flowers for buttons. With her swift steps in soft, red boots, she looked like a pantomime boy, treating this as her own stage, taking him exactly where she wanted. Upstairs, downstairs, in my lady's chamber.

'This is the interactive bit,' Hen said. 'Just to give kids and people like you an idea of what a difference clothes can make. Here you can get an idea. They leave things for people to try on. Don't worry, I won't make you do it.'

They were in a room with a stripped wood floor, displays of curios, turquoise walls, and free-standing mirrors, in which he could see himself looking rather down at heel. He ignored his own image and watched Hen. She was wrapping a boned bodice round her own torso, pulling in the laces at the front.

'A bustier, for someone without a lady's maid,' she said before putting on a hooped skirt and tying it round her waist. The skirt had seven hoops of cane sewn inside the cotton, the broadest hoop at the bottom. It fell in a circle round her feet, swaying and moving as she walked round the room.

'These are the undergarments of an early Victorian lady,' Hen said. 'They were designed to make her walk upright. See?'

He could see. A lady would walk upright with her skirts moving in front and behind. She would flow, she would glide on invisible feet with easy grace.

'Not suitable for trains,' Hen said. 'But it does make a lady walk tall, and turns a woman into a lady. If you couldn't add to your own height or status, you could always use volume to make an entrance.'

'What's the modern equivalent of making a statement like that? I mean making an entrance purely by using your clothes?'

'Nudity, I suppose,' Hen said. 'That's the only way left.'

'Works for me. Would you like to demonstrate that, too?'

She grinned at him. He thought for a moment she would respond to the merest suggestion of a dare, strip off her clothes and run through the august halls of the Victoria and Albert Museum naked as a rose. The idea was appealing: he could see her taking the challenge. Hen grinned wider. Then the phone in his pocket rang, in tune with the one in her bag. Both fumbled; each of them walked to opposite corners of the room and answered the summons, Peter because he could ignore his phone once or twice, but never indefinitely, Hen because hers never usually rang at all. It was strange and suddenly extremely funny to watch someone speak into a mobile phone while wearing a hooped petticoat. It was if time had moved sideways, leaving them marooned somewhere in limbo. Murmured voices on mobiles in a panelled, Victorian room. Hen said, 'Yes, I'm sorry. I'll speak to you as soon as I get out of here.' On his own phone, Peter thought Thomas Noble's strident voice could be heard from the other end of the building, saying what the hell was he doing pissing about in the middle of the day and would he please go somewhere he didn't have to talk in whispers? Where was he, in church or something?

Of one accord, they listened and replaced their phones. Hen took off skirt and bodice, leaving it where she had found it for the next member of the public, and walked out of the room towards the exit. Both seemed in need of air; Peter was glad to follow her, otherwise he would have been lost. Got to go and see a lover. Come here first, it's on the way. Wear clothes. What?

Outside, winter drizzle marred the view of Brompton Road. Hen looked bemused and upset. Peter wanted the grin back, took her arm and led her, unresisting, down the grand steps, across the deafening lanes of traffic to the other side. The sudden noise was disorientating after all the respectful silence of the museum, making him wonder which was the real world. Starbucks beckoned, a hundred yards away.

Rain hung like glitter on her hair as she sat, waiting for coffee. Peter thought *at least I'm good for something*, waiting impatiently in line for the laborious making of cappuccino. He added pastries: she looked as if she needed sugar.

'What's the matter?' he asked gently.

'My father,' she said. 'My very angry father.'

'Can I help?'

She was tearing a croissant into very small pieces, spreading crumbs.

'I don't think so. You're a stranger.'

'No,' he said. 'I'm not. Not any more.'

He had read too much.

*Continuation of cross-examination of Henrietta Joyce
by Marianne Shearer, QC.*

MS. I'd like to go into your family background, Miss Joyce.
Not a lot, only a little.

Interruption: Is this relevant?

MS. Highly relevant, your Honour. It's relevant to establish
what exactly motivates this witness to conspire with her
younger sister in the creation of a tissue of lies and false
allegations against a man she did not know. Family relationships are the key to such motivations. I'll be brief.

All right, Miss Joyce. Angel was the favoured child, wasn't
she?

HJ. I don't see how this is relevant. I refuse to answer
questions about our parents.

MS. You must answer the questions I put to you. And you're
on oath. Angel was the favourite, wasn't she?

HJ. If she was, she deserved to be.

MS. That's not what I'm asking, Miss Joyce.

HJ. That's what I'm answering.

MS. Very well. I'll ask another. Why did you keep your parents out of the loop after you brought Angel back to
London? Why not enlist their help?

HJ. Angel didn't want that.

MS. I'll ask her, in due course. I suggest *you* didn't want
that. You knew that they would have made their favoured
child tell the truth, didn't you? Whereas you had no interest
in that. You were using her to get your own back on them,
weren't you?

HJ. That really is nonsense. If I wanted anything, I wanted
to protect them all.

MS. Oh yes, I can see that. Save Angel's disgrace by crying rape and kidnap. Bit of a power kick, wasn't it, keeping them in the dark, wasn't it?

HJ. They weren't kept in the dark.

MS. They must have resented their exclusion, didn't they?

HJ. I was doing what Angel wanted. I did that as far as I could.

MS. What *you* wanted. What made *you* feel the more important one, for once. The little dry-cleaning assistant takes charge . . .

CHAPTER ELEVEN

William Joyce came back home from the storage warehouse that was the foundation of his modest fortunes, cold and hungry after an early start. He shared shifts with his manager. They had remarked on how the punters were already putting their unwanted Christmas presents in store. Mr Joyce told anyone who would listen that his business was based on the fact that people owned so many *things* without the space to keep them; it thrived on an insufficiency of attics in modern houses and a need for ownership. *Things* equal a sense of prosperity. As long as people dwelt in places too small, moved house, changed jobs, divorced, had temporary existences, worked overseas, renting space for storage provided that extra attic or garage. WJ's self-storage units provided bigger space for vehicles, machinery, spare parts, heirlooms, furniture, redundant cookers awaiting further use, tricycles, three sets of county archives, endless book and record collections, surplus stocks and at least one set of prosthetic limbs, but the bulk of the customers stored rubbish.

Hired space for it by the square foot, per week, month or year. Storing rubbish was good business. Will Joyce neither minded nor cared what people wished to store, provided it was legal and non-infectious. He liked to see them return, collect their keys and check on treasured possessions, even if he wondered why they valued them. He was proud of keeping things safe in the old hospital buildings converted for the purpose on the roundabout outside town; it had made a good living for three decades. He was pleased with his own business acumen which had made him see the opportunity before anyone else did all those years ago when the place stood empty. We facilitate materialism and preservation, he would say. We rent out space in metal containers and that's an honourable enough way to make a living, although not exactly a riveting subject of conversation. Except to Hen, he remembered. She considered the featureless, anonymous storage facility as a magic place where people stored dreams of how they wanted to live, silly child.

The storage buildings maintained a cool temperature, with cold, concrete floors, painted grey. An industrial estate had grown up unpicturesquely around it. Privately, William enjoyed the place, but today he was cold to his bones and he wanted the warmth of his extraordinarily comfortable house.

That was where Ellen Joyce had always excelled. Comfort: soft seats and good linen, thick towels, clean clothes and heavy curtains, colourful tapestries on the walls, a love of fabric and the homemade. No clutter or fussiness, nothing too precious to handle, everything durable, no sharp edges, always a relaxing place to land. Plus something ready to eat or something cooking, or at least that was the way it had been in their solid brick-built nest before the fledglings arrived and left. William Joyce wanted it back; he wanted to forget the in-betweens and enjoy it again. As long as Henrietta stayed away, they would surely come to enjoy it again. He worshipped Henrietta, but not when she was the reminder of all their failures.

He went upstairs, feeling the warmth seep back into his bones. As long as everything stayed as it was for the time being, with no new reminders of old nightmares, no shocks or alarms, they would gradually accommodate themselves to their new freedoms and they would manage. The house was back in order without Hen in it. She could not live and let things alone. Hen 'helping' was a running sore. They were better by themselves with no more interruptions.

William loved order, hated anything superfluous. Better to forget and move on. The Joyce family did not store rubbish because everything in their house was either pretty or necessary. He could see the clear lines of the place beginning to emerge, and the shadows ready to lift in the spring.

There was a knock on the door.

Delivery for a Miss Joyce, the man said.

Henrietta's father stood on the doorstep and said there must be some mistake. A Miss Joyce, or Miss A. Joyce? Failing to add that Miss A. Joyce was dead.

A Miss Joyce, the man from Federal Express said. Sorry, misread it. Maybe to Ms H. Joyce, from Ms H. Joyce. Says so here, on this label, black and white. Where do you want it? I've been waiting five minutes and I can't take it back.

Where the hell am I supposed to put it? You've got the wrong address.

No, I haven't.

The FedEx man had already wheeled it out of the back of his van. It was the size of a broad, squat coffin, which gave William a turn as soon as he had answered the door, still with his coat on. The van blocked the street going up to the sea; a car hooted behind it and another car which had turned right from the front began to reverse impatiently, so that out of a corner of the other ear which was not listening to the FedEx man, he heard the sound of a furious engine noise and found himself waiting for a crash. The van had a peculiar resemblance to an ambulance in size and stripes and emblazoned emblems announcing its own urgency, but was mercifully without a siren. William thanked the stars that Ellen was out, although he bitterly regretted it. Damn Henrietta, what kind of joke was she playing, getting stuff delivered here?

The car behind the FedEx van hooted again and the delivery man said, Where do you want it, and without listening to William saying, I don't want it at all, he hauled the thing up the steps and over the doorstep. Not a coffin, a trunk. It was too bulky for one man, and against his better judgement, Mr Joyce found himself helping. The trunk blocked the narrow hallway and bumped against Mrs Joyce's framed tapestries: no one could pass either side. William panicked about her not being able to get in, panicked at the sight of it, so he and the angry delivery man hauled it upstairs and put it in the room on the left of the landing, which was Angel's old room. The house was deceptive from the outside, looked small, but expanded like a TARDIS into many rooms leading off from narrow spaces on three floors. The trunk was more like a wardrobe, heavy but feeling lighter than Angel had been when they hauled her down on a stretcher – but somehow still similar. It was as if she was being delivered back in a container, still dead.

Then the FedEx man said there was another couple of items. William was too stunned to reply and one way or another he dragged two, less heavy material-coated wardrobe bags upstairs as well. They seemed to fill the room. By this time, William was angry and breathless. He slammed the front door behind the man and listened as the van roared off up the street towards the sea, in the general direction of where his wife would be sitting in a bus shelter instead of being at the door and telling them where to put it. William was trembling with rage.

Delivery for Ms Joyce, meaning the one left alive. Hen, no doubt, interfering again, getting rid of the last of Angel's things, sending stuff back, blocking up Angel's room trying to shock them, was that it? He put on his anorak emblazoned with his own logo, 'WJ Storage', and went out to fetch his wife, as angry as he had ever been. She would be in that bus shelter the other end, the one where he and she had their best conversations, ever since their first courtship there, forty years ago. There was nowhere else to go then, except the back seat of his Dad's borrowed car. Hen didn't know that.

Right, who am I? He asked himself on the way. Will Joyce, likely lad, married young, soon after that looking for a business opportunity and a family. What did he get? A business, a marriage that wouldn't produce babies, and a wife he would love for ever and ever. And there was Hen, making a point, blocking up Angel's room. She must have meant it; she wanted to take over that room as if Angel had never been there, remind them of her own existence, show her resentment about not being needed, teach them something. He stood on the seafront, with the wind howling around him, and phoned her number on the mobile phone he hated. Heard her whispering and saying, Dad? Is that you, and him shouting back, come down and get all that crap out of here, and her saying, Can I call you back, as if it was nothing important and she hadn't done that to them, had all that shit delivered to take up Angel's room, how could she?

I'll call you back, she said. I'm in a museum.

Busy.

He walked onwards, and oh, hell, why hadn't he done the obvious, and redirected FedEx to his own storage store, said take it there, whatever it is, and leave it, that's what it's for. And why did he take it in? Because it had her name on it? He was in shock. Mother was going to be very, very upset, just when she was getting better. Thank God she hadn't been indoors.

William sat in the shelter with his wife, taking her cold hand and letting her enfold his colder wrist, and then the phone went again. Cold though it was, it was less cold than it had been. She had brought her tapestry with her, and fingered it, gently, as if the stitches would work all on their own and the sight of her, just doing that, made him feel angrier. She would not like what she was going to find at home, Hen using the place as a dump; it would disturb the fragile equilibrium. He was furious with Henrietta for not understanding anything, being busy, for God's sake, and then that damn phone went again. He had to detach his hand to shout into it. He shouted for a long time.

A quiet male voice, asking not him not to shout the way he was shouting already, which made him shout even louder. Can we talk, the voice said, calm as cold custard, whoever it was, but at least it wasn't Hen, saying she was busy.

I'm a friend, the voice said. Can I help? Only Hen's a bit upset, so perhaps you can tell me.

She's UPSET? What do you think we are? How do I tell my wife that the house is full of her junk?

There must be some mistake . . .

MISTAKE? Hen never makes mistakes, not her. Never. She sent it on purpose.

Can you leave it where it is for the moment? Just close the door? I could come tomorrow, and perhaps help you sort it out.

YOU can come, whoever the hell you are. I just don't want Hen here. What's your bloody name?

Peter.

William did not know why the voice made him feel better. He had always wanted a son, but it had been the daughters who had been available.

'Do you think,' Peter later said to Hen, 'that I've got the gist of this? Your father thinks that you've chosen this moment in time to dump the remnants of Angel's things on them? Or that you've had stuff delivered to them to taunt them out of their misery, or make your presence felt, knowing they would hate it?'

'I don't know what he thinks. Only that he's very angry. That he thinks that I'm being spiteful, using them in some way. Getting my own back for being rejected.'

You're a user, aren't you, Henrietta. You used your own sister to bolster up your own importance didn't you? You have to be indispensable.

Oh Lord, sitting in Hen's pretty, if dilapidated, kitchen, the last thing he wanted to think of was Marianne Shearer's cross-examination of a primary witness of reported fact, and of how, between them, they had made the jury suspicious.

'This isn't what I imagined,' he said. 'This isn't the way I thought you lived.'

She shrugged, more than slightly restored on the way home on the bus, with all that talking in the meantime.

Saying thank you all the time, for speaking to my father when I couldn't.

'You've only seen the basement,' she said. 'I live on this level, work on the other two. I used to share this flat with Jake.'

'Jake?'

'The man who got me into this business. He lives with his son in Watford now. I moved in three years ago when he was finding it difficult to manage the stairs, and became his assistant. Then his eyesight got worse. It's his house. I pay him rent which covers everything. He should sell it, really, but he wants to keep it for his son. And he wants his business to go on.'

Peter was remembering another bit of Marianne Shearer's cross-examination of Henrietta Joyce, found himself paraphrasing it out loud.

'She said, "Miss Joyce, You live with a seventy-year-old man, don't you? You wormed your way in to his affections for free accommodation, didn't you? Basically you're a squatter, and that's what you took your sister to."'

Hen nodded, still upset, and then amused. 'Yes, she did say that, didn't she? She was flinging in anything to undermine my credibility. I don't even know where she got all that from. Angel stayed here a couple of times before, so I'm guessing it must have been garbled, second hand information gleaned from something Angel had told Rick Boyd. Angel liked to do me down, it seems. I didn't *live* with Jake. I camped in the dressing room downstairs until he went, which was when Angel was away with Rick. I didn't want him to go. I wanted to look after him and learn as much as I could, but I suppose it meant there was space for Angel. Angel liked it here when she visited before . . .' She hesitated, leaving something out. 'She didn't like it so much when I brought her back here.'

MS. If she wanted to go anywhere, Miss Joyce, she wanted to go home, didn't she?
HJ. No, she didn't want to go home. There would be nothing for her to do, and she was too ashamed.
MS. She was or you were?

Peter wished he could get the cross-examination echoes out of his head.

You needed her, rather than her needing you. Otherwise read as Miss H. Joyce is a sponger, a feeder on the frailties of others. He was looking round the room and not quite getting it. He was in an old-fashioned attic under the eaves of a house where he had only seen the cellar. It was one of the warmest rooms he had ever sat in, with yellow-washed walls, an old table, painted blue, a minimum of fittings and equipment, three mismatched chairs with cushions, crockery that looked as if it had come from a boot fair, and good coffee. A boiler hummed in a crooked cupboard. It's a sort of patchwork kitchen, Hen explained. You can see why Jake couldn't rent out this house commercially. Something old, nothing new, plenty borrowed and much of it blue. Probably needs rewiring, for starters. The bathroom's ancient. All Peter could think of was how comfortable it was. She was suddenly a little formal, like a person who was aware of having revealed too much and wanting to retreat, confused by gratitude for having been helped. Are you sure? she kept saying. Are you sure?

'So, your father thinks that you deliberately upset your mother by sending a trunkload of clothes down to their house. He thinks you were sending back Angel's things, although he doesn't know what's in there. Alternatively he just thinks that you're using the family home as free storage, violating their space. Actually, he doesn't know who sent the stuff.'

She nodded. 'Neither do I. I was just shocked by the anger. It's not like him. He's never shouted. He's a quiet man. I can't believe I just handed the phone to you. I'm sorry. The least I can do is find you a suit. Are you sure you want to carry on with this? You don't have to, you know, you really don't. I don't know why you volunteered. Why are you so good at calming people? Is that legal training?'

'Am I? Three questions in one. Bad cross-examination technique, unless you want to confuse. I spoke to your father because I hate anyone shouting. I shall go there tomorrow because I'm intrigued and I fancy a day by the sea. And having a calming influence doesn't come from legal training, which teaches you how to wind people up, it probably comes from being the middle one of five children.'

She propped her elbows on the table, rapt with attention.

'Really? Fantastic. Lucky you. Brothers? Sisters?'

'Two brothers, two sisters. Lots of hand-me-down clothes. I could have come out as a cross-dresser.'

Now she laughed. 'I'm sure it can be arranged,' she said. 'We've got to find you a suit, haven't we?'

'It'd save me going home to fetch the one I have,' he said. 'You heard my boss, dear Thomas, giving his opinion that this gentleman I have to see this evening would be unlikely to give the time of day to anyone improperly dressed.'

'I bet Thomas is wrong, but he pays your wages, I suppose.'

'He might, if we ever find Marianne's things. Anyway, I have to respect his opinion. He isn't a fool.'

He had described Thomas and Thomas's dilemmas on the long way home, when they had both been talking like trains running. Everything. The unfolding of the skirt, the attitude to Rick Boyd, words tumbling out. Not only talking, but also comprehending, Peter thought, still slightly amazed at himself for volunteering to act as family conciliator in a disagreement the nuances of which were beyond him. Yet. They moved down to the dressing-room floor, which, like the kitchen, enchanted him. It almost made him wished he could sew. Become a tailor, sitting cross-legged, working in isolation in a warm room full of cloth. No confrontations, no problems other than unpaid bills and a shortage of thread.

'Some of my male clients give me things and I can never resist men's shirts,' Hen was saying. 'A good suit's great for recycling. Better cloth than you usually get in the average female fashion item, the best wool seems to go to the gents. We could send you out like a peacock. Smoking jacket? Maybe not. A suit is advised and a suit it shall be. Try this.'

She was half hidden behind the row of what looked like black. He took a suit from her hand. 'Put it on,' she said. 'I'll stay here.'

The suit was charcoal grey, far kinder than black and it did not fit, either perfectly or at all, but it still transformed him. At least the trousers were a trifle long, better than the oddness of being too short. His existing white shirt would do. Hen also found a tie from stock.

'I love ties,' she said. 'I take them apart and plait them into belts. Yes, you'll do. Miss Shearer's paramour might recognise quality.'

In you, she wanted to say. Kind, impulsive, calming, curious you. You look delicious. Instead she suggested a further cup of tea. It was late in the afternoon by now, dark outside and the colours of the room in the spotlights made it difficult to leave. Peter hitched up the trousers of the suit with exaggerated care as he sat down at the work table, touching the rough surface of it with enjoyment. A person could get to like good clothes.

'Are you sure about tomorrow? I've given you the address? What will you do when you get there?'

'I don't know. See what gives. See what's the matter. Bring the stuff back with me, if that's necessary. I can't help thinking this all connects.'

She was spooning sugar into his tea as if she wanted to fatten him up, ignoring the last remark. He was not sure if that was deliberate.

'You could kill two birds with one stone. You know my father has a storage business? Of course not, why should you? Anyway, he does. He'll also have a list of just about every other storage place in the south east. Things get shifted around, they work together and talk to each other. You could get the information somewhere else, for sure, but he'd know best. He can preach sermons on the subject of storage. Then your Thomas Noble could ring round the lot and see if Shearer deposited stuff.'

'Thomas is convinced she left everything with a friend,' Peter said. 'Possibly the Lover.'

'Hmm. It would take a good friend and secret lovers don't make good friends. He'd have to hide it, wouldn't he? Don't you think she'd rather rely on someone she paid? Look, are you really sure you want to do this tomorrow? You've got so much to do.'

He grinned. 'As you said, I can make it part of my investigations. Ask your dad.'

'He likes a problem. Don't have a bad impression of him,'

Hen said, anxiously. 'He's the nicest man in the world really. Out of his depth, sometimes, with all these women around.

'He's an innocent. He can't believe people can be as bad as they are. He should have talked everything through with a man, but neither of them could talk to anyone else.'

'Could have done with a son, then?'

She smiled. 'I wish. Of course, which father wouldn't? But in their case, if they wanted children, they had to take what was available at the time. Those were the rules. Look at the time. You'd better go. Can't be late for the Lover.'

'Regroup tomorrow evening?'

She saluted. 'Yessir. Watch out for that suit. Are you going straight there? No deviations to parade your finery?'

'Nope. What do you mean, "what was available?"'

'Nothing.' She was hurrying him out. 'Tomorrow? Come for supper? I can cook, a bit. Least I can do.'

Yes to that. He would love to eat a meal in that kitchen. There was a brief hesitation on his part. He had talked too much, perhaps presumed too much. He felt as if she could hear the other questions buzzing in his head.

How do you get blood out of a fifty-year-old silk skirt?

And why did you send a copy of Angel's post-mortem report to Marianne Shearer?

'Thank you,' she said, touching his arm. 'Thank you from the bottom of my heart.'

'For what?'

'For telling me things. Trusting me with that damn skirt. Doing this. You don't know what it means.'

I might try water first. A little liquid detergent, over a clean towel. But I'll take a tiny piece out of the hem and test for colour fastness. Lemon juice. I don't know, but I'll get it out.

After the front door closed, she hurried back upstairs to

the attic kitchen. Damn, damn, damn. He had been alone in there with the carpet bag she had left behind for the very first time today, a day she had vowed to travel without it. The bag that went everywhere, like an extra coat, because she did not dare let it out of her sight.

It was stashed in the gap between the old butler sink and the equally old cooker, obviously untouched. Hen took it out. As if Peter Friel would snoop. He had the advantage of her. He had met her on paper long before he had ever seen her; he had other yardsticks to judge her by. It made him act as if he had known her for ever, made his mind up about something. The same was not true in reverse.

A trusting soul, a natural confider who believed in two-way traffic to truth and maybe talked too much. Told her all about working for Thomas Noble; Rick Boyd coming to call on him in Lincoln's Inn Fields, all that. Asking for the return of his property, enquiring about a possible bequest. She listened to Thomas's irritated, precious voice on the mobile as he gave directions and dress code for Peter to visit the Lover, Peter mimicking it all afterwards, cleverly but kindly, so she could picture the man. Getting her involved, as she had involved him more closely than she had ever intended because she had reacted so badly to the shock of her father shouting. Offering to go home, instead of her. Sharing grief, but why? Hen did not see herself as the object of a sudden passion, how could she? She was not used to anyone wanting to help. Spontaneously. Especially a lawyer, all of them cut from the same cloth as Marianne Shearer. Also a grown man with brothers and sisters, nephews and nieces; she remembered the egg on his jacket the first time she met him. He was nice. Maybe normal people were nice.

She checked her watch and looked for another coat. She

would go and see this Thomas Noble she had identified at the inquest as a small, self-important man. Explain that she had everything Rick Boyd wanted, or at least some of it. She spread things out of the bag, on to the kitchen table, deliberately slowly.

Photos of Angel, au naturel, legs spread, inserting the handle of a carving knife inside her own vagina, face to camera, terrified, still smiling. Photos of Angel, presenting her buttocks, pulling the cheeks aside to ease the passage of the bottle up her anus, her contorted face visible between her own, thin thighs. The broken bottle hurt more, she said, but I let him do it, Hen, I let him. I can't have anyone see these, Hen, they're his. I can't let anyone know what I let him do. I couldn't bear it, Hen, I won't be examined, *I won't, I won't, I won't*. I was such a fool. *Don't* touch me. Don't try. If you tell anyone about what I let him do, I swear I'll kill you.

Another digital photo. Angel, naked, sitting grinning, eyes vacant, with her elegant hands with their long fingers spread wide on the table top, nails varnished, waiting like a cat so anxious for food it would sidle up to a snake. Waiting for her hands to be admired. At the very least, Hen thought wryly, evidence that someone else was present, if only to take the picture. Another picture, showing that miniature axe. NO, Angel shouted. No. No one must ever see this. I let him. I didn't know what he was going to do, but I let him do it. It didn't even hurt. Not then. I was telling him I could always sew, that I wasn't worthless, and he said, which finger do you use most? I said that one, I suppose.

These were the souvenirs that she had scooped up from the hidden places in that damp cellar in Birmingham and put in the carpet bag along with everything else, plucked from corners Angel never examined. All his emails and letters to the other women, their photos, nothing like as bad. Addresses, details of who they were. Those she had given to the police, while the photos of Angel stayed at home. She had set the hunters on R. Boyd, and kept the pictures back, because of what Angel said. 'If I've got to go to court, Mum and Dad'll see these, won't they? We *can't*, Hen, we can't . . .'

Also inside the bag was a copy of the Pathologist's report on Angel Joyce.

Overdose of narcotics, diazepam, tranquillisers, facilitated by alcohol.

No abnormalities to heart or lungs. Deceased has history of non-fatal, extraordinary, physical damage. Spindle-like object inserted as far as the womb, possibly amateur abortion. Torn sphincter, indicative of gross interference, healed. Significant vaginal scarring, possibly glass.

Not a newsworthy inquest. Unlike that of Marianne Shearer, no one was interested in Angel Joyce by the time it came to an inquest, except her mother who had cried silently throughout the Pathologist's respectful, jargon-filled rendition. Then screamed until she was taken away. Hen was thinking, we didn't protect her after all. She had learned thus much about inquests. All the Coroner wanted or needed to know was Cause of Death. Not Why, *How*. Cause of death was a self-inflicted cocktail of an overdose. Verdict: Accidental Death while balance of mind disturbed. End of case.

The copied report shivered in her hand, along with the memory of the scene. Her own shame at what else she had done, such as sending a copy to Marianne Shearer after too much thinking about it, an act of spite and an early Christmas present. Hen was ashamed of herself, put her head in her hands and wept. Because Richard M. Boyd was back, like the miasma he was.

Wanting his souvenirs. Wanting the evidence of what he had done, so no one else could have it. Seeking out anything that Marianne Shearer had preserved, angry with her for not proving him innocent, plus anything else she, Henrietta Joyce, had withheld. He must be afraid. He must feel ill at ease, to go and ask. Richard M. Boyd. After his release, he had insisted on the return of all his property. She had been asked if she had anything and choked with rage as she tore up the letter, then wrote back, saying everything was with the police or his lawyer, M. Shearer. What did he believe? Maybe he thought Marianne Shearer had everything, the full possession of the facts. It had taken Henrietta Joyce right up until now to realise that Ms Shearer had never been in full possession of the facts. She had only been armed with her ghastly belief.

What to do? Take it all to Thomas Noble. Keep Rick Boyd away. She could feel his hatred, drifting over the courtroom, burning her as his counsel made a right royal fool of her. Grimacing, rather than smiling as if in pity, the most contemptuous thing of all.

Take it to Thomas Noble, the messenger. Tell him it had some bearing on the death, *get rid of it*. Then think about the trunk delivered to her father. Hen hesitated. She had automatically repacked the carpet bag and put it back where it had been. Then she hefted it out again. She had lived with it long enough.

The blood on the skirt could wait. She wanted out. The new knowledge of that bastard wandering round with his own mission made her twitch. He wanted what Marianne Shearer knew and he wanted what was his and he knew where she lived.

He had been here before, to collect his Angel.

And she had been waiting.

CHAPTER TWELVE

Thomas was reading.

Continuation of cross-examination of Angel Joyce by Marianne Shearer, QC

MS. We'll leave the business of you supposedly having been raped, but I will come back to it. I can tell it's a strain on you. Are you OK, Angel? Bit pale this morning, are we?

AJ. Fine.

MS. As plain as ever . . .

Interruption from Counsel.

MS. My Lord, if you'll let me finish my sentence. I was saying as plain-*speaking* as ever, OK? I make no allusions to Angel's exceptionally unangelic appearance. If your Lordship would stop interrupting, we might get on with this trial, right?

OK, Ms Angel, how did you lose that finger?

AJ. He cut it off.

MS. When was that?

AJ. I don't know. Not exactly. I'd done my nails and—

MS. You don't know when? A memorable experience, surely? Losing a finger. As well as doing your nails.

AJ. I was waiting for him to come home. I'd found some nail varnish, varnished my nails. Last thing I'd got left, really, always had nice hands.

MS. And in he came and chopped off your first finger? Just like that? With an axe?

AJ. We had an axe to get into the squat. A little one. I don't know where it was.

MS. You didn't know where it was? Did he know?

AJ. *Hesitation.* I dunno. There was always something sharp about the place. Something to hurt. Sharp things. Like glass.

MS. Sharp things that weren't available when he was absent ? Things with which you could hurt yourself?

AJ. Yes. He hid them until he came home. Then he got them out.

MS. He hid the sharp things from you, did he?

AJ. I suppose so. We had an axe, anyway. Put away somewhere safe. Only a little one.

MS. Like the one you used to trash the other flat?

AJ. I never did that. I might have done, but I never did. I liked it.

MS. Oh, you liked it, did you? So why did you trash it?

AJ. I didn't. Whenever I was out of my head, I slept. When he went away, I slept and went to work. It was like that.

MS. But the sharp things were hidden when he went away?

AJ. Yeah.

MS. He hid the sharp things to save you from harming yourself, didn't he, Angel?

Pause. Witness confused and looking round.

AJ. Did he? I didn't think that was why. He always hid things. I wasn't supposed to look.

MS. Tell us about when he cut off your finger with the little axe.

AJ. *Animated.* I'd found this old nail varnish. My nails were all cracked and bitten, but they looked great when he came home. I told him I'm going to work with my sister, cos I'm good at sewing, and he said, what for? And I said, to sew. And he said, you can't make anything. And I said, yeah, I can. I'm not worthless, you know, I'm gonna leave you. She'll give me a job. And I showed him my nice nails, and he took a picture, and he said, which finger do you use most when you sew? That one, I said. And he hit it with that little axe.

MS. A little axe? You're sure about that?

AJ. Yeah. I had my hands on the table, showing my nails, and—

MS. How much had you had to drink? Or smoke? Or snort?

AJ. *Excited.* He brought back weed, and vodka. I don't know how much.

MS. Definitely an axe?

AJ. Yeah. Because I said I was leaving. I didn't see him get it out.

MS. Right. You said it didn't hurt much at the time?

AJ. No. It did afterwards. He put salt on it.

MS. And, much later, after your sister Henrietta came to collect you and took you back to London, the finger was examined? Not the rest of you, because you refused, but the finger?

AJ. Yes. I remember that.

MS. And examination showed that it wasn't done with a sharp blow from an axe. Examination showed that the top knuckle of your right index finger was sawn off, possibly with a large pair of scissors. He didn't think you were a danger to yourself with scissors, did he?

AJ. *Whispers.* I mended his clothes. There were always scissors.

MS. Proper, professional scissors, which you turned on yourself, Angel. You did, didn't you?

AJ. I don't know. *Witness becomes restless. Calms down.* What he didn't know is how you use all your fingers to sew. You use them all. I can still sew. Hen made me. So he didn't win.

MS. You could take off your own finger with an industrial-sized pair of dressmaking scissors, couldn't you Angel?

AJ. I suppose. I don't know.

MS. Are you aware that when the flat was searched by the police, no axe was found, but there was a pair of scissors? *Interruption by HHJ McD. The witness cannot possibly answer that question.*

MS. Quite right, Your Honour, I take it back. Better adjourn here, Your Honour, don't you think? Give the witness a rest.

AJ. *Screaming.* You don't believe me, do you?

MS. I can't possibly answer that question.

Dear God. Scissors.

Thomas found the huge scissors he used in his office for cutting open harmless paper sacks, tamper-proof envelopes of the sort used by banks, as well as for the destruction of the cardboard boxes in which his wine deliveries arrived. These boxes had to be reduced to tidy fragments to go out with the ordinary rubbish. Cutting them up tidily was a process he enjoyed.

He spread his left hand on the desk and held the scissors in his right hand. They were the size of small shears and comfortably heavy. With three fingers and thumb, he opened the blades, keeping them far away from the spread hand, and closed them, slowly. Yes, he supposed it could be done, with the right kind of madness and the right pair of scissors.

This afternoon, Thomas had found it difficult to resist the manuscript of the trial for several reasons, viz. a) he was restless and he did not have enough to do, b) the Lover inspired him to read it for clues, and c) it was appallingly interesting. He had leafed through selectively, looking for *her*, vowed never to bother again, and still he was drawn, if only to those pages where he could hear her talking. He had no interest in the evidence-in-chief of the witnesses, answering questions from the Prosecutor, only in the pages containing her name. Such a ruthless bitch, making it quite obvious that the silly girl was lying, with her frightful cross-examination technique, asking several questions at once, confusing but effective with a slow witness. He was wondering why she was never stopped, remembering how she could mesmerise with conversation alone, what a fast talker she was, with a way of deflecting interruptions. He was missing her again, on tenterhooks about Peter Friel and the Lover, found himself wanting to tell her about it, until he came across this bit about scissors and dropped the pages to the floor. It was important to put them back in the box, alongside a learned discussion on the law of kidnap, before going to find his own scissors. It was like putting Marianne away, to sleep with a cloth over her head. Thomas was glad it was almost time to close the office and go home, leaving her there.

He was still examining the scissors for size, peering at them with his hand clasped behind his back, when down-stairs rang up and said, Ms Henrietta Joyce to see you. Dear God, again. A real-life Joyce? A spectre rising up from the printed paged of a transcript, which was all that was left of Marianne Shearer as far as he knew. *Pretty and harmless,* downstairs said in her own code. *Smells OK.*

He was hiding his own weapons when she came in. How peculiar. H. Joyce, not A. Joyce. Funny little thing with an interesting coat and an enchanting carpet bag, and, as he discovered to his relief when he shook her hand, she cer-tainly had all five fingers. The right Ms Joyce. The same name; the person to whom Peter Friel had taken the skirt. He simply had not made the connection before. What the hell was going on? Outmanoeuvred and excluded, angry again, and yet, oddly, he could not take exception to her physical presence. She was . . . what was the right word for her? Nice, and strangely familiar. Racking his brains. She was not the one Marianne had described as that silly little bitch, but the sister of same. *Stood up well to cross-examination,* Marianne said. *Better than some. A miracle I got her on the stand first, they must have been mad to let me.*

This one walked like a princess, full of natural charm. The right kind of diffidence and a perfectly crazy coat. Like something made out of a man's wool pinstripe, pieced together with big, bone buttons. He craved it in a different size. Also the red boots.

'Thank you for seeing me, Mr Noble. Where would you like me to sit?'

'Anywhere you like. I don't expect you'll be staying long, we close soon.'

'Yes, I know that. It's very kind of you to see me at all.'

She perched on the edge of the armchair, with no sign of permanent occupation, still wearing her coat, ignoring the fire and everything else that might have impressed her. So far, so good.

'How can I help?'

His standard response, while wondering whatever it was for. A woman appearing out of the pages of a transcript, beautiful but businesslike, smaller than he could ever have imagined, with a nice, electric voice he seemed to have heard before. The sister of a nutcase who has scissored off her own finger. Only the last joint of it; he must remember that.

'I don't know if you can actually help, Mr Noble, but I wondered if you could. I gather Mr Richard Boyd, who thinks Ms Marianne Shearer, deceased, may have kept something of his, visited you recently. I don't know if that's true, but if he comes back, could you give him this?'

She gestured towards the bag at her side.

'He may thinks it's his,' she said. 'He may think Ms Shearer had it. Not the bag, the contents.'

'Is that all?'

'Just about.'

He cleared his throat to hide deepening confusion and a faint feeling of going mad.

'Is there anything of hers in there? Anything that could explain her death? Anything I should see?'

She shook her head. 'No, I don't think so. It might be better if you didn't look.'

'I don't understand. You want me to act as messenger to this Rick Boyd, whom I do not know, just like that? I'm a lawyer, Miss Joyce, not a delivery service. A lawyer acting as ex officio executor in the estate of Ms Marianne Shearer, a lady you've encountered, I believe, in a professional context?'

To his surprise, she smiled. It was a delightful smile, showing small teeth and a wide mouth and crinkles round her eyes. A face of premature wisdom, he decided, falling into one of his sudden, unaccountable *likings* for highly individual women. In Marianne Shearer's case, it had proved more dangerous than falling in love and he was glad to find he still had the capacity. The smile on her face grew broader and more rueful, until it turned into a small, natural laugh, directed at herself.

'Two questions in one,' she said. 'I'm sorry. I just love the idea of a professional encounter. Puts it into context. I never quite thought of it that way. Witness and interrogator, that's all it was. Professional. Personally, I could never bring myself to refer to her as a "lady". Could we start again?'

He was smiling in response to her smiling, beginning to enjoy himself, forgetting scissors, fingers in pies and Peter Friel's gross impertinence in not telling him where, exactly, he had taken that skirt and with whom, precisely, he had left it. Or not telling him the context of how she was otherwise involved. He was entertaining small thoughts of jealousy at the same time. Peter got to her first, and Peter was in demand with the Lover. Beggars cannot be choosers. A gay man who preferred the company of women had to take what he could. Live by the hour. He sat back. So, to his relief, did she. Intriguing.

'I love this square,' she said. 'Although it isn't really a square. It was a field. Then a building site, I suppose. Some of the oldest buildings in London. What a great place to work. I knew where you were, because it's so close to the Sir John Soane's Museum. I can't imagine how you manage to do any work here at all. Me, I'd spend all my time looking out of the windows.'

'I do,' he said.

There was a brief, relaxed pause. He noticed the big fat scissors still sitting on the desk. He worked it out, briefly. Her testimony had preceded her sister's. She would not know, might not know what was suggested next, but clearly, huge scissors sitting around, ready to chop, held no fear for her.

'Can I be clear?' he said. Rules of cross-examination, ask one question at a time. Never ask a question when you don't already know the answer, something learned at law school, never much used in his practice. Up until now, he waited for people to tell, rather than recite to them what he needed to know. For her, he would make an exception.

'You're Henrietta Joyce. Your sister killed herself, accidentally or not (oh God, more lawyer speak, always hedging bets), rather than continue to be cross-examined by Marianne Shearer. You were yourself *professionally* mauled by Ms Shearer, who is my deceased client, in her very last, important case. You're some kind of expert in old clothes. My colleague, Peter Friel, consulted you in the matter of a dead woman's apparel.'

Why couldn't he stop speaking like this? *Apparel? Deceased*, rather than 'dead'?

She was shaking her head. Rain fell out of her hair. Marianne always had good hair, even when flattened by a wig. Good hair, ugly face.

'None of which explains why you're here. I'm inadequately informed, Miss Joyce. Enlighten me.'

He was doing it again. Old-fashioned speak, his best defence against being charmed. Wasted on the Lover, though not on her.

She was smiling again. Thank God for an interval between smiles, otherwise a smile became a rictus, no wonder you never got smiling portraits, the longest pose to hold. Thomas never could rid his mind of irrelevancies. He wanted to look out of the window into the new dark, and did it anyway. Taking off her coat she followed and stood beside him.

At first glance, Lincoln's Inn Fields was obscured by blinding rain, bashing against the windows with a thudding sound. Almost a squall. Then the shape of trees and shrubs took shape, swaying in the wind beyond the railings guarding the fields and, although dark and feeling like the middle of the night, the pathways in the fields were full of life. People criss-crossing, going-home time, offices, everything, emptying out with scurrying human beings aiming themselves elsewhere and out of the place where they would linger on the grass in summer. If you looked long enough, you could imagine it. As it was, he could see the beautiful shapes of winter, bare branches, grey shrubs, elegant street lamps casting pools of wet light, could have watched for ever.

'I'm so lucky,' Thomas said, gazing. Such an instinctive remark, he didn't realise he had spoken it out loud. 'So lucky to have this.'

He had forgotten where he was, turned to her and remembered.

'How can I help?' he asked, thinking, one question at a time. This time, he meant it.

'Oh, look,' she said. 'Just look.'

He looked and saw a jogger with a dog, tripping round the paths of the Fields with a basset hound at his heels, going faster than he on small, wobbly legs, caught in the light of the intricate lamps as a comic freeze frame, jogger defeated, dog triumphant, plodding along arrogantly. They both admired the dog first.

'So handsome,' Hen said.

They stayed where they were, looking for similar delights, watching as the hound went out of vision and the other people continued. Easier to talk near a window, like talking in a car.

'I brought you some incrimating photographs, Mr Noble, and I shouldn't have done it, really. They're the original photos of my sister in the extremes of her own sort of torture. I think Rick Boyd is desperate to find any of the evidence left over from his trial. Anything which might still incriminate him and anything not revealed which shows what he is. Marianne Shearer would have plenty of material like that, wouldn't she? Things she *could* reveal. He's still afraid. He was acquitted, but he was never proved innocent. Anyway, I wanted to give them to you because Peter told me that he's been here already. He went to the initial inquest, too. Rick Boyd wants what he thinks Marianne Shearer kept, even her memories. He'll want what he knows I have. He wants the physical evidence of anyone else's knowledge. Fear neutralised everyone else, except Ms Shearer and me. I don't know exactly what he wants. Only that he'll come back, now she's dead, either here to this office, or to me, to get what he thinks is his, so I thought you might be able to give him this, and say leave us alone. Get him off everyone's back. It might be enough. Then he might disappear again. Otherwise, he might hurt anyone else who gets in the way.'

'What did you say? Hurt whom?'

'Two questions in one sentence,' she said, sadly. She knew she was losing the thread and losing the audience. She had got this all wrong. The contents of the carpet bag were her responsibility and hers alone. It was unfair to involve anyone else.

One last try.

'Rick Boyd can't bear anyone *knowing* about him. Angel said it would never be enough for him to be acquitted. He would still know that someone *knew*. Had knowledge they could use. As long as Marianne Shearer was alive and kicking, I felt safe. Because someone else, a powerful someone else, knew all about him. He would never take the risk of harming me, because Marianne Shearer would know. Someone else would know it was him and would know why. Now I'm the only person who knows. Her knowledge was my insurance policy, and heaven help me, I made sure she knew. She had copies of everything in this bag.'

Thomas interrupted.

'Ms Shearer would never have revealed personal information about a client. That's entirely against professional ethics.'

'Rick Boyd wouldn't know about that, Mr Noble. He was relying on her to subvert the rules, after all. Perhaps he hounded her for what he thought was his. *That* might be relevant to her death.'

Thomas was trying to follow, not getting the full meaning, but sensing some of it. He had already decided that much as he liked her on first sight, there was absolutely no way he was going to keep that carpet bag, whatever it contained. His dramatic imagination already envisaged a desiccated fingertip and he shuddered. He could hear the door downstairs bang shut as the staff from the other offices left to run home through the rain. The building felt empty. He was not going to stay alone in this room with whatever was in that bag. A dead woman's knowledge was worse than a dead woman's skirt. She looked at him wisely, as if guessing his thoughts.

'Only photographs,' she said. 'Snapshots of Boyd's systematic debasement of my sister. She really didn't lie during that trial, Mr Noble, whatever Marianne Shearer made her look like. I didn't lie, either. I've never seen the point of it, but then I've never had to. I hide things, though, I keep quiet. Easier than lying.'

Thomas was rallying himself to speak, but she held up her hand.

'I know, I know, and I quite understand. I shouldn't even have suggested it. I do apologise. I'm not your client, I'll take the bag home where it belongs. And I know it might not seem like it, but I'm trying to protect more than me. Because Rick Boyd won't give up. He won't believe you don't have what he wants. He's a perverted con man, so he thinks everyone else is, too.'

Thomas sighed in exasperation, not knowing quite what to think, only that he wanted the bag out of the room as much as he had wanted Peter Friel to take away Marianne's clothes, even though it might have been a dereliction of duty. He shrugged, to hide a sense of confused shame. Remembered Peter and felt a rush of spite. These two were friends already: he could feel it in his bones. If she wanted to protect anyone, it would be him. Let fucking Peter Friel take charge.

'If it worries you,' he said as mildly as he could, 'perhaps our mutual friend Mr Friel could take charge of it for you. He's obviously younger and stronger than I.'

'Ah,' she said. 'That's exactly what I don't want. He'd be a bit of a red flag to Rick Boyd.'

And I wouldn't? Thomas thought. Not young enough, not competitive enough? Too bloody old to be involved?

He took off his spectacles and wiped them, another ploy.

'And, with respect, you are not my client. Marianne Shearer and her heir are my client. I must also answer to the Coroner. I can't consider anyone else.'

She gathered her whole self for departure, after what was obviously the failure of an errand. Thomas remembered his manners, and then his duties, while helping her into her coat, pausing to wonder from where she had got those artful buttons. Bone, fingers and skin were on his mind, as well as the sensation of the heavy scissors in his hand. He began to gabble, the way he did when he felt guilty, remembering only the duty towards the client that Marianne understood better than anything else.

'How are your researches progressing with the skirt, Miss Joyce?'

She paused at the door, with the carpet bag in her hand, smiling again. He wanted to go with her, not be left alone in this office with everyone else gone.

'I think it's 1930s, and rather valuable. I told Peter there must be more. Best I go home and get the blood out. I'll send a proper report, I promise.'

'I'll pay you for anything you can find. Listen, before you go, do you think this Rick Boyd could have anything directly to do with Marianne's death?'

She paused, mid flight.

'Like pushing her off the balcony? Blackmailing her? Hounding her to death? Something like that? No, I don't think so, although he's capable. He'd get someone else, if he could. But she did have deadly knowledge, didn't she?'

He waited until he knew she would be out of the front

door and then went to the window, wanting to watch her go and see which direction she took.

She went left, first, towards the tube station at Holborn, walked almost out of sight in that direction, hesitated and then came back slowly. Oh, God, he thought, she's thought of something else. Maybe he should call her back, but she didn't return to the door of the office, she paced up and down. Then she disappeared out of sight, coming up the steps towards the door. He waited for the sound of the out of office hours bell that he never answered.

He turned off the light in time to see her cross the road diagonally, into the nearest entrance into the Fields. Her hair gleamed in the lamplight as she padded from the glow of it into relative darkness. He wondered about her route. Then he saw the man come out of the light from behind her and loop a scarf round her neck, like a lover, keeping her warm, pulling her close.

Not so lonely, then, Thomas thought. Already spoken for.

He turned away for a moment, turned back.

She was falling.

No, not like a lover. Not like a close friend.

An enemy.

And over there, somewhere, a man in that coat.

CHAPTER THIRTEEN

Sticky soil, holly scratching the cold skin of her face. Blood
stuck in her throat and swelling inside. Trying to cough, gasp-
ing for air, stumbling down into soil with him behind her at
first, twisting something round her neck. She could feel rough
wool, knitted wool, too heavy, too clumsy, man-smelling.
Why? A thick rope, looped round her neck, pulling her back-
wards, stumbling, losing balance down into the flowerbed.
Then the man astride her, face dark with fury, the light
through the tree, him holding both ends of the rope thing
and pulling. Her neck jerked sideways, no, no, not like this.
She was trying to push herself up, hands sinking in wet soil.
No breath. Save the effort, let him fall on her, roll away, twist,
turn. Then the stench of dog faeces as she pulled her hands
out of soil and filth, reaching towards her neck to scrabble at
the scarf, she knew it was a scarf now, trying to stop it tight-
ening. The scarf was the enemy; no, he was the enemy. She
could feel the soil from her hands on her neck and smell the
stink. She heard from a long way off the diesel throb of a

taxi, only yards away, prayed for running footsteps and then nothing but her own breath and his words, BITCH, BITCH, BITCH. Her eyes were wide open now. He was pulling at the scarf, half kneeling with one knee on her chest, badly angled for his task. At the sight of her staring eyes, he paused to release one hand and slap her face so hard that her teeth clashed and she grunted, came back to feeling alive. Angry, so angry. The slap unbalanced him: the scarf was too thick and soft to do the work. Hen jabbed her filthy fingers into his eyes, once, twice, three times, then raked her nails down his face and then it was him who screamed. The baby.

He fell to one side, lifting his hands away to save his own eyes with his face streaked with soil and dog dirt. The earth smelt of vomit. Thomas's high voice was shrieking anxiety. He was kicking ineffectually at the torso of the man as the man rolled away, yelling at him bizarrely, YOU PIG, YOU GREAT FAT PIG, GET OFF . . . the figure rolled free, out on to the path, heaved itself upright, staggering with his face covered by his hands, and stumbled away. Someone else had stopped to watch, but no one prevented him. Lincoln's Inn Fields had its share of drunks and addicts, better leave them alone.

A woman's face loomed over Hen's. Other sounds came into focus, another taxi, Thomas twittering, oh dear, oh dear, oh dear.

Are you all right down there? the woman said, and it seemed to Hen such a strange question to ask of a person sitting in a municipal flowerbed in a busy London square at a still innocent time of day. She had a great desire to giggle as well as release a long delayed scream from her burning throat. Instead she said, yes I think so and to Thomas, no, don't touch me, you'll get dirty. Thomas helped her to her feet, pulling her by the coat rather than touching any part of her skin. They moved into the light. He was in his shirt-sleeves and shivering. The scarf was still round her neck. They moved to the nearest bench and sat apart while she unwound it. Looped, not knotted, easy to remove, even with shaking hands. The air in her lungs felt wonderful. Thomas was proffering a handkerchief. It made her want to cry.

'Do you want me to call the police?'

The instinctive answer was no. She said so. Thomas seemed relieved.

'You'd better come back in,' he said. They got up, stiffly, moved in the direction of the office. Another jogger puffed by, oblivious to another daily drama. Thomas stopped.

'Where's the bag?' he asked.

'There. Over there.'

It was stuck in the branches of a shrub by the side of the entrance gate, looking as if it was waiting for collection. She could not imagine how it had got there, tried to remember herself trying to hit him with it. Wanted to think she had done something to resist, satisfied with the thought she might have made him bleed, but doubting that her short, practical nails had done much damage. The dog dirt was the real weapon, and oh, she must stink. Once inside, Thomas locked the door behind them, and when back in his room, he pulled the blinds down against the view. Hen spent some time in the office lavatory and came back with a cleaner face and hands, but the smell still lingered. Vomit, dog faeces, urban sewer in urban flowerbed. Above all, she wanted to go home. So did he. He was still in shock, as much as from what had actually happened in front of his very eyes as from his own response.

'Thank you for saving me, Mr Noble,' she said. 'You were incredibly brave. I wouldn't have been brave enough to wade in like that. Thank you for saving me.'

Thomas preened slightly, still in shock, moved to be the subject of gratitude for doing something that had taken him by surprise. He knew he had no physical courage and he knew very well that he had hesitated for a second before running out of the office and over the road, hoping someone else would get there first. Just as he knew she had saved herself. The whisky glasses knocked together noisily as he put them on the table untidily, but yes, perhaps on the whole, he had not done too badly. Peter Friel could not have done better, surely. What a silly thought.

'Shall I try and raise Peter Friel?' he asked. 'He has gallant instincts.'

She shook her head. 'No, I don't think so. He has plenty enough to do. And more, tomorrow.'

She was quite irritatingly almost peaceful, as if she had merely tripped and fallen. It infuriated him. The whisky slopped from the bottle on to the desk.

'For God's sake, woman, what's the matter with you? You're supposed to be weeping and wailing and screaming and . . . not like you are. Did you know who that was? Why are you just so . . . together?'

She took the glass he offered her with a steadier hand than his.

'How very kind you are. I'm fine, Mr Noble, really I am. I'm fine because I know who it wasn't. It wasn't Rick Boyd. That's all that matters.'

'All? He tried to strangle you.'

She nodded agreement.

'Yes, I suppose he did. With a knitted wool scarf. It would never have worked. Or taken too long. Too much stretch in it, you see. Entirely the wrong material.'

Thomas could only admire her, while remaining full of

wonder for what he himself had done. Kicked a client; how often had he wanted to do that?

Maybe later he would be brave enough to go back for the scarf.

The wrong material. Who would have thought?

She placed the unblemished carpet bag by the side of her chair, ready to depart.

'I'm sorry about that,' Thomas said, pointing towards it. 'But I still can't take care of it. Are you sure you're all right to get home? I'll come with you, get you a taxi.'

The client needed a drink.

'The bitch,' he kept repeating. 'The bitch.'

'Yes, but,' Rick was saying soothingly, 'yes, but why did you do it?'

'Has she poisoned me?'

They were standing by the basins in the urinal belonging to a Fleet Street pub with an interior so old and dark that no one would notice what anyone else looked like, even less the state of their clothes. A pub favoured by builders, shapeless tourists on the history trail, clandestine lovers in the interval between work and home, no dress code to speak of. A place of authentic, centuries-old gloom, extending back as far as the gents', the atmosphere issuing an invitation to plot and conspire. Rick Boyd dabbed at the very minor scratches on Frank Shearer's face as if the man were his innocent son, offering words of comfort and genuine wonder.

'What made you fly off the handle like that, Frank old son? I mean, like what were you doing there in the first place? We were meeting here, weren't we?'

Frank had been crying when he called from his mobile. Come and get me, Rick, I can't see. Where the fuck are you?

In the lav, end of Lincoln's Inn Fields. I just hit this bitch, and she, she . . . the bitch.

No, you come here. Turn right outside, down that narrow road at the end and you're in Fleet Street. Go left, it's down on the left. You know where it is. No one'll notice. Promise.

If Frank had turned up in a state bad enough to be embarrassing and pursued by a copper, Rick would have melted away and left him to it. As it was, Frank was a bit bruised and battered and dirty and smelly, with the reek of three days' drink on him mixed with the rest, but not as bad as a tramp. It was not anything like the pervasive scent of someone who had not washed for weeks. Frank had not been entirely sober since he met Rick and the days blurred. Took a day off work yesterday and spent it with him, getting smashed and angry, had not slept the night before, and a few extra supplements, provided by Rick, made him delusional. So terrified of being a loser again that he saw shadows in the light and despair in the shadows, fit to fight a dog and kill a ghost. Even a pretend ghost. If Rick had pity in him, he might have felt it, but since he did not know what that was like, he did not feel it now. All he felt was the sense of triumph that came when he conned someone so completely, amazement that it worked mixed with alarm when it worked as quickly and comprehensively as this. Plus caution, because things had to be worked out all over again. You could never stick to plan A when the vic was smitten. Didn't matter what they were smitten with, whether it was with himself, or with their own insecurities or with fear of loss, with sex, with anything. It was the way they just lay down and invited you to fuck them as soon as they were filled with dreams, new fears, new insecurities and unaccustomed pleasures. Amazing. As if they had not lived before they met him. Frank was like that.

Plan A was to persuade Frank Shearer to part with a large sum of money to eradicate all traces of Marianne Shearer's mythical child. Such an invention. Plan B, so outrageous he had hardly contemplated it up until now, was to harness Frank, to do something he wanted done. He was shaking his head at the very idea. Frank took the gesture for something indicating compassion and he was weeping again. His eyes were like pissholes in the snow; he looked as bad as any weeping woman, although in Frank's case supplication did not move Rick to hurt him, the way it did with a silly bitch.

'Start from the top,' he said soothingly. 'You were coming here, to meet me for a drink and a chat, where the booze is cheaper than bloody Mayfair and you went through Lincoln's Inn Fields? Past nice Mr Noble's. Were you going to go in?'

'No, Rick, honest I wasn't.'

'Told you, Frank, you can't trust that bloke. I said we'd go together, ask him what he was up to. You can't believe him when he says he doesn't know where anything is. Where your lovely sister's hidden her stuff. He knows more than he says. Didn't you trust me? You can't tell him what we know. You'll get nothing. Why did you go by his office?'

'It was on the way. I did think maybe I should ask him something. No, I didn't, it was just because it was on the way.'

A expression of fear on his face, not wanting to admit that yes, he did want to talk to T. Noble. Rick decided to let that one go.

'Anyway, I stopped outside. Other side of the railings, looking up. That's where I went first, to hear about my "good fortune". That's what Thomas Noble called it. I stood inside those railings, looking up. Newspaper in my hands, thinking, yes, she's dead. I wanted to remember what it felt like, so I did it again, and then I saw her.'

He blew his nose on a paper towel. Rick reached for another. Harsh, blue paper, no luxuries here.

'The bitch. She was walking up and down. She was like I was, first, walking up and down and thinking about going in. Carrying a bag, pacing, thinking about it. Like she didn't know whether she should or she shouldn't. Then she couldn't. I watched, and I thought, it's got to be her. Hesitating like that, cos she knows. It's her, I thought, that's Marianne's girl. Then she went up to ring the bell. Went up there to claim everything that's mine. Mine. Only she didn't. She came back in through the gate where I was standing, and I thought, you bitch. Its you. You're the bitch who wants to take it all away.'

Rick dabbed at the mark on Frank's red face, threw away the paper towel. There were plenty of those for the price of a pint. Too early in the evening yet for this place to stink of misdirected pee. Frank had a penis the size of a stub and managed to pee like a horse. Possibly the only time the bloody thing grew. Rick was well hung, better than a donkey, but he could keep his own pee pees inside for hours and hours. The result of long hours of surveillance, he'd told Frank, and Frank, bless him, believed.

'OK, Frank. So you thought she was the long-lost daughter who'd read a newspaper and come to claim. Bollocks, old son. With respect. Why wasn't she just a bird, wandering up and down, early for something? Going out with some bloke in there, been stood up, whatever? What made you think she was anything to do with anything? What made you see red and hit her?'

'It was the way she walked,' Frank said. 'She looked like she owned the fucking world. Like Marianne did. I knew it was her. I thought, that's the bitch who thinks she's going to inherit. It was the way she looked. She was hanging around outside there, like she didn't know whether she should go in or not. I'd seen Thomas, looking out of the window, like he was waiting for someone. Then he went away and then she came. I thought, *you're coming to claim. You're coming to claim.* And then she seemed to know I was there. She turned round and came straight towards me. Like she was going to tell me to fuck off. Like women do. I lost it.'

Rick Boyd smiled. Don't tell the man that you had never quite let him out of your sight in three days. That you did not trust him to make a meeting in a cosy pub deliberately chosen for being out of his territory and closer to your own. Suggested also because its persuasively dark interior and proximity to the lowering buildings of the Law Courts made it an ideal place to sit Frank Shearer down again and feed his growing paranoia. Don't tell him how you yourself had stood well back and watched the man make a complete ass of himself in a full scale explosion of stupid violence. The paranoia had already taken hold. Made him make connections where there were none. Don't say, look mate, if you're going to hurt someone, make sure it hurts bad and make sure it makes you happy. No point hurting anyone unless you enjoy it. Even better if they enjoy it too. Even less point if you come off worse. What a fucking idiot Frank Shearer was, but a rich, delusional idiot, sublimely suggestible and with very useful propensities if used as a weapon. He could certainly pack a punch if only he could aim right. A heat-seeking missile, fuelled by a serious hatred of women. Rick could take a bet that this wasn't the first time Frank had had his face scratched. Probably couldn't get it up, blamed everything on them, although the way Frank told it, they were all gagging for him. Or they would be, when he was rich.

'The bitch,' Rick said. 'What a bitch. How old was she, would you say, Frank?'

'I don't know. Not a kid, a young *laydeee*.'

He spat the last word. Lady Muck. He still smelt, slightly; still belligerent from the drink at lunchtime. Better cut this down, Rick thought; otherwise he'll lose the job, and don't want that, not yet. Got to get him to pledge me at least ten thousand to find this daughter or son and get rid. He's got to believe I can do that. Or believe he can. Or I can point him in the direction he's already taken. Use him to get that bitch. Oh shit, I can't believe this. Too good to be true, what else can I get him to do? His voice was soothing.

'Only, if she did happen to be Marianne's bastard, she wouldn't be that young, would she? Because Marianne would have been a kid herself when she had it. So it's got to be thirty, I reckon. Plenty of boys and girls of that age knocking around, pacing up and down, whatever. So why the fuck did you leap to the amazing conclusion that this was *It*? Why was this one a bigger threat than any other bitch?'

'It was the way she walked,' Frank said stubbornly, sensing criticism and ready to cry again. 'And because she was there.' He was snivelling now. 'And cos she came straight for me.'

Rick wanted a drink, very badly. Patted Frank down like a good old friend who could never doubt him.

'We'll check it out, Frank. Told you I've got all the contacts. I'm nearly there. Never mind. I reckon she deserved a slapping, whoever she was. We'll find her. We'll sort her out.'

'She pushed dog shit in my face,' Frank said. 'No one does that to me.'

'There are different ways to connect, Frank.'

Rick really could have laughed, but that would have been unkind. God was sometimes good, but Christ, he worked in mysterious ways.

Peter Friel was finding it very difficult to see a connection between the man he faced and the woman he had known. Abrasive, aggressive, throaty-voiced, harsh-mannered, wily Marianne Shearer was so vulgar in her naked ambition that her sheer physical presence pushed one aside. She could spit contempt without actually spitting, while this old man was softly spoken, mellow, almost deferential in his guarded politeness and it was difficult to see what they might have had in common, apart from the attraction of opposites. He had the feeling that Stanton, QC, otherwise known as the Lover, would have loathed Shearer in an ordinary social context, would not be seen dead with her, despite the flattery of her being so much younger. He might have been ashamed of her had she been his daughter. What the hell was this paragon doing with a middle-aged harridan like Marianne Shearer and her plain, pug face? Old habits dying hard? Her availability, their athleticism, mutual sexual peccadilloes or what? Peter tried not to let his own speculations surface, although he did not resist a tendency to stare. Distracting himself from the scrutiny to which he himself was being subjected was not so difficult. He was sitting in a room he would remember for ever at the end of a long day of visual feasts. He was in a world apart, sitting in a parallel universe. Peter found he was memorising details to pass on to Hen, and to Thomas. It was indeed cruel of the Lover to deny Thomas the sight of this room. Thomas would ache for it.

The Lover's top floor apartment was safely within the confines of Lincoln's Inn itself, set off to the side away from the main square, overlooking a courtyard thoroughfare on one side and Chancery Lane on the other, as if it formed a boundary between two worlds. How he had come by this and managed to keep it away from the grasp of all those lawyers greedy for priceless office space in this precious square mile was something Peter could not comprehend, but every one of the Inns of Court had leasehold anomalies and hidden gems guarded by old or privileged retainers. The three gates to Lincoln's Inn were locked at night with massive doors. There were smaller doors contained in the larger doors for keyholders only. The idea of stepping through a door within a door had always delighted Peter, and now he felt he stepped through another door beyond. The Lover could look down into the courtyard and see the lights in the warren of offices go out, one by one, until only the ancient lamp lights were left. No one would see him looking. No one would see who came in with their own key. An excellent trysting place.

'Excuse me, sir, I'm a little overwhelmed. It's odd to be inside a place . . . so unusual. I've passed through a hundred times and never realised that anyone lived here at all.'

'I don't live here,' the Lover said. 'I live at home. In a large house, with an exacting, extended, adorable family whose admiration I wish to keep. My family has its squalid side, as in arguments, tragedies, noise, utilitarian architecture and the unattractive machinery of everyday life. I detest everyday life. You don't need to know where I actually live.'

'No, sir, I don't.'

'Good. I've come here, at least once a week for more years than I can remember, at first when I still worked, and later, gratefully, for the hell of it. Officially, I stay overnight for the committee meetings I still attend. Once you've finished looking at everything, perhaps we could get on to the matter in hand. I promise you there's nothing more than you can see.'

A large, low-ceilinged room, spanning the top of the building, windows each end. An open door to a small bedroom with a huge Biedermeier bed, dressed in cream linen. An upright wardrobe in walnut, the contours framed in black. On the far side of the main room, a kitchen area rather than a kitchen, and, naked to the eye, a splendid bath half hidden by a painted screen. No modern planning permission would allow for any of it.

'I understand the need for privacy, sir. I'm not Marianne Shearer's executor. That's Thomas Noble. I don't have any obligation to reveal anything, nor inclination either. But I do have a job to do that she herself seems to have set out for me, which is to find out why such a woman took her own life and where she left her personal possessions. Including her instructions, her wishes, her clothes, her computer, her records of work and her phone. I was hoping you could help me. Mr Noble was hoping you would be the custodian of it all. My personal curiosity's another matter and believe me, I've plenty of that. She was kind to me, once. I know what she was wearing when she died and I know all about her last case. None of that gives me an excuse to pry into how you live.'

'No, it doesn't. I suppose she broke every bone in her body on the way down from the sixth floor? The very least I'd have expected of her. Thorough. Death with a degree of style. Her own timing, but what a mess she must have made on the pavement. At least she avoided the tree, that would have been extremely undignified. Do you think she arranged the photographer in advance? He would have taken better pictures if she had. I wish she'd asked me. I could have told

her exactly what to wear. I did wonder if that skirt was supposed to break the fall. Pity, it was one of my favourites. Also
hers.'

Peter looked down at his own feet, planted on an exquisite
carpet which covered half of the fine wood floor. Either old
or reclaimed. There was another carpet hanging on the wall
behind him, gilt mirrors on the walls either side, the constant
risk of seeing himself, and the apartment, reflected. It was
like a room from a small palace or a bijou hotel in Venice,
requiring invisible servants of the utmost discretion or none
at all. He wondered, like the pedant he felt, who kept it clean.

'I could probably get you the Pathologist's report in
advance of the inquest if you want to know the details,' he
said carefully, reading an expression of sheer distaste on the
Lover's face. 'I don't know what was fractured on impact.
You may be right, perhaps everything dissolved. I can only
tell you there was very little blood on the skirt she wore. She
upholstered it from the inside. Most of the bleeding was from
the head, as far as I know. She died on impact.'

The Lover waved his hand dismissively, as if to say he was
not really that curious. Peter could suddenly see what the
two of them had had in common, which was a merciless
objectivity that left no room for sentiment. Neither would
have any time to waste on pity.

The Lover adjusted himself in his winged armchair, tapping his elegant fingers on the angled wings of the arms. The
whole room was a poem of wood, fabric and mirrors. Oak
floors, deco panellings. The owner of it was in love with
another era and another way of living, but not entirely ruled
by it. There were touches of modernity, in the form of a
small but elaborate sound system, and the blessing of comfortable heating. What was certain was the old man was not

wedded to the decade or year in which he lived now. In manners, dress and attitude, he belonged elsewhere. When he smiled he was powerfully attractive, an old rogue of a beast. It was equally clear to Peter that he himself had somehow passed a test, and the Lover wanted an audience.

'This place,' he said, 'is a respite from the ugliness outside. I have an aversion to ugliness. I missed my real vocation, which was to design clothes for beautiful bodies. Preferably for androgynous yet feminine bodies like Marianne's, but there was precious little scope for that when I was first apprenticed as a mere boy to Hartnell. Ghastly economy clothing and no sign of it ending, then. So I took to the Law, devoted my life to another kind of ugliness. Disputes about patents, designs, ephemera, the protection of same. I hate cheap, I was inordinately well paid. I always knew when something was original and authentic.'

Peter picked up the crystal glass which stood on a small rosewood table by his chair. He wanted to hold it up to the light to see the colour of the pale wine reflected in one of the mirrors. Instead, he sipped.

'She liked Sauvignon best, lately,' the Lover said, noticing. 'As long as it did not come from New Zealand. In some things she had very little taste, as well as quite unreasonable prejudice.'

There was nothing unharmonious in this room, Peter was thinking. Maybe Marianne Shearer, visiting mistress, was allowed to bring a little of the ugliness of her own world, simply by way of contrast. No new object here, except the CD player, and over there the fridge, hidden by another screen. Peter presumed that the lavatory, hidden behind the only door, worked perfectly.

'If you can't tell me anything about how Marianne died, or

where she hid her intentions, sir, perhaps I shouldn't take up any more of your time.'

Peter felt a longing for anywhere else, a place of lesser perfection where people lived messier lives. He wanted to be in a fully functioning kitchen with children yelling offstage, and then felt guilty. He had no idea what this man's life was like or what made him what he was. Perhaps Marianne did.

'I quite understand if there's no need to bother you further, but thank you for the wine and the sight of this room. If you ever look down, you might see me craning my neck upwards, wishing I could come back or tell someone about it.'

Stanton, QC, laughed softly, a wicked laugh. Peter remembered Marianne Shearer's gaudy cackle. They would have made strange music together.

'She told me you were a born diplomat,' the Lover said. 'She said you might have been an excellent liar, if only you'd tried. You aren't her son by any chance, are you?'

Peter put the glass back on the table with great care. There was hardly a suitable reply.

'I don't think so, sir. I'm one of five, with marked resemblances to one another and to our parents. If there's nothing else, perhaps I should go.'

'One of five, are you? I have five. I made five. Such gorgeous creatures. Grandchildren, too. Hence mess, hence discretion.'

Peter got to his feet. He saw himself in one of the mirrors and heard Marianne laughing.

'Please stay,' the Lover said. 'Please stay.'

He swallowed.

'I need you for a while. Please stay.'

CHAPTER FOURTEEN

The Lover turned on the music. The sound of it drifted round the corners of the room. He sat centre stage and softly lit.

'I met Marianne when she was very young. Still a student, young and raw and looking for a place.'

Peter was calculating. Perhaps forty-five to her twenty, something like that. Miss Shearer, drawn to an older man.

'She was allocated to be my pupil. I gather you were once hers. One hopes she behaved better towards you. We slept together, which is a polite way of putting it, since we never actually slept. It was deliciously incestuous; she was the same age as my eldest daughter and quite irresistible in her naive belief that screwing senior men was a short cut to influence rather than ridicule. Women were still called chicks in those days. She was an ugly minx, so ambitious she shone with it like the grease on her skin, nothing she would not do. Poor creature: all we men wanted was an extra orifice, an extra mouth when our wives – my second wife by then – were busy with our children. She said it was love. I said how can it be? She became a nuisance, I got her thrown out of our set of chambers. Told her crime would suit her better, because she would understand the tarts and the crooks. Still, there was a charm about her. She would never dress like anyone else.'

The Lover rose from his chair and refilled the wine glasses with a flourish. He detoured towards the CD player and altered the volume to background noise only. Peter struggled to detect exactly what the music was.

'Then she got pregnant and pretended it was mine, but I knew it wasn't. I might have taken risks, but not that kind. I called her a liar. She went like a lamb. She knew she'd gone too far. A quiet termination and back to business. She said, you wait, I'll show you. I'm going to be big news, I'll show you what I'm worth one day. Then she disappeared. I never asked where, never tried to find her, but I missed her.'

He smiled at memories. Peter did not.

'I met her five years after I threw her out, walking through the Temple. She was as sleek as a seal with her hair cut in a cap, walking as if someone had trained her to dance. A grown-up woman with success in her eyes, and she said how do I look, Lover boy, do you still not want me? I invited her here. She came in dressed in a real Lanvin evening jacket. High-necked, satin. Her mother or grandmother might have had such a thing. Held together by a single button, yellow silk, cross-cut, topstitched heavy-duty thing. Of course I wanted her.

'It came to be a ritual. Every week, Miss Marianne Shearer came to this room where I take refuge, supposedly at the end of a day of my committee meetings. She dressed; she undressed. I am always besotted with beautiful clothes, while my dear wives never cared. She was the ideal model. She loved what I loved and I loved to dress her. She was the perfect shape, she could bend double, pliable as the cloth, and still, nothing she wouldn't do, no position she could not reach. We would dress in our best; we would meet, undress, dress, eat a little, drink a little and dance to the light of the silvery moon. Where else is there to dance to the music of one's choice? Away from all the ugliness, while each presents their best, their very best?'

Peter was silent. The music was definable. A muted, big band sound.

He leant forward, imagining Marianne Shearer waltzing across the room. Did they roll back the carpet? Did anyone hear? Did she laugh at their charade? Did they laugh at one another, did she tease him and which of them dictated what they did?

'What did you talk about?'

'Ah. There was an unspoken rule that we didn't dwell on anything unpleasant. Bar gossip, a little character assassination here and there, the nicer things we had seen and done. Music, news, clothes, the latest abominable fashions. I would find her something new to take home with her sometimes, to wear next time. She was a collector, so was I; I collected for her and paid in clothes. She really was the most glorious undemanding mistress. She was a reason to shop. Every evening a joy, a respite from ugliness for both of us. I'm sure you can understand. You must need it yourself, don't you?'

Yes, not quite like that, a walk in the park.

Peter took another covert look around. Other than the sound system there was no machinery, no TV: no doubt the Lover abhorred such things, too.

'How did you make contact between times?'

The Lover looked surprised.

'Contact? Why should I want regular contact? I wanted nothing to do with the ghastly criminal side of her life. We made the next appointment before we parted and always kept it. She had my number for emergencies. There was only once, I think.'

'Did she ever talk about her work?'

'Rarely. Sometimes. Mostly she left it behind. Sometimes we danced for hours and that was all. I was her thing of beauty and she was mine. It was as if when we were here, we had all the time in the world.'

Ugliness banned. Peter recognised the tempo of the music just before it drew to an end. A quickstep, dancing music. Somehow he imagined it would be Strauss, for waltzing. He was in the wrong century and the Lover was addicted to the decades of his youth. The reverie and the storytelling ended with the music. Peter wondered if at the end of her weekly star turn, Ms Shearer took herself home in a taxi, or was sent away with a new dress. It sounded to him like a peculiar, repressive abusive fantasy, but what did he know, only that he pitied her when perhaps he should not. Old Moses here would return to his fuller life, restored and benign. She might return to hers refreshed and dignified, still precious, desired and cherished, a creature of loveliness. Perhaps these were moments of glory and perfection that could make her immune to need. Enough. She would go back to fighting and winning and guarding a collection of clothes, and, once a week, she would be beautifully perfect. Each to his own. It made him sad. What about the joy of talking in bed, about anything and everything, planning a future with five children? Daring to love someone surely meant venturing out and shouting about it.

I was her thing of beauty and she was mine.

The Lover seemed to sense that the narrative had come to an end and with it his self-indulgence. He could see Peter struggling to absorb what he might not be able to comprehend.

'Please don't judge, Mr Friel, you're far too young and it's so unbecoming. We all find our moments of contentment, whichever way we can. Don't judge her or me by your own, cheap standards. We had ours, and kept them. Thank you for listening.'

Peter bowed his head. He was a born listener, hated to be thanked for listening, because being invited to listen was a privilege. It occurred to him that the narrative was unique. Marianne could never have told anyone about these glamorous moments; nor could the Lover. He was not judging, except that such necessary, lonely secretiveness appalled him.

'I should like to come back, sir, if I may, and I wouldn't be indulging you, only myself. But for the moment, I need to know what Marianne Shearer left with you. I need to know what she was like before she killed herself.'

The mood changed in the absence of the music. The Lover turned his leonine head towards the mirror on the wall and ran his fingers through his magnificent white hair. Did these two exist to admire one another, or simply to admire him? Plain Jane with sculpted body, brushed up nicely in sophisticated frocks, kneeling to suck cock of an old Adonis? Could do worse. There must have been Love, there *must* have been. Peter could not bear it otherwise.

The Lover was suddenly businesslike and efficient, but still retaining his place, centre stage, the designer not only of clothes, but of his own life. Colder than an ice sculpture, equally impressive. A man resuming his alter ego as lawyer, albeit reluctantly.

'Of course. I have something here. Not her goods and chattels, you understand, she kept nothing with me, there simply isn't room – she came and she went, that was the arrangement. She brought herself and left no trace of herself. That was what we both wanted.'

'Both' . . . I hope it was both.

'And didn't talk about ugliness? About cases, clients, winning, losing, rapists, paedophiles, gangsters, drug runners, pornographers, her stock-in-trade?'

'Very little. She alluded to it, sometimes. Said there was nothing she wouldn't defend, as long as there was the slightest chance of winning. I applauded her for it. I liked her craftiness, her lack of sentimental morality and her good, thick skin. All I know is that the last big case upset her. When was that? Last summer, it was hot and she was cold. She was *distraite*. Not herself. It was if,' he said, laughingly, 'as if she had acquired the *inconvenience* of a conscience.'

'Does conscience have obvious symptoms?' Peter asked.

'Like a rash, or a pimple on the nose? I don't think so. I would have seen, since she would always expose every inch of herself. It was the fact that she was so preoccupied.'

'You told Thomas Noble she was doing research into her own family history, and it upset her.'

'Yes, so I did. What an attentive little queer he is.'

'There was talk that she was going to write a book. That she was commissioned to write one about her cases, dishing the dirt on everyone.'

'She would never have done it,' the Lover said. 'No one wants the truth, especially her.'

He took a deep gulp of the wine, moved across and turned on the music again. This time it was Cole Porter.

'She was silent in my arms for six months. Thinner, easier to dress. I know she was moving house. I know she hoped I would come to her, rather than her always to me. I said no, and then she said, there's something I want you to do for me. I said why? She said, because the child I once said was yours was never terminated, *It* was born and given away. Adopted, but alive. Marianne said she kept dreaming that she had seen *It*. Or, someone who was exactly like what she imagined that child would have become. I have no idea if she approved of this spectre, or if it was a vision that appalled her. I suspect the latter, hoped it was the former. In any event, it distressed her mightily. She was convinced she had done this person great harm.'

The Lover gazed at Peter intently, taking in every detail he might have missed on the initial inspection, although this time his regard was almost fond.

'I did think that the creature of her imagining might be you, although I now see it's impossible.' He smiled. 'I can't see any son of Marianne's, or indeed mine, wearing a suit as ill-fitting as that. No insult intended: I appreciate the effort you made to wear it. Nor does she appear to have done you any harm. Don't lawyers wear decent suits these days?'

Peter laughed, amazed by such attention to detail. Very Marianne Shearer. These two would have had such fun sitting out in public, watching the passers-by, but instead hid away and merely reported to one another the stylistic horrors of the ugly present.

'There's a huge advantage in a wig and gown, sir. It doesn't much matter what you wear beneath; a suit, yes, but any old suit will do. This one was borrowed, but I'm told the cloth is good. This baby . . . this child, how old would it be now? And did you believe her?'

Two questions in one. He could tell it was irritating and watched the Lover pausing to arrange his answers in order.

217

'The child would be about your age, thirtyish, I suppose? Hence my optimism about your identity. Yes, I believed her, because she believed herself, but whether said infant still existed or had ever existed except in her mind, was another matter. I also considered that she might well have reached the age of fantasising about what might have been. There comes a discontented stage when one's achievements, however considerable, are simply not enough and one dwells on what one cannot have.' He shrugged. 'Both sexes have these menopausal morbidities. Latterly, she kept asking me about *my* children, what they were like; she'd never have done that before. It was none of her business.'

'Just as this . . . child, was none of yours?'

Peter had moved his chair to sit nearer. They could have touched.

'No. Except for the fact that I wanted to establish beyond doubt that the child was not mine. I encouraged her to trace it, and she had all the means to do so. I believe she did exactly that, over several months. Getting closer, she would say, getting closer, and then I would change the subject. The last time I saw her, she said she had found two distinct possibilities. She refused to say more. She looked exquisite. A Jean Muir dress, early seventies, not my favourite epoch, but quite wonderful. We danced, Mr Friel, we had better things to do.'

Peter felt hot in this room, a feverish reaction to the almost laughable callousness of the Lover, who had risen, busily, but as elegantly as ever, to fetch a small case from behind where he sat. The case was pigskin, with buckles. He sat back in his chair with the case on his lap, his left foot tapping in time to distant music.

'The instructions,' Peter murmured.

218

'Arrived on the day she made the front page of the newspaper,' the Lover said, without emotion. 'We were supposed to meet that evening. I saw the newspaper first, came anyway because I thought it must be a mistake. The instructions were here when I arrived. The least I could do was follow them to the letter. It hasn't been difficult. She was very precise.'

He handed Peter a photocopied, typed sheet, and then shut the satchel and fastened the buckles, as if to say, that's all you're going to get for the moment. Peter read a document that could have been written in code.

Sure now I know who it is who's haunting me. I can't bear it, Lover, I can't.

There's 2 of them.

Better be buried before anyone knows.

Wait a week before contacting Thos Noble @ L Inn Fields. (tel no on list, over.) Speak to Peter Friel re anything psonal. More dogged, might write the book, good at guessing.

All in transcript, one copy anyway. Can't remember which one. I put the reasons in my own transpcript.

U don't want to know why. Only I know I've never done anything good, bt as bad things go, this takes the ticket.

The Storage place (no is on list) will wait for instructions from you to send things on where they belong. Quote ref QCANl/609, they had address. Do this 10th.

Bye, Lover. It was never yrs, but I was. Only one I can trust, because you've been as cruel as me.

Sorry, fgt you don't do text. It gets into spelling.

PS. Don't let man called R Boyd in. A life trasher. Give other parcel to PF, no, R wld kill him. Tell him to find good journalist? Tell the truth about Boyd. Get the bastard. Tell someone it wasn't all my fault.

While Peter was reading, the Lover turned up the music. Peggy Lee, belting out I'm a WOMAN, W-O-M-A-N, Say it again. Say it *AGAIN*.

'What other parcel?' Peter shouted into the sudden volume of noise. He was looking for the bulky case out of which that single sheet had appeared, but it had vanished, and the Lover was waltzing all by himself, across the floor, his polished shoes gleaming.

'It's on the way to you,' he said, with an over-the-shoulder smile. 'Second class post. That's all for now, dear lady, good-night.'

To Peter's embarassment, the Lover bowed like a courtier.

'Go away,' he said, 'and let me dream of her. Let me do a little cross-examination of myself to music.'

On that note, Peter left. He felt as if he was running away.

Henrietta Joyce was where she needed to be. Safe at home, doing what she wanted to do best. Making something out of nothing. Sewing, cleaning and mending, the most absorbing activities she had ever found, herself her mother's daughter. She had let herself in through the front door, raced up to the top of the house, tearing off her grubby coat. She stashed the bag back in the kitchen. In the tiny bathroom, she scrubbed her whole body clean, found her favourite warm bathrobe, the one in Liberty print with a soft towel lining which made her feel dressed, descended the stairs to the dressing room with a bottle of wine. She locked the door to the room behind her. Hen hated locking doors. It was against nature, but natural this evening. Once she was seated at the table in her warm room, insulated by the comfort of colourful cloth, she breathed easier. She displaced the taste of whisky with a mouthful of warm red wine.

A failed errand, a mugging. A feeling of having escaped something which energised her. Hen wanted to work. If she did not get back to work soon, she would be bankrupt. A forgiving bank manager would only go so far. She had no money for stock, even the cheapest kind. Work was the panacea for all ills. Work with her hands gave permission for the thoughts in her mind to percolate and assemble themselves into something like order, possibly even to the extent of forming conclusions. Work cleared the mind and let it fill again at its own speed. Like draining dirty water out of a bath to fill it with clean, the equivalent of draining the solvent out of the tank downstairs to see what residue remained, discovering that it had done the work and given up the information about what had made the stain. The solvent was working, the dead moth eggs would drop out. Pacing up and down had the opposite effect. She was seriously sorry for anyone who could not take refuge in work. Get busy.

Nothing came clean unless she was busy.

She was yearning to make something new, starting from scratch. She was a self-taught, mother-taught dressmaker, good at cobbling together something from nothing, not a trained designer, but she could try. She was a craftsperson who belonged in the back room, messing about. This time she was going to start at the beginning. Hen was imagining a garment that might have suited Marianne Shearer.

Supposing she was sitting over there, next to the tailor's dummy, saying make me something. Make me a dress to die for, sorry, die *in*.

I would ask her what she wanted, Hen thought. That's what I always do. Ask, and find out what they don't want, in order to discover what they really do. Marianne Shearer was refusing to speak. Just something gorgeous then. Vintage cloth, definitely no frills, streamlined. Not a shroud. You know the colours. Fit for a Scorpio. Do you have a picture of what you want, a photograph, perhaps? You've been looking and admiring all your life, haven't you? You dressed up as a child and spent all your adult life wearing a uniform. Hen jotted down the rough measurements she was guessing and then quickly started to cut the pattern of a bodice from brown paper. It would be simple, with all the detail round the neck. Not a costume, something dramatic to go with the skirt.

She laid the paper pattern on a flattened roll of lightweight cambric. Ideal for cutting a template for the customer to try for size. A pound a metre, different weights, Hen always had muslin for wrapping and cambric for cutting. The material was clean and stiff, like paper; it would hold line and shape without drooping, crisp enough to show errors in the shape which a drape would disguise. She dressed the dummy with one half of the cambric bodice and started to fashion a collar. The collar would be like a fan, which stood up at the back of the head, making a frame. It would be a foil for the pleated fabric of the bloodstained skirt, almost like the ruff framing the head of a medieval queen, but not white; red, purple, even black. Yes, a black ruff would work. She liked moulage, making something on the dummy rather than on a flat surface. The real designers would have a series of dummies tailor-made for each rich client. She was not a designer; she was messing about. By the early hours of the morning, she had a cambric pattern for Ms Shearer's jacket. The line was severe, the upstanding collar a piece of sheer frivolity. She would stiffen the cambric with starch.

Always make it in cambric, try it for size, make another

paper pattern, do it again and again, fitting it to the body, the dummy, the body, long before taking scissors to cut into a priceless piece of cloth. A stiff satin would do well; a tight-fitting bodice above a free-flowing skirt. The customer would have to walk tall and hold her breath. A jacket for standing in rather than sitting, or eating. Hen had often thought there was a breed of designers who actually hated women and wished to punish them via the discomfort of their clothes. This garment was not designed for comfort, but then neither was the client who would want to wear it. It might never get further than cambric or paper.

She looked at the time, refreshed and weary. No thoughts had assembled themselves, but at least she was functioning. The ghost of Marianne Shearer melted away. Hen let herself out of the room and went downstairs. Soak the collar template in starch down there, check the place over the way she always did before sleep, even when she was aching for sleep. Wishing sometimes that moral dilemmas were soluble in chemical solvents and only presented the same problems as stains.

Ms Shearer's skirt was where she had left it this morning. The tiny fragments she had cut from the inside of the hem had soaked all day without the slightest alteration in the colour; a successful experiment showing that this solvent was safe for the rest. The light in here was bright and the bare room was cold and cheerless after the warmth upstairs, despite the sweet antiseptic smell. The lace cleaned yesterday was dry. The skirt hung like a brilliant flag. She took a last look round, thinking the holiday is over, the work will be coming back soon.

The newly cleaned, de-infested teddy bears sat where they had sat drying for days. Angel's old teddy bears, to be restored for Mum and Dad, if they wanted them, now nice and dry. She looked closer.

The teddy bears had no eyes.

She remembered Angel taking out the eyes. She went back upstairs and turned the music on, loud.

Chapter Fifteen

Later than midnight and the music had stopped.

Wake up, old man, wake up. Talk to me.

He had been pirouetting round the polished floor and then he had fallen. Marianne had liked salsa; the Lover did not care for it himself, and could not remember why he was trying to remember the few steps she had taught him, pleased with himself that he did. Oh, so clever. He had staggered, recovered enough to career across the room until he hit the bed and sprawled on it, still dizzy. Mildly shocked, with his heart not even pounding until he opened his eyes, minutes or seconds later, and saw that man leaning over him in double vision. An awful coat, pushed up to the elbows, as if he had something to do which should not be done while wearing an overcoat, like dancing.

Where's her stuff, old man? Where is it? What do you know?

A voice in the background saying, come away. What are we doing here anyway?

It's your sister's shag. Where's her stuff, you old bastard?

A face, too close to his own, spittle on his skin, angry, shouting in a low octave no one would hear, as if anyone would hear. The distant music, and his own voice, his Loverly, mellifluous voice saying, go away, you silly little man, in his best accents, using his hand to push that other body, his fist encountering solid muscle.

Confused now, beginning to be afraid but not enough to mask his contempt for anyone who came into this place without an invitation, the Lover sat up wearily, then turned his head to the other person in the room, the one he sensed, rather than saw, and said, 'Who is this clown?'

'Don't,' the figure said, knowing something he did not. 'Don't provoke him.'

There was a disgusting smell of stale beer.

'Where's her stuff, old man? That bloke came from Noble to find it, didn't he? I followed him, and now he's gone home, and you're on your own.'

Desperately awful, dear, but easy on the eye. Dress sense? Unbelievable.

Her stuff, where's her stuff? Where's her paperwork? Where's the stuff she was going to put in a book? If you haven't got it, where is it?

Spitting the words; gobs of spit landing on the Lover's face.

Stop shouting at me.

Look, I'm Marianne's dearest. She loved me, old man, she loved me. I want my legacy, and he wants his money, all of it, not some of it, do you hear me?

Marianne loved you? How ridiculous.

He found the thought of Marianne touching this creature amusing. She would despise you. She did, didn't she? She would despise you both.

He thought it, he might have said it, whatever he said, his voice sounded high and shrill to his own ears and he felt as if he had fallen not on to his own soft couch, but down into a pit from which he would never arise. A huge hand slapped him into silence, cutting off contemptuous laughter.

Tears sprang into his eyes and he roared, *You stupid little prick.*

He, they, left him then. He could hear them, banging around the room, pulling open drawers. He heard a glass smash, then another, the noise of the fruitless search of someone who did not know what they were searching for, sensing the one pulling the other back, somehow smelled the presence of rage and caution and the rattle of breathing which might have been his own. He sat on the side of the bed where they had lain, countless times, let the spittle remain on his face, refusing to wipe it away in the same manner he and she had let the sweat dry in its own time. Oh, he had been proud of her, once, why had he never said it? The same face loomed over him. Write it down, the voice commanded. Write down where everything is. The notepad from his briefcase was held in front of his eyes. He nodded.

He took hold of his own pen and wrote in large, shaky letters, NOT PETER. Then he let go of the pen, and pulled the man's hair, hard, holding a fistful of it, and not letting go although the texture disgusted him, grabbing it for purchase as he butted him on the forehead, twice, still not letting go until he felt drops of blood on his face. He had known how to fight, once. Then he let go. He felt the hands circle his neck, almost without surprise, heard again that distant shouting and let himself go limp.

He was aware of nothing much now, except that it had been a mistake to laugh, and he was face down on the bed with his buttocks exposed, and a searing pain as something sharp ground into soft flesh.

One voice said, make it look like a rent boy didn't get paid. Another voice pleading, no, no, stop. The sound of retching and whining. No music.

He laughed at me. He hit me first.

Then . . . silence. Pain and silence and only the sound of his own breathing. Focusing his thoughts on something else, the way he did to maintain control, never letting anything drift. Controlling his mind the way he had ever since he was a boy and lost everything. Remembering what she had said once, *if you're ever going to get murdered, make sure they leave their DNA all over you. Such unequivocal evidence.* He was faintly proud of writing NOT PETER, as if the DNA wasn't enough to exonerate the person who had not done this. She had liked the boy, would never have wanted him implicated, shame she had never had a son. However unecessary the writing had been, it was still a nice touch and the least he owed her. Were they sent by her to kill him, or had it been entirely unintended?

If he moved now, he might bleed to death. It would be better to lie still and wait for someone to come. He decided to move, all the same, because he could not bear the thought of anyone finding him like this.

Undressed.

Jan 12. Morning.

The cold was intense, as raw and grey as it ever became, with a fierce wind tugging at coats. Snow was forecast and the arrival would be a relief. People scurried on to the train and did not want to get off. They were cross and defenceless because close-packed streets and ordinary clothes were not keeping them either safe or warm. Peter Friel was glad he had not been born in a city. The very idea that it sheltered you was just another illusion. He had been born a country boy, sent out to school in sensible vests, and it still amazed him when Londoners reacted to cold, ice and snow as if it had never happened before.

It was another emasculating lack in himself not to own a car, since a non-car-owning male was far less useful or desirable, he was told, but he hated cars and loved the thinking times provided by trains. He could retreat into his own skull on public transport, even when hemmed in by other bodies; he could read or think even when hanging from a strap in a swaying carriage or he could lose himself in watching. His father said if Peter could speculate on investments the way he did on crowd observation, he might make his family rich. No chance of that. Peter felt almost childish and irresponsible on a train and he was looking forward to seeing the sea, as if this was a holiday. He allowed that anticipation to overcome the seriousness of the mission and his profound disappointment with all of them. Because of a terse, hardly informative phone call from Thomas Noble, he was angry with Hen for not trusting him with whatever she was prepared to take to Noble herself and he was relieved that she had been, in Thomas's brief words, sent home safe. He was angry with the Lover for being extraordinary; he was furious with Ms Shearer, QC for everything, including her own humiliations, and he was trying to preserve a little righteous anger with Hen's parents whom he was, after all, going to see. He was irritated with himself for not knowing quite which way to turn, for not phoning Hen and deciding to do only what he had already promised to do today. He knew enough about law to know that it was usually best to concentrate on one thing at a time and to allow everyone to speak at their own pace, in their own time, especially if truth was required.

The task of the Prosecution in the trial of Rick Boyd had been to establish the truth. The transcript of the trial, the distillation of evidence into printed words on paper, moved him. He was remembering the frustration he had felt when the law was discussed, similar to what he felt now. Can you kidnap a person without kidnapping them, so to speak? Has there ever been a case before your Lordship where the kidnap is only the result of the victim's naiveté, rather than deception, and where there was no force involved because she went willingly? Albeit she went seduced by hopeful promises which are only now called lies? Could you kidnap a person without force, by seduction only? Kidnapping, my Lord, surely involves the active subjugation of will, and there was none of that here. Just as the infliction of grievous bodily harm cannot be made out as a punishable offence when the only perpetrator is the victim. My client has been framed by facts, my Lord. Some of the facts may be indisputable – the woman went with the man; she became ill; she was hurt – but the inferences drawn from these facts, such as any of this being my client's fault, are riddled with doubt. Peter could hear in his imagination exactly the way Ms Shearer would have argued a powerful closing speech, if ever they had reached that point. If Rick Boyd had ever given evidence and been revealed in cross examination. If Angel had not died of her own free will.

The train sped through the station where his sister lived and he had the sudden urge to get off and find the noisy sanity of children in her crowded house. An hour outside London, it was emptying fast and careering towards Dover. The sky lightened and the threat of snow was far behind.

Despite himself, and the monstrous scenarios that were forming in his mind in a mushroom cloud of an explanation of why Marianne Shearer might have killed herself when she did, he looked forward to seeing where Hen had lived. Curiosity, a clue to the enigma she was, perhaps, or simply something to endorse the powerful need he had to believe in her.

His thoughts deviated to wondering if Marianne Shearer had really formed some master plan before she jumped. He decided it was unlikely that she had, or at least not any plan which bore close inspection. If she were mad enough to jump, she would surely not have been sane enough to plot the details with her usual finesse. It followed from this thinking that he wanted to tell Hen that Marianne Shearer might not even have planned the course of Rick Boyd's acquittal, since no one in a trial could ever have the exclusive power to do that. It just looked as if she had controlled it while really it was a procession of accidents with its own momentum. He wanted to explain that it was not entirely her fault. Peter got out on to a platform and smelled the sea.

After the warmth of the train, the fresher cold took his breath away and he plunged his hands into the pockets of his coat. There was only one colour for a coat and that was black. He was still wearing the borrowed suit because it was big and comfortable and he thought he would ask Hen if he could buy it. A red woolly scarf was his only colour, worn like a badge. It was like setting out to interview a client or witness in prison, with him always hoping he could like or admire something about the person at some level or other, even if he only liked their shoes, because that always helped. There was also something else intervening which made him feel increasingly uncomfortable. He felt like a suitor, come to woo the parents of a beloved and wishing their approval, without quite knowing from when and where that feeling had arrived. He was nothing of the kind. He was searching for words for what he was. An interfering arbitrator, come to make peace. He turned off his mobile phone.

The route to the house was as easy as she had described. Go the long route, she said, because it's easier to explain and you see the sea soonest. Walk through the town down to the front, turn right, continue along, turn right at the end of the street, it's three doors up, and oh, by the way, if you see a woman with white hair sitting in one of the bus shelters you pass en route on the sea side of the road, bring her along, she might be my mother. Peter looked as he walked and saw no one either waiting for a bus or sheltering from the wind. The sea was magnificently churlish, speaking to him with the subdued violence he had met in many a prisoner. He turned into the correct side road and stepped up to ring the bell. There was a small Christmas tree lit in the window next to the door which was flung open as if whoever indoors was waiting for a signal.

A big man and a small woman crowded into a narrow entrance to greet him, competing for the privilege. He was standing on the bottom step of three, just about level with their waistlines, which despite the disparity in overall height appeared to coincide. One with a long torso and short legs, and the other with long legs and a thin middle leading to a long neck, bypassing the bosom entirely. He could see no resemblance to Hen at all. A blast of warmth hit him.

'How kind of you to come all this way. I'm sorry to have sounded so brisk, yesterday, only . . .'

'Silly old bugger . . .'

'Honestly, we get so upset . . . Come in . . .'

'I was in the bus shelter when it came and I didn't know . . . I'm not going to do that any more. I get so cross. I think, if only Angel . . .'

'Stoppit, Mother. Oh come in, it's cold out there. Who are you, anyway?'

'My name is Peter Friel . . . I spoke to you yesterday.'

'Yes, I know the name, but who exactly are you?'

Peter smiled at them. They were the kind of people it was easy to smile at. He remembered them now, from the single day they had come to court and taken their daughter home.

'I'm an arbitrator,' he said. 'I help sort things out.'

'Of course, of course, come in, cold out there, come in.'

And then he was in, hauled up steps and into an over warm room with a blazing fire, and his eyes getting accustomed to dark and light and an onslaught of colour. Rubbing shoulders with tapestries in glass, slinking in like a stranger on what felt like false pretences, smothered in words, but welcome. It occurred to him, humbly, that they welcomed him because they needed him and they had needed someone like him all along. An outsider to talk to. His coat was almost forcibly removed.

The fire blasted out heat and the room was an oasis of comfort. The coffee lived up to its own smell and biscuits were proffered with urgency by Mrs Joyce, both of them talking at once, as if he knew everything already. He let it flow.

'I shouldn't have got so angry,' Mr Joyce was saying. ' I really shouldn't. I never get angry at work, even though people irritate me, so why should I get angry at home? It was just the last straw, you know. Henrietta always thinks she can fix things, always took it for granted she could. She thought she could cheer us up by staying with us at Christmas, but she was just a reminder, you know? Acting as if she owned this house, when she hasn't lived here for years, getting stuff delivered here, as if we were her postbox. She *knew* it would have to go in Angel's room.'

'That's not so bad, Father, she wasn't to know, was she? And it is her house, always will be. Just like it was always Angel's house, only Angel never really went away.'

'. . . And she would have come back in time, if only Henrietta hadn't gone and fetched her and made all that fuss. She'd have come back with her tail between her legs, like any girl who's been left by her bloke and it hasn't turned out right. She could have come home whenever she wanted, couldn't she mother?'

Not if she was debilitated, depressed, wounded, ashamed, deprived of a mobile phone and without the price of a train ticket.

'*I* would have gone and fetched her myself, wouldn't I, Mother? Even it meant driving up there in one of the vans.'

Mother was silent. She began to fidget with the hem of her skirt, then clasped her hands in her lap. Her face was lined with grief, but also with determination, a person in command of herself, wanting to say something but biding her time. She poured more coffee into Peter's cup. He sensed a person who would pile on a second helping of everything, whether asked or not. Love was food and food was love. The house was a cocoon of colours. A little cloying on a hotter day, perhaps.

'But no, Hen wasn't having any of that. It had to be her doing the business, taking Angel back to that wretched place of hers in London, setting her to work *and* getting that bloke charged. I ask you! All right, he was a bloody bad lot, excuse my language, he really was, and a bit violent with it, maybe, but he's not the first and he won't be the last. He was always very polite to us, wasn't he Mother?'

She remained silent.

'The evidence suggests he was a sadist, Mr Joyce,' Peter said, quietly.

'Yes, so I gather, but I still think it's best to keep these things in the family. Not go running to the police because you've let yourself get messed up. No, you dust yourself down and get on with it. Me, I felt bad because it looked like we'd never taught her how to spot the rotten apple, but he fooled us too, didn't he, Mother?'

She nodded. 'He seemed a nice man,' she said. 'That's why we gave them the money.' She turned to her husband, anxiously. 'Do you think Hen might have been a little bit jealous about that? After all, we never gave her any.'

'Didn't need it, did she?' he interrupted. 'Always wanted to make her own way, you could never get Hen to take any-thing, could you? She'd never ask, would she? Why should it bother her? No, it was Hen knowing best, before she's even met him. And then keeping Angel in London when she should have brought her back here.'

He turned to his wife. 'But maybe you're right at that. Maybe Hen did resent the money, but to be fair to her, Mother, I can't see it myself. She always knew that Angel would need more because she didn't have the brains.'

Peter was beginning to understand why Angel might have preferred to stay with her sister than crawl back here into this smothering forgiveness and lack of comprehension. To be cosseted by a mum and dad who would never, ever be able to bring themselves to believe what had happened to her. Dad radiated angry innocence, blustering with a shame he could not understand, a horror that this was his fault. The impo-tence of the male provider, failing to solve the problems of his children with blundering love alone. About the mother, Peter was less sure. Her face was wiser than his. Dad had a sudden burst of temper, which seemed to be his alternative to tears.

'That bastard *corrupted* her. She was so sweet, my Angel. She was a star. She'd have been a lovely mum herself, like Mother here. Only he comes along, and he does the business and he wasn't even proud of her. Oh bugger, I could kill him, but God help me, I could have gone for Hen too. Why did she make her do it?'

'Do what?' Peter asked.

'Stand up and tell everyone. Tell the police, go to court and talk about it, for Godsakes. Angel wouldn't have wanted to do that. And not tell *us*. Tells us when the trial's happening, and a copper comes round and tells us to stay away, because we might be witnesses, so we can't go to court and God knows what. But we went, didn't we Mother? In the end. We had to, you know. And it was us she wanted then. Only we couldn't help her, it was too late. If only she'd come home first. Oh God, I miss her. Sorry, excuse me.'

He was fumbling for his handkerchief as he stumbled from the room to pound up the stairs, blowing his nose. His footsteps sounded away into silence and Peter could hear the echo of a man who found it impossible to sob in public, whoever he needed to blame. Six months since that death, not long, no real time at all. A burning log fell from the over-built fire into the slate hearth. Mrs Joyce moved nimbly, seized a pair of tongs and put it back on the flames with the rest. Peter was feeling the heat. A long moment of silence. Then she turned towards him and pulled a face. He thought he could see a touch of her daughter in her then, even more than in the colours in the walls, the pictures, the tapestries and the vivid green of her skirt that looked as if it had been made from something else. She was either wearing it back to front or the seams were odd. Her hands were still, now, and she gazed back towards the fire.

'Well, Peter, you're good for him, I'll say that. He doesn't do tears or temper very often, more's the pity. He'll be back down soon, so if I were you, I'd pretend it didn't happen. Would you like another biscuit?'

'Please.'

Another silence. The fire popped. He waited.

'I know why Angel went off with that Rick Boyd, and I know why she didn't come back, and I've got some idea of what happened to her,' Mother said finally, flatly. 'At least, I don't know, but I can guess. I know that we got it wrong, every single one of us; Hen, too, I think, if you don't mind my saying so, you being a friend of hers. A special friend, I hope, she deserves it. You had to love Angel, you really did. She was put on God's earth to be loved, she really was. Hen was put on earth to find her own way, heaven help her and I hope I had something to do with that.'

'A lot,' he wanted to say.

'But we did treat Angel differently, and we did love her best, heaven help us. You love the one who needs most, can't help it. And to have Angel die in her own room, when she might not have died otherwise, was hell on wheels, Peter. It was never going to be all right, or it was never going to be all right for a long, long time, and Dad's right, in his own way, too, that it might have been better to say nothing and let the bastard loose. I sank like a stone, Peter, for I loved that girl, you can't help that, love's where the devil takes you, you love one better than the other, and the trick's not to show it. But, I tell you now, they were both of them wrong, I mean Hen and Angel's dad, were wrong, you know. She wasn't corrupted by that young man, however bad he was himself.

She was way before him, and I'll always wonder if Hen knew that. I'd rather she didn't, if you know what I mean, just as I'd rather Dad didn't know either. He'll be down in a minute.'

She rearranged her skirt. She had dressed for the occasion. A sweet waft of her own scent drifted towards him. Soap and lavender, a definite taste of fresh from the bath.

'I don't know where or how she'd learned this *knowingness*, but she always had it. I don't know why, some girls just *do*. They go on heat early. Always experimenting with herself. Painting her nipples with my lipstick when she was a kid, shaving her pubes as soon they grew hair, fascinated with her own anatomy. She must have discovered masturbation sooner than most, anyway discovered something other kids didn't know. She had a need for sex, such a craving need the boys could smell it; it worried me sick, but it had the effect of frightening them off. That kind of over-maturity, it does repel, doesn't it?'

'I don't know. Could go both ways.'

She nodded. 'Well, it would attract if you happened to be pretty with it. And had the faintest idea of what you were doing. Instead of not being popular, being rude to people, being on the outside. Drawing attention in all the wrong ways, and getting the wrong result. I'd've rather she'd gone with dozens of boys than stayed in her own room, wanking. Her Dad never knew, of course, but I heard. It calmed down of course, it always does, I suppose. Angel never got what she wanted, really. It broke my heart.'

Peter was wondering quite what all this was about. Mrs Joyce looked at him shrewdly.

'Too much information, eh? I'm sorry about that, but I've never been able to talk to anyone else about it and you're here. Nothing stopped Angel being a sweetheart, she'd have

238

given you the shirt off her back, but she did need protecting. And I could see the look on your face when Father was downplaying what that man did. He's wrong, I know, but he only does it because he can't bear the thought of her really hurting. And, as I said, I'm not sure if it's fair to say that Rick Boyd corrupted Angel. She had corruption in her. There was nothing she wouldn't have tried. After all, she died with her legs spread, lips and tits smeared with lipstick, oh, never mind, that's how I found her in the morning. I had to wash her before I called Dad, like I did when she was a kid. Poor baby. I don't know if that was her own pose, or one she'd learned from him. More coffee?'

'No, thank you,' Peter said, quietly absorbing his own shock.

Footsteps sounded down the stairs. Mrs Joyce got up and loaded the tray, as if her part was finished. How well do parents really know their children? Peter thought. How well do the children know one another and to what lengths would all of them go to protect each other?

Mr Joyce had recovered himself. He took the tray from his wife, put it to one side and ushered her back to her seat.

'C'mon, pet,' he said. 'I'll see to those. I like to see you just sitting.' .

'I'm not good at that,' she said, smiling at him fondly as if there was no one else in the room. 'I shall have to learn, shan't I?'

A grandfather clock ticked in the corner of the room. Peter waited, curious to see where they would go from here, deciding it was up to them. The silence was not uncomfortable as if the warmth of the place took away any feeling of urgency.

'Well, well,' Mr Joyce said. 'I don't know if that's cleared the air, or what. We'd better be honest, with you, Mr. Friel.

We were angry with Hen over this, and it looked like sending down all this stuff was her trying to tell us something, shock us out of our misery. Being a bit vindictive, I thought. She can be like that. Well, I thought, anyway. We went back into a bit of a state of shock, you see, when that woman committed suicide. Brought it all back, as if it had ever gone away. Kids, eh? Who'd have 'em? They're all you want, and then you don't know them at all. Never know what you're going to get, not even when they're your own. I suppose we took even more of a risk, didn't we, Mother?'

'No, we didn't. No more than anyone else.'

'What do you mean?' Peter asked.

'They were adopted,' Mrs Joyce said. 'Didn't you know? Angel and Hen, both of them were. We got them when they were only ten days old.'

CHAPTER SIXTEEN

'Both of them?' Peter said, keeping his voice on an even keel. 'That was very brave of you. Who came first?'

'Henrietta, of course,' Mrs Joyce said, proudly. 'Mind, we'd had to wait long enough for her. It was like being vetted for being a spy. I think they even looked to see if you had anything hidden under the carpets. Very secret and private it was then, not like now. It was a church adoption society. You didn't even know the name of the mother and the mother was never to know who we were. Anyway, we got her at ten days old, and it didn't take us long after that to decide, in all fairness, there'd better be two. Didn't seem right to raise one on her own, when we'd got so much to give. So Angel arrived. We were so lucky.'

'So were they, Mother, they were lucky to have you.' Mr Joyce leaned forward and patted her hand, the gesture covering Peter's loud fit of coughing, which took him by surprise and brought them back into the present. They both looked towards him with genuine concern. He could imagine that every babyish cough or whimper from one of their daughters would be examined instantly.

'Did they know?' he asked, when the coughing stopped. 'About being adopted, I mean? Only it's never been mentioned, not in the court case, not anywhere.'

'Yes, they both knew early on. That's what we were advised to do. Didn't bother Hen either way, she wasn't curious or didn't seem to be. We were her mum and dad, and that was that. But we probably set about it a bit wrong with Angel. She had bad dreams over it, she thought someone was going to come and take her away again. We made up for it by telling her she was very special, in a very special way. We told her she was ours because we loved her and chose her right from the start. I said most mums and dads didn't get to choose their kids, they just happened; they could just be accidents and what made her special was that she was there, just because she was loved and we really, really wanted her so much, we'd had to fight to get her and we were never going to let her go. I suppose that set in the rot at school, because she got up one day and told the rest of them they were all accidents and their parents couldn't possibly want them the way hers did. Bless her. She took everything literally, Angel did.'

'Not sure Mr Friel wants to know about this,' Mr Joyce muttered, but his wife was in full flight in front of an objective, deeply interested audience who was, in his stillness and irrelevance, a sounding board.

'Maybe not,' she said firmly. 'But I do, and so should you, 'cos I think that's where everything started, you know? Kids don't discriminate, they really don't, until one of them stands up and yells out about being different, especially if they're saying they're better. I only wanted to remind you, dear, that it was Hen broke up the fight. Hen always looked after her. There, that's me done, but I need to know, love, what you want me to do. Talk too much, or not talk at all. It's one or the other, I'm afraid, no in-betweens.'

'Talk,' he said, tersely. 'Please talk. Talk me to death.'

She had risen to take up the tray again, carried it aloft over his head, brushing his arm as she moved.

'I'll not do that, love. I prefer you alive, for a good long while. And I'd like Hen to come home for a bit, whenever she's ready. And I'd like that room back. I'll agree with your there, she shouldn't have sent that stuff down. It was, oh I don't know, rude of her.'

'She didn't send it, Mrs Joyce. Somebody else did. She has no idea who. That's why I'm here.'

She put down the tray again and then picked it up, like a shield, a person who always carried something or other about with the same ease she wore her clothes. She did not believe him, but she was willing to forgive mistakes.

'Oh, really? Tell her I've given up the bus shelter, will you?'

She nodded towards the door to the stairs.

'That's man's work.'

Angel's room, beyond the stuff that stood in the entrance, was a pleasant room, apart from the frills. If not the best room in the house, it would have to rival it, larger than Peter imagined, but then he had been thinking of a child. He wanted to see the other two storeys of this house, Hen's room, the parental room, and he could not ask, thought instead of how he himself could root himself here and never want to grow up and out of it. He could also see why the arrival of so much luggage would anger anyone. The baggage was not quite as he imagined it: he had been thinking ahead of untidy, rubbishy bags, because those were the sorts of items that had always accompanied him whenever he moved. Instead there was a neat old trunk of big proportions, and a couple of garment bags. Difficult to see what all the fuss was about, except for the sheer bulk, the intrusion into the room, the fact that they did not look as if they belonged, and the covering of purple and orange FedEx logos. FOR A JOYCE FOR H JOYCE, other labels, too, H and A JOYCE, package prepaid, deliver on X. There was a set of far older, worn-out luggage labels on the trunk, overwritten by the purple and orange.

'I didn't even look,' Mr Joyce was saying. 'I'd only just been able to persuade Mother to take a look at Angel's kiddy stuff, you see, and I knew it would be too much for us to look at whatever Hen was sending of hers. So I phoned, like I did. Spoke to you. I'm sorry again for being so angry.'

'Hen didn't send these things,' Peter said again, louder this time. Peering over the trunk and around the garment bags, he could see it was a pretty room, without a sniff of death in it. There were toys on the white bedspread, pale pink walls and a smell of pot pourri. It felt as if the door to the room had never been opened in the whole six months since Angel had died there. Aged approximately thirty years and still a precocious child. Mr Joyce had stopped at the door.

'What do you mean, Hen didn't send this stuff? She must have done, it says so. Probably didn't want it messing up her place.'

'The labels aren't entirely clear, are they?' Peter said pleasantly. 'Perhaps we should take a look.'

Mr Joyce choked and shook his head.

'Or perhaps *I* should take a look, while you and Mrs Joyce make us another cup of coffee? And then we can decide what to do with it all.'

Joyce nodded gratefully and went back towards the stairs. His dread of the mysterious delivery had already imparted itself to Peter, who could feel his fingers tingling, and felt his own reluctance making him cautious, as if he were a bomb disposal expert without the necessary training. Or as if opening the old trunk would release a cloud of germs. He was back in Thomas Noble's office, unpacking that skirt. It was if unpacking stuff was his new role in life and becoming an uncomfortable habit.

He took the trunk first, because it looked more dangerous than the garment bags lying harmlessly on the floor. The trunk had three hasps securing the lid; it was like an old seagoing trunk, reinforced canvas banded with wood, heavy in its own right and not padlocked. The hasps moved easily, although the metal was pitted with rust. There was no ominous creak from the hinges of the lid as he opened it to the sweet smell of lavender far stronger than the bowl of pot pourri by the bed. It was almost overpowering, so that Peter edged round it and went to open the window. A draught of wonderful damp air and the smell of sea cleared his head; if he had his way, he would throw open every window in this house, however cold it was, and let the draught at least begin to clear the shadows. He could see Mrs Joyce doing that, soon. He went back to the trunk, plunged his hands into tissue paper.

Clothes, exquisite clothes, carefully, recently packed in a state of pristine cleanliness. How would he describe this if he was compiling a list of contents for a jury to consider, and this was exhibit A? *Female apparel, of an old kind, in unusual fabrics. Some items requiring repair. A consignment of ladies' garments of a kind not currently worn. Vintage unknown. Value not easily determined. Label stuck inside lid of trunk says 'My*

245

mother's clothes.' That was as accurate as he could make it on examination of the first three layers, and that was as far as he cared to go. His hand closed round an object that he pulled to the surface and found he was holding a bar of soap. *Female apparel interlayered with wrapped tablets of soap,* then, with something heavier at the bottom. Shoes? Documents? That was the general idea. Peter knelt by the garment bags and unzipped the first. Coats, made of velvet, cotton, silk, trimmed with fur and beaded collars, not everyday coats. In the second bag, he found what he could only describe as *costumes,* suits, but frivolous suits, all made to fit a slim body. He zipped up the bags and closed the lid of the trunk. Then he examined the outside surface of it, wishing he had the detective's magnifying glass. He was perfectly sure that it was not his place or his task to examine everything in detail. To do so felt entirely wrong; it was not his and he might do damage. Someone else had to be present when all this was unpacked, whatever there was inside the pockets and down at the bottom of the trunk. Peter sat on a dead woman's bed and regarded the clothes of another woman, who was also, undoubtedly, dead, and briefly mourned them both.

The first priority was to get this stuff out of here. He went down the stairs, rehearsing his lines. The Joyces were waiting for him.

'I think it's all been a bit of a mistake,' he said. 'Looks like a mis delivery of a whole lot of theatrical costumes, nothing to do with you at all. No personal effects, nothing dangerous.' He knew he was lying. 'I wonder how that could have happened?'

They looked puzzled and relieved. They needed someone else to take charge; they would do whatever he suggested as if it were an order and he was the merciful official for whom they had been waiting.

'Best thing to do is get it all out of here and into a storage place until I can get FedEx to sort out the problem,' Peter went on. 'And you'll know how we should do that, Mr Joyce. You have a company, don't you? It'll be my expense.'

Mr Joyce clapped a hand to his forehead.

'That's what I should have done in the first place.'

'You're always saying that,' his wife said, shaking her head.

'And, perhaps while we wait, you won't mind my picking your brains about storage . . . Hen says you know all about it.'

It was midday before the white van arrived at the command of the master of the house. In the meantime, Peter had eaten sandwiches, admired the tapestries on the walls and learned plenty about the benefits of living where they did and running a business like theirs. Peter wanted to go, but he knew he could not until he had seen the trunk and the garment bags safely stowed anywhere else than this. Part of him also wanted to hang around the parents and listen to whatever else they might tell him about their adopted daughters, but the moment for that had somehow passed and the talk was easily neutral. They chatted like starlings about storage, the place where they lived and the price of eggs, albeit without the same spontaneity, until a man with the WJ logo on his sweater turned up with the van and Peter helped him load. Then Mr Joyce drove Peter, himself and all the misdirected baggage away. This time, Peter knew they were carrying the equivalent of high explosive. The mushroom cloud of a fanciful explanation that had tickled his fancy in the train was forming itself into newer, outrageous shapes, like the clouds in the multicoloured sky long after the threat of snow had gone away. What a beautiful day it was. Joyce was listless and thoughtful in the face of it, dabbing at a smeared windscreen, until encouraged to talk about business.

'Storage is magic,' he said. 'You can't do anyone harm, you see. You give them their own space, a unit however big or small they want, and they keep their own key on their own peg. You keep it clean and tidy and cool, give them peace of mind. I just look after it. They can come and visit stuff whenever they want, and we never interfere. If they stop paying and don't make contact, we have to threaten to use the duplicate key in the safe and send the stuff to auction. It doesn't usually happen, unless someone gets ill or . . . dies and I can afford to give them a bit of time to sort things. The only people we have to let in are the police, with a warrant. Bit awkward when folk get divorced and we don't know who should have the damn key, and oh, the stories. That's what I like, quarrels over stuff nobody needs, because that's what it mainly is, like the stuff in the back. Rubbish, eh?'

Peter smiled agreement and held on to his seat. If he ever again got a motor, it would be a medium sized white van. They ruled the road. Everyone else got out of the way of the white van.

'What if someone comes in and asks for the key to someone else's storage unit?'

'If they haven't got the number, and we don't recognise them, they're out of there. No way. Legal letters proving ownership, maybe. That's why we keep the keys.'

'Security?'

'Video, outside and inside in every corner of the place, except the interiors of the units. Most people bring stuff in themselves, self-storage, see? but it can be done by removers and we can send it on. You can see everything from the office where we keep the keys. John or me's on duty every day from eight until eight, except Saturdays. We lock up and leave it for the night. Not much of a robbery risk, really. Place is like a warren of a fortress, and why rob a place unless you know what's in it? It's nice that you're interested, Peter. Can't usually get anyone interested in a business like this. Hen was the only one who ever was, she worked here. Said we had to have a special unit for clothes, so we do. Do you have intentions towards my daughter?'

'I don't know yet. Only honourable ones.'

Mr Joyce gave a bark of laughter.

'Well, that's honest, at least. If you mess her about, I'll not make the same mistakes as I did with Angel, I'll just come along and punch your lights out. Wish I'd done it to him. I would, now.'

They had driven two miles into countryside Peter failed to notice, past roundabouts and out-of-town supermarkets, down a hill into the vicinity of Mr Joyce's empire. A sprawled building of dull ugliness, two storeys high in parts, the dimensions difficult to detect, an anonymous blot on the landscape, a red-bricked and metal-windowed eyesore, looking like the disused military hospital it once was, the sight of it depressing him and cheering Mr Joyce mightily. It was his, after all. There were large metal containers, each the size of a small bathroom and each with its own, padlocked door, lined up in rows next to where he parked the van in front of the building. These containers looked like portable lavatory cabins, arranged into a set of miniature streets.

'Chinese containers,' Mr Joyce said, proudly. They export so much stuff in these, and we never send anything back. Very solid and cheap to buy. Would one of them do?'

'No. Somewhere inside.'

Despite the front office, with heater and counter and seats and clipboards and video screens, a place where Mr Joyce was obviously at home, Peter bristled in the atmosphere of the place. There were notices, NO GUNS, AMMUNITION, WEAPONS, FOODSTUFFS ACCEPTED FOR STORAGE. His criminally orientated mind thought only of what other contraband could be stored here, such as laundered money, drugs and burglary proceeds, things hidden to be kept from recognition by anyone else. A man came into the office, sheepishly requesting his key so that he could search among his stored possessions for a missing passport he had left in a drawer, and innocence prevailed again. Now, where shall we put this? On to a trolley for passage from here to there, number, ready for Peter to push easily but clumsily to a new home. Row D, but they don't go in order, we've expanded since we started; that was once F, and the one leading off is Z, it's all on the cork board. Pins in different colours, all with numbers, bit of a puzzle, unless you know where you are. Used to be an isolation unit, I think, lots and lots of separate rooms and do you think this needs a de luxe suite? Cost per square foot.

'I don't suppose anyone else can know the inside of this place like you do?'

'I do, John does, Hen, too, I suppose, she used to play here. Is this big enough? Nothing will perish in there.'

It was cold, cold, cold, walls of painted brick and concrete floors. Dozens of metal cells of various sizes, reached by neon lit, glaringly white corridors punctuated by heavy swing doors, reminiscent of the old institution it was and full of the spectres of human luggage on stretchers. Peter had the urge to uncoil a piece of string after himself, so that he could feel his way back. It reminded him of a vast and empty school after everyone had gone home shrieking with the glee of the newly escaped, with distinct overtones of a prison, a place of a thousand locks and keys. They passed a separate room housing an archive, a room for spare parts of washing machines, smaller rooms for personal items, all guaranteed free of damp, mice and other vermin; if such destructive creatures, or anything live lurked inside the metal sheds, they would be able to escape. The further they penetrated into the bowels of the building, the colder it grew, or perhaps that was his imagination and the depressing realisation that he would have to come back here one day soon and find it all over again. With Hen.

The selected space was at the furthest end of the complex, reached long after he was lost following Mr Joyce who strode ahead, talking over his shoulder and mistaking Peter's silent curiosity for genuine interest in something more than the way out. That one's full of books; that one's stock for a little mail order business; that one, I don't know. Gets full, after Christmas. They reached a metal container in a room big enough to house five trunks let alone the one. The trunk was unloaded, convenient handles on either side. There were hooks for the garment bags left hanging against the walls forlornly. Even the trunk looked lonely, as if pressed into service after a long time and then abandoned again. The metal door was closed, the padlock secured and the key pocketed. Peter felt he was walking away from the depositing of a coffin containing a body that was only preserved for a post mortem. It was chilly enough for a mortuary.

Abandoned goods, packed with care, looking forlorn and undignified as if saying we were intended for better things and finer settings than this: we require a room with a view. Shutting the door on them seeming like cruelty. Like everything in this place, it might be mainly rubbish, but it was rubbish with attitude and meaning.

Mr Joyce drove Peter back to the station where they shook hands, firmly, even warmly. The seat on the train seemed sumptuously warm, with the peculiar privacy of public transport. He was full of sad anger, looked at the number on the key he had insisted on keeping and felt his wallet lighter by a hundred pounds. Who was he to tell that he might have deposited the cream of Marianne Shearer's wardrobe into anonymity, where it could stay safe and undisturbed, as long as he paid? The stuff in the trunk must have been hers. The trunk was the vintage of trunk she might have borrowed and carried with her from New Zealand when she came here to study and make her fortune. It looked old enough, with the old labels bearing her name still affixed over even older labels, and all so blurred it came from another lifetime. Why had she ordered these things to be delivered to the Misses Joyce? When had the Lover followed her instructions? Who to tell, who to tell?

To whom could he tell his own, monstrous theory of a shameless woman who died of shame?

Come back, he said and tell me. Tell me what you thought. No answer.

Transcript, transcript. She talked about the transcript in the note she left for the Lover. She must mean the transcript of the Rick Boyd trial, and in all Peter's own reading of his own copy, rationing it, never wanting to dwell on it, there was something he missed. Something in a copy. Tell who? Tell Henrietta Joyce about her bequest, and Thomas Noble about the possible existence of documents at the bottom of that trunk? No, not until he knew why. A good lawyer only served one master at once, conflicts of interest to be avoided at all costs. Unfashionable notion though it was, Peter knew the first master was conscience and the second the client who paid you. He wanted to see Hen, but he would see Thomas Noble first.

Leaving the mobile definitely off, he went straight to Thomas Noble's office, maybe to begin with a request for advice. It was four forty-five when he came out of the train station at Charing Cross into the winter dark. He pushed through the crowds heading home for the weekend, surprising himself by noticing which day it was, and walked slowly, like an old man with a head full of new secrets which were heavy to carry. The bitch, the elegant bitch, leaving everything in code. Marianne Shearer, pupil mistress, cunning, unhappy vixen and the best-dressed tart in London. He was also remembering that the Lover had sent him something by second-class post.

There was a reception committee at Noble's office. The lamplight fell on the empty benches in Lincoln's Inn Fields where the snow had fallen and melted. The whole room was in turmoil again and the fire was out.

'I told you he would come along eventually,' Thomas said to the other two present. 'He's famous for turning up in the end, however long it takes, although it doesn't always follow that he's there when needed, or indeed that he follows instructions to the letter.'

He waved towards the police officers, one man, one woman, plain-clothed and standing still. The man was older, the woman younger, both interested. Thomas vibrated with fury. His posture announced that enough was more than enough.

'*Think* I've persuaded them out of arresting you,' he said. 'But only just, dear. I told them you were sent to interview the old boy, and maybe put a little pressure on him, but not to *kill* the poor sod in such a conspicuous manner. Marianne said you could be trusted to be docile, whatever your method of cross-examination. You'd have let him keep his trousers. He tried, poor dear, he really tried to preserve his reputation. Alas, I knew you had no such tendencies, either to the arcane or brutal, however strapped you are for cash, but these police officers might think otherwise. Oh, of course, you're not up to speed, are you? You leave your mobile off. I've been robbed and the Lover's dead, and him in his Sunday best, too.'

Peter was blinking in the light, shaking his head slowly like a dumb animal. He felt unsteady. He felt he should proffer his wrists for the handcuffs. The woman came towards him.

'So this is NOT PETER. My, my. Could you face me, please?'

He turned towards her, not caring who the hell she was. There were tears behind his eyes and he could not stop them.

She touched his chin and tilted his head, inspecting him in an almost motherly fashion. He was entirely obedient, overwhelmed with sadness.

'So this is Peter. Don't worry, Peter. The person who throttled his ex-Honour and shoved a glass into his arse had the grace to headbutt him first. Or the other way round. Left enough blood and traces. There's no corresponding wound on you. We'll need a sample, but you're not under arrest. You don't strike me as a likely rent boy, anyway. Just sit down and tell us about it.'

'I should never have put them together,' Thomas said. 'They were made for one another.'

'Who do you mean?'

'Oh, Marianne Shearer's paramour and this young idiot, of course. I'm lousy at making introductions,' Thomas said regretting his flippancy as soon as he spoke. So unbecoming in the circumstances. The woman officer looked at him with no attempt to disguise her dislike.

'Such a sense of humour you have, sir. Quite refreshing, really. I expect we're supposed to be grateful. You're actually quite good at making introductions. After all, you call us here this morning because your office has been burgled by someone who stole confidential information, and you give us a link straight away to the body of a distinguished old bloke found halfway down his own stairs not half a mile away. Then you introduce us to your colleague who might have been one of the last to see the poor sod alive. You're doing quite well, so far.'

Thomas whimpered. In terms of client confidentiality, he was failing miserably and had already said too much. He must remember his duty to his client and remind himself that he could still take pride in that. It always came first; it was his own religion. His grasshopper mind had diverted itself to the complications of Frank Shearer's inheritance. Insurance policies, etc, the inadvisability of a verdict of suicide: the omnipresence of Marianne Shearer. Anything in this nightmare that could be turned to some advantage and redeem him. He did not care about the death of an old, rude man.

'Of course,' he said, 'this new homicide raises other questions than the identity of the culprit. Such as the obvious connection to Marianne Shearer's death. If the Lover was murdered, doesn't it follow that she might have been too? At least it casts a doubt on her suicide. Some jealous type, out for them both? A relative of the Lover, perhaps, outraged by his double life? Does for the mistress first?'

'I don't think there's any doubt about Ms Shearer's suicide,' Peter said.

'Oh, Peter, do shut up. You've done enough damage.'

'It certainly opens up other possibilities,' the woman officer agreed, reluctantly, watching a whole new trench of impossible work coming in her direction. She had been cross-examined by Marianne Shearer once and loathed her. No tears were shed in the police service when MS jumped. Looking at these two, she knew she was right to hate all lawyers. Snivelling wretches, never anything else but trouble. She was going to get out of this as soon as she could. She had no place in this story.

'I think she committed suicide,' Peter repeated, refusing to be sidetracked, but not adding that he might also know why. The sadness dogged him. It was going to get worse. He shook himself and faced the woman.

'I left Mr Stanton at about nine in the evening. He was alone and . . . dancing.'

She nodded.

'I bet he was rueing the day he ever met that bitch Marianne Shearer,' Thomas said. 'I know I do.'

'Do you?' Peter said. 'I don't. Nor did he.'

I was her thing of beauty and she was mine.

He turned to the woman.

'I'll make a statement whenever you want. Samples, now, if you like. I can only tell you that I met Mr Stanton for the first time yesterday evening. I see Mr Noble has already told you why I went to see him, but I'd rather not include that in the statement. It's not relevant, is it? Do you have any idea who killed him?'

'Whoever it was didn't quite kill him, Mr Friel. He bloodied him and stuck a glass in him. Looks like he dressed himself and died on the stairs.'

'Poor man.'

A moment's respectful silence, but only a moment.

'There's a connection,' Thomas said heavily, directing his

remark to Peter. 'There's got to be. First Miss Joyce, mean-
inglessly mugged out there . . .'

'You didn't tell me that.'

'. . . while you're at the Lover's. Then my office gets burgled, someone takes away his address and my notes and
makes a mess of my desk. Looks like a person or persons is
on a bit a spree, so to speak . . .'

He sensed that no one was listening. He leant against the
window, looked outside into the fields, and sighed.

'And it used to be so peaceful here,' he complained. 'The
only arguments we ever got were people queueing for the
museum or disentangling dogs.'

Peter decided his first duty was *not* to Thomas Noble or
his client. He turned back to the woman.

'If I could come to you tomorrow?'

'Yes, tomorrow,' she said. 'It can wait until then. We know
where you are.'

Two deaths, no . . . three. It could all wait.

She actually smiled. Peter could suddenly see Rick Boyd,
smiling from the dock. That vacant, friendly face, rising up
behind the image of Marianne Shearer, falling from the balcony.

Rick Boyd, who never quite got what he wanted.

Continuation of cross-examination of Angel Joyce by Marianne Shearer, QC

MS. That's right, Angel. Have a glass of water. I asked you to speak up, not to shout.

AJ. You don't believe me.

MS. It's up to the jury to decide if they believe you or your sister, Angel. Just tell the truth.

AJ. I am telling the truth.

MS. Of course you are, as you know it. Subjective and objective are two different things.

Interruption.

MS. We'll go back to the indictment, shall we? How often did you say you were raped, Angel?

AJ. Every time I begged him to stop.

MS. Do you mean every time you begged him to start? How did he get you to agree to anything?

AJ. He smiled at me. And he asked me to smile.

Chapter Seventeen

He was not smiling. He was fingering pieces of paper and definitely not smiling until he was ready.

No seduction upon which he had ever embarked had succeeded so quickly, or so badly. He should have done his homework, should never have assumed Frank would resemble his own sister. Frank Shearer had required so little. All it had taken was promises and then the threat of promises denied. Nurturing Frank had involved a matter of hours, pandering to Frank's worst fears, requiring the minimum of pretence and reinvention on his own part. It always depended on the raw material. He could never have known what Frank was like. Frank could have been as cold and persuadable as his clever bitch of a sister, with vanities and ambitions of the same intensity. He could have been as cunning and ruthless. Instead he was a powder keg of the most stupid, volatile, senseless violence and a fucking liability.

Rick had to concede, though, that brother and sister did have a fair bit in common. Hidden passion versus the obvious kind. They were both incredibly naive. They both fell for him and were willing to do anything, which was quite right and what he was owed. The difference was that while Marianne Shearer made it her business to believe everything she was told, and act upon it decisively in due course, banning any doubt about the client from her mind with fierce loyalty, exactly as she should, she did at least weigh the evidence before she absorbed it for later use. She manufactured her own anger, controlled and refined it into venom only as necessary and added in her own contempt for silly women one dollop at a time, while Frank, the throwback, believed everything he was told, took it without digestion like a dog wolfing food, and acted on it immediately. Then it was light the blue touchpaper and retire. A useless ally in a cold war, a literally bloody liability. All Rick had to do was to make sure it was Frank who drew the blood and none of it got on him. He checked the sleeves on his camel hair coat. The cuffs were wearing thin, but this material didn't shed much. It was too old.

They were in Frank's place, and Frank had cried off sick for the day. Or at least, Rick had done it for him. The beast was in the next room, hunched in his bed, waking up to cry and vomit, authenticating the validity of the excuses Rick had made in his most authoritative tones, learned from the likes of Marianne Shearer, to the manager of the car showroom. *I'm his brother. I'm afraid he's frightfully ill and sends his apologies. Yes, of course he'll be back tomorrow, and of course he'll make up the time. I'm so sorry.* Oh, those patrician, barristerial voices, like those of priests and preachers, they worked all the time; voices which brooked no argument or contradiction and were so easy to mimic. Voices which countered the verbal abuse directed back by saying, *I beg your pardon? I don't understand. Please explain.*

Manners maketh man and accents made him heard.
Always better than shouting.

So, Frank was ill and staying in bed all day today, damn
right he was. He had mugged a girl and nearly killed a bloke,
all in the space of a few hours. Phenomenal. Such fun. Rick
sat back in this filthy armchair, still in his coat, and considered it. The first was to blame on delusion and paranoia, the
second, pure misjudgement. Weeping, blubbering, already
bloodied, big ol' Frank, rallying with alcohol like that, and
then going off beam again.

Let's check on Noble's office, see what he's hiding. I know
how to get in: I've sat and watched them punch in those
numbers on that keypad by the door. He was up for that, and
then . . . I only suggested we call on the old boy, Frank. I
always had his number, from her diary I looked at when she
was out of the room; and look here, there's an address on
Noble's desk. Your sister's shag, who might just have the
stuff we need. I just said, let's call on him since we're in the
area, why don't we? Just up the road. What else to do when
the pubs are shut? Old geezer might give us a drink. She had
a lover. The lover might know about the kid, like where she
lives and does she know, as well as knowing about where all
those valuable goods and money and furniture are, which
Thomas Noble says are lost, even they're yours, now. It all
belongs to you, really, Frank. He might have taken them.

The mere hint of riches not his own triggered Frank into a
frenzy, didn't it? That room, that taste, that opulence, that
privacy. Plus a man lying on a bed, calling him ugly and
saying his sister never loved him. Whoah.

Maybe Frank would not go to work tomorrow either. Not
with a face full of festering scratches and that contusion on
his forehead.

Rick Boyd got to his feet and aimed for the kitchen of this horrible place. The man lived like a pig, with a clean avenue between bathroom and bed, where the daily suit and clean shirt was always ready between one day and the next, with Frank's remaining sixth sense telling him that personal hygiene and presentation were all that mattered. You couldn't sit in his chair without something sticking to you.

Rick retrieved the clean lint and saline fluid he had got from the chemist, moved towards the smell of Frank's room. Wounds must not fester. He dabbed at that big face with the stinging fluid until Frank woke up and screamed. There, there, he said, and Frank, said, Mummy, Mummy, is he dead?

The man who called you scum? I hope so, Frank, my darling. You know that one about dead men not telling tales? Go to sleep, baby, go to sleepy sleep. Good boy. When you get your money, we'll go fifty–fifty, right?

The contents of the pigskin case were disappointing at first. A copy of M. Shearer's instructions, all in a kind of code, and a bundle of what looked like part of the transcript of Rick's very own trial. He had taken it out and leafed through quickly in the dreadful light of Frank's tiny flat. I want to come home with you, Frank had sobbed into Rick's shoulder, What did we do? Christ, even before they had got to the end of Chancery Lane and the sight of a taxi. No way, let's go to yours, not having your DNA in mine, and please don't mention we. It was all you, love, it was all you, Mr Mighty Man. You did it, you great ape, never mind, I'll look after you. I loves you, Frank.

He went through the contents of the case again. A copy of the transcript including the bit about kidnap, beginning with reams of law, marked, 'Send to Peter Friel'. Rick remembered him, silly little tosser on the other side who never got a chance to open his mouth. He threw it aside, then picked it up again, almost fondly. He had been so important then, so much a celebrity that every word that was spoken in his trial was written down. He could remember Marianne, taking exception to the written record of yesterday on each following morning, insisting on examining the record precisely, pointing at it with her long red nails. That's not what was said, she would say, they've made a mistake, I said it that way. The inference is missed. She could waste half an hour every day that way, making it longer and longer, infuriating everyone. Wasting the patience of the absent jury, tearing the heart out of witnesses in waiting. Then apologising in the same tones he used with Frank's boss. Using her presence to make sure they didn't notice they were being conned.

He went on to these funny instructions, marked 'Copy to', which worried him. Send a copy of this shit to Peter Friel? What was she on about? That courtroom had been stuffed with copies of everything.

What was perfectly, glaringly clear from that note, though, was that Marianne was going to write a book, maybe had written it already or was getting someone to write it. And the Lover had put ticks on a list of what he was supposed to do, which included sending a whole lot of stuff to H. Joyce, addressed to Angel's parents' place. Whoah, what was this? So that was where everything was. A lot, a very expensive delivery, a vanload, maybe.

Rick sat back and remembered that house. Sitting there and being interviewed by that stupid old dad who didn't think anyone was good enough for his slag of a daughter. Not good enough for Angel? Angel wasn't halfway good enough for him; Dad got it the wrong way round. He deserved far better than Angel and Angel only got what was coming to her. As far as Rick Boyd knew he had never done anything wrong in his life, it was the others. That stuffy room with a fire, everything ordered and tidy; Angel's anally retentive dad talking about his storage place; he had even offered Rick a job in it. Who did he think he was?

Yeah. Dad puts everything we don't need in storage, Angel said. He hates clutter and he's got the space.

Better go and get it. See what was in it, before anyone else looked, but how to get in? That's just what Marianne would do out of spite. Send it all to Hen Joyce, get her to run with it, the way she had run Angel. Put it together with what she had and get him put inside again.

Maybe not take Frank. Maybe just leave him here, covered in DNA. Frank's worth a fortune and Frank does dirty work. I don't make him, he just does it, it's not my fault. And Frank still thinks he's got a serious rival for the old inheritance. If he goes apeshit with her, so what? I run away and let him. Fucking H. Joyce had obviously got together with Marianne Shearer somehow. Plotting behind his back like she did with Angel, using what was his to make another case against him, writing that book. Rick went back and looked at Frank. Frank could drive, and he had access to cars. He would have to do. In the meantime, he would give Frank another pill and settle down to think in this dirty chair.

Think of a plan. Where to first? He couldn't go to her place alone, it scared him.

I'm sorry, my brother has developed pneumonia.

Are you caring for him?

I care for everyone in my charge. They do not always appreciate it. They don't always know what's good for them.

Peter was tired. It was akin to the tiredness of a week in court, when he would burn the midnight oil between the days, working up to a fatigue that would create bad dreams in which he would see himself a naked laughing stock unable to speak. He was heavy with sadness when he needed to be optimistic, and the anxiety which afflicted him was nothing to do with himself. He wanted to see her, needed to see her in situ, while on the way he was working out how to ration the information, spare the pain and the surprise, and yet wanting her to suffer it. Hen might be lovely, but she was also crafty. If he rationed information with her, kept anything back, it would only be revenge for her doing the same thing to him, to her parents, to everyone else involved with Angel, doing harm in the name of doing good. As he walked down her street, he decided against withholding anything. Repeat verbatim, spare nothing, keep nothing back. Wherever it was going to go with her, that was the way it was going to be with him. He was too tired for subterfuge anyway, too shocked to manage it. He would be calm truthful and precise, and tell her to lock her doors. If there were any questions, they would be asked and answered one at a time.

Instead, he stumbled into her arms and wanted to cry. She held on to him, with her arms round his back, holding him tightly. She was so small, so bitterly strong. You need food, Peter, she said. Come and eat. He could hear her mother's voice, and was glad of it. The mother who raised her, the one she thought she knew.

Yes, Hen said, she taught me to cook, too.

Up those stairs, to sit in that kitchen he liked. So different from the seaside house, a palette of bright, primary colours, clashing together joyfully, without any of the harmonious forethought of that other place. Tunes in his head, a mind full of interiors.

He ate what was put in front of him, a casserole with

unidentifiable ingredients, hot and strong, with crumbly tomato bread.

Ate. Talked. Repeated, verbatim, as if he was making a comprehensive report on the last twenty-six hours. As accurate and complete as if he were a shorthand writer preparing the transcript for the next day of a trial.

An honest and impartial witness, omitting nothing, except his own emotional reactions. She followed his example, remaining silent until he had finished, although her face registered shock, surprise, anger and sorrow, even a smile when he described her mother's hospitality, and by the end, she had crumbled her half of the loaf into very small pieces which she rolled between her fingers, as if trying to make them disappear.

'Then I came here,' Peter ended. 'That part you know.'

'Thank you,' she said. She raised her glass. 'Let's drink to the dead. And to lovers everywhere. May they do a little better than those two. And to adopted children everywhere – the lucky ones.'

She was too controlled, he thought, wishing he could stop analysing and simply watch. Too controlled because she has had to be so. Like me, in a courtroom, and I am sick of it. We should all be shouting and screaming, dancing with outrage and staging some sort of riot, joining in a lynch mob, instead of waiting for the due process of law and rational thought.

'Rick Boyd,' she said. 'I feel Richard Boyd right in the middle of this. Especially the bit about the broken glass. What you lot would call similar fact. Rick Boyd, a man without a centre, put on earth to mess up lives. Not worth analysing, because there's nothing there. Not worth punishing, because he would never understand why, but eminently worth destroying. I should have killed him when I had the chance.'

She brushed her hands through her hair, blinked repeat-
edly. This was no point to cry or to blackmail him with tears.
It simply wasn't fair. Nothing was bloody well fair. He was
looking at her differently, as if the knowledge of her parent-
age and her parents' opinions made her pitiable. Let him try.

'Look,' she said. 'This is the time you walk away. This is
the time you *should* walk away. Give up the job with Thomas
Noble, get the poison out of your life, forget that damn trial
and everything else, especially Marianne Shearer. And me. I
shouldn't think less of you if you did, I'd still think you're the
best thing to come out of the whole business. Give up thinking you're in some way *responsible* for that trial. That's why
you're here, isn't it? To make up for a personal failure. I
don't want you contaminated any more. I don't want you in
our kind of danger.'

'Yes, I do feel responsible, I *am* responsible. And if I say I
can't walk away, even if you pushed me, can't, don't want to,
I'm not going anywhere and I'm insulted by the suggestion
that I should, what would you say then?'

She considered it, frowning. Peter took off his spectacles
and rubbed them assiduously with the linen napkin she had
left on the table, suddenly realising he had seen it before. It
was the one he had given her. Oh, the magpie. He had an
absurd desire to see Hen unpack that trunk full of clothes. It
might be like a child with a dressing-up box.

She smiled a shaky smile.

'Then I'd say we'd better have a full discussion, in which I
fill in a few holes. It's a pretty uncomfortable garment I'm
making at the moment. Do you want to see it? I've been
trying to get to grips with Marianne Shearer's bosom. I need
to do something with my hands.'

He did not understand, but nodded. The aching fatigue

had receded. They took the wine down to the dressing room and sat either side of the table. He liked this room as much as the attic kitchen. It was a soothing place, with an atmosphere of calm, contented industry, reminding him of a much loved library. There was the dummy by the table, the torso dressed in one half of a bodice with half an upstanding collar extending above the headless neck. It looked hopeful and comical rather than sinister. She took the bodice off the dummy and sat with it on her lap. Then she threaded a needle.

'I'm making one half first, to see what works. It's bit like putting together a story, one half is easy, until you get to the next bit and it doesn't hang together. Should I start by saying I have absolutely no idea why Marianne Shearer would send me clothes from beyond the grave? Oh, I forget, she isn't buried yet. It's shattering and disturbing. Why should she want me to have anything of hers? Because I made her feel bad? Because I sent her Angel's post-mortem report? Because she thought she did us wrong? Because she wanted to be liked?'

She shook her head and stabbed the needle into the cloth.

'That's starting with the second half. Lets go back to Angel and Boyd.'

She got up and dragged out the carpet bag from its new place beneath the suits. She rummaged in it and withdrew a pile of photographs, spreading them on the table in front of him, waiting while he looked, ready to take them away again. Photos of Angel, spreadeagled, masturbating and smiling; a photo of Angel's lacerated backside; a photo of Angel's shaven and bloody vagina exposed by her own hands. Pornographic photos of Angel screaming and smiling, and lastly, a photo of her raised hand with the missing fingertip, making a salute in front of her face. Hen took the photos away. His face was ashen.

'I took his camera, too,' Hen said, 'but I think it's these he wants back. He may think Marianne Shearer had them.'

'But they should have been exhibited at the trial,' Peter said. 'They would have nailed him. They make a nonsense of any idea of consent or cooperation. Why didn't you hand them over? No woman consents to that.'

'Not even a woman as sexually curious as my little sister. Or as corrupt, as my mother hinted. I always knew that hunger in her, and that self destructive kick, but I knew it never went anywhere near enjoying pain. She was terrified of physical pain, but oh, did she want to please. These were taken when she was past caring.'

'They should have been exhibited,' Peter repeated. 'You were withholding evidence.'

'It wasn't my evidence to withhold,' Hen said. 'Just as it wasn't in my power to force Angel to have the intimate examinations which would show the extent of the injuries. I was pushing her far enough as it was. She was only ever going to go through with it if the worst of it didn't come out. She said she would die if Mum and Dad ever knew. She thought it would kill them. Better they didn't know and disbelieved her, than if they knew and still didn't believe her. She didn't want anyone to know. I couldn't change that. Besides, there seemed plenty of evidence of the abuse without including the pictorial record. No one could deny the missing finger. Then there were the other victims, all that similar fact. We could rely on the others, we thought. There was mountains of other evidence against him in the beginning.'

'Until it all got whittled away. Until the kidnap charge was slung out. Did she actually want him to be convicted?'

She hesitated. 'I sometimes wonder about that.'

'But that means no one in that courtroom knew the extent

of it,' Peter said. 'Not judge, jury, the prosecution or the defence. Not me, not even Marianne Shearer.'

'Not even Marianne Shearer, but Marianne Shearer *should* have known. She knew Boyd. She knew each and every allegation made against him. She knew his history, his habits, his proclivities. She knew the type of victim, the pattern, she knew more than anyone, and she denied knowing, to herself, at least, all for the sake of *winning*. She denied what she knew.

'That's why I sent her Angel's post-mortem report. There's a graphic account of the scars. I wanted her to know what she denied.'

Peter picked up a needle from a colourful pin cushion and attempted to thread it with black cotton. It was a long time since he had done such a thing. He was trying to remember if his mother had ever taught him to sew.

'I did so many things wrong, right from the beginning,' Hen said, watching him. 'Or I did so many wrong things. Sending that post-mortem report was one of them, but earlier than that I cocked up mightily. I should have called the police to the flat, rather than taken her away. There were still traces of blood on the table, there were still the filthy sheets she slept in, but I couldn't let her stay there another minute. I bundled up evidence like that,' she gestured towards the carpet bag, 'all his letters and his camera, and we went. Gave him plenty of chance to sanitise the place before he was arrested. I gave stuff to the police selectively. And I let her get cleaned up; it's the first stage on the road to recovery, isn't it? Getting cleaned and dressed.'

'Wasn't she dressed?'

'Scarcely. It was November, bloody cold.'

'He was arrested in that flat,' Peter said slowly. 'He didn't move on when he came back and found she'd gone. He wasn't expecting it.'

'No, he wasn't. He cleaned up for himself and he took away the axe, but it would never have occurred to him that Angel would send them. None of the others had, they were found later, they didn't volunteer. More than that, it would never have occurred to him that he'd done anything wrong. She was his. Even if he didn't want her any more, she was still useful and she was still his. Rick Boyd, you see, was always innocent. I didn't know him, and there were aspects of Angel I didn't know and couldn't predict, either.'

She sewed three small stitches and put the cloth down. Peter remembered Mrs Joyce's surprising confidences in the absence of Mr Joyce. The tapestries on the walls, which must have taken years to sew, the need of certain women to keep their hands busy.

'Rick Boyd wanted total exoneration,' he said, 'and he didn't get it. He got a disgraceful half-win and emerges from prison with the mark of Cain still on him, only technically innocent, still personally outraged. The only person who held out against him was Angel, led from behind by you. The only *two* people who knew the full extent of what he did were you and Marianne Shearer. Marianne Shearer, who was supposed to be going to write a book, and could have got him rearrested. Someone, something, was harassing her before she died. And now there's only you. You both had something he needed to destroy. Knowledge and evidence. The Lover knew where the evidence was, even if he didn't know what it was. He's dead, too. He was . . . played with, tormented a little before he died. Maybe he came across with more information than he gave me. Doesn't this suggest Rick Boyd? He's out there and you need protection. Either you move from here, or I don't leave you alone until I see the police tomorrow. You can't stay here by yourself. He wanted what Marianne had; she's dead. He wanted what the Lover might have had and I don't know what the Lover might have told him. Now there's only you and some of Marianne's possessions. He can't know where they are.'

His voice tailed off. Hen smiled at him gently. He could see himself as he imagined she might see him. Long and skinny in an ill-fitting suit, playing with a needle he could not thread without spectacles, not exactly the protector of choice.

'I won the three-legged race, once,' he volunteered. 'My school reports said I was "resourceful".'

And Marianne Shearer branded me a wimp. And trusted me with something precious.

'Thank you,' Hen said, without any argument. 'I should like that very much, although what I really want is forgiveness. For the wrong things.'

He shook his head, the weariness coming back to hit the back of his neck like a cudgel, making him realise he would soon be slurring his words and there was nothing more to be said or done before morning. No stamina, that boy. There were dark hollows below his eyes.

'You have my bed, and I'll sleep here,' she said. 'We've got to sleep, we're dead on our feet. I'll just check there's nothing overcooking downstairs.'

'I'll come with you.'

'There's no need. And I don't want you staying on false pretences. I want you to stay because it's late and you're tired and I can press that suit in the morning and find a clean shirt. Not because Rick Boyd's going to turn up here in the middle of the night. He won't come here.'

'I'm coming with you.'

'He won't come here,' she repeated.

Peter followed her downstairs to the basement. It was

cooler, full of the chemical smell which revived him, but only a little. There was so much more he wanted to ask. The place was a laboratory for cleaning. Their footsteps sounded loud on the stone floor. He watched her detach a piece of cambric from the clothes line and lay it flat. It would be easy for a thief to gain access here, but there was nothing a casual thief would want to steal. Marianne's skirt hung on the overhead pulley, accusingly. Not even the eyeless teddy bears held any appeal.

'Why wouldn't Rick Boyd come here?' he asked. 'He can get in anywhere. Squats, other people's house, the Lover's perhaps. He just walks in to other people's lives.'

Hen was standing by the light switch, ready to usher him out, pausing before moving.

'He won't come here,' she said, 'because he came here before. The one week he was on bail, he came to find Angel. She was waiting for him upstairs, hiding in the dressing room, dressed in her best. She would have gone with him, but I found him first, down here. He came in the back.'

Peter moved to stand close to her, touched her arm gently. 'And?'

She shrugged.

'I chucked a bucket of dry-cleaning fluid all over him. It was fluid out of the drain from the tank. It blinded him for a while. I pushed him out. I should have killed him.'

She turned out the light and Peter followed her up the stairs. Again, he felt he was following in the footsteps of someone he did not know. Hen spoke over her shoulder.

'He won't come here,' she was saying. 'So you're safe with me. Rick Boyd may hate me like poison, but as long as he's on his own, he's still afraid of me.'

CHAPTER EIGHTEEN

Wake up, Frank my lad. We've got things to do. I think we'll take a Mercedes.

C'mon, it's a Saturday, the place is closed. I found where Marianne put her stuff. It's OK, Frank.

Peter slipped out of the house in the dark of early morning and hit the street running. He could forgo a pressed suit or a clean shirt until he was home. The most ominous thing she had said was that Rick Boyd was afraid of her. He could make himself believe she was safe where she was and that Boyd was afraid of the place. He must be, otherwise he would have come back long before and would not return to the scene of a previous humiliation without an ally, and Rick Boyd had no allies; no ally or friend mentioned in the whole of that trial; men like that did not. He made others conspire with him, though: that was what he had done with his series of hapless women. Peter went back to his own flat in a state of suppressed panic he could not fully explain either to himself or to anyone else, except by saying that he had to see what was in the post. And then the nine o'clock appointment with the police to make a statement and say his piece about all the rest as well as he could. In the growing light of day, it all seemed as woolly and ephemeral as dawn mist.

Tube quicker than taxi for the route to Camden on a Saturday morning. Hen had promised she would not move. She had plenty to do indoors, she said. There might even be customers.

Thomas Noble, another early riser, had already phoned. Peter found himself looking round the carriage of the underground train, so prompt, so efficient at this hour, so half full of silent listeners, he wanted to hide inside his coat so that his own thoughts would not be overheard.

Would *sir* like the services of a solicitor to accompany him on his visit to the police station? I'm not au fait with these situations, not my kind of law, but I think I might owe you that. Early morning sarcasm. No, thank you, Peter muttered. I know what I have to say. Besides, you would alienate them and I need them to listen.

Whose side are you on, Peter?

I didn't know there were sides.

You know what you were hired for.

To find out Marianne was murdered, rather than suicidal, isn't that what you want, what the client wants? I thought you said it was to find out why.

Why was an obscene word in an early morning train bearing passengers in and out of town to open shops, markets, weekend businesses, anything, whilst bearing home the night shift. Whatever had been sent by post should have arrived. Snail mail. Why on earth had Marianne Shearer failed to commit her intentions to email? Too easy? Perhaps her laptop was at the bottom of the trunk. He should have paid the price and towed it all back, not left it lonely.

His flat was stuffy and warm. He hated it on sight, but then he had never loved it, or any place he had ever lived alone. It was not home, it was a stopgap. The post in the front door was disappointingly small. A manilla envelope, A4-sized.

An envelope, punctiliously addressed in a sloping hand. *To Peter Friel, Esq.* in the Lover's old-fashioned hand. Inside it, a few pages looking for all the world like a part of the transcript of the trial. All that trouble to send him something he might have missed from the original volumes which still lurked in the corner of his room; in a corner of Thomas Noble's office and in several other damn corners; a big, paperwork reminder of failure.

A single sheet of paper clipped to the front.

You never read anything properly, Peter. This is Why. *Look after the relics.*

Peter changed his clothes in his colourless flat, feeling homesick for where he had been, wishing he had not slept in Hen's bed without her. He could not stop to read now, stuffed everything in the knapsack he used in lieu of a briefcase and ran for the next appointment. He was dressed in jeans and the same dusty black coat, his boots were worn. He thought how the Lover would be appalled, and wished there could be a chance to meet him again. It was piercingly cold: Peter went back for his gloves. Concentrate on one thing at a time. Make the statement, set them rolling, pray for them to believe him, and then get back to Hen. Get Hen to join him. West End Central Police station was close to the station where they could take the train. He wanted her to see what was in storage long before it was given to Thomas Noble.

They kept him waiting. It was the fate of a witness to be

kept waiting. There would be a certain pleasure in keeping a witness as to material fact waiting even longer if they also happened to be a lawyer – although he doubted if there was anything contrived about that. It was Saturday morning, and a pall of resentment hung about the place. Peter remembered from the original police report in *R* v Boyd, that this was the station where Hen had first taken Angel, over a year ago. Police stations did not change. They could be painted in different colours and vain attempts tried to make them user-friendly, but it never made them different. He never went inside without feeling he was under arrest, although to his knowledge he had never committed an offence worthy of that. Drunk and disorderly, perhaps, cheating on train fares in the critically poor days of student life. He was only ever guilty by proxy. Guilty of not doing enough. He waited and read what Marianne Shearer had sent him.

The last questions and answers spoken before they had stumbled towards their respective beds, while Hen found towels and toothbrush for him, her efficiency never quite deserting her, haunted him too. Do you suppose *anyone* loved Marianne Shearer? she asked. Do you suppose *he* loved her? I hope he did. Can you die of not being loved, or want to die because you aren't? No, he had said. I don't think anyone loved her, or not in a way I understand, she took what she could. And, Hen, why did neither you nor Angel ever mention you were adopted children?

She was handing him the towel. Angel never mentioned it after getting into trouble for shouting about it in school the way she did. Besides, it would have made her look even more like a natural victim, somehow. Nobody else's business. As for me, it was never relevant. I thought I was lucky to be chosen, never curious because my own mother was dead, my father told me.

He was beginning to read when the officer came to fetch him. She found a studious young man, not looking like a lawyer, nodding to himself, beginning to understand.

Ann, the work-experience girl, came back on the Saturday morning because she was bored. It seemed better to be out of the house and Henrietta Joyce had said come back some-time over the weekend, so she was taking her at her word. Eleven o'clock on a Saturday morning seemed a reasonable time. The street was only half busy; the specialist shops mostly closed, still recovering from Christmas holidays and the dearth of trade in January. Ann did not notice this; she was thinking of the sad fact that her mother did not under-stand her and never, ever would in a month of Sundays, and if anyone had a chance of understanding the mess of her life, it was Henrietta Joyce. Hen Joyce actually talked to her. Hen was OK, and Anna did not think she would mind being messed about. Hen wouldn't point out that her hair was dyed all wrong and her skirt didn't suit her plump legs, like Mum did.

It turned out she was right. She rang the bell, spoke into the intercom and was told to come upstairs, there was plenty to do. Weekends were not sacred in this kind of business and the company would be good. While she waited on the doorstep, she saw a Mercedes cruising down the street. A silver machine, erratically but slowly driven, as if the person behind the wheel did not know where he was going, or if the two of them were having a row. Her parents drove around like that sometimes.

'I was just making tea,' Hen said. Today she was wearing a scruffy boiler suit. 'Milk no sugar, wasn't it?'

As if there had been no intervening days, she sat down and

felt at home in the dressing-up-box room. It was nice here. There was a radio burbling music on the big table, not Ann's kind of music, but OK-ish, not classical at least, something which made her want to tap her feet without much effort while letting the rest of her stay still, and oh, heavens above, Hen actually asking her opinion, showing her something hanging off the dummy.

'What do you think of this bodice thing? Is it worth doing, do you think? I wanted something that could look good with jeans, something you could button or leave undone. Something that could be worn by all ages, that someone like you could wear, or someone as old as me.'

'Cool,' Ann said. 'Really cool, but where's the other half?'

But then Hen was no longer listening, just like any other adult. Her head was cocked to one side and she was listening for something else entirely, such as the sounds of her own house or whatever else was going on in her weird head. Then Ann watched her put a finger over her own lips, miming *shhh*, rather than saying it, moving closer to the door she had left open behind her, closing it and listening harder. A voice shouted a cheerful greeting up the stairs, comfortably far away. Two sets of footsteps.

Hide, Hen mouthed, then whispered, '*Hide*. Hide now, and stay where you are until I say come out, OK? Just do it. Here. Just *hide*.'

She pushed back the rack of evening gowns and garments that hung to the floor. There was space behind, *aired clothes need space around themselves, don't squash them up*. A stuffy space, all the same, warm and dark and rustling with noises as she pushed her way through, so it made Ann want to giggle as she was shoved in there, saying What? like it was a scene from a play, or something. Get right back and stay there, OK. OK, OK, OK, Hen was sounding like her mother and she was being ordered about again, but it was more than that. It was Hen's face told her it wasn't a game. So she curled herself up into the smallest foetus shape she could make of herself, backed against a warm wall, seeing nothing but the light of the dressing-up room where it penetrated for a few inches between the gaps in the garments which did not quite sweep the floor. She held on to the skirt of something to lower herself down, let go quickly. It was some kind of taffeta and it made a noise. She heard Hen go back and sit at the table. Then the men came in.

Anna could see one set of polished shoes. An attractive voice, greeting cheerfully.

'Hello, Hen. No, don't phone out, please. Be polite, for God's sake. Meet my friend, Frank. Be nice to him, he's not too well at the moment.'

'Hello, Frank. What was it you wanted to buy? Either of you? Why don't you just get out of here?'

Frank's voice, slurred and dreary. His shoes taking the place of the other shoes.

'Where's the lumpy little girl, then, the one at the door? I fancied her. You're not that bitch are you, naaa, you can't be, what are we doing here, Rick? I dunno.'

The sound of someone sitting down heavily, moving the wooden chair so it scraped on the floor, dumping a great weight inside itself.

'I didn't think you'd have the nerve, Rick,' Hen was saying quietly. 'Fancy you coming back, after last time.'

'Couldn't have done it alone, Hen, not after that. But I've got a friend, see? Makes all the difference. Adds weight, if you see what I mean. So where's the lumpy girl, then? Frank likes them young.'

'You mean the one who delivers the paper and goes away? You're out of luck, Rick Boyd. So's your friend. Get out.'

'Are you my fucking niece?' That other, druggy voice.

'We're all related to apes, aren't we?'

Then they hit her. They stood round her and hit her. Ann could see the movement of their feet. Or maybe one was hitting, soft, breathy blows, and one was watching, she couldn't tell. Enough to stay hidden back among the clothes and listen, easy does it, Frank, easy up, Frank, she only scratched you, she's got things to tell us, like where's the stuff?

She's not the one, Frank, lay off, sit down, you've got to drive. I WANT TO KNOW WHERE MARIANNE PUT HER STUFF. Can you hear me? WHERE IS IT?

Frank sat back in the same chair. He was the one with the dirty boots, not the polished shoes.

'She's not?'

'Of course she fucking isn't. But she knows who is. Get a grip, Frank, just relax.'

Turning back, talking softly, Where's the stuff? Where did you put it? What did Marianne send to you?

Her voice, too calm, almost inaudible.

'I don't know. She didn't send it to me. She sent her clothes to Angel.'

'She got her shag to send stuff to Angel, yes I know that. But what about the stuff she sent to you? What about the stuff you sent to her? Where's my camera, where's my notes, where's my photos, where's my Angel, where's my fucking LIFE?'

Silence. The screaming voice seemed muffled by the presence of all the clothes. Ann shrank further back.

'My fucking life, you bitch. You took it away. What did you do with what you took? Is it here? Shall I get Frank to look? Shall I get him to tear this place apart?'

The voice was rising, going out of control, returning to a whisper. Someone beat the table with a fist. Anna could feel the vibrations of small and large objects scattering and falling to the floor. A reel of cotton rolled away beneath the long garments and came to rest touching her foot. The tiny contact made her want to scream. There was a brief pause while the other man mumbled.

'Tear it apart, Rick? Why should I do that? What am I doing here, Rick? If it isn't her, what am I doing here?'

'Shuttit. You wanted a woman, didn't you? You can have her when we've finished.'

'Why, Rick? What's this got to do with me?'

'Oh, look what I've found. A big pair of scissors. Shall I start with these, sweetheart, snip, snip, snip, or let Frank have a go with his big, bare hands?'

'There's nothing here,' Hen said quietly. 'I sent everything to Marianne Shearer. I wanted her to know. I thought she would need it for her memoirs. Did you kill her too?'

'I've never killed anybody. Not my style. If they choose to jump or take the pills, or move when they should stay where I tell them, that's up to them.'

He was back in control, as if she had said something flattering, a suggestion of his own prowess that mollified him. Then he sighed.

'Better get on with it then. Hold her still, Frank.'

There was the decisive clip of scissor blades, *clop, clop, clop*. The big scissors, used for the proper cloth, not the small scissors for clipping silk threads; those had their own, small sound. The massive scissors went *clop, clop* when you practised with them, not *clip, clip*, like the Chinese scissors she used for silk. There was a single, sharp scream. The feet moved, busily. Then they sat, one of them tapping his feet.

'All right,' Hen said. 'I know where it is.'

'At last,' Rick said. 'I thought you'd never say. It's all in Daddy's little attic. Like I thought. Daddy hates clutter.'

'You won't be able to get it out,' Hen said. 'But I could. Shall we go? They close soon. I want to help, Rick, I do. Always fancied you.'

The scissors fell to the floor. A large hand scooped them up, and they all went away. The draught from the door they slammed behind them sent eddies of curly auburn hair drifting across the floor towards Ann's hiding place. She clutched a handful of Hen's hair and whimpered. It was all like noises in your head that had nothing to do with you. It was long after all the footsteps had died away along with the voice of the other man, whining, and the downstairs door slammed, that she uncurled and crawled out from behind the dresses and coats. She went on her hands and knees across the objects strewn on the floor, pulled herself up over an overturned chair and leaned against the table. The bodice on the dummy was ripped to pieces; there were small spots of shining blood on the table. The only other things left were the sewing machine and the heavy old phone. There were hats littered on the floor.

The phone rang. She fumbled for her own mobile in confusion and only when she couldn't find it picked up the receiver.

'Hen? Is that you?'

'No,' she said, beginning to cry. 'It isn't Hen. It's me.'

Thomas Noble hated to work on a Saturday, but it had been an extraordinary week. Nothing had been achieved except the complete and utter wreckage of his peace of mind. He was still no further forward in the matter of the sorting out of the estate of Ms Marianne Shearer, QC and he seemed to have done nothing but disservice to his client. Nor could he do anything to explain matters to him, since Frank Shearer was not at work. It would have been the perfect morning for an informative discussion with Peter Friel about his own frolics and what, if anything, they had revealed apart from somehow resulting in the death of an old lawyer, for which he, Thomas Noble, could not be held accountable, but Peter Friel was booked in with the police. Nothing for it but to tinker round the edges of the problem, spring clean his own room and restore order again.

He had detoured into the museum on the way, simply to calm himself and prove that there were some things that had not changed and surely never would. The blood red of the walls in one of the rooms, the way the building was designed to let light into its own darkness and show the facets of all the fragments of Greco-Roman sculpture the man had collected. The room where the Hogarth paintings were artfully displayed on panels which swung from the wall to reveal another sequence behind, the sheer ingenuity of it, the whole place a monument to the rare and beautiful, gathered into a very private, comfortable house. It might also have represented a vivid kind of kleptomania, a devotion to the grand and the obscure, and it always gave him the feeling of being let into a secret.

Sir John Soane, architect and collector, probably manic. The oasis these rooms created put into perspective the horrors of burglary, homicide and suicide, because after how ever many hundreds of years, it was all still there. Thomas had never entirely believed in death, because in this place that he visited at least once a week, it was irrelevant. Collectors like Sir John Soane and himself would last forever. Someone would remember Thomas Noble for his fine collection of porcelain that covered every inch of his home.

Marianne was a collector. He had seen it in her. She had disliked his eighteenth-century porcelain, but admired him for collecting it, the way one collector respected another without questioning why they did it.

Restored by the kindred spirit of Soane, he went into the office with a lesser amount of dread, using the new code for the lock on the door and breathing easier as soon as he got the smell of Saturday morning emptiness in the absence of the few weekday personnel. The post was in the box behind the door: it made him feel vaguely important to act as delivery boy between the floors, and be, for the moment, in charge of something apart from his own china. There was still something to celebrate, and still his personal view of the Fields.

Marianne, collector. Hence the frightful skirt. He felt that the least he owed her was to make sure she was buried in something decent, although preferably not the skirt in which she had jumped, however much restored. A decent, elegant shroud was what was required. Thomas reminded himself that the arrangements for the funeral were his responsibility and already well in hand for whatever date available after the body was released. Toxicology reports, all that. There was no one but himself to agitate for the speeding of the process. Dear Frank couldn't care, and Frank was way off beam anyway. Not at work, not anywhere. Except lurking in the Fields, the other evening. Thomas put that out of his mind.

Ever dutiful to his client. If it had been Frank who had mugged Henrietta Joyce, it was not for him to say.

He was ripping open an envelope addressed to himself in what he diagnosed as a foreign hand. Sloping too far to the right, big loopy letters, not used to writing in English. There was an invoice inside, written out in the same hand in the same uncertain letters, using the sort of printed invoice form you could still just about buy from small stationers. The sort of communication he privately preferred, since you could read it at leisure and argue a discount before the immediate command to reply.

To To *Miss Shearer.*
From *Monika*
For *The dress*
Sum *£300.*

There was a phone number scrawled on the top. Not a person who used a computer, a reminder that half the world still preferred to write. Thomas entirely forgot his nervousness about entering his recently burgled, still untidy office, and dialled the number. He got that angry, sad voice he had heard in Marianne's flat, the voice of the woman who had phoned when Frank was there, some bloody old woman, going on about a blasted dress while dopey Frank unpicked cushions.

'Yeah? What you want?'

'Ms Monicker, I've got your invoice. As I said, I'll make sure it's paid by return, although it might take a day or two. Is there anything else I should know?'

'What?'

There were background sounds of children yelling.

'Anything else? Anything else I can help you with?'

A pause.

'Can you collect the other stuff?'

The noise increased.

'What other stuff was that?'

'All that stuff she left with me. She brought it round while she moved. Only for a week or two, she said. What am I supposed to do with it?'

'What kind of *stuff*?' He hated that word.

'Paper and books and stuff.'

'Could you describe it more accurately?'

After a while, he put down the phone.

Eureka. He did a little jig round the room. How like a cunning collector to leave her personal possessions with someone unknown and careful. How like Marianne to dump stuff, not on a friend, but on someone who needed her money and therefore someone she would feel free to abuse, like a backstreet Ukrainian dressmaker.

Case solved. He had never really needed Peter Friel at all. There was so much to be said for not being proactive all the time. Everything comes to those who wait.

Cross-examination of Marianne Shearer by Ms Marianne Shearer.

Name, date, d.o.b: Irrelevant.

Q. Ms Shearer, tell the court, what's the best thing you have ever done in your life?
A. Given birth to a daughter. Only really positive thing I ever did. Failing to abort her. A negative achievement, but I enabled her to live.
Q. I didn't ask for details. Please give one answer at a time.
A. Right.
Q. And what do you regard as the worst thing you've ever done in your life?
A. I killed her.
Witness is distressed.
Q. There's no room for hysteria, Ms S. Pull yourself together. What do you mean, you *killed* her? With your bare hands?
A. Please ask one question at a time.
Q. Why should I? You don't. How did you do it?
A. Oh, perverting the course of justice in the interests of justice. Humiliation, degradation for real and by proxy. I encouraged someone else. I continued the destruction he began. I made it inevitable.
Q. You're being obscure, Ms S.
A. Am I?
Q. It's for me to ask the questions. You either killed your daughter or you licensed her death, which is it?
A. I entered the conspiracy, it amounts to the same thing.
Q. Does it? Of course it does; the responsibility's the same, so pleased you haven't forgotten your law, but did you

behave this way towards this person *because* she was your daughter?

A. No, I didn't know then who she was.

Q. She was just a another girl, Ms S, and you just *helped* in tearing her apart, is that it?

A. Yes.

Q. So it didn't matter if she was just someone else's daughter?

A. No. No, I mean not then.

Q. So you're getting all weepy and conscience-stricken just because it was your daughter? You have to wait to kill your own flesh and blood before thinking about what you've done to other daughters and sons?

A. Yes.

Q. What does that make you, Ms Shearer?

A. It makes me criminally irresponsible. Like some terrorist who'll kill anyone but family. It makes me a heartless winner with nothing, *nothing* to be proud of. It makes me as amoral and dangerous as Rick Boyd.

Q. Well, you are, aren't you?

A. Can you clarify, please?

CHAPTER NINETEEN

They didn't believe him, perhaps because he was stuttering. They thought he was constructing a story out of thin air, all speculation and no proof. Until Peter came up with names and someone phoned someone who knew all about Rick Boyd, in the form of another disgruntled police officer who had left the courtroom on the last day of that trial in his company. The one like Peter, who never forgot, and remembered Marianne Shearer as a kind of murderer. The ignominy of that defeat and its aftermath had not improved his credibility, either, and even with him, it was half belief. No one wanted to believe that Rick Boyd still existed. They sent a car for Ann, who would not open the door at first. It all took some time.

How long to drive from London to the emptier stretches of Kent? Depends on traffic. They would not let Peter go. They might send along the one policeman on patrol between two townships on a cold Saturday afternoon, but not on suppositions like this. After all, Peter, think about it; who knows who took Ms Joyce and where they went? How well do you know her?

Mr and Mrs Joyce had gone out together for the day, for the first time in many months, their answerphone message said. WJ Storage closed on Saturday afternoons. Sunday was the busy day when the storing public arrived in numbers to reunite themselves with the contents of the attic, adding to and subtracting from the rubbish.

Rick Boyd held the remains of Hen Joyce's hair and forced a pill into her mouth as soon as they got into the car. Keep her quiet for an hour. He pulled the hat down over her forehead. She pouched the pill into her cheek, like a hamster, storing it, and feigned sleep. There was, after all, nothing to say. She was leading them on to her own territory. Frank drove badly, cursing and swearing. Neither of them was fully in control; they had lost the plot and they were at odds. Hen thought of embroidery stitches and her mother. The magic number for cross-stitching on linen is two. The basic stitch on linen is done from left to right, bottom to top, like handwriting, slant-ing over two threads and up two threads. Chain stitches, particularly useful for *joining the edges of fine linen* ... Herringbone stitch, the sort that is used to sew the label in your coat. Nun's stitch for lingerie.

Perhaps my father will be there to rescue me. Perhaps there will be a party, waiting for us, with lights and music and everything. In between reciting descriptions of stitches to herself, she listened to the men talk. Nervy, angry arguments, strange snatches of conversation, while the man called Frank drove too fast, and braked too hard. They woke her up for directions. She had been mumbling in her sleep about what was in the storage room, key no 3611. Jewels, she muttered, money and treasure and clothes and papers and everything, all sorts of things that Marianne Shearer left for Angel and me.

WJ Storage, disused hospital, place of contagion and safety. Rooms within rooms, cells within cells. She knew it well and she was well known to it. It had seemed her father's kingdom when he had started it and she was a child. She had been in awe of its vast emptiness. No one else's mum and dad had access to so much space for playing hide and seek. Gradually, it became fuller and more of it was out of bounds to anyone but her. Other children did not want to play, not even Angel who had been willing until she got scared of the dark corners. Such a safe, sanitised, but still diseased place that no one wanted, Dad said. Because of ghosts? No, no, no. Because it's ugly, superfluous, wrong shape for anything and jerry-built. You can't open the windows and people died here. She and Dad were the only ones who loved it, although Mum had her moments. She made the front office cosy.

Towards the end of the journey, listening, reciting descriptions of stitches and remembering the geography of the place where they were going, she was less afraid, because she *was* the only one who knew it.

They parked the car and went towards the office at the back, past the Chinese containers. Hen's hat, a green beret designed for a man with a large head, was rammed down over her hair and stuck to her scalp. Together with the boiler suit and its many pockets, it made for a businesslike ensemble, suitable for collecting storage or moving house. They were amateur kidnappers, careless with angry excitement, never checking the prisoner's pockets, her mood, her co-operation, assuming her docility; they were pirates in pursuit of some buried treasure, ready to kill the messenger once they had found it. Hen was conscious of aches and pains and blood on her scalp. The one called Frank had taken the scissors that Rick Boyd had handed to him. He used them to prod her in the back on the way downstairs and he giggled at himself as if a man holding dressmaking shears was really as ridiculous as that. Driving the car had given him confidence. He was punch drunk, but he still carried weight and he pinched her arm with the sort of affection that made bruises as he swaggered across the car park with the intoxicated gait of a bow-legged, brain-dead cowboy coming out of the bar.

John, the manager of twenty years, was packing up to go home early, the way she knew he did on Saturdays. Hen knew he did that and he knew that Hen knew and Dad didn't, a harmless conspiracy entered into a long time ago, when she used to help out. The three of them shuffled in like Siamese twins with an escort, the scissors in Frank's pocket bumping against her hip, Rick standing apart and behind, pushing Frank into the line of the video cameras first while ducking to avoid them himself. Frank waved to camera, while clever bugger Rick turned his head. John the manager was not an observant man. He was simply pleased to see Hen.

Just got to get something from Zone A . . . Dad left it yesterday.

Fine, I'll be off then. Hen had often been left in charge. Hen knew how to lock up after, and he was out of here. Hen could do no wrong. Hen was the boss's daughter.

There was no rescue posse. The place was dead. John had never been clever, only reliable. The boss's daughter could have whatever she liked and never told tales.

You haven't got a fucking key?

No, I've got all the duplicate keys, so we'll try a few, shall we? Peter Friel's got the key, and I know exactly which unit, so we might have to try a few. I didn't load it in here, he did. And he didn't remember the number, but it's one of these, right, down here, this zone. Look, there's no need to hold on to me, there's no one else here, I'm trying to help you, right?

Right.

Hat down, she led them slowly along the straight lines of daylight-free corridors, with the small, signal lights winking from the walls – the same endless passages where she had once raced as a ten-year-old. Rick Boyd kept his head down, Frank looked around like a big bear off territory.

Left at the end, right, left again, down that set of doors, I think, then on the left.

She was going faster. Nearly there: they were breathless. Hen stopped at a door on her right, gestured for the keys Rick carried.

Could be this one.

He opened the door and almost fell through it. It opened inwards. Frank went in first, like a sniffer dog. Rick Boyd stood back, holding the door, ushering Hen in front, always keeping up the rear and blocking escape. If only there were not two of them. Frank's scissors weighed down the jacket of his suit. The lights in here were dim, emergency lights only, until someone found the master switch – Hen was not about to tell them where she was.

They were in the neglected archive store, full of documents on unstable, free-standing metal shelves not bolted to the walls, a cheap storage job in a place so much ignored it scarcely mattered if it was safe. Rick stayed where he was, half inside the dark room, half outside, letting his trouble-shooter go first, waiting and watching as Frank moved in, looking for treasure which was his, not hurrying, ambling down the central aisle of a room hired by a local authority, as if he had been sent to value it. Other people's stuff always fascinated Frank. Hen darted to one side, behind the back of the stacks, moving parallel to him, getting ahead, gauging the distance. Then she used all her strength to push. The central stack of ledgers swayed briefly and fell, hitting him even as he turned to watch in dull astonishment. While the noise reverberated in tune with his brief grunt of surprise, Hen was back by the door. She could see Rick Boyd's hand still curled round the edge and she flung herself against the metal while he still held on. He was only just beginning to retreat when the door slammed against his hand.

He roared like an animal and tried to pull back. Hen seized the inner handle, opened the door fractionally and slammed it again. And again, and again, until it closed without resistance and she leaned against it. Listening to shuffling and a keening noise, then nothing.

She moved to the opposite end and turned on the lights. She looked around for any kind of weapon, searching in her pockets. Then she waited, she could easily wait. Frank had the scissors in his pocket after all, and they were the only weapon she feared. She doubted he was dead; he was not the first to fall between these shelves. She feared the scissors more than she feared the man. She had watched him run away before: she knew his smell now. For Frank she felt nothing more than an enraged puzzlement as to why he wanted to hurt her at all, and why the fool was letting himself be led by someone who ran away and left him. For a few seconds her mind wandered into speculation while she struggled to control her breath. The most dangerous things in her pockets were a reel of thread and two packets of needles. The only weapon she had was the place itself.

There was everything useful in here. Rubbish was useful.

There were other weapons everywhere. Rick Boyd would find them, but Rick Boyd would not know his way in the dark, so she would have to find him first. In the car, she had been thinking of what he wanted, and what he was. Wily, cowardly, sadistic, obsessive, wanting something, but not wanting to be caught. Using the man Frank as a shield, thinking ahead to let Frank take the rap, making Frank strike the blows. It would be Frank's blood on the Lover, Frank's picture on the video camera, Frank in the frame, and maybe Rick would be worse without an ally like that, he did not have anyone to take the blame any more, and therefore not a lot to lose. Rick thought he was immortal; Rick would change tack and make himself believe that there were no consequences to whatever he did. It was Frank who was supposed to do the damage. Now it would have to be him. He would either stay and fight for Marianne's mementos like a wounded savage, or the bully would run away as soon as he could find the way out.

However had he persuaded Frank to do this? Easy. She shivered. He had persuaded Angel to live in slavery and conspire in the mutilation of herself. He wanted any evidence of that eradicated: he wanted any knowledge of that destroyed. It was madness with a kind of sanity; it had nothing to do with conscience. He would not give up on what he wanted yet; he would not have run away. She should stay where she was and hide, but she could not stay still: she had never been able to do it for long, even when playing hide and seek. The door of the room remained shut, Rick Boyd on the other side or further away. The only sound was Frank moaning. Hen went towards him and looked down on him dispassionately.

He was sprawled beneath the metal stack, with the shelves lying across his lower back and buttocks. The stack had

296

housed old folders, catalogues and anonymous directories that were spread around him. His chest was flat against the floor, his arms outflung and his head turned to one side. There was no visible blood in the dim light. He did not seem to know where he was or why, and his predicament was not clear to him yet. Maybe then he would start screaming and waste his energy. He seemed like a man who wasted his energy most of the time. A waster, a loser.

If he used his little intelligence, in time he would be able to worm himself out from beneath the stack, unless his back was broken. Either way, it was difficult to care. She wanted to ask him something. She bent over and spoke into his one visible ear.

'Why did you want to kill me, Frank? What have I ever done to you? Tell me, and I might help you.'

When he muttered, she had to stoop further to hear, repelled by the smell of him. Sweat and fear, booze and dope, the ingrained dirt of the not-washed, the familiar smell of a Rick Boyd victim, lost to himself, all dignity stolen, like Angel.

'He says you're Marianne's daughter. He says you'll get it all. You . . . get it all . . . I get nothing.'

'Who the fuck are you?'

'Shearer. Frank Shearer. Marianne's brother.'

She kicked him without force, shaking her head, almost laughing.

'You've been conned by the best, Frank.'

She left him and went out into the corridor, leaving the door open.

Seek and you shall find. Do not misjudge the psychopath because you do not know how to judge or predict him. In the dim light of the corridor, she saw a lone gleaming spot of blood on the floor. Encouraging; almost cheering. As long as she made a single wound or broke one little finger bone, they were more like equal and he might be afraid. Hen hesitated, considering which way to go next. Getting the hell out made the most sense; getting back to the office and the phone and then out, running like mad, that made sense. She walked left to where the corridor reached another of the endless junctions. Her boots sounded loud on the concrete floor: she leant against the wall and took them off. Then, in her socks, she quietly followed where she thought he might have gone. Rick Boyd had an uncanny instinct for weakness, an innate taste for what was precious and valuable and a powerful urge to destroy it; he might have an equally unerring sense of direction.

She paused in a pool of brighter light at the junction, listened to the silence and examined the pockets of the boiler suit yet again. There were needles and linen thread as strong as fishing wire, a thing for unpicking stitches, safety pins, a small perfume spray, but no mobile phone that was always in the bag she carried. She wondered what the spray was doing there, wanted to throw it away in disgust. There was nothing in her pockets useful for anything but the making of cats' cradles. She could not overpower him, she could only run away from him, and she would not do that.

They had taken seven keys to seven separate units. Rick Boyd had them all. He would try them one by one but he did not know what he was looking for. He would only know that Hen had led them into the wrong place.

Hen knew exactly where the trunk was stored. Zone A, suitable for clothing, metal containers inside rooms and one of the more expensive areas. Odd to think there was storage and luxury storage, some units guaranteed more air- and watertight than others, with better light. There was no equality in stored rubbish; if you wanted it safer than houses, you paid more. By a process of elimination, using the numbers of the keys, he would find it in the end, might have found it by now, but would he recognise what he found? There was a washbasin in an alcove on her left, washbasins in many of the corridors, not always with running water. The clue to Rick Boyd's spoor was in the pinkish water still in the basin and the drips below. She took strength from reminding herself that she had hurt him. It was cold in the centre of this enclosed world and she was conscious of hurting all over. It was the chilliness of the place, even in summer, that had stopped her playing hide and seek and it seemed to be freezing her now. She moved faster. Then paused again.

She was in a hallway of twelve metal containers, the size of shower rooms, forming their own streets in what once might have been a spacious hospital ward. The containers that were being used had locked padlocks hanging from the metal hasps of the doors: the empty ones had the locks hanging free. The padlocks varied in size. The one she took was as big as a fist, cold and heavy to the touch. She had always laughed at these padlocks. They looked impressive; they comforted the customer who held the key, but for all the weight the mechanism was primitive enough to be unlocked by a child with a penknife. It was the weight of it that counted, the feeling of security and that was why she wanted it in her hand.

Left, right, away from the centre, through another set of swing doors, another washbasin, another pool of light. Past three open doors showing stacks of furniture, rammed into the space, books in another, the contents of a child's bedroom in the third. He had tried them all, dismissed them, until he found this and he was not sure about it. He was oblivious to inspection, no longer cared who saw him, framed by the light inside his metal cell. Instinct must have told him he was in the right place, but his instinct for what he wanted seemed to have deserted him. Perhaps he could only smell the presence of Marianne Shearer in here, realised that all he had wanted was the knowledge that was in her mind. Hen had a sudden flash image of something seen in a film, long ago, a picture of a man raiding an ancient tomb for treasure, not knowing what he should take away, until he fell prey to the curse.

He had used a knife to slash at the cambric wardrobe bags bearing the purple and orange delivery labels with the distinctive Joyce name. The beige cloth was torn, not to ribbons, only enough to have created a jagged inspection hole. That effort had wearied him; the discovery that the blade of his kitchen knife was dull against tough fabric, his left hand was not strong enough and the contents were not what he thought they were. The knife had dropped to the concrete floor. He had taken off the windcheater he had worn and used it to bind his other hand. He was sitting on the trunk, holding his wrapped hand between his crossed legs, bent over himself, his head bowed, exposing his neck. The heel of his foot beat a tattoo against the edge of the trunk, masking any noise she made. The sound she heard first was a light *thump, thump, thump* of indecision. Someone kicking against the cold.

Hen paused long enough to consider if there was enough time to pull the door closed and use the new padlock and key she carried to lock him in from the outside but the padlocks were fiddly; she would have to be quicker than he. She might just do it, but she could not take the risk. A piece of scarlet cloth protruded from the hole he had made in the wardrobe bag, and that angered her. She could not take the risk of leaving him locked in here with all his destructive strength, because what would he do but destroy it?

She stepped forward with the padlock held firmly in both her hands, raised them high and smashed it down on the back of his neck.

Rick Boyd slumped sideways. She could not believe it could ever be as easy as that, as easy as it had seemed to be with Frank. Better to hit him again and again, but revulsion prevailed. She did not want to be close enough, nor repeat that sick sensation of metal against flesh and bone, nor become like him and take pleasure in it. She pushed him off the trunk, aiding his own, agonisingly slow sliding to the floor. Cat got your tongue, Rick? Never silent for long, surely. He lay on his side. She pulled his damaged hand from between his legs, unwound the windcheater binding and tossed it aside. She avoided looking at the purpling lump of flesh, grasped the back of his shirt and dragged him towards the door. The shirt rode up over his perfect, washboard abdomen, the contours visible in the harsh neon light of the unit, making her feel sick. He was beginning to move, struggle, and murmur incoherently. She tied a sleeve of the windcheater round his good wrist, knotting it tightly. She pulled the rest of the noisy nylon windcheater through a metal strut on the back of the door and secured it with the padlock. When he came round, it would be the padlock he would see: he would have one badly injured hand to free himself. Enough to buy time.

She tore strips from the wardrobe cloth; didn't he know this kind of material was easier to tear than to cut? She could tie his feet with that. Her own feet and her own limbs were icy cold. She wanted to stitch his mouth shut with linen thread, but the needles she carried were wrong. No, it was bad enough to touch him at all. Scissors would have been useful: she could have snipped off his fingers, one by one.

Rick Boyd opened his eyes and looked at her, the way he had stared in court with all the old arrogance of injured innocence. He winked, slowly.

'Hello, Angel,' he said. 'It was always you I wanted.'

She wanted a knife, then. She sprayed the perfume into his mouth and eyes and watched him choke. He screamed and tried to lift his hands to rub it away, hitting the injured hand against his chin, clumsily putting a finger into his mouth, biting down and screaming again. His body contorted, still powerful, and then as awareness dawned, he was quieter. He opened his inflamed eyes, blinked and stared as if realising for the first time that what he saw was not what he expected to see. He twisted and saw the padlock anchoring him to the door and began to groan, softly. She was not smiling at him. Only Angel had smiled.

She was not smiling or responding at all, except for staring back at him, her face a study of disgust.

'Where's Frank? Where's my friend?'

'Friend? You have no friends. There's only me. Stay still while I touch you. Don't look.'

She tied his ankles with strips of canvas. There were spasms of movement rather than resistance. He closed his eyes: she did not trust him. Hen went back to the first of the units he had tried en route to this one to fetch whatever she could find. A real rubbish unit with old household stuff awaiting further use, soft objects padding out the hard. Ironic, really, that she should find black bin liners labelled 'Curtains/blankets'. They promised warmth and suffocation and she staggered beneath the weight. The whole contents of this packed unit shifted ominously as she pulled them out, disobeying all the rules. *We never, ever touch anyone's things, unless they've absolutely stopped paying for the space.* She laid a weighty set of mismatched curtains across his torso, pinning him down with cloth. His eyes were blue and also inflamed; they mirrored his terror. There. He was immobilised for a while. There didn't seem too much hurry about anything any more. Hen would have liked him not to be there. He got in the way.

'Please,' he murmured. 'Please.'

There was no satisfaction in his pleading. It was not what she wanted.

'What did you say to the last woman who said *"Please?"*' she asked him.

His body shook. Warmth flooded him from the suffocating material. He bared his teeth in the effort not to scream. Sweat rolled from his thick hair down the side of his face. He whispered, 'I'm sorry.' She shook her head.

'No you aren't. I just wanted you to know what it was like.'

She told him she had the scissors from Frank's pocket. Told him she was considering doing to him what he had done to Angel. Or would he prefer her to cover him with something else? There was plenty of polythene in here, dangerous to children. No hurry. She thought of asking him, *Why?* but it seemed pointless. There was no *Why* to Rick Boyd.

She was sitting on the trunk watching him watching her, not enjoying the raw fear of him, the passive distress, simply noting the fact that yes, he did know how it felt now. The colour seemed to leach from his mesmerising blue eyes, like blue flowers losing lustre and intensity.

Footsteps sounded down the corridor, coming towards them. At last, she was thinking, will someone come and save me from myself? The footsteps were plural and hurried, not recognisable, although she thought she could decipher the click of female hooves and the more ponderous ones of a male. Hide and seek taught footstep recognition, as well as how to hold your breath.

Rick Boyd heard, too. He began to scream for help in a high, piercing girlish sound that was peculiarly pitiful. Hen's last, irrelevant thought was that the scream did justice to his size. It worked very well on an audience.

There were gasps of horror from the doorway behind her. Then her father's sad, angry voice.

'Oh God, Hen. Why can't you leave things alone? What have you done now?'

CHAPTER TWENTY

Continuation of cross-examination of Marianne Shearer, QC, by herself.

Q. Can you clarify, please? Make it clear, please, why you're so ashamed of yourself that you really want to die?

A. I've told you. I conspired to kill my own daughter. Death's the proper penalty.

Q. Oh, come on. Was there malice aforethought? Recklessness? An intention to do her serious harm? Any of the ingredients that would make this homicide rather than misadventure?

A. Are you trying to help my conscience?

Q. Too late for that, since you never had one. I'm only trying to understand it for posterity. You won the case by use of your forensic talent, so what? That's what you do, isn't it? Conscience never bothered you before. You're a professional left wing liberal; you don't believe in hanging.

A. There was recklessness and there was malice. I humili-ated the witness. I made sure she was marooned and isolated. I took away all the supports that could bolster her. I undermined her sister and made the jury laugh at her. Then I set about her until she lost control and came across as a spoiled child. I drove her to desperation and she killed herself.

Q. Why so cruel? You could have won without that.

A. I hated her. She reminded me of myself as a girl. She made it so easy. And I wanted to win. I had to destroy her, so that Boyd wouldn't have to take the stand. The case had to be demolished before that. I didn't want to call him. He would have been a dreadful witness, such an obvious liar.

Q. You knew he lied?

A. Oh yes. I couldn't take the risk of him lying in public, it would be obvious as soon as he spoke. *They* had to be diminished first.

Q. Ms Shearer, your career has been made by bullying and undermining witnesses. You've made a fortune out of dirty tricks. What made this exceptional?

A. Because I did it to someone who might have loved me. The only one. Whom I might have loved. Mine. She reminded me of me when I was powerless. She was so easily had. She began to haunt me, even before I'd finished with her. I'd forgotten my daughter's date of birth, forgotten it, or put it out of mind, until I remembered it on the last day. When Rick Boyd shook my hand, and shouted after me, did I know she was adopted? I remembered it. I thought he knew. It was as if I had conjured her up, and then, well, there she was. Not what I would have wanted her to be. There she was. Crucified. I put in the nails.

Q. Such sentimental shit. A woman like you, being haunted by a baby you'd never given a damn about?

A. When the trial was over and I knew that this girl was dead because of me, I had to find out. Everything I've ever done went up in flames.

Q. Like what? Like defending people by subverting others? Your life work and bogus idealism? Same thing as defending the innocent?

A. I never cared about innocence or guilt. I wanted to win and it's easier to do it working with the wicked. Truth has all these inhibitions, lies don't. I used my left wing, anti-authority liberal credentials to feather my nest quickest and win, win, win, no matter what harm and who got hurt. I'm a sham, a complete sham.

Q. So what's different? Why can't you go on being a sham?

A. Because I've lost sight of everything about me which might have been decent. Because I know I can't ever do it again and there's nothing else I can do. Because I could never look at myself in the mirror and feel proud of what I was unless I was dressed in my best. And now, even in my finest finery, I can't bear to look at all. I see her.

Q. But it was Boyd who tortured your daughter, wasn't it?

A. I fetched the axe. I always fetch the axe. Or the nails, or the scissors. The murderer's little helper.

Q. Speak up. The jury needs to hear you. Say it again.

A. I can't live with it. I want to kill myself before it kills me.

Peter read this portion of the transcript while sitting in a bus shelter. He could see a bus shelter was a good place to be, a sort of spiritual home for a soul in transit. The shelter a half lively sea caught between moods. It was a grey mid morning with a sky which seemed at first perfectly colourless until he looked more closely, and then it was everything from pink to black, and the sea itself a spectrum of colours from creamy white through brown to blue, graded by constant movement into fractions of colours. The waves, almost too lazy to be as cross as they looked, approached the shingled shore with fake aggression, and then when they broke into foam, nibbled at the shingle, withdrew as if sated or defeated and then came back, starved and curious, looking for somewhere to go. Waves with parents, pulling them back into the deep and saying, you are too young yet. Come home.

He was piecing it together. He would never know when Marianne Shearer had written this, or when the copies had been added to the transcripts that had been sent from Ms Shearer's chambers to himself, long before her death, and to Thomas Noble the day after she died. Whatever happened, it had always been there to be found by anyone who looked. She had wanted them to know, later rather than sooner, deprived them of anything else and then, in case no one looked at all, sent him a reminder. He would have got there without her. He had almost finished his reading.

She had been kinder to him with the copy sent by post via the Lover, which ended with a postscript. She had added to his version a longer recitation which she would certainly have interrupted if it had come from a witness hostile to her cause, or anyone who stood in the way of winning.

I don't know why, Peter, believe me.

I can't do anything straightforward. I was reading through the transcript (for the tenth time), and I thought I'd continue it. Why couldn't I just write it down?

I was thinking of her before that trial, and there she was, as silly and small and malleable as me, the self I hated. This is crap. I was looking for her, thought I recognised her, got a detective, costly, but so easy. Its all about birth certificates. I did it to prove I was wrong, but then, horrors, I found out I was right. I got as far as finding out that Angel Joyce was adopted, one of two.

So silly Angel it was. NB, I hoped it was the other one, Henrietta, because she survived. I found out all about her, too. What she does etc. I wish I had a sister like that.

I knew what I had done, and to whom, by the time Henrietta Joyce sent me the post-mortem report. Thank her for underlining it.

I had delivered my daughter to suicide and granted her tormentor the freedom to do the same to someone else.

The shame makes me squirm; it's like I've drunk the acid I've been pouring down other throats all these years. Got to stop myself doing any more harm.

They were right, all those mothers. It's not the same if it's yours. As if all the others weren't somebody's child too.

Tell me I've still got style.

Peter got up and walked against the wind as far as the next shelter. People said hello and he said it back. He admired her lack of self-pity. He had been acting as interlocutor, again, between Henrietta Joyce, her parents and the law. It was a role he had wanted, in case she needed him, which he doubted she did. You are always too late, Peter: you always get there too late. You're a post-hoc thinker, a lawyer, not a doer.

He was being a doer, now. He was waiting for a white van

to take him back to London. The loose ends were unravelling and ravelling again, like unpicked knitting wool about to be made into a new garment. He had enjoyed the learning of new facts, like how, thirty-odd years ago, an original birth certificate was superseded by another in the case of children adopted at birth. The first, with the mother's name, remained in the archives of the agency of adoption, and the one created by the adoption order remained with the parents. Birth certificates were unalterable, but you could have two; one you saw and one you did not know about. No one need know the birth mother's name, not then, neither daughters – nor sons – or substituted parents. It could stay secret.

He had been afraid that Hen had known all along.

She didn't know. She could not have known, could she?

The van arrived.

January 17

Pray stand for Her Majesty's Coroner !

All stood.

The Sergeant bowed. They all bowed as the Deputy Coroner for the county ambled in like the best man at a shotgun wedding, determined to make things easy. Not much of a crowd, witnesses only; therefore the usual pall of worry attendant on any sudden death but without the sharper, more unpredictable overtones of grief. The Coroner had served this court for twenty-five years and detested wastage of effort when there were no relatives to mollify. After all, the deceased was not local.

Thomas Noble imagined that as he grew older, all the funerals and all the inquests might meld together in one, long memory with only occasional highlights. He could write a style guide to funerals and inquests, including how to show the necessary respect, what to wear, etc. He was keeping his powder dry for the next one that would surely have a better attendance than this miserable gathering. The ambience and decor of this room was familiar, dressed as it was in the same, anonymous style, but he was slightly off familiar territory here and he felt conspicuous. Acting as moral support for the new clients, grateful for the mercy of working for *nice* people, although why Marianne Shearer had left a will – hidden along with a laptop, a phone and various other invaluable sundries in the back room of a Ukrainian dressmaker – leaving the bulk of her estate to Mr and Mrs Joyce, was a tad beyond his comprehension. Conscience was a strange thing. A client was a client; one did one's best.

Tut, tut. He supposed the powers that were had scoured the length and breadth of the land to find a living relative willing to own Rick Boyd. Perhaps the absence of same was his problem. Either the man had never had loving arms around him or perhaps he had hacked them all off, long since. That handshake of his alone would do it; he could see Boyd shaking off a whole arm and eating it. The two Joyces stood so close they could have been formed from the same substance. Unlike himself, they had authority in this room; they were local, and therefore beyond reproach. The Coroner nodded towards them like an old friend; everyone nodded to one another.

'Perhaps I can begin with a brief recitation,' the Coroner said, 'of the facts as I know them. Who do we have here? Ah, yes, Mr and Mrs Joyce, thank you so much for coming along. There was no one else to identify the deceased, very obliging of Mr Joyce in the circumstances. Could we agree on the salient facts? Is there anyone here representing the deceased? No?

'I must remind you that my duty is to pronounce upon the cause of death, rather than why. I have no comment to make on the circumstances of the death or the penultimate reasons why it occurred when it did, only what caused it. Which disease took its own moment to strike, if you get my drift. The fact that Mr R. Boyd appears to have precipitated his own demise is not my business, or the business of this court. Here are the facts and the pathology.

'Mr Richard Boyd and an accomplice who remains at Her Majesty's pleasure, embarked upon burglary in a self-storage unit whilst it was closed to the public.'

There was a pause to consider the enormity of this. He made it sound like public sodomy and Thomas wanted to giggle.

'It would appear that they had prevailed upon the manager to give them keys to several individual units and it would also appear that they argued as robbers do, although in what order they argued and struck one another is subject to conjecture and criminal proceedings. Mr Boyd's accomplice was found in one unit, with a blood alcohol level off the stratosphere, the deceased was found in another. They appear to have injured one another in a series of fights. Mr Boyd, the deceased, had superficial injuries to his skull. Two of the digits on his right hand were broken.

'Alerted to the burglary, Mr and Mrs Joyce (well-respected proprietors of WJ Storage), attended the premises.

'The deceased was comatose when tended by the ambulance service. He died, at a moment that cannot be exactly specified as yet, of systemic heart disease. Post-mortem analysis revealed long-standing heart problems. He could have died at any time.

'The cause of death was heart failure. There are possible

ancillary causes; the condition is historically exacerbated by abuse of steroids, substance abuse, abuse by anything, including electric shocks, nicotine, cannabinol derivatives, you know what, but essentially he died from a genetic disease of the heart. Possibly precipitated by shock: with similar, post-mortem symptoms as those found in suffocation, such as petechiae under the skin, but the man was a walking time bomb. Ours is not to reason why. Blocked ventricles kill in time.

'We can surmise that a better way of life may have assisted the deceased to live longer, but then again, it might not have.'

Praise be, Thomas said to himself. He was already thinking of the shop he had passed while walking through the unfamiliar town en route to here. An antique shop with interesting porcelain displayed in the window, including a small, silver jug, not quite his style, but definitely appealing.

Inquest adjourned for six weeks.

They stood outside, arm in arm, she with an embroidered hankie pressed against her face. Elderly parents, he noted, must have been well on in years before they acquired their kids.

'Oof, Mr Noble, I thought he was going to ask questions, I really did. Like what Hen did to him first. Like how I took her away, to go and phone and everything and left him with Father. Poor lad, silly boy.'

The sun came out and illuminated Ellen Joyce's pale face. Such a deceptive glint in her eye, almost triumphant. Father patted her elbow that had the effect of quietening her without him making any request. Father, Thomas noted, at least knew not to trust any lawyer with indiscreet words or admission, especially when the lawyer was your own. They smiled at one another. Yes, Thomas thought, they really are nice people. I would not cross either of them. They would cut me up in little pieces and put me in bags and store me away until everyone had forgotten about me if I crossed them. He shook them by the hand and promised to speak soon. Father's handshake was remarkably strong for a man of his age, but then he had been lifting and carrying and burying things for half a lifetime.

'Thank you for coming,' Father said, echoing the Coroner. 'It'll be all right, you know. Half the police force store stuff with me. And he wasn't much of a loss, was he?'

Walking back through the town in search of the shop, Thomas reflected that his reasons for attending this formality of an inquest were perfectly sound. He was protecting the interests of his clients and Peter Friel would not have been good for this occasion. The facts would have worried him. He would have managed to feel sorry for Rick Boyd and he would have questioned the manner of his dying. Peter's great imagination would have gone into overdrive; he was like that. He would want to know the truth of it while Thomas himself definitely did not. If it was Hen Joyce or her father or her mother or all of them together who had smothered that bastard with stored rubbish, he definitely did not want to know. There were remembered fragments of Mrs Joyce's statement that could easily be forgotten. *He seemed to be having a fit, he was very cold. My daughter and I ran back to the office leaving my husband to try and keep him warm.*

On balance, Thomas decided it was definitely Dad. A dutiful man doing his duty, saving society the expense of another trial and saving his daughter from ever having to give evidence again. Such a practical man, hated clutter, would do anything for his daughters, wasn't going to take any more risks. Thomas found the shop he had seen before and secured for himself the purchase of a small silver jug. A sweet thing with a fat little belly embossed with flowers, standing solidly on three slender legs. Not Georgian; an excellent copy. Thomas loved a good fake, but what a mistake it was to think you ever got a bargain out of town.

One more inquest to go. What a shame the Joyces would not get a hundred per cent of the estate.

'This is definitely the best,' Hen said, 'as well as the oldest.'

'What is it?'

'A Delphos gown, designed by Fortuny, early nineteen hundred. He made a lot of dresses, invented all sorts of new ways of dyeing and printing textiles, but this sort of gown was a hallmark, I suppose. Often made in black, much rarer in red, like this. It's a featherweight multi-pleated silk sheath which just flows over any shape, so light it would float away if it wasn't weighted with tiny Venetian glass beads at the side and the shoulders and the hem. You'd have to kick it gently as you walked. Sarah Bernhardt and Isadora Duncan probably wore one of these. It's a miracle. Looks simple, is anything but. Like that skirt. A woman assumes exceptional importance when wearing this dress.'

'Not for everyday use,' Peter said. 'Might go to her head.'

'No, but durable if well kept. There's no strain on the seams, no strain in wearing it, so it doesn't wear out. I reckon if she wore this she might have covered it up with that Hardy Amies cape. Dark blue, floor-length, rather severe and wintry. Or this Trigere cashmere evening cape, it's sort of shadowy grey, floating warmth, could almost double as an elegant dressing gown. But look at this slip of a thing, isn't it clever? The sort of garment you keep forever and wear again and again in all sorts of different ways.'

'Looks nothing to me. An underslip? A black petticoat?'

'Wash your mouth out, you philistine. An underdress, more like. It's Hartnell, heavy crêpe de Chine, with a simple high-waisted bodice, V-shaped over the bust and thin straps over the shoulders. The skirt's made of panels, giving it shape and the hem's extra deep and heavy, to keep it all in place. It never rides up, the creases hang out, the hem gives it the weight and sort of releases it do its own business. She packed this up with the gowns she could wear with it, one gown over another. There's one in cream lace, up to the neck with three-quarter sleeves, don't know what vintage, greatly discreet. Then there's this wraparound dress, Ossie Clark, 1970s. See? Diaphanous material over a soft, solid base. Wonderful soft ruffles at the neck, edged in satin with satin ties and flared sleeves. Hardy Amies and Ossie Clark. Quite a mix of generations. She had no brand loyalty, that Marianne Shearer. She liked the best and she liked it useful. The fewer fastenings the better. There's a beaded black flapper dress, House of Adair, it's got no zips or hooks, just glass bugle beads and seed beads in silver, gold and fuchsia, quite fragile really, already repaired, I reckon she might have danced in that. Or someone did.'

She was in full flight and Peter was listening.

'But I still don't understand her taste. It's truly eclectic. She likes silk and wool and jersey, she doesn't mind innovation or the relatively modern, and she likes all sorts of different shapes in the end. Big shapes and no shapes. Look at this, entirely different. It's typical Christian Dior. A white silk and satin ball gown flocked with black carnations. Boned bodice, skirt too big for a taxi. She could certainly dress to surprise, this lady. And in all the colours.'

'And what is Miss Joyce wearing today?

She put one hand on her hip, turned her profile away from him, posing.

'A Charles Creed suit, circa 1953. Lightweight herringbone tweed jacket with huge lapels and padded shoulders, fitted dead close to the waist. Fastened with three enormous buttons, detail repeated on the cuffs. Skirt like a pencil. You have to hold your breath in this and you'd have to bend at the knees to pick up anything off the floor, but apart from that it's quite comfortable really. A real power suit. I prefer the Valentino pink chiffon evening gown with the ostrich feather stole. Great with a tan, but not with buzz-cut hair like mine.'

She sat down. Peter winced at her almost bald head. The crew-cut hair, beginning to grow, was a vast improvement on the tufted and bloody scalp he had first seen outside WJ Storage. She refused to discuss it. It needed restyling, she said. Hair will grow. A finger wouldn't; it was so much better than what I thought he would do.

'No,' she went on. 'I can't guess her taste. She's got all sorts of labels, all nationalities, French, English, Japanese, American, as if she was picking the best from all decades. Diane von Furstenberg, Sarmi, Missoni, Hartnell, Chanel. She goes from demure and severe, like this, to vamp. There's a very girly thing in mint-green organdie, a floor-length shirt-waister I wouldn't have thought was her at all. She's got the labels, and she's got the fakes. Not fakes, but handmade copies. Things she must have got made. The Fortuny's genuine, though. Belongs in a museum.'

'Or on the back of a woman who needed to feel important. Like that suit you have on.'

Hen flushed.

'I'm not criticising,' he said. 'But I prefer your own label.'

She moved out of his line of vision. Reluctantly he kept his eyes fixed on the new racks of clothes crowding the dressing room. How had all that been marshalled into a trunk and two wardrobe bags, and then expanded to such sweet-smelling volume? He could taste the scent of lavender and soap. Hen was taking off the suit: he could hear her doing that from the rustle of it and the sound she made when she let out her breath. A constricting suit, fit for a funeral where no one either sat, or cried. She came back into his line of vision, clad in denim. Ms Shearer might never have worn denim.

'Did you ever know,' he asked, 'where you and Angel came from?'

'The stork brought us,' she said. 'The stork brought along a selection, and we were chosen because we were lovely. That's my version.'

'Yes, of course the stork did. Via an adoption agency who kept the birth certificates. You parents probably never even saw them. But whatever her name, your mother might not be dead. Marianne Shearer's detective found the originals. Do you want to know any more?'

'No, not now. Perhaps in a year or two. I've got too much else to do and what would it achieve? I'll settle for the stork and what I've got. Is it wrong to feel so liberated? Am I so frivolous that happiness lies in the conservation and repair of all these brilliant clothes? Yes, I am. My sort of aunt has dictated my immediate future and I'm bloody grateful. Do you want more tea or shall we bypass that and go straight to the bottle?'

'You were right, you know. She did have her clothes made, quite apart from what she collected. The everyday clothes were all handmade.'

'Why did she leave me this legacy, Peter?'

'Because you were the one who tried to rescue her child?

Because she respected you? I don't know. Nobody knew her. Let's go out. Have you tried on every single thing?'

She blushed.

'Not the underwear, of course, but yes, most of the others. I've got to make an inventory. I had to see what condition they were in, trying them on is just one way to check. She was a good conservator. I had to check for repairs. They aren't really mine, you know.'

He laughed at her embarrassment, at the excitement she could not conceal. She leant over him and kissed his cheek.

'Peter, you're the only man I've ever met who likes shopping.'

He stood up to hug her. That was easy. He was thinking how strange it was that all of Marianne Shearer's collected garments, the priceless and the ordinary, should be her size.

Loving her a little helplessly, and wondering how he could ever make a person of such self-sufficiency need him. Wondering if he would ever break that lifelong habit of arriving too late, such as arriving outside that terrible storage building with a phalanx of police after dark, only to discover the ambulance already there. Still wondering, too, after what he had been told, exactly how it was that Rick Boyd had come to die.

She was like a very adult child who has been given a dressing-up box. The joy of it was unseemly on the eve of a funeral. He felt Ms Shearer might approve.

'I think the lingerie was made by nuns,' Hen said. 'Convent-made items from between the wars. You can tell by the stitching. Nun's stitch. My mother taught me. I like the irony of Marianne Shearer's negligee being made by nuns.'

CHAPTER TWENTY-ONE

January 14th

Pray stand for Her Majesty's Coroner.

They all stood. This Coroner bounded into the room like a greyhound let out of a trap, all businesslike energy, noticing quite a crowd and the eye of the world on him, determined to be heard and admired for clarity, rather than producing fodder for journalists. If they thought he was in any sense corruptible or persuadable, they had another think coming. He knew his verdicts; he was not going to be swayed by any other consideration, such as other people's money. That was not the business of this Coroner's Court, but oh, dear me, what an unpleasant woman she seemed to have been and so utterly selfish in the manner of her dying. Such an attention-seeker. His sympathies, such as they were, were with the people who had been forced to watch and pick up the pieces. Photographer, policeman, the ambulance man with the shovel for the brains. Not fair. Not his business, but still, more interesting than most and oddly moving, so disturbing he was more impatient than ever.

'Mr Noble, I understand you're representing the deceased in the absence of her sole relative who is in prison at the moment? Yes? Fine. DC Jones for the police? We established continuity of the body and identification last time, didn't we? I suggest we do a short cut on the narrative, since there's not much disagreement about the facts.'

The front row in the wooden benches nodded like mechanical dummies and the crowd on the plastic chairs at the back found themselves nodding also.

'May I remind you all that the purpose of this court is to establish the cause of the death of Ms Marianne Shearer, the deceased. How, not why, except insofar as it influences the verdict. We're looking at the death, not the life. Let's start with you, DC Jones, if you'd take the stand. Just the salient points, please. We're not here to entertain journalists.'

'I swear by Almighty God to tell the truth, the whole truth and nothing but the truth . . .'

He looked as if God would strike him down if he did not. He speeded up his delivery to keep pace.

'The deceased took a suite in the Imperial Hotel on the evening of December 28. She had a small suitcase containing nothing but personal effects, toiletries and nightwear. She left her credit card at the desk and requested nothing further from the staff. At seven thirty the next morning, she was seen sitting on the balustrade of the balcony of her room by a chambermaid who had stepped out of the next door room she was cleaning to have a cigarette. The maid saw a woman. She said to Ms Shearer, hello, are you OK, you'll get your skirt dirty, would you like a cigarette? The maid, sir, had limited English and has since left the hotel's employment. Ms Shearer is reported to have said, No thank you. Then she jumped. Mr Paul Bain, a photographer, who happened to be

321

walking to work in the street below, also saw Ms Shearer stationary on the balcony. He recorded her last movements with his camera.'

'We should have Mr Bain at this point,' the Coroner said.

One man shuffled out of the witness box, and another shuffled in, the latter looking embarrassed. The Coroner looked at him with concealed curiosity, as if he was examining a curious species of lizard, and Bain shrivelled under his scrutiny.

'Won't keep you long, Mr Bain. You took your snapshots and remained at the scene, did you?'

'Yes.'

'How long were you standing there before she jumped?'

'Less than a minute. I just looked up and saw her there.'

'No doubt you moved to get a better angle?'

Sitting in the first row of the plastic seats at the back, next to Hen, Peter could see Thomas Noble bow his head. Bain remained silent.

'Mr Bain, the suggestion's been made that there was another person in the room behind Ms Shearer. Did you see any other person either on the balcony or in the room? A shadow, even?'

Bain looked at Thomas Noble, who looked away.

'There were net curtains behind her, billowing out slightly. A bit theatrical.'

'I wasn't asking for your comments on how it looked. Did you see anyone else? The merest suggestion hinting at the presence of someone else behind her?'

'No. I couldn't see into the room at all. She was the only person on the balcony. She didn't look back into the room. She looked sideways to the next balcony, and then she jumped.'

He began to shake. It was not quite what he had wanted to say.

Then the Pathologist, intoning details without relish, respectfully, the bloodiness downplayed with scientific terms. It seemed almost polite of him to mention that the deceased had normal heart and lung functions and was free of any notable disease; it sounded as if he was complimenting her. Thomas remarked later that it was if he was saying she wasn't in bad nick for her years and still had good legs, too. All in order, apart from being dead. Injuries: ruptured spleen, severed spinal cord, multiple fractures to the skull, as if, the witness said, she had twisted mid air, defied the gravitational pull of her own weight and allowed her skull the first impact with the ground. Death instantaneous: cause of death multiple injuries, some twenty of which would have been individually sufficient to achieve the end result. Insignificant traces of alcohol in her blood. No medication.

Perhaps she really was trying to save the skirt, Peter thought. You don't have to hear this, he whispered to Hen. Yes I do, she said. She deserves that I do. I wish she had been drunk.

It was the Coroner's choice how much or how little he said about all the other information at his disposal. He was not there to reveal the life, only to reach and deliver a reasoned verdict. No one cared about this woman except the journalists; he was free to say as little as he liked, and still he faltered.

'Facts dictate that the deceased killed herself by jumping from a height. She appeared to have dressed for the occasion. Did she fully intend the consequences of her actions, or was she acting when the balance of her mind was disturbed, by which I mean, was the mental state of the deceased such that her actions were unpredictable, the result of loss of mental balance, something she would not have done unless her mind was disordered? If you take the example of a person who climbs to the top of a tall building while under the influence of drugs and then leaps off because he thinks he can fly, that is death where the balance of the mind is disturbed or at least confused, if you take my meaning. It may look like suicide, but it isn't suicide according to law. That dead person intended to fly, not to die in the attempt. A person who takes too many pills when drunk and depressed, for instance, is not a suicide, either. That's closer to death by misadventure.'

He cleared his throat, which had become oddly constricted.

'Suicide requires more elements than disorder. For suicide to be the proper verdict in this court, it must be proved beyond doubt that the deceased intended to die, *planned* to die by self-infliction, gave notice of that intention and really meant to carry it through. Suicide, in the strict legal sense, is the act of a rational mind.'

He paused again, upset by his own words.

'I wouldn't have considered a verdict of suicide here in the absence of evidence from Ms Shearer herself as to her intentions. I have never given a verdict of suicide without some form of suicide note, however deliberate the actions of the deceased. It's the most distressing verdict of all. Why? Because it leaves the survivors, the family and friends with a colossal burden of guilt. They should have known; they should have prevented it. They bear the accusations, the mistrust of the deceased whom they thought they knew and they did not offer help. They are rendered impotent. I cannot approach such a verdict lightly.'

It was strange, Peter thought, how much it mattered.

Nothing to do with heaven and hell. How much it would have mattered to the Lover. How much it mattered to himself, although he scarcely knew her. They would all have preferred death by misadventure or the act of a disordered mind. The voice went on.

'Suicide is the proper verdict. Ms Shearer was possessed of a highly rational mind. She left an abundance of suicide notes in various protracted forms. She showed her intentions in the plans she made which I do not have to describe here. The verdict is suicide, beyond reasonable doubt. The only thing I can say to comfort those who admired her is that it does seem to have been, in her case, a peculiarly positive act.'

'What did he mean, "positive"?' Thomas said later, facing them both across the table and wafting away the steam from a cup of foul-looking herbal tea. The late February rain streamed down against the windows of the coffee shop and the traffic rumbled by on High Holborn. The table by the window was too small for three and too low for comfort. Thomas adored Hen's suit. So good of her to dress formally for an inquest she need not have attended. He supposed she had come to support Peter, in case he should be called to give evidence. It had not happened: thank God for a coroner of such discretion, even if his verdict depleted an estate.

'Positive?' Thomas repeated. 'How did he make a positive out of such a negative? Still, I liked his style.'

'I can see what he meant,' Peter said. 'Rick Boyd is dead and Frank Shearer is in prison. Marianne's wealth will be fairly distributed. That all flows from the suicide. Seems pretty positive to me.'

'And I met you,' Hen said to him. 'Positive so far?'

'How so?' Thomas asked her. She turned towards him. She

never usually looked at anyone other than Peter if Peter was there to be observed. Couldn't quite take her eyes away from him, leading to the conclusion that there was no accounting for taste. Perhaps *that* was the positive result the Coroner meant.

'He dresses better than he did,' she said. 'Not that I care what he wears.'

The man doesn't stand a chance, Thomas thought, not a cat in hell's chance. If she had her way, they'd be breeding five children before he knew it. A woman was so incredibly determined once she had made up her mind.

She was laughing at him the way Marianne had laughed; in a way that made him feel part of it.

'I don't understand,' she was saying. 'I'm glad I was there, and wish I wasn't. I wanted to mourn, but I can't do that. Would she want to be mourned, do you think? Mourned or respected? Anyway, it was a reminder, oh I don't know, of what a small amount a court case covers. You only get half the story. That's all you ever get.'

Peter leant forward, suddenly earnest.

'Oh, I don't know,' he said. 'There's a different dynamic in a criminal court. I mean the thing has its own wheel, turning on a bloody uneven surface, generating sparks and punctures, subject to weather conditions, drivers, highwaymen, rain and fog. Think of the logistics of getting a number of people to turn up at the same place and time, think of the egos who take the reins, and the lame horse, and the capacity for accidents. Think of someone without a compass and someone with one. Luck and incompetence in combination. The wheel stays off or on. The thing can sabotage itself. I can't have you blaming *her*. Not entirely. It isn't all sabotage. There was plenty of truth in the verdicts. Marianne Shearer owed you nothing.'

He turned to Thomas.

'She would have wanted her brother to have a decent defence, you know. Whatever he did. Shall I do something about that, or will you? Someone must.'

No *should*, must.

Maybe he did have a cat in hell's chance.

She was looking at that honest face of his, with her mouth half open in admiration, shaking her head as if she had suddenly encountered a wonder of the world.

'You're right,' she said. 'Marianne's victim. Boyd's victim. Everyone deserves a defence.'

Her profile was a beautiful version of the same profile, her shape the same shape. She sat the same way. She would suit the clothes.

Some mistake, surely, some quirk of the light.